W9-ADY-424

Also by Sadeqa Johnson

Yellow Wife

And Then There Was Me

Second House from the Corner

Love in a Carry-On Bag

THE HOUSE OF EVE

BY SADEQA JOHNSON

SIMON & SCHUSTER
New York London Toronto Sydney New Delhi

Simon & Schuster
1230 Avenue of the Americas
New York, NY 10020

This book is a work of fiction. Any references to historical events, real people, or real places are used fictitiously. Other names, characters, places, and events are products of the author's imagination, and any resemblance to actual events or places or persons, living or dead, is entirely coincidental.

First Simon & Schuster hardcover edition March 2023

SIMON & SCHUSTER and colophon are registered trademarks of Simon & Schuster, Inc.

For information about special discounts for bulk purchases, please contact Simon & Schuster Special Sales at 1-866-506-1949 or business@simonandschuster.com.

The Simon & Schuster Speakers Bureau can bring authors to your live event. For more information or to book an event, contact the Simon & Schuster Speakers Bureau at 1-866-248-3049 or visit our website at www.simonspeakers.com.

Interior design by Wendy Blum

Manufactured in the United States of America

10 9 8 7 6 5 4 3 2 1

Library of Congress Cataloging-in-Publication Data has been applied for.

ISBN 978-1-9821-9736-0
ISBN 978-1-9821-9738-4 (ebook)

For my Mother and her Mother

In loving memory of
Paula Marise Johnson

THE HOUSE OF EVE

PART ONE

Each story has a monster in it who made them tough instead of brave, so they open their legs rather than their hearts where the folded child is tucked.

—Toni Morrison

Chapter One

Philadelphia, October 1948

MOMMIES AND DRAGONS

Ruby

My grandma Nene always said that early was on time, on time was late, and late was unacceptable. Fatty was unacceptably late again. Knowing full well that I had some place important to be. I didn't mind staying with Grandma Nene overnight once a week so that Fatty could clean offices. All I asked was that she be home in time for me to catch the bus to my Saturday enrichment classes. And for the third week in a row, Fatty dragged her heavy feet through Nene's apartment door fifteen minutes behind schedule, calling out in her high-pitched voice, "Ruby girl, I'm sorry. Let me tell you what happened."

My cousin had more excuses than a hoe going to jail, and I didn't have time to entertain her colorful tales this morning. I had one hour to get all the way down to South Philly, and I twisted up my lips in a way that I hoped conveyed how annoyed I was over her lack of consideration.

"You got my carfare?" I thrust my hand in her face, but Fatty brushed past me in the narrow hallway, past the crooked family pictures that hung in mismatched frames, through to the small L-shaped kitchen. I stomped behind her as she snatched back her pageboy wig and tossed it on the counter.

"Your mother said she'd leave it for you."

A baby cockroach scurried from under the toaster, and Fatty smashed it dead with her palm.

"You gonna make me walk all the way back in the opposite direction? Just give me twenty cents."

"I would if I could," she said, scrubbing her hands at the apron sink. "But I'm broke as a joke girl until next Friday."

My scalp heated. "Grandma ain't got no money round here? What if my mother forgot?"

"Chile, I talked to Inez last night, she said she would. Now quit wearing out my nerves. If you leave now, you'll make it." Fatty reached into the icebox and cracked open a can of Schlitz. She tipped it to her lips and took a long swallow, then exhaled in a way that suggested that she had been thirsting for that beer her whole way home. After another hungry swig, she undid the buttons to her blue uniform down to her waist. The rolls around her middle sighed with relief.

"Did Nene take her medicine?"

I snatched up my school bag, nodding my head with frustration. "She's been sleep twenty minutes. Her next eye dosage is at eleven."

With the front door open, I could smell scrapple frying from the new neighbor's apartment on the first floor. She had twin babies who kept up a chorus of crying all night long. "I'm not doing this for you no more."

Fatty belched, then called after me, "I said I was sorry. Damn girl, what you want? Blood?"

I slammed the door in response, then felt bad, hoping I hadn't disturbed Nene.

The piece of toast I had prepared for my journey was now cold and stiff with butter. I shoved the bread in my mouth as I ran down the two flights of stairs and out onto 28th Street. A dampness clung to the air from last night's rain, and I had to sidestep wet leaves that had gathered in potholes.

I had been marked tardy for the last three weeks in a row, and Mrs. Thomas said if I was late to one more enrichment class, she was writing me up. I wondered if Fatty was messing with my future on purpose. Everyone, even Fatty, knew how prestigious it was to be selected to participate in the Armstrong Association's *We Rise* program. As one of twelve Negro students chosen from across the city of Philadelphia, I was competing to receive a full four-year scholarship to Cheyney University, the oldest historically Negro college in the country. To earn it, I had to be impeccable in every way, and being on time was a requirement. If I wasn't awarded the scholarship, I could forget all about going to college for optometry. No one in my family had been to college, nor could they afford to send me. I refused to let Fatty's disregard for time muddy up my future. Especially since she hadn't even finished high school.

Out on Columbia Avenue I passed by the Temple of God, where women dressed in white from head to toe stood greeting the congregation by the storefront entrance. It was the only church in the neighborhood that met on Saturday mornings, and I avoided eye contact, lest one of the women think I was curious about being saved by their Lord and try coaxing me to join them.

I hurried on, rounding the corner onto 33rd Street. In the middle of the block, I could see four men huddled in folding chairs in front of Process Willie's barbershop. A backgammon set hunkered between two of them, and they all clung to paper cups, probably sipping brown liquor that kept them warm so early in the morning. Their wrinkled clothes and befuddled expressions suggested that they had been carrying on all night long, and I knew that meant trouble.

I buttoned up my jumbo knit sweater hoping that would make me invisible to them. But I wasn't fast enough. As soon as I stepped down off the curb, I heard the first one call.

"Girl, you fine enough to make a grown man cry."

The one next to him grinned wide enough for me to see that he was missing a tooth. "Yes, Lawd. Shaped like a Coca-Cola bottle. Got me thirsting for a drink."

"Bet she taste sweet like candy, too."

The one closest to me reached for my hand, but I sidestepped it.

"Whatcha in a rush for? Big Daddy got everything you need right here."

I shot him the most evil eye I could muster as I slipped past them. The men continued to wolf whistle, and I could feel their eyes fixed on my behind. It was times like this I wished there was a button that would erase me. Not to die or nothing. Just so I wouldn't exist. At the very least, I'd like to take a pin to my oversized tits and pop them like water balloons. Making me flat like a pancake, and as boring to watch as a teacup. Maybe then my mother would see me for who I was and stop calling me out my name.

We lived in a rented apartment on the corner of 33rd and Oxford. It was the third place we had called home in the past two years. Across the street from us was a huge park that we wouldn't dare venture into. The closest I got to the lush greens was from our front porch, where I sat in a rusty folding chair and watched red-faced men play golf, their blonde wives parked with their children and packed snacks on nearby blankets, blasting the latest hits by Tony Bennett and Percy Faith.

Skipping up the cement steps of our redbrick building, I fumbled for the keys around my neck. None of the doorbells ever worked, and I had to jimmy my key in the deadbolt several times before it turned. Whenever it rained, the door jammed and I had to shove the heavy wood with my shoulder to pry it open. As I moved up the creaky stairs two at a time, I could feel my blouse sticking to my back. Whenever I got nervous, my face and back broke out into an annoying sweat. The bus would arrive in twenty minutes, which gave me time to change into another top that didn't need pressing and sneak some of Inez's perfume.

The front door of our apartment opened into the canary-colored kitchen, and I smelled a cigarette burning. I dabbed the sleeve of my sweater against my forehead and swallowed down my unease.

Inez always left money for me in the same hiding place: wrapped in a paper towel and slipped between two steak knives in a kitchen drawer. I slid open the drawer, breathing a sigh of relief when I saw the napkin. My fingers curled around it, but it felt light. I shook the tissue free, then moved the other knives around, hoping the money had slipped out somehow. But found nothing.

A new wave of sweat moistened my hairline as I tried to think of what to do next. There was no loose change laying around the apartment; I had used the spare coins last week when Inez hadn't left the money. I had no idea how long it would take for me to walk from North Philly to South Philly, but just the thought of crossing the city on foot made my head hurt.

My unsteady fingers gripped the upholstery stuffing that was loose in the kitchen chair, trying to make a plan, when Leap, my mother's latest boyfriend, strolled into the kitchen with a cigarette fastened between his nicotine-stained teeth.

"What are you doing here?" fell from my lips.

He cocked his head at me. "You my woman now, too?"

"You usually at the barber shop on Saturday morning."

Leap drifted to the sink and turned on the faucet. He let the water gush out for a few seconds, and then he picked up a glass from the dish rack and filled it. While he sipped, his eyes roamed over me. Leap's wandering eyes always made me self-conscious. Usually I avoided him as best I could, but in that moment I didn't look away.

A baby-blue satin scarf was tied around the sides of his processed hair, knotted at his forehead. He had smooth, cherrywood-colored skin. A rope chain hung from his neck, and his T-shirt was untucked from his drawstring pants. He thought he looked like Nat King Cole, but he wasn't nearly as cute.

The kitchen felt cramped and hot with both of us standing there. Leap leaned over the table and tapped his cigarette into the glass ashtray that sat among scattered bills. I could hear the wall clock ticking, and the toilet running from down the hall. Leap had forgotten to jiggle the toilet handle again after he flushed.

"What you in here rummaging around for?"

"My mother said she'd leave twenty cents for my carfare down to Lombard Street. You seen it?"

"Naw." He dragged.

"Well, can you loan it to me till she get back?"

A slight smirk played on his face. "What you gonna do for me?"

My bus arrived in ten minutes, and I could hear each precious second ticking away on the kitchen clock.

"What you want?" I chewed on my fingernail, spitting out flecks of pink polish.

Leap stamped out his cigarette. "A kiss."

"Huh?" My stomach sank so low I forgot to breathe.

"Just a quick one. No harm in that, and I'll give you a quarter." He flashed me a smile. His gold crown glinted from the upper right side of his mouth.

That was ten cents each way, plus five cents extra for a pretzel and juice on our break. Inez never gave me extra for food. I usually just sat in class hungry. My schoolbag had gotten heavy; I hadn't realized I was still holding it.

The stress of it all was getting the best of me. I was desperate to get to my classes, determined to earn my scholarship, so that I could stop depending on Inez's creepy boyfriends to keep a roof over our heads.

"Just a peck?" My voice cracked, hating that I was in this position, and Inez even more for putting me in it.

"Yeah."

"On the cheek?"

He reached into his pocket and flipped the quarter in the air with his thumb and pointer finger, caught it and slammed it down on the table. "The lips."

I shivered.

Leap folded his hands behind his back, squinting his eyes the way I saw him do to Inez when he wanted her to give him some sugar, as he called it.

Shame flooded through me. Gulping down my nerves, I willed my feet to move around the chrome kitchen table toward him.

The only thing standing between me and getting to the program on time was a kiss. A measly little kiss. I could do this. When I closed my eyes and leaned up, I could smell a mixture of last night's whiskey and this morning's cigarettes reeking from him. I held back my gag.

Leap pressed his thick lips against mine and my knees knocked against each other. In an instant I felt his slimy tongue force my lips open. When I tried to pull away, Leap cupped one hand over my left breast and used the other hand to grab my behind, tilting me up against him. I squirmed but he just held me tighter, thrusting his thing up against my thigh over my skirt.

"Stop," I whined, pressing my elbows against his waist, trying to free myself. But his grip was unbreakable.

Just then, the front door swung open. Leap stumbled back and pushed me away, but he wasn't quick enough. Inez's big eyes roved between us like a madwoman's.

"What the hell?" she shouted, dropping the brown grocery bag. I heard something crack as it hit the linoleum floor.

Leap backed farther away from me with his hands up, like she was the police. "She came on to me. Talking about needing bus fare. All up on me before I could stop her."

"Liar," I hissed. "It was you."

"Get the fuck out of here." My mother put her arm in the air like she was firing a warning shot. Soft tendrils from her ponytail had come loose. We shared the same walnut-colored skin tone, but hers had turned apple red.

I turned to Leap, waiting to see how he'd react, glad that my mother was finally taking my side. But then I realized: she was looking at me. She was speaking to me. I was the one she blamed. Her eyes sliced into me like a butcher knife.

"Now! Fast ass."

I palmed the quarter, and when I got to the front door, she pushed me in the back of my head. "Got no business all up in my man's face. Stay in a child's place."

She slammed the door behind me so hard that the impact shook the hinges. I stumbled down the steep steps, reaching for the banister to catch myself from falling. Once outside I tried to shake the whole scene from my mind, but I kept feeling Leap's fingers clawing me, kept feeling Inez's fury burn my chest, as I ran the three blocks to the bus stop.

About a half block away, I could see the bus pull over to the curb, and I ran faster, pumping my knees under my skirt as my bag slapped hard against my hip. I called out, waving my hands to get the driver's attention. A few feet away, the door cranked closed, but I was near enough to bang on the metal siding with my fist.

"Please, wait!" I hollered.

But the bus driver pulled away from the curb like he didn't hear me. Like I didn't matter. Like I didn't exist. I hurled my schoolbag to the ground, then bent over and spit the overwhelming taste of Leap from my mouth.

CHAPTER TWO

Washington, D.C., October 1948

THE LINE

Eleanor

Eleanor bustled across Howard University's campus, clutching the letter in her right hand. The return stamp was crested with the Alpha Beta Chi emblem, so she knew it was what she'd been waiting for: a response to her interest letter to join the sorority.

She had watched the girls move about campus with prominence all of last year. They were glamorous, always with their matching lavender scarves, tight knit sweaters, sleek high heels and glossy curls. They did meaningful work, like organize mobile book drives for children in the rural South, draw picket signs to support Mary Church Terrell in her tireless fight to end segregation in public accommodations and collect food for the poor. But most importantly, they were the baddest steppers on the yard. When they twirled their pretty heads, called out, stomped and clapped, everyone stopped at attention. While there were other sororities on campus, it was clear that the ladies in silver and lavender were the pinnacle of the pile, and Eleanor, now a sophomore and finally eligible, was eager to join them.

She moved across the lawn, careful not to walk over students studying or relaxing on the grass between classes, and dodged up the steps to her dormitory, accidentally trampling on a young man's boat-sized foot.

"Oh, I'm so sorry," she shouted over her shoulder as she hastened down the first-floor corridor to her room on the left.

Her heart was beating fast with anticipation, and she tried to steady herself by placing the letter over her chest. This *had* to be her invitation. The one that would change her life. Make her shiny instead of dull. Popular instead of overlooked. A part of a vibrant group instead of plain and solo.

She did not know where the funds would come from for her initiation fees; after all, the money for books and supplies for the past three semesters had bled her parents dry. But the details didn't matter. She'd figure it out. Eleanor's fingers shook as they slid under the flap of the linen envelope, loosening the glue on the seal. A matching piece of stationery slipped into her hand.

October 01, 1948

Dear Miss Quarles,

Thank you so much for your application and inquiry for the sorority Alpha Beta Chi. We appreciate your dedication and enthusiasm for our members and mission. Although you have great spirit, we had a strong pool of applicants and cannot offer you a place on line this year. Please keep up your community presence, study hard, and we invite you to try again next year.

Yours in sisterhood,
Greta Hepburn
President of Alpha Beta Chi, Incorporated

Eleanor's vision went blurry and she blinked several times before reading the letter again, this time more slowly. She mined through each word, searching for it to say the opposite of what she'd first read. By the third time through, her eyes were warm with tears. She hadn't read it wrong; she'd been rejected. Eleanor was crumpling the letter in her hand just as her roommate, Nadine Sherwood, burst through the door.

"Why do you look like someone died?"

Eleanor flung the crumpled correspondence into Nadine's gloved hand. After smoothing it out and dragging her eyes over it, Nadine dropped the sheet into the wastepaper basket next to the chest of drawers.

"I could have spared you the trouble if I had known you were going out for the ABCs. Why didn't you tell me?" She removed her wool suit jacket while simultaneously kicking out of her peep-toe heels.

"I wanted to surprise you."

"Honey, everyone knows they only pick girls with hair straight as a ruler, and skin paler than a paper bag. Where have you been?" Nadine took a seat on her twin bed, tapping her gold cigarette case. "Sometimes you act like Ohio was another planet."

Eleanor had heard those rumors before about the ABCs, but she had written them off as just that. One because it was just plain foolish to judge a girl's worth by her skin color, and two because she knew at least two girls who'd got in and did not fit that description. "Millicent's an ABC and she's a shade browner than me."

"Millicent's daddy is a judge. She comes from old money." Nadine lit up her Chesterfield. "Her mother is an ABC, and both of her parents attended Howard. It's called legacy."

Eleanor hadn't realized that. This way of life was all new to her. She turned from Nadine and studied herself in the wall mirror that hung to the right of the door. Her eyes were still stained with tears. She had warm bronze skin, a broad nose, high cheekbones and a decent head of hair. That's how her mother, Lorraine, always referred to it when she ran the hot comb through it every Sunday before church. Eleanor had been told that she was good-looking, but she'd never considered her skin color a plus or a negative. It just *was*.

Honestly, she hadn't even known that Negroes separated themselves by color until she stepped foot onto the all-Negro university's campus a year ago. Eleanor's house in Ohio was wedged between Italians and Germans; a Polish family lived just up the block. The Negroes in her hometown were too busy getting along with everyone to pit themselves against each other.

"What am I going to do now?"

"Forget about those stuck-up hussies and come to the dance with me tonight."

Eleanor blew out her breath. That was Nadine's response to everything. Go to a party. It was a wonder how she got any studying done at all.

"I have to work."

"You are always working. College is supposed to be the time of your life and you never let loose. I don't think you've been to a good party all year."

"I have to keep my grades up. My parents didn't work their butts off to get me here to waste it away doing the Lindy Hop, Nadine."

Eleanor wanted to add, *I wasn't born with a silver spoon in my mouth like you*, but Nadine didn't deserve that. She had always been sweet to Eleanor, never making bones about their differences.

Nadine got up and thrust open the closet they shared, though the reality was that almost everything in it was Nadine's. After pushing around a few tailored frocks, A-line skirts and silky blouses, Nadine tossed a scoop-neck dress onto Eleanor's bed.

"I can't fit into this anymore. Looks like it's just your size."

Eleanor pressed her lips together to keep them from breaking into a smile. It was a beauty. Belted at the waist. The perfect blush color. Satiny material soft to the touch.

"Stop trying to tempt me." She turned away.

"Dancing will release those blues from your bones." Nadine teased her, crossing the tiny room back to her bed. "And just so you know, no one does the Lindy Hop anymore."

Eleanor shook her head and reached under her bed for her one good pair of wedged shoes. After a year of wearing them a half size too small, they had finally stretched out to being somewhat comfortable. Her shift started in thirty minutes, and with the library on the other side of campus, she needed to get moving.

Stubbing out her cigarette, Nadine fixed her with those haughty eyes. "I'm not taking no for an answer."

Eleanor caught herself sizing up Nadine's slender features. If what Nadine said was true about the ABCs, she could have easily checked the hair and complexion box requirements, though she didn't appear the least bit interested in social clubs. Nadine had lived in Washington, D.C., all her life and didn't have to work as hard as Eleanor to fit in. Her last name opened doors for her, without her having to lift a finger to make a single connection for herself.

"I better go."

"Tonight. Ohio," she hummed her pet name for Eleanor. "I'm going to wait for you to return, and then hound you until you put on that dress."

"I didn't even put in for a pass to go out this evening."

"I'll take care of the dorm matron," Nadine shot back.

Eleanor nodded in exasperation, and then closed the door behind her. How could she focus on going to a party when her confidence was so injured? Eleanor couldn't remember the last time she wanted something as much as she'd wanted to join the ABCs. She had worked extra hard on her application, spending over a week on perfecting it. Her GPA was well above the requirement, and she had volunteered several times at Harrison Elementary school for her community service. What was worse, it had been the first time she had put herself out there, after that trouble she had gotten herself into her senior year of high school. Only for it to blow up in her face. On paper she looked like the model candidate.

Not in the mirror, you aren't.

She picked up her pace, trying to dampen the flicker of self-doubt that had started whispering to her when she arrived at the university. In her distraction, she wandered through the Founder's Square, treading over the university's limestone seal. It was believed that if you walked over the mark without reading it, you'd earn a semester of bad luck. Eleanor stopped. She couldn't take any more bad luck.

The campus library was just ahead, and Eleanor walked through the doors and up the marble steps to the second floor. Her boss, Dorothy Porter, stood on the other side of the glass wall in the collection room, holding a magnifying glass to her eye. Her tight curls were pushed away from her forehead, and she wore a polka-dot dress that hit below her knees.

"Has a new flat arrived?" Eleanor asked as she dropped her bag.

The collection room was always kept cool and dry, providing a stable environment for the assemblage of rare manuscripts, pamphlets and books that Mrs. Porter curated in her role as an archivist.

"It's a letter written from James Forten, of Philadelphia, addressed to William Lloyd Garrison, dated December 31, 1830," she spoke in a hushed voice, as if talking at full volume would destroy the delicate paper in her hand.

Eleanor read over Mrs. Porter's shoulder, knowing from working with her for the last year that she dare not touch the naked sheet without washing her hands.

"Forten was a wealthy Negro sailmaker. A stunning piece to add to our manuscript puzzle." Mrs. Porter's eyes shone. "I'll need you to codify this."

"Freeman. Biography. Philadelphia?" Eleanor looked at her boss expectantly.

"Yes, and then by decade and gender."

Mrs. Porter slipped the flat paper into a clear polyester film sleeve and then passed it on to Eleanor. "We have a private viewing of biographies and portraits for a donor in Boston next month. I'd like your suggestion on which pieces we should display."

Eleanor whipped her head toward Mrs. Porter in surprise. This was a first, and it patted a layer of salve over the sting from the sorority's rejection letter.

Mrs. Porter was very protective of "her collection" that she had spent two decades amassing, and her zeal for her work was astonishing.

Eleanor had arrived at Howard as an English major with the mind that she would become a teacher, but that had changed only a few weeks into her first semester, when she'd first met Mrs. Porter.

Eleanor had been studying in the library when a voice behind her asked, "Would you mind lending me a hand, dear?" A woman—Mrs. Porter—had stood in a plaid suit with a bulky shopping bag in each hand. Eleanor had taken the heaviest one from her and followed her up to the Moorland Room.

"Careful with that." Mrs. Porter chastised her when Eleanor thumped the bag on the table. "You never know what treasures can be found on the floors of people's basements."

The contents in the bag were odorous, but that didn't sway Mrs. Porter from gently going through all the pieces with the care of a mother hen. There were letters, a diary, photographs, dusty books, rusty trinkets and newspaper clippings. Eleanor asked Mrs. Porter what the assortment was for as she had a propensity for antiquated things.

"My goal is to build a collection that would reflect all of our history. Comprehensive Negro history." Mrs. Porter beamed.

Her enthusiasm was contagious, and after just a few moments together, Mrs. Porter asked, "Have you read *Incident in the Life of a Slave Girl*?"

"By Harriet Jacobs? It's one of my favorites." Eleanor grinned. She had been a self-proclaimed history hound since her eighth-grade teacher introduced her to the writings of Claude McKay, Alice Dunbar-Nelson, and her husband, Paul Laurence Dunbar.

Mrs. Porter had instructed Eleanor to put on a pair of white gloves and then placed a weathered newspaper clipping in her hands. Eleanor had looked from the piece between her fingers to Mrs. Porter with her mouth agape.

Mrs. Porter confirmed. "An original advertisement for Jacobs's capture. It ran in the *American Beacon* newspaper on July 4, 1835, in Norfolk, Virginia."

Chills surfaced up Eleanor's arms as she pored over the ad offering a $100 reward for Harriet Jacobs's apprehension and delivery. Unexpected tears welled in Eleanor's eyes as she recalled Jacobs hiding in an attic of her grandmother's house for seven long years before finally escaping north to freedom. Eleanor's gaze locked with Mrs. Porter's as an understanding passed between them. From that moment on, Eleanor was hooked. Before her first semester was over, she changed her major to history, with the goal of becoming a library archivist, just like Mrs. Porter.

Curating a collection was a first step and she responded brightly, "I have a few ideas."

"Wonderful. I've left a stack of card indexes for you at the circulation desk that need cataloguing. I'll be in my office charming away monetary donations."

Mrs. Porter picked up several new bags brimming with books and headed up to the third floor. When Eleanor arrived at the circulation desk, she found the list of patrons with overdue books who needed to be telephoned. Between the calls and Mrs. Porter's assignments, she had more than enough work to keep her mind occupied.

The library was the most peaceful place on campus, especially for someone like Eleanor, who had grown to prefer the company of books to people. Though deep down she knew that she desired both, which is why she wanted to join the ABCs, and the new wave of rejection tugged her bottom lip into a pout. Perhaps she should consider going to the party with Nadine. It had been a long time since she dressed up and she had always loved to dance. But no, she had several chapters to read for her philosophy class. The time she'd spent working on her application for the ABCs had put her dreadfully behind on her studies. And it had all been for nothing. Eleanor cast that thought aside and turned to her library work.

After an hour of sorting and filing indexes, the steady sound of crinkling paper pulled her attention away from her task. At the table across from her, she noticed a growing pile of balled leaflets. Her cheeks warmed, and she had to rest her elbows on the desk to steady herself. The Back was back.

The Back belonged to a boy. He always sat in the same cushioned chair, at the same wooden table. He had wide shoulders and dark hair that curled tightly at the nape of his long neck. Eleanor often daydreamed about what it would be like to give those shiny curls a tug. In the many months that she had admired him from her post, she could not recall ever catching him full frontal. Spotting Mr. Back at his regular place always made her day a bit brighter.

An hour or so later, as Eleanor was making a list of stationery supplies that needed to be ordered, she heard footsteps as someone approached the circulation table. She looked up and was met with broad shoulders, tightly curled hair. It was him. Mr. Back.

"Sorry to trouble you, ma'am. But can I sharpen my pencil?" Eleanor's tongue lost the ability to speak. She had caught his side profile a few times, but that had not prepared her for him up close, in her personal space. Oh Lord, faced front Mr. Back was *fine*.

"Does it work?" His slightly slanted, inky black eyes looked puzzled. He had smooth skin and soft lips.

"I'd be happy to." Eleanor regained her composure. She took the pencil from him, thrust it into the sharpener and cranked the metal handle. Suddenly worried about her own appearance, she wished she could catch a glimpse of herself in the reflection of the sharpener. Were her eyes puffy? Hair in place? She turned back to him, pencil in hand.

"William," he said.

"Excuse me?"

"My name. It's William. William Pride."

"Oh, Eleanor Quarles."

"How long have you been at Howard?"

"I'm a sophomore. You?"

"Third year of medical school. I did my undergrad at Howard too."

Eleanor kept her face cool, even though her insides did a pirouette. He was going to be a doctor. A Negro doctor.

“Well, I’ll be here all day if you need your pencil sharpened again.” Her voice cracked, and she tried to cover up her nervousness with a hearty laugh.

“I’ll remember that.” He winked and turned for his table. Eleanor went back to filing, the whole time trying to focus on the papers in front of her instead of staring at William Pride’s beautiful back.

Chapter Three

THE SWEETEST THING

Ruby

I arrived at Thomas Durham Public School forty-five minutes late, with the feeling of Leap's vile tongue and nauseating scent still on me. My enrichment instructor, Mrs. Thomas, had locked her classroom door when I tried to enter, so I sat on the hard bench in the hall trying to overhear the lesson on college essay writing. I couldn't see the blackboard through the frosted glass, or hear the student's responses, but Mrs. Thomas had a voice that carried, and I jotted down what I could gather.

My blouse had discolored with wet rings under the armpits, and my stomach wouldn't settle down no matter how many times I rubbed it. For two long hours I waited, feeling completely disgusted with myself. I'd endured being slobbered on by my mother's boyfriend, and where had that gotten me? I was still on the outside of the classroom while everyone else was in. Finally, the door pulled open, and my cohorts filed out. As some snuck furtive glances my way, it felt like they had known what I had done with Leap, and I squirmed shamefully on my seat, avoiding all eye contact.

Two years ago, back in eighth grade, we had been selected for *We Rise*. The program provided tutoring and mandatory Saturday enrichment classes, along with vigorous testing throughout high school, to prepare us for college. As the best and the brightest, we twelve were competing for only two full scholarships. The ten who were not awarded the highest opportunity would be given a modest stipend to attend a trade school and continued support for job placement. I couldn't afford to be one of the ten who didn't qualify and be stuck living hand to mouth with Inez, begging Fatty for money, and being prey to Leap. This was my only way out. Failing to get the scholarship just wasn't an option for me.

The last students trailed by as if I were nonexistent. But as their shoes echoed down the hall, I was sure of what they were thinking: *How come she's always late? I don't have to worry about her nabbing the scholarship over me. Careless. Stupid. Not even a threat.*

"Miss Pearsall," my teacher called, in her firm voice. She'd seen me through the window in the door.

I pushed my bag over my shoulder and walked into the classroom while Mrs. Thomas got to work erasing the blackboard. She kept the shades up for the various gardenias, ferns and snake plants she had perched along the windowsills. A horn honked outside her window, and two dogs barked in succession. The room smelled of honeyed tea and the vanilla candle that always burned.

Mrs. Thomas closed the door behind me, and then took a seat at her long wooden desk. Her dark brown hair was rolled away from her face and pinned off her neck. She wore a string of pearls with a gold broach, and matching droplets hung daintily from her earlobes. She was the most proper Negro woman I had ever met, and disappointing her hurt like a hole in my tooth.

She motioned for me to take a seat. "Miss Pearsall, do you realize that there are many Negro students up and down the East Coast that would give anything to be in your position?"

"Yes, ma'am."

"Then what is your problem? I warned you last week."

"I know, but . . ."

"There are no buts." Her voice bit into me as she leaned across her desk. "There are no second chances when it comes to us. If you want to escape your current circumstances, you have to work like your tail is on fire."

My right knee shook, and I bit down on my bottom lip.

"Potential without focus and full commitment bears no fruit."

"Yes, ma'am."

She leaned back in her seat, moving some papers around in front of her. "Instead of the field trip to Hahnemann Hospital next week, you will stay here and make up the work you have missed."

"No, please. I can make that work up from home."

"I'm sorry, Ruby. I cannot allow you to attend. It will look as if I am showing you favor to the students who are here every week on time. Now, go home and decide if attending college is really what you want."

"It is, ma'am. More than anything."

"Then show up and work like your life depends on it. Now you're dismissed." Her chair scraped against the floor as she stood up and pointed to the door.

I walked out feeling like a stone was lodged in the middle of my chest. The field trip had been planned for weeks. My class was going to shadow the medical staff as they made their rounds. It was my chance to connect with real doctors, and I had blown the opportunity.

As the door to the school building slammed behind me, I could feel Leap's scaly fingers squeezing my breast and the memory made me walk faster up Lombard Street. Like I was trying to outrun a ghost. No matter how many times I had swallowed since the kiss, I swore I could still taste him. When I got to the traffic light on the corner of Broad Street, I coughed, then spit him out on the sidewalk, not caring that I wasn't being ladylike and that someone might see me. All that nastiness had been for nothing.

I trudged north on Broad Street until my head cleared. It didn't feel wise to go back to Inez's fury—plus, Leap was most likely still there. I didn't want to look at either of them, and I certainly didn't want to hear the bed springs and moans that came after their fights, drifting through the thin walls as Inez gave up all her sugar. Instead, I hopped on the streetcar and then transferred to the bus that took me to 29th Street. As I walked over to Diamond Street, a breeze rustled through my hair and I pressed my bangs back against my forehead.

My aunt Marie's apartment was two houses from the corner, a few feet from a paint store. At her front door, I glanced over my shoulder like she taught me to do before pulling my beaded key chain from around my neck. Her apartment was three long flights up, and I knocked twice to announce myself before twisting my key in the lock.

The old furnace burning in the middle of the room gave off a damp odor that was only partially masked by the cinnamon potpourri simmering on the stovetop. Aunt Marie's eyes widened as she waved me in. She sat on the saggy sofa in her flowered housecoat, with the telephone tucked between her ear and shoulder. A pen and receipt pad in her hand.

"644, 828 and 757. And Joe? No jiving this week. Don't make me kick your ass."

Aunt Marie dropped the receiver back into the cradle and smiled, showing off the gap between her two front teeth. She was Inez's older sister, though they were nothing alike.

"Your mother dropped your stuff off."

"What she say?" I chewed my nail, and glimpsed three shopping bags by the wall that overflowed with sweaters and shorts, recognizing pieces that I hadn't worn in years. It looked like Inez had swooped up everything I owned, regardless of size or season.

"That you been smelling your piss."

Aunt Marie ran her hand over her short, gray-speckled hair, and asked me what happened. I loosened my shoes and told her about needing carfare to get to my program, and how Leap offered it to me.

"For a kiss?" She sucked hard on her teeth. "He a grown-ass man. That all he do?"

I nodded my head quickly, leaving off him pushing his thing against me. Aunt Marie was known to settle problems with the .22 she kept on the floor beneath the couch, and I didn't want her troubled on my account.

"Triflin' as shit. Inez over here talking about she done finally found a good man to settle down with. Ain't nothing good about a man who got eyes for a girl 'bout to turn fifteen." She pushed herself to stand and reached out her jiggly arms to me.

Aunt Marie was tall and stout like a tree, and I sank into her strong girth.

"Stay as long as you need, hear?"

"Thank you." Relief made me burrow deeper into her embrace.

"Everything going to be all right." She lifted my chin. "You eat?"

"Not much. Just a few bites of toast for breakfast."

Aunt Marie started walking to her bedroom in the back of the apartment. "Some tuna in the fridge. Eat as much as you want."

From the living room, I only had to walk two steps and I was in what passed as her kitchen, though it was really all one big room. I pulled down a plate from the shelf and smeared the mixture of tuna with cubed boiled eggs and diced onions on two slices of white bread. I took a big bite, and then carried the rest of it back to her bedroom. Aunt Marie dropped the needle on her record player, and out crooned Dinah Washington. From her vanity, she talked to me through the mirror while I sat on the edge of her bed.

"Gotta perform at Kiki's tonight. Promised I'd get there early and help set up. You be okay here by yourself?"

"I reckon I'll manage."

"Your paint supplies still over in the corner under the bay window. Just don't mess up my floors."

Aunt Marie's eggplant-colored bedroom always made me feel like we were backstage at a theater. She had wigs and mustaches, makeup and lashes, feathers and boas, top hats, ties and tails. I chomped down on my sandwich while she applied blush to her umber-colored cheeks and bright red lipstick to her wide mouth. She cocked her head, while I told her about Fatty being late and me not being able to go on the field trip next week.

"Do I need to ride down there and talk to someone about this?"

"No, I got it." My jaw tightened.

I knew she meant well, but Mrs. Thomas wouldn't take kindly to me siccing my aunt on her. Besides, Aunt Marie wasn't the type of person Mrs. Thomas would understand. She'd probably faint at the sight of my big-boned, gun-toting, numbers-running aunt. People like Aunt Marie and Mrs. Thomas didn't mix. Her showing up to fight my battle would only push me farther from Mrs. Thomas's favor, and I was already barking up a thin tree. I just had to accept my punishment and move on.

Humming along with Dinah Washington, Aunt Marie slipped on a stark white men's dress shirt that hung from her closet door, then handed me a pair of gold cuff links to fasten for her. After stepping into men's trousers and a checkered sports jacket, she finished the look with clip-on chandelier earrings.

"How do I look?"

"Like you the big money McGillicuddy."

She chuckled. "Only way to be my little money McGillicuddy is to keep your head in those books. I'll straighten out Fatty. You just do what those people tell you and get that scholarship."

I wiped the mayo from the corner of my mouth.

"Oh, and Shimmy coming by here to look up underneath the sink."

"Who's Shimmy?"

I followed her back down the hall, taking in a whiff of the spicy cologne she sprayed on her neck and wrists.

"My landlord's son. Too cheap to hire a real plumber. Always sending that boy to do the work round here. And don't nothing ever get done."

I slid the metal chain across the doorframe after she went out, and left Dinah Washington playing to keep me company. Inez wouldn't let me store my paint supplies at our house. Said seeing my stuff all over made her nerves bad, but all things concerning me put Inez on edge. At Aunt Marie's, I kept all my art in a metal wash bin. My beige apron had splatters of dry paint down the front, and I slipped it over my neck, then clipped my bangs back off my forehead with bobby pins so that I could see.

The sun had traveled to the other side of the street, making the room dim. I yanked on the rusted string of the brass floor lamp, then spread the worn sheet I used as a drop cloth underneath my feet. My easel wasn't more than a few scraps of wood that Aunt Marie had found and nailed together for me. Paint was expensive, so I had only the three primary colors: yellow, blue and red, but I was a master at mixing the right combination to create almost any color I wanted.

As I stared at the blank canvas trying to figure out where to begin, I could feel my shoulders slip down my back. It was always like that. To paint was to breathe easy. When I picked up my brush, all my problems magically washed away. I had started painting about two years ago, after my *We Rise* teacher took us on a field trip to the Philadelphia College of the Arts for a class on oil painting. Louise Clement, a young art student, was our teacher. I had never met a Negro artist before and found myself intrigued by the way her face lit up as she talked about her work. While Louise explained color theory and brush techniques, most of my classmates' eyes had glazed over with boredom, but I listened with intensity. After the three-hour workshop, I produced my first piece of art. It was a pastel painting of tall willowy branches reaching for the light of the moon. Louise stared at my painting for so long I had begun to sweat, worrying that I had done it all wrong.

Then she touched my shoulder and said, "Art is the friend that you can always return to. It will always be there to heighten your feeling of aliveness. Keep going."

As our class packed up to leave, Louise gifted me a tote bag containing a few tubes of paint, four brushes, and three small canvases.

Most times my approach to making art was to let my brushes guide the way to unlocking what was inside my heart, so I dipped the flat brush in black, and streaked it across the white page creating a tangle of darkness in the sky. It didn't take long for me to get lost in the sweep of gray, then scatters of blue, disappearing into what I called Ruby Red's World, where I had complete control over everything.

Dinah Washington was singing "I Wanna Be Loved" when a hard rap against the door snapped me back.

"Who is it?" My voice came out husky.

"Miz Marie, it's Shimmy."

I wiped my hands on my apron and swung open the door. A pale boy with curly brown hair stood under the fluorescent hall light. Our eyes touched and the air around me felt sticky and warm.

"Who are you?" His cheeks flushed beet, and his emerald-green eyes stared at me two seconds beyond politeness.

"Ruby. Marie's my aunt."

"Shimmy Shapiro."

I stepped aside to let him enter.

He smelled like cedar with a hint of the potatoes I pictured him having for dinner. I felt unkempt in my splashed apron and wished I had left my bangs curled over my wide forehead.

His eyes lingered over my canvas and paints, then turned his focus to the kitchen. "This sink here?"

I nodded and he rolled his shirtsleeves to his elbows and hiked up his dungarees. After placing his tool bag on the table, he got down on the floor. He pushed aside the makeshift curtain that covered the plumbing and pulled out a bucket. I could smell bleach, and see a bottle of vinegar and a small flask that probably contained corn liquor.

With his head underneath the sink, he called to me. "Can you hand me that flashlight?"

I looked down at the stick hanging from the top of his bag and unclipped it. Our fingers brushed against each other as he took it from me.

"Are you an artist?"

I blew out a nervous giggle. "Wouldn't say that."

He rooted around and then pulled his head out and sat up.

"Is it fixed?"

"No, I don't have the right tools." He took off his gloves and wiped the sweat on his forehead. "Can I have a drink of water?"

Each cup I picked up was either chipped or faded, and I didn't want to feel shamed in front of this white boy. I chose my tin mug with the dent next to the handle.

He leaned against the sink and sipped, while taking in my homemade studio in the corner. "You look like an artist to me. What are you painting?"

I glanced down at my bare feet. The pink polish had chipped on my big toe, and I covered it with my other foot.

"Nothing really. Just passing time."

"Can I see?"

Ordinarily, I didn't show anyone besides Aunt Marie my work, but there was something about the way he asked. It had a sweetness to it that blotted away some of the sourness from my awful day. Timidly, I turned the easel his way. He moved in closer to me. Then put his hand on his chin and studied it, almost like he was at a museum.

"It's beautiful but moody. What's got you sad?" He stared at me with intense green eyes. His expression was thoughtful, and I could tell that he was actually interested in what I had to say.

"Who says I'm sad?"

"The contrast in colors, here and here."

"You an art critic or something?" I turned my easel away from him.

"No, but I've taken a few classes at the art museum. And I know I like it."

I wasn't used to compliments. His appreciation of my work made me feel foolish for turning the easel, so I dropped my hands and allowed him to see. He took in the painting again.

In the middle of the page was a large head with grossly oversized bloodshot eyes. I had exaggerated the hair, making it wild and so big that it clouded and shaded out the sun. Down in the right-hand corner was an oak tree with a knothole in the center. Peeking from the hole was a small blue bird searching for the light. Shimmy stepped in closer, tracing the bird with his fingertips. After several seconds passed, he uttered the word "lovely."

I wrapped my arms around my middle, suddenly feeling exposed.

"The bird says it all."

The tiny bird was the only object on the page that was bright and in full color.

"Thank you," I mumbled finally, having not realized that I had been holding my breath until the words left my body.

"May I?" He reached for my paintbrush.

I nodded and then he dipped the brush in my smear of yellow and dabbed in a streak through the big head's hair. It added the perfect contrast to the bird's blue.

"If you don't like it, you can cover it over with black."

"No, it's nice." My heart was thumping like I had just taken the stairs two at a time. Shimmy stood so close to me that we were almost touching. The way he stared at my painting made me feel like he was peeking at my soul.

He finished his water and then put his cup in the sink. Turning for the door he said, "I better go. Tell your aunt my mother will send someone by. Guess I'll see you around, Ruby."

"When?" The question escaped from my lips too quick for my brain to stop it, and I wanted to grab the word and shove it back inside. There was no reason for me to see this white boy again. Even if he did like my art.

"I work at Greenwald's candy store." He offered a boyish grin. "Come by tomorrow for a malt?"

"We'll see."

Shimmy hesitated in the hall. "If you come, it'll be on me."

"I can pay for myself."

"Of course, I didn't mean—"

"Thanks for looking at the sink," I said quickly before closing the door.

Dinah Washington stopped crooning, and I replaced her album with Billie Holiday. "Lover Man" filled the room as I stood over the sink. Shimmy's mug was the only dish in the basin. I picked it up, and without thinking, rested the rim against my bottom lip.

Chapter Four

BLACK MECCA

Eleanor

Eleanor ran a tube of coral lipstick across her lips, and then dabbed her wrists and neck with a lilac-scented eau de toilette. She fixed her hair with two rolls pinned on top and left the back down in drop curls. When she stood back from the hanging mirror in her dorm room, she was unable to believe what she saw. The dress Nadine had laid out for her clung to her curves like a second skin. The low neckline accentuated her graceful shoulders, and the satiny blush material seemed to illuminate her face, giving her a healthy glow. Eleanor hadn't felt beautiful in a long time, and she stared at herself in awe.

"What did I tell you, Ohio? Don't you feel better already?" Nadine reached over and buttoned the tiny clasp at the back of Eleanor's neck.

"We'd better get going before I change my mind," Eleanor teased. Glancing around their room. "Why do you have to make such a mess, girly. You know things out of order wrecks my nerves."

Nadine had gone through several frocks, nylons, heels, gloves, and they were all scattered about her bed, and some covered the floor.

"I have a hard time making decisions." Nadine picked up her purse.

"I should probably stay back and tidy up. Your clutter is a perfect excuse not to go."

"Please, not after all my hard work." Nadine put her finger on Eleanor's back and playfully shoved her out the door.

The hallway was filled with fragrances of fruity perfumes, talcum powders and hair pomade, as many girls buzzed about. Some had on their good trench coats, silk stockings and scarlet lipstick, prancing down the hall on their way out. A few sat in the lounge by the roaring fire, waiting for gentleman callers to drop by. Then there were the ones that were nowhere to be found, tucked in their rooms with snacks smuggled from the cafeteria, the radio turned low with a book opened. If it hadn't been for Nadine and her relentless harassment, Eleanor would have been one of the latter.

As the pair signed out at the front desk, their dorm matron, a thick woman with gray streaks in her hair, pushed back her glasses and spoke through clenched teeth: "Please remember to conduct yourself like ladies at all times. Your future husband could be anywhere, and I wouldn't want you to taint your reputation with bad behavior."

"Yes, ma'am," they replied in unison, scribbling their names on the night ledger.

The Coedikette, their handbook of rules, made it very clear: students were only permitted two off-campus passes per month, and requests needed to be made in writing at least one week in advance. When Eleanor asked Nadine how she could have possibly secured one for her so quickly, Nadine replied with a mischievous grin, "If I told you, I'd have to shoot you."

The girls walked to the edge of campus arm in arm. Nadine insisted on paying for a taxicab, because her parents would be cross if they found out she was on the bus after dark. The cracked leather seats in the cab smelled like coconuts. When the driver turned onto U Street, Eleanor gazed out the window at all the well-dressed people in hats and long coats strolling up and down the brightly lit street. They passed the Murray Casino, the Ford, the Dabney Movie Theater and then pulled to a stop in front of the Club Bali at 14th Street.

"Have a good evening, ladies." The driver stood on the street and held the car door.

The flashing red-and-yellow sign above the club, coupled with the song "Caravan" by Duke Ellington floating from inside, gave Eleanor a surprise jolt of excitement at the base of her spine. She had not spent much time off campus at all.

Eleanor followed Nadine down the skinny stairs into a dance hall lit dimly with Gothic wall sconces. There were square tables in a U-shape hugging the dance floor. The band played "It Don't Mean a Thing," and couples were shaking their hips, snapping their fingers and patting their feet to the rhythm. Groups of girls stood in safe clusters with their eyes darting about, hoping a boy would ask them to dance.

All the tables were nearly full, but Nadine spotted a fellow from high school at a table near the center.

"Showtime," she said, smiling at Eleanor, and then sauntered across the room.

"What you know good, Clarence?" Nadine placed her long fingers on her hips and spilled her cleavage forward.

"Nadine Sher-rr-wood," the brawny man stuttered, gazing at Nadine like she was an answer to his prayers.

"Are you going to just stare at me or invite us to sit down?" she purred.

"So-so-rry. Please." He scrambled up and offered them both seats. Eleanor squeezed in next to Nadine as she made quick introductions.

"How-www have you been?"

"Peachy." Nadine leaned in so that he could light her cigarette. They kept up a steady stream of conversation while Eleanor fanned her throat.

"It's hot in here," Eleanor said to no one in particular. She was suddenly parched and could barely move an inch without bumping into Clarence's friend, whose breath smelled of rotten cheese. He hadn't said much, but he wouldn't take his eyes off her lips. This was a bad idea. She should have followed her own mind and stayed in. Eleanor looked around the room for the waitress, and that's when she saw him.

Mr. Back from the library. William. He turned toward her before she could render her eyes away. He smiled, and she gave a small wave in response. William waved back and then he was making his way through the crowd. Eleanor dipped her head, hoping he wasn't coming to their table, while also wanting nothing more. She tried to turn her attention to the conversation Nadine was having and busied her hands by opening and closing the clasp on Nadine's cigarette case.

"Finally going to fancy a smoke?" Nadine mocked her, and stuttering Clarence took her humor as a cue to inch closer, warding off the boys circling.

Heat rose up Eleanor's neck as a shadow was cast over her.

"Eleanor?"

He had abandoned his sweater for a tweed jacket and a spear-point-collar shirt. Blue sure looked mighty good on him.

Curving her face up, she grinned. "William, right?"

"What are the odds of running into you twice in one day?"

"Pretty slim I'd imagine."

The trombone player whined out a long curdling sound as the band leader sang a finale of high notes.

"Would you like to dance?" He held his hand out to her.

She flushed and her fingers shook as she extended her arm. "I'd love to."

Nadine pinched Eleanor's thigh under the table in excitement as she lifted out of her seat. William did not let her hand go once she rose, and his palm was warm against hers as they moved through the swarm of people. His fingers were smooth like they hadn't known a day of hard work, not stiff and rough like her father's—like most of the boys Eleanor knew from back home, in fact. The quartet was loud, and Eleanor was grateful that the music drowned out the thumping of her heart.

The moment she stepped foot on the parquet dance floor, the band slowed the pace. Couples brushed against each other. William took a step toward her, draping his arm around her waist, as if it was something he had done countless times before. He smelled divine, like bark, or maybe bergamot. Whatever it was smelled masculine.

"I didn't expect to see you here tonight. I've only ever seen you in the library." William's voice was sultry at her ear.

She gulped. He had noticed her before? "My roommate dragged me out."

"Let me guess, you'd rather be home studying?"

"How'd you know?"

"You work in the library."

"What's that supposed to mean?"

"I bet you spend more time with books than people," he teased, showing perfectly stacked teeth.

"Sometimes they are better company."

"Well, Miss Eleanor, I'm glad you came out. Everyone needs a break." He spun her around and then dipped her. "It's good for the soul."

"What makes you so wise?" She lifted her head so that the light caught her eyes.

"Experience."

They danced with ease, quickly spinning and bopping through three songs that felt like one. By the time the band took a break, Eleanor's brows were clammy and she was sure her curls had flopped. While they applauded the musician's set, a string of loud voices turned everyone's attention to the front door.

"Say what? Say who? Say what? Say who?"

Through the crowd marched a single file of women dressed in lavender shirtwaist dresses, with silver belts. People parted a path for them as the ladies swayed their way onto the dance floor, moving their arms and legs in a synchronized movement. The drummer, who had been about to leave the stage, gave a few tap, tap, taps. The girls clapped their hands to his beat, and then called out in unison.

"Say Alpha Beta Chi, that's who."

The ABCs threw their hands in the air to hoots and applause. A few girls blew kisses, then broke away from their formation to greet friends and admirers around the dance hall. Eleanor gritted her teeth. She'd actually managed to put her dismissal by the ABCs out of her mind when dancing with William. Now it all came flying back.

William touched her elbow. "May I get you something to drink?"

While William ordered drinks, Eleanor stole a glance at the ABCs' pledge line. These girls were outfitted in white dresses rather than the customary lavender. They wore silver ribbons in their hair. They stood against the wall, hands clasped in front of them, their stony faces waiting for instructions. Pledges on the line were to be seen but never heard as they assured their loyalty to Alpha Beta Chi. The pledgees wouldn't earn their silver belts and the right to wear lavender until they crossed over in six weeks' time. Eleanor should have been one of them. She couldn't help feeling a twinge of envy as her eyes swept their faces, confirming that Nadine had been right: all the girls were light and bright.

William returned with an Orange Crush for Eleanor. "Salut." He raised his glass of beer. Eleanor took a sip of pop, happy for the distraction of his attention.

Suddenly, a shrill voice calling William's name interrupted the moment between them.

They both turned to see Greta Hepburn, president of the ABCs and homecoming queen for two years straight, gliding in their direction. She nearly fell into William's arms as she pecked him on his cheek.

He looked startled by the affection. "Good to see you, Greta," he said, taking a step back, forcing her to drop her embrace.

Greta flung her soft wavy hair over her shoulder and turned to Eleanor. "I assume you received your letter?" She looked as if she was trying to muster sympathy, but it never reached her honey-colored eyes.

Eleanor nodded, desperately wishing that Greta had kept her mouth shut in front of William.

"Better luck next year. Stay persistent," she cooed, then twirled to William. "I'm so thirsty. Would you be a doll and get me some punch?"

"Sure," William said. "Eleanor, anything else?"

"No, thank you."

William walked off as Greta moved so close that Eleanor could smell expensive department store perfume.

"How do you know William?"

"We just met."

"He and I go way back. We practically bathed together as children," she laughed. "Our families are very close."

Eleanor didn't know what to say, so she nodded and sipped her drink. William made his way back toward them grinning. Was the affectionate look for her or Greta? It was hard to tell with them standing so close to each other, but it was probably for Greta. Eleanor had to admit that Greta was a sight. Everyone on campus said so. Eleanor had never seen her without every hair perfect and in place. She reeked of money, dressed in the most eye-catching clothes and carried herself like she was the prima donna of Howard. Greta's skin was so white the only thing that identified her as a Negro was that she attended Howard with the rest of them.

"Here you are." William extended the drink toward Greta, and as she reached for it, her elbow slipped back behind her, knocking against Eleanor's glass and tipping the bright Orange Crush down the front of her borrowed frock.

"I'm so sorry," she shrieked, but didn't move to do anything about it.

William stepped in and handed Eleanor his embroidered handkerchief. "Are you okay?"

"Fine."

Just humiliated, she thought. The band started playing again.

"William, let's dance." Greta grabbed him by the arm. William looked at Eleanor.

"I'm going to pop into the ladies' lounge to clean up. You two have fun," Eleanor offered, walking away before anyone had a chance to respond.

When she peered at herself in the long mirror, she saw the wet spot soaked down the front of Nadine's frock. Now she'd have to spring for dry cleaning. Greta had bumped her on purpose, Eleanor was sure of it. Was it not enough to reject her from the ABCs?

Eleanor dabbed at the neckline with a wet paper towel, at least thankful the drink hadn't been tea or Coke. Still, she was ruined for the night, and knew the best thing for her to do was to return to her dormitory. There was time enough for her to get in a few chapters of philosophy before bed if she left now.

On her way out, Eleanor glanced at the dance floor, where Greta swayed, her arms wrapped around William's neck. They made the most handsome pair, looking like a couple right out of a magazine.

We practically bathed together as children.

It was just as well. There was no way that William Pride, a future doctor, could be interested in a girl like Eleanor. He had all but declared her a boring bookworm on the dance floor. Eleanor patted herself on the back for not getting too swept up in the easy nature of his hands around her waist and the kind voice in her ear. William had been polite to call on her, but it meant nothing.

She took one last look at the dance floor. Nadine was shimmying on one end, and on the other, Greta leaned in and said something that made William chuckle. Eleanor headed for the door. It wasn't until she landed outside and felt the cool night air graze her knuckles that she realized she was still clutching William's handkerchief.

Chapter Five

ACTING UGLY

Ruby

Sunlight flooded the apartment, making it hard for me to sleep in. I rolled over on the lumpy pullout sofa to the sight of Aunt Marie sitting at the table with a piece of frozen beef against her face.

"What happened?" My wool blanket fell to my hips.

"Right before closing, I had to sucker punch a fool who couldn't hold his liquor and was running off at the mouth."

"You all right?"

"Looks worse than it is. Just mad at myself for not ducking." She winced through the gap in her teeth. "I don't know who let him in, but I could tell he was trouble by the way he sat through the show jeering all night. Management gon' to have to do a better job screening folk. Kiki's is a safe haven for us."

By "us" she didn't mean just our people, she meant her kind of people. The kind that wore what they wanted and kissed who they wanted. She let the meat down, and I could see the swirl of black and blue marbling around her left eye.

"What you need me to do?"

"Run on over to 31st Street and pick up a few things."

When I slid my bare feet onto the cold hardwood floor, I immediately started to tremble. The furnace had gone out, but I could still smell the embers. The chill made me sneeze over and over again until my eyes watered.

"Reach up in that cabinet over the sink and take a spoonful of cod liver oil," Aunt Marie commanded.

"I'm all right," I responded, trying to avoid taking the nasty concoction that smelled like fish. It made my breath stink and hurt my stomach.

"Sweetness, I'm not asking. Can't have you sick up in here, not on my watch."

I'd stayed with Aunt Marie enough over the years to know that there was no point in arguing with her, so I grabbed a spoon and the bottle and sucked down a dose of the nasty fish oil. My stomach churned, and the aftertaste lingered on my tongue even after several gulps of water.

"That a girl." Aunt Marie moved the meat back up to her eye. "Make sure you dress in layers."

I nodded while making the effort to suppress another sneeze, worried that she'd make me take something more. I ruffled through the paper bags that contained my things, Inez's words, "fast ass," echoing from each bag. I had been right: every piece of clothing I owned was crammed in.

Seven years. That's the amount of time Inez had played mother to me. From the time I was born until third grade, Inez was just Nene's daughter. The pretty lady who smelled like honeysuckle and wore slingback heels, who came around on the weekends to drink beer with my cousin Fatty. Then Nene's glaucoma worsened and she fell and fractured her hip. Two days later she was declared legally blind.

A week after her prognosis, I could tell that something was wrong by the way Nene's bottom lip quivered as she crushed me to her breasts. "If I could keep you, sweetness, you know I would. But Nene's getting old, and she the only mother you got. Be patient with her."

That's how I found out that this Inez lady was my real mama and I had to move a few blocks over to the apartment that she shared with her boyfriend of the moment.

Inez clearly never wanted me with her, though. I missed Nene and our routine something fierce. And everything I did in my new home set Inez off. If I poured too much Karo syrup on my pancakes, she'd slap me. Ask her a question while her man was present, I got cussed out. And God forbid one of her suitors took his attention off her and put it on me; that meant there would be a meeting of my behind and the thick leather belt she kept on the back of her bedroom door. Most of her mad moments were followed by a drop-off at Aunt Marie's till she got her "nerves together."

But Inez had never sent me packing with everything I owned. Not until this thing with Leap. My throat ached as I belched up the awful taste of cod liver oil.

"Some hominy grits in the pot for breakfast." Aunt Marie's voice brought me back.

I nodded. My black pants didn't need pressing, so I slipped them on with a plaid blouse, loose cardigan and flats. When I first moved in with Inez, she had joked that my forehead was as big as a skillet, and that she could fry an egg on it. Her laughter was relentless, and from that moment on I never left the house without my bangs almost down to my eyelids. I pressed them down against my forehead, and the rest of my hair I tucked into a bun.

By the time I was ready to go, Aunt Marie had changed into her flowered housecoat and was standing at the hall mirror spreading a layer of toothpaste over her black eye.

"When you go to Sandler's deli, don't let that mean lady with the mole serve you. She likes to give us the tough cut a' meat. Wait for the other lady with the blonde wig, even if she's with a customer."

Aunt Marie handed me a crochet shopping bag, her handwritten list, and three dollars, folded in a handkerchief that she made me pin to the inside of my blouse, close to my heart where someone would have to hold me down to get to it.

"Count my change, hear?"

I undid all three locks on her front door. Outside, the October air felt good on my face, and I was surprised that it was warmer outside than it was in the apartment. Across the street was a filling station, and as I passed by, a bearded man leaned out the window of his car and stared me down.

"Baby Love, you too fine to be walking these streets alone. Let me give you a ride." He was old enough to be my father and had the same gold crown on his tooth as Leap.

I crossed in the opposite direction, bristling at the sound of him calling after me, turning back to make sure he wasn't following. Satisfied, I walked two blocks over to 31st Street, where Jewish shops and businesses lined both sides of the street for a four-block radius. Shoppers could buy everything from fresh bread to fruits and vegetables, sweet treats and jewelry. The whole street was closed on Saturdays. The people who lived in the neighborhood mostly shopped the stores on Sunday, before or after church. Aunt Marie didn't believe in church, and Inez didn't much either. We only went when someone died or was getting married.

I moved through the storefronts, procuring everything on the list, with five cents to spare. From the moment I stepped foot onto 31st Street my eyes kept finding Greenwald's, and I debated back and forth if I should stop by. Greenwald's candy store was in the middle of the block, with two red-and-white poles that made me think of peppermint sticks twirling on either side of the door. I had never been inside. Some of the white stores on 31st Street felt off-limits to me, and Greenwald's was one of them. Before Nene went blind, she used to churn homemade ice cream for us by hand, or we'd buy three pieces of candy for a penny from the corner store.

A bell chimed to announce my arrival in the shop. The noise startled me. I suddenly felt stupid for being there and turned to walk back out, but then the sound of my name rooted me to the black-and-white checkered floor.

"Ruby?"

Sure enough, it was Shimmy. He stood behind the laminated counter wearing a candy-striped apron and paper folded hat, beckoning me forward with the wave of his hand.

"You came." His voice wavered.

"Aunt Marie sent me for her provisions." I lifted up the shopping bag as proof, and then glanced around the store.

It was smaller on the inside then it looked from the street and smelled like cake frosting. Neatly arranged shelves lined the wall filled with glass jars containing wrapped taffy, sugared jellies, bubble gum, licorice sticks, lollipops, malted balls, fudge and things dipped in swirls of marshmallow, peanut butter, toffee, caramel and chocolate. It felt like I had stumbled into a sugarcoated dream, and I wanted to touch and taste everything.

Shimmy picked up the white towel and wiped down the top, though it already gleamed. "What can I get you?"

I pointed to the homemade ice cream that sat in a clear display case.

"What flavors do you have?" It was a dumb question, because each canister was plainly labeled.

"Chocolate, butter pecan, vanilla, cherry vanilla and strawberry. My favorite is the cherry vanilla."

I nodded toward the cherry vanilla, and he scraped the metal scooper against the creamy goodness.

"I'm just paying for one scoop." I put up my hand, but he ignored me, and added a second helping to my bowl.

We were alone in the store. There were three silver barstools against the counter, but I didn't move to sit. A jukebox with shiny metal castings, tubes of cellophane and bright colored lights sat under the window. I had spent very little time with white people growing up. Especially ones my age. There were the sisters that I had played with on Saturdays while Inez cleaned their house, but that was it. Aunt Marie would be fit to be tied if she found out about this foolishness. I was contemplating taking the ice cream to go, but then Shimmy interrupted my thoughts.

"What do you say?" He grinned expectantly.

I put my spoon to my lips and let the coldness dissolve on my tongue. "It's good."

"Just good?" He reached into the display and took some for himself.

"You gotta pay for that?"

"Nope, it's one of the perks of working here." He dipped his spoon and brought the ice cream to his lips. Some got caught in the crest of his mouth.

"You need a tissue." I pointed.

He smirked. "You can have a seat."

"I'm okay."

"Ruby, relax, this is practically my place." He gestured to the stool.

"You sure?" I looked around again, so unaccustomed to occupying white folks' spaces.

"Mr. Greenwald is a nice guy."

I hesitated and then slid onto the stool. Shimmy leaned across the counter and our silver bowls touched.

"Cheers," he said, shoveling a big helping into his mouth. A faint mustache stretched across his top lip.

The bell chimed again, and I turned to see a pale lady dressed in a red felt hat enter the shop. Her dark eyes found me sitting at the counter and her thin nose turned up, like she was inhaling milk that had surprised her by going sour.

Shimmy straightened to a stand. "Afternoon. What can I get for you, Mrs. Levy?"

A long silence passed between them, and I didn't know if I should get up or just leave, so I kept my face in my ice cream bowl. Not wanting to bring attention to myself, I didn't even lift my spoon.

"I'll have a half dozen chocolate turtles and a handful of licorice." Her voice was careful and deliberate.

"Coming right up." He moved to retrieve the treats.

"How's your mother, Shimmy?" I could feel the woman shooting daggered looks my way. Beads of sweat broke down my neck.

"She's fine." He wrapped her chocolates in wax paper and then wrapped them again in white paper that he sealed with a red Greenwald's label.

With her goods under her arm, the woman walked past me and stopped at the door, gawking unabashedly at my full bosom. I lifted my shoulders and lowered my head farther into my bowl.

"Be careful of the company you keep, Shimmy. *They* are a danger to good Jewish boys like you." She huffed, sweeping the door closed behind her with a loud thud.

Shimmy slipped the money into the register.

"Sorry about that," he offered, but I was already up out of my seat. The woman's distaste for me had robbed me of my appetite. What was I doing here anyway? Besides making a fool of myself. I pushed my half-eaten bowl across the counter.

"Don't go." Shimmy reached out and grabbed my arm. His touch was both warm and clammy.

"This isn't my world." I snatched it away.

"Look, Mrs. Levy is just sore because her husband is cheating on her with the woman who works at the deli."

I paused. "I just came from there. Which lady?"

"Alma, the one with the big mole on her chin."

"She always looks so mad. I never let her serve me."

"That's because she wants him to get a divorce, but he refuses because they have two boys."

"That's a shame."

"It's all over the neighborhood, and her oldest son has been acting out in school."

I shifted on my feet, feeling a bit of pity for the rude woman.

"Come on, let me play something for you on the jukebox. Sundays are slow and if you leave me alone, I'll be forced to eat that whole barrel of ice cream." His green eyes pleaded. I had never looked into eyes so clear, so bright with hope.

I sighed and made a show of sitting back down. He clapped his hands together, then strolled over to the jukebox in the corner.

"You work here every day?"

"Only Sundays, Wednesdays and Thursdays after school."

"Must be nice to eat all the free sweets you want."

"Definitely a plus. But I do have to be careful that all that sugar doesn't ruin my figure." He held up his arm and made a muscle. He was more string bean than potato, and the sight of his flexed arm set me into a fit of giggles.

"What, you disagree?" He lifted the other arm and made the same motion, and I chuckled even harder. "What song would keep that smile on your face?"

I felt myself blush. "Got any Nat King Cole?"

He dropped a coin in the slot, pressed the button and out came "A Blossom Fell."

"That's one of my favorites. How did you know?"

"Lucky guess." He flashed his teeth.

The familiar music put me at ease, and we finished our ice cream. Our conversation flowed from the lyrics of our favorite songs, to what we hated about school, and landed on our weekly radio shows. We both agreed that *The Fred Allen Show* was our favorite and Shimmy cracked me up with his impersonations as he told joke after joke. The foot traffic into the store was slow. One man came in with five small kids, but he was so busy trying to please each with their favorite treat that he didn't pay me much mind. Time seemed to drift away from us as Shimmy exhausted every song I knew on the jukebox, and then played a few of his favorites. When I said to him that I had better go, he asked me to stay a while longer.

Aunt Marie was sure to be looking for me by now, but I told him one last song. "Make this your finale."

"I saved the best for last." He pressed the button on the jukebox and out came "Rock and Roll" by Wild Bill Moore.

I only recognized the song because last weekend Fatty had brought home the 78 and played it nonstop while trying to teach me how to dance the jitterbug. I snapped my fingers to the beat, wiggling around in my seat.

"What do you know about this song?" I asked, because it had so much soul. "Are you trying to impress me?"

"Have I succeeded?" He tipped his chin.

"Just a little." I moved my shoulders and hummed with the lyrics.

You can have my money, you can have my honey
but let me rock and roll.

Shimmy leaned forward, drumming his long fingers on the countertop. He was so near that our elbows touched and the smell of him made me heady.

"There's something about that horn and the strong backbeat that makes me feel on top of the world." He turned his face toward mine. There was a thin streak of ice cream under his bottom lip.

"I agree." Without thinking, I licked the tip of my finger and wiped the streak away. Our eyes locked.

Just then, the shop door opened and in walked a graying man with a potbelly, wearing the same hat that Shimmy wore.

"Didn't I tell you about playing those immoral records in here?" he said, chastising him. Then he saw me, and his eyes darkened like rain clouds. "No sitting allowed," he roared.

I tripped over my own foot trying to stand up.

"Mr. Greenwald—" Shimmy mumbled, taking a step back.

"Shimmy, you should know better."

Mr. Greenwald was a bear of a man, both tall and wide. He stood over me with his teeth clenched. Before he could say anything else, I rushed past him and out of the store. I knew what men like him were capable of. I read the newspaper and watched the news. It wasn't until I made it halfway down the block that I realized my mistake. I had forgotten Aunt Marie's packages. If I went home without her food, she'd have my head. I had no choice but to turn back.

An uneasy heat rippled down my back, and I paused at the door of the shop. As I was getting up the courage to go in, I heard Mr. Greenwald yelling.

"You can serve *them* quickly, but they can't hang around and definitely can't sit at my counter. You know that, boy. My old man must be rolling around in his grave." He tsked through his teeth. "I received several calls of complaints."

"She's, she's my friend," Shimmy stammered.

"You can't be friends with the likes of her. I thought you had more sense, boy. Don't end up like your father."

Mr. Greenwald paused when he heard the bell on the door and turned toward me with a smile. "Welcome to . . ." He stopped when he realized it was me, and his face furrowed. "You again?"

"I forgot my bag, sir." I scooted into the store, avoiding Shimmy's gaze, grabbed Aunt Marie's shopping bag and went back out the door. I heard Mr. Greenwald lock the door behind me and then slap the closed sign on the window.

Church had let out and brown-faced families ambled in their Sunday best, heading home for lunch before afternoon service. I trudged up 31st Street with Aunt Marie's purchases, trying to stomp off Mr. Greenwald's comments and the image of his snarl. I was a paying customer, and he did not have to treat me like dirty chewing gum stuck to the bottom of his shoe. It wasn't like I didn't know that white people hated us. It was a fact of life. Everybody I knew lived in cramped, drafty apartments and paid rent to white folks who did little to make the place livable. The adults I knew worked low-level jobs for white people who paid them too little for too much work. Fatty cleaned offices, my mother did day's work for families who couldn't afford a full-time maid and Nene used to take in laundry and cook to make ends meet.

Their lives were my window, and I knew from an early age that cleaning up after white folks wasn't the path for me. I was going to be an optometrist so that I could discover the cure to fix Nene's glaucoma and bring back her sight. I would be the first in our family to go to college, and when I came home with my various degrees, it would serve as proof that my father's family had been wrong about me. And that Inez had been wrong about me, too.

Aunt Marie told me that when Inez had confessed to being pregnant at the tender age of fifteen, Nene cried and then slapped Inez across the face, saying, "I'm glad your father already went to be with the Lord, otherwise you'd drive him right up to the pearly gates yourself."

Once Nene calmed down and came to grips with reality, there was only one thing for her to do. Insist that the boy do his honorable duty. Junior Banks was a good-looking young man, and his parents owned Bankses' funeral home. They lived on the corner of 16th and York, in a row house with a wide front porch.

"At least you haven't disgraced yourself with a common little nigga," Nene had said—Aunt Marie had shared the whole story with me last summer over a game of cards and a few too many glasses of home-brewed hooch.

When my father's mother, Mrs. Banks, opened the door, she didn't even invite Nene and Inez in for tea. She just stood there, holding her storm door closed like she didn't want them to see all the finery inside her house. Like they might try to steal something.

According to Aunt Marie, after Nene had cleared her throat and delivered the news, Mrs. Banks took one look at Inez, in her well-worn coat and wide-brimmed hat that made her look more like a sharecropper than a respectable young girl, and laughed in her face.

"There ain't no way that Junior would lick his chops at the sight of you. Go find some other fool to claim your bastard." Mrs. Banks was apparently still cackling when she closed her door.

Inez holed up in their apartment while Nene tried to figure out their next move. Aunt Marie told me that she was the one who went back a few days later and banged on the Bankses' door, with the intention of knocking some sense into whoever answered. It was Mr. Banks who stood in the doorframe, informing her that Junior lived in Baltimore now and couldn't possibly be the father.

He handed Aunt Marie a small envelope, "for your troubles." And then he closed the door.

Inside was enough money to cover two months' rent, and the matter was dropped. Six months after I was born, word traveled that Junior Banks had proposed marriage to a respectable woman.

I knew where the Banks lived, and I walked by their house on occasion, just to look at the well-kept porch with the hanging potted plants. When I earned my degree and became a doctor, I pictured that they would be down on their knees begging my forgiveness for abandoning me. They would see that I was good enough. Smart enough. Worthy of the last name, Banks, that they made sure Inez did not include on my birth certificate.

I was determined to prove myself, to give Nene her eyesight back—and to never have to depend on a man to keep a roof over my head like Inez. That's why I worked so hard in the *We Rise* program and had to secure that full scholarship. Falling short was not an option, and this new friendship with Shimmy was a distraction that I couldn't afford. I had to put him and those magnetic green eyes out of my mind. It wasn't like I needed Mr. Greenwald or the rude woman to point out that Shimmy and I were not intended to mix. It was something I was born knowing.

For the next few days I kept my head in my schoolwork, and Shimmy brushing yellow on my painting and playing Wild Bill on the jukebox far from my mind. Then on the following Friday, I was sitting on Aunt Marie's front steps when I looked up to see Shimmy emerging from the paint store on the corner, his hair falling over one eye, the other one fastened on me.

Without thinking, my hand reached up to touch my bangs, to make sure the wind had not blown them out of place. Open in my lap was a paperback copy of *Twelfth Night*, an assignment for my advanced English class at school. From the corner of my eye, I saw Shimmy slip closer. He was walking next to an older man who was favoring his left knee.

"Pop, I'll wait for you out here."

"I won't be long," said the man, looking straight ahead at the front door of the building. His face was shiny, his grip on the banister clumsy, and I caught a whiff of hard liquor seeping from his skin. I had seen him before, but hadn't known he was Shimmy's father. He was Aunt Marie's landlord, and he came by to collect the rent money. The man had a reputation for being a drunk, and spent time up in Mr. Leroy's apartment on the top floor drinking, sometimes until he passed out. Even in his liquored fog he was still a stickler for his money. He didn't trust his tenants to pay at the end of each month, so he collected his money weekly.

Shimmy stood a few feet from the iron railing.

"Hi."

I didn't look up from my book, even though I could no longer make sense of the words on the page.

"Whatcha reading?"

I held up the cover. Willing him with my mind to go.

"I read that last year. Decent for Shakespeare."

Then I couldn't help myself. "Which of his is your favorite?"

"Probably *Romeo and Juliet*."

"Why?"

"I'm a sucker for a forbidden love story." He swept his hair out of his eye and smiled.

My face betrayed my resolve by breaking into a grin. "I'd never peg you as a hopeless romantic."

"Mind if I sit?"

I looked up the street to see who was watching. Two boys played kick the can, and a black dog sniffed the trash cans looking for food. Ms. Edna's second-floor window was open, but just because I didn't see her, that didn't mean she wasn't lurking. On this block someone was always paying attention.

"It's not a good idea."

He lowered himself onto the step two spots below me and peered up at me through his lashes. They were long and full and a shame to waste on a boy who already had so many good features.

"I don't want you to get into any more trouble." I turned my face toward the sky.

"Sorry about Mr. Greenwald. I didn't know he'd act like that."

"I shouldn't have expected anything more."

A blush crept up his neck and bloomed in his cheeks. "Of course you should have. Let me make it up to you."

I pressed my lips together, searching for a hint of the Chap Stick I had applied earlier, but it had dried up.

"Just forget it, please."

Shimmy reached into his pocket and held out a tube of lavender paint to me. "Now you can add a few flowers to the tree in your painting."

No boy had ever brought me a gift before. They took things from me, though. Brushed up against my behind in the hall at school, looked up underneath my skirt on the stairs, always with their hands out trying to get a free feel when adults weren't looking in the schoolyard. And then there was Leap, and the men on the street. Shimmy was so different.

"Thank you. This means a lot."

"Come listen to some music with me tomorrow night at the Dell." His voice was hoarse.

"Are you crazy? Deaf or dumb?" I blew out a laugh, while flipping the tube of paint over in my hand. It was the good kind that would dry fast.

"I'm serious."

"How are we supposed to get away with that? I can't even come in your candy store without being thrown out like the evening trash."

He put his hands together. "Let me show you. I'll meet you right here at eight."

His eyes bored into me for so long I had to look away. What I should have said was *absolutely not*, but before I could stop myself, I whispered, "What if someone sees us?"

"I'll have my father's car." He ventured up a step closer to me. His cedar scent made it impossible for me to think straight.

"Shimmy, you don't owe me anything. The ice cream was nice but—"

"Come on Ruby, don't make me beg."

I sighed. No matter how hard I wanted to deny it, I enjoyed Shimmy's company. He was smart, funny and easy to be around. And we did like the same music. I had never been to the Dell. What was the harm in two friends listening to music?

I looked up at Ms. Edna's window again to see if she was spying, but it was still empty. If Aunt Marie found out, I was as good as dead.

I exhaled. "Okay, but we can't be out in the open. Pull into the side alley."

"I'll be there."

Chapter Six

WELL

Eleanor

The next morning, Eleanor tucked a copy of *Our Nig: Sketches from the Life of a Free Black*, by Harriet E. Wilson, into the front compartment of her envelope purse. Mrs. Porter had leant her a first edition, published in 1859, with the directive of caring for the book like she would a newborn. Nadine was still in bed with her satin sleep mask pulled over her eyes, and Eleanor tried not to trip over her mess of clothes on the floor and close the door behind her as quietly as possible. As she passed the dormitory's front desk, the freshman girl monitoring the door called out to her.

"Quarles. This came for you." She extended her hand.

Eleanor unfolded the paper as she continued outside. It was a letter from the bursar's office directing her to stop in today before the office closed at noon. The detour would make her late for her shift at the library, but she didn't have a choice.

The bursar's office was on the first floor of the Administration Building on the north side of campus. When Eleanor arrived, a man with a jet-black mustache and square shoulders reiterated what she already knew: the remainder of her tuition was past due.

"Would you be able to make a payment today?" He tapped his ink pen.

"No, sir. What other options do I have?"

"Shall I inform your parents?"

"No, please don't." Eleanor did not want her parents working themselves even harder on her account. She quickly calculated how much was in her bank account, and what she had under the mattress in her room. It wasn't a quarter of what she needed.

"Can I work for it?"

He pushed his bifocal glasses up his thin nose and took a closer look at her file. "I see that you already have a job at the library. We aren't at liberty to give students more than twenty-five hours of work release. You're already at your max."

"Well, what am I supposed to do?"

The man leaned back in his seat and looked Eleanor over. He sighed before flipping through a binder until he found a business card.

"Would you be willing to take a job off campus?"

"Yes. Anything. I'll do what needs to be done." She gripped the counter.

"Are you familiar with Ware's?"

Ware's was the city's first Negro-owned and -operated department store. Nadine shopped there. Eleanor had accompanied her once when she was looking for a dress to wear to Homecoming. It was by far the classiest shopping experience in D.C., and Eleanor had been wowed by the racks of high-end fashion and the finest selection of accessories she had ever laid eyes on.

"Yes, of course."

The man handed her a business card. "Ask for Gloria, and tell her I sent you. She's looking to hire a new counter girl. Once you have secured the job, come back so that we can put you on a payment plan to pay off the semester. It will need to be paid in full before you register for winter classes, no exception."

"Thank you, sir."

"Go on and make Howard proud."

Eleanor had no idea how she was going to work a second job, all while archiving the collection with Mrs. Porter and keeping her grades up, but she would have to find a way. As a child, Eleanor had been lulled to sleep by the sound of wooden spoons whipping against metal bowls, and the smell of butter, sugar and vanilla bubbling through her house as her mother baked through the night. Then with little sleep, she'd drive up and down Route 10 selling her savory cakes and flaky pies to save for Eleanor's college education. The least Eleanor could do was handle this.

The stop put her ten minutes late for her shift, and she apologized to the clerk she was relieving. Slipping her bag under the circulation desk, she decided to start with shelving books. Saturdays were always slow, and since it was Mrs. Porter's day off, she'd have time to write her essay arguing how the novel *Our Nig* was a response to Harriet Beecher Stowe's *Uncle Tom's Cabin*. Preparing her application for Alpha Beta Chi had Eleanor behind, but if she could get a few thoughts down while she was at work, she'd make a dent in catching up.

Eleanor arranged the books on the cart by subject and then section. The feel of the textbooks in her hand, and the syrupy, musky smell that came from the pages as she rolled the cart across the carpet, grounded her. One of the things she liked about working in the library was that everything had a proper place. Eleanor had always felt most at ease when things were categorized, neat and organized.

A telephone ringing at the circulation desk interrupted her trance, and she hurried over to answer it. She was in the middle of helping the patron over the phone when she glanced up to see William Pride, and that glorious back, sitting at his usual table in his regular chair.

He must have sensed her presence, because he turned his head slightly, and when he saw her, he dropped his pencil, pushed back his seat and stood.

Eleanor cradled the phone between her ear and shoulder, watching as he moved in a loose turtleneck, perfectly starched pants and polished wing-tip shoes.

She put up a finger to signal that she'd be right with him, and then jotted down the patron's book request.

"Yes, ma'am, I'll check the shelves and give you a call right back. So long." She hung up and turned her face to William. "Did you need some help?"

"Are you all right?" He leaned his elbows on the counter.

"What do you mean?"

"You left in such a rush last night. I never thanked you for the dance."

"I had to. My frock was soaked from Greta's drink," Eleanor said, immediately regretting mentioning her name. She hoped she didn't sound bitter or jealous.

His jet-black eyes softened. "I looked for you."

Eleanor remembered. "I didn't give you back your handkerchief. I'm planning to wash it by hand."

He waved away her words. "Give it to me on Friday. I have an extra ticket to the Lincoln Theatre. Would you like to be my guest?"

"Me?" Her eyes fluttered.

"Don't tell me you have to study either." He tilted his smooth chin, and Eleanor pictured her lips pressed against the tip of it.

"I believe I'm free," she said, smiling.

William pushed a piece of paper toward her, instructing her to write down her dorm information. "I'll pick you up at seven."

A few days later, Nadine unrolled a curler from the front of her hair. She sat on the edge of her bed in a satin slip watching Eleanor with a look of shock. "William Pride asked you out?"

"Why is that so surprising?"

"When did this happen?"

"Saturday. And I was able to get a pass to leave all by myself." Eleanor stood looking at the dresses on her side of the closet.

"I went to Dunbar High with his younger brother, Theodore—Teddy. He was in my biology class and so easy on the eyes," Nadine chuckled. "I'm surprised you said yes—you never say yes to anything other than an extra shift at the library."

"Ha ha ha. It's just one little date."

"The Lincoln Theatre is a big date, Ohio. Those tickets aren't easy to come by." Nadine stamped out her cigarette and walked to where Eleanor stood at the closet. "What are you wearing? You know William Pride is studying to be a doctor."

Eleanor pulled out her pine-green dress with the Peter Pan collar. It was the nicest one she owned, sewn by the hands of her mother's best friend. She hadn't worn it much, and instead had saved it for a special occasion. The last time she put it on was for the ABCs interest meeting, and remembering their rejection put a frown on her lips. Nadine interrupted her thoughts by taking the dress from her and hanging it back in the closet.

"While it's a darling dress, Ohio, you said William Pride and the Lincoln."

"So?"

"A girl going out on the town with a handsome doctor-to-be needs something slightly more sophisticated." Nadine rummaged around until she held a royal-purple swing frock with cap sleeves and a fitted bodice. It was even more beautiful than the last one Eleanor had borrowed.

Eleanor's face reddened. "I don't need you dressing me. You see what happened to the last frock you lent me." She thought about the ruined dress at the back of her closet. With her tuition payment past due, she had no idea when she'd have the extra money to carry it to the dry cleaners. But Nadine brushed her comment aside.

"You know fashion is my forte. Besides, William Pride is a big fish. We need to pull out all the stops so that you can reel him in."

"Who said anything about reeling anyone in? He's just being polite. A penance for his good friend Greta Hepburn spilling pop all over me. *We practically bathed together*," Eleanor mocked Greta's shrill voice, and Nadine tipped over from laughing.

"I doubt that he's thinking about her, Ohio. Like I said, tickets to the Lincoln don't come easy. If they were such good friends, why didn't he invite her?" With both hands, she presented the sparkling frock.

Eleanor knew she would be daft not to take it. Sighing, she slipped into the dress. Then allowed Nadine to brush pink blush onto her cheeks. When she looked in the mirror, a giddiness came over her that she couldn't deny.

"There. You are as stunning as Lena Horne in *Stormy Weather*." Nadine beamed.

Members of the opposite sex were not permitted past the front lounge in the girl's dormitory, so when William arrived to pick Eleanor up, a junior who lived down the hall knocked to let her know.

"Last looks." She faced Nadine, tugging at the petticoat under her frock, making sure everything was smooth and in place. "What are you doing tonight?"

"I'm meeting a gentleman caller later to go to the shake show at the Cave." She shimmied her shoulders.

"Isn't that after curfew?"

"Don't worry about me. You just enjoy yourself, Ohio. I'll be back by morning." She gave Eleanor one of her wicked grins.

Even after rooming together all last year, Eleanor couldn't figure out how Nadine got away with breaking all the rules, while never paying the consequences. When Eleanor turned the corner into the lounge, she noticed two girls pretending to read on the sofa, but their eyes kept floating up at William.

He stood by the fireplace, wearing a tailored navy suit. A stingy brim fedora centered on his head, with a slight tilt forward, lending him an air of mystery. When he moved to greet her, she inhaled that same mysterious scent. She decided it was more bergamot than bark.

"You look lovely." He took her gloved hand and kissed it, sending tingles up her wrist. "Shall we?"

Eleanor linked her arm around his steady bicep, happy with herself for listening to Nadine's dressing advice. Outside, the sun had set, stripping the warmth of the fall day with it, but as Eleanor walked next to William, her skin felt humid. She loosened the top button of her coat. Passing men said hello to William, and he shook a few hands as they walked through the yard.

"You seem to know a lot of people," she commented.

"I lived in that dormitory right over there." He pointed, then reached into his pocket for the key.

Eleanor didn't know much about cars, but his, parked beneath a red maple tree, was far nicer than the badly corroded Chevy that her father drove. Inside, the car was still warm from his ride over, and as Eleanor settled in, she realized that she could stretch her feet forward without them sinking through rusty holes in the sheet metal like they had in the old Chevy. In William's car, even the floor mats were plush. She folded her hands so she wouldn't fidget. Being this close to Mr. Back, alone on a date, was making her more nervous than a long-tailed cat in a room filled with rocking chairs.

"So where did you say you were from?" William switched gears and merged into traffic. The engine revved softly, and it felt like the wheels barely touched the street.

"Ohio. Not far from Cleveland" was the best way to explain Elyria, which most people had never heard of. "You?" Eleanor asked, not wanting to reveal that she already knew he was from D.C.

"Born and bred right here in the nation's capital."

Eleanor watched the city pass her by through the window. She loved how vibrant and pulsing D.C. was in comparison to the drab, industrial town of Elyria. "It must have been nice growing up in such a thriving city, with everything right at your fingertips."

"Hard to say since it's all I know. You must be from a small town."

"Tiny is more like it."

"Well, sweet people usually come out of tight communities." William winked, and his attention made her feel gushy all over.

He circled the block a few times, and then found a parking space on

12th Street at the corner of T. The theater was a brick building, with "Lincoln" spelled out brightly in lights. The white billboard held the names of several upcoming acts. Pictures of past performers, including Pearl Bailey, Ella Fitzgerald, Cab Calloway and Duke Ellington, were posted in oversized frames along the wall around the entrance. While they stood in line, Eleanor watched the crowd of well-groomed men and stylish women chat excitedly as they waited their turn to enter. William produced two tickets from the inside pocket of his jacket and handed them to the usher. They walked through a second set of doors, and her heels sank into the thick burgundy carpet. The usher stopped at the third row.

"How is this?" William turned to her.

Eleanor looked up at the wide stage. She could almost touch it. She had never sat so close to a performance. In fact, she'd hardly been to any performances at all, outside of the Christmas shows in her church's basement back home.

"It's perfect," she said with a smile. It really was.

Once they were comfortable with soft drinks, the heavy velvet curtains rolled back, and a man dressed in a black suit wearing a top hat crossed the stage. He entertained the audience with his impressions of movie stars and politicians. Once he had the crowd fired up, he paused from his antics and introduced the main event.

"All the way from Newark, New Jersey. She's been called Sassy, the Divine One, one of the greatest voices in the business, I give you Miss Sarah Vaughan."

The crowd burst into applause. Eleanor could not believe her eyes as Sarah Vaughan pranced across the stage in a gold, beaded, slim-fitted dress that dazzled under the lights. Then Sarah put her mouth to the microphone, declaring in a tiny voice, "I must apologize in advance. This morning I came down with a cold. So, we will just see what happens." She shrugged her shoulders and smiled. Then out of her mouth came a voice so voluptuous, it embraced Eleanor with every leap and swoop. Vaughan sang every song that Eleanor had heard over the radio, and then a few more. It wasn't until she took her final bow and disappeared behind the curtains that Eleanor felt like she could breathe again.

"That was magnificent." She turned to William, touching her hand to her chest. "The best I've ever seen. Thank you."

His eyes glistened. "It's my pleasure. You seem as big a fan as I am."

William reached for Eleanor's hand to help her from her seat, and she felt warmed by his touch. They poured out of the theater toward the exit sign. Some patrons turned right for the front door, but William guided Eleanor left, and then down another set of stairs that led to a ballroom. A five-piece band was onstage playing a familiar tune.

"Care to dance, baby?"

Eleanor nodded, liking the way *baby* sounded on his lips. They walked to the center of the room, stopping under a twinkling silver ball. When he reached for her, their bodies collided with a familiarity that both delighted and surprised her. William moved like a man who was comfortable in his skin, and Eleanor swung her hips to match his tempo. Then the music slowed to a soft whine, and William stepped even closer. With her right hand in his, he pulled her to his chest. Eleanor could feel his heart racing against the swell of her breasts, and when she relaxed her forehead against his cheek, she had never felt so complete.

They stayed like that. Her hand tucked inside his, hips sighing against each other's, until the world went still. Eleanor didn't even hear the music, only the sound of William's ragged breath against her ear. When she finally opened her eyes, and caught the clock over his shoulder, the silent spell was broken.

"I need to go. Curfew."

William raced down U Street, and they hustled back through the yard.

"I'll be right out." Eleanor tossed him her best smile, hoping that he'd be okay with waiting for her.

In the lobby, her dorm matron looked up from her crossword puzzle. "Just in the nick of time." She tapped her watch.

"May I have a few extra minutes to thank my gentleman caller?"

"Don't stay too long and appear desperate for his attention." Her voice was stern.

Outside, William leaned against the metal railing with his hat in his hand. He was so breathtaking in his suit and overcoat that Eleanor could hardly stand to look at him full on.

"My dorm matron runs things like a martinet. That woman is way too serious." She met him at the bottom of the stairs. "I bet they don't even pay her well."

William laughed at her joke. "Well, I'm glad I got the princess back to the castle on time."

"If only my dorm matron was as sweet as a real queen." Eleanor batted her eyes and then remembered. "You must want your handkerchief back. I can run and—"

"I'll get it next time." William's eyes locked with hers and blood rushed to her temples. He wanted there to be a next time.

"You up for that?"

"Only if you promise to watch the clock. Otherwise, I'll be expelled from the kingdom, and we can't have that." She giggled, loving the way his face honeyed into a smile.

"Tomorrow then?"

Eleanor bit her bottom lip, for she wanted to say yes, but she was starting her new job at the department store.

"I work a full shift at Ware's," she explained.

"So, I can pick you up from work then?"

"Really?"

"After standing on your feet all day, I can't have you out there waiting on a bus, baby," he said smiling, and she noticed a dimple on his left cheek.

"Well." Eleanor gazed up at him. "Until then."

William leaned his face toward hers, kissing her cheek. His lips marked her skin. What she wouldn't have given for the nerve to grab his chin and kiss him right.

"Good night."

Eleanor could feel him watching the curve of her behind as she walked up the stairs, and after months of staring at his back in the library, it made her giddy that it was his turn to take in her backside. When she reached her room, she slid open her top drawer for his handkerchief. It still smelled faintly of bergamot, and she draped it across her pillow.

Chapter Seven

TREADING WATER

Ruby

Aunt Marie wasn't home, so I had the place to myself as I got ready to go out for the evening to meet Shimmy. We had spent all of Saturday afternoon cleaning the apartment, and my fingers were stiff as I combed through my hair. She'd had me scrub the grease-splattered wall behind the stove with vinegar and water until the chipped paint peeled even more. Then I mopped the cracked linoleum floors. There were so many buckling crevices that the floors were never really clean, but I did what I could. After Aunt Marie sponged down what passed as the bathroom, together we scooped the smut from the furnace and dumped it inside an old tire in the backyard with the other piles of neighborhood debris.

Before she left for work, we shared a hot dinner of okra, corn and tomatoes, but in all our hours together I never asked for permission to leave the house. Partly because Aunt Marie would have told me no, and more specifically because I was leaving to see Shimmy, a white Jewish boy who on every day of the week was off-limits to me. It wasn't like we were planning to go steady or anything, we were just meeting as friends, and I thought it best not to get Aunt Marie's panties all ruffled into a bunch over nothing. In hindsight, I probably should have said something, because I could feel guilt knotting up in my chest as I slipped a sloppy joe sweater over my head. Bobby socks and saddle shoes finished off my look.

I had inherited a pretty decent hand-me-down wardrobe from Inez's white employers, and was handy with a needle and thread so I could make my own adjustments. As a final touch, I clipped on a pair of Aunt Marie's pearl earrings and spread on a thin layer of her pink lipstick.

Aunt Marie only wore cologne, and nothing I fingered on her nightstand smelled remotely feminine, so the mixture of Ivory soap and Jergens lotion would just have to do. That was one of the many ways Aunt Marie and my mother differed. Inez had sweet-smelling lotions, talcum powder and toilet water for every day of the week. She even wore perfume to clean up after people. Told me it made her feel like a whole person and not just some hired *jigaboo*.

It was near eight when I got downstairs, and night had fallen. I toyed with my bangs, fluffing then smoothing them as I watched the street. Loose newspapers, candy wrappers and soda cans tumbled against each other, rustling over the concrete, swept through by the wind. I could hear the baseball game on in one of the first-floor apartments, and the fragrance of slow-cooked pork turned my stomach sour. I knew it was my nerves.

I had never done anything so crazy before. Sneaking out. I was being reckless and foolish, going God knows where with this boy. No good could come of it, and I was just wasting precious time when I should be studying the six functions of angles and better understanding my trigonometry. But then I saw headlights, followed by a light blue Ford Crestline. The car slowed to a crawl and then turned into the side alley. It was Shimmy.

There was still time to walk back up the stairs and forget this whole thing. Instead, I counted to ten, then took a long exhale and opened the front door.

As I hurried down the steps and around to the side of the building, I glanced about, praying that no one who knew Aunt Marie had seen me leaving the house unchaperoned this time of night.

The narrow alley was nothing more than a slit between two buildings, and smelled like cat piss, fish grease and beer. I had to sidestep a broken bottle as Shimmy leaned over and pushed the passenger door open for me.

"I'm getting in the back seat."

"Why?"

"'Cause if you want to hang out, we gotta be smart." I pushed the front seat forward and slipped into the back. Shimmy pulled the door closed behind me and then slowly tunneled the car through the alley.

I squatted down in my seat so that I couldn't be seen through the window. If anyone saw Shimmy driving, they would think he was riding alone.

"So glad you came. I didn't know if you'd show." His voice cracked as he spoke over his shoulder. If he had only known how many times I'd thought of reneging.

"How are we going to pull this Dell thing off?"

"You'll see."

I didn't know if I should just trust him or demand to know more. The most comfortable way to sit without being seen was with my legs stretched to the left and my head and torso to the right. The seats were plush and smelled smokey, like new leather with just a hint of pine. I couldn't help but run my fingers over the buttery cushion, quickly realizing that this was the finest car I had ever ridden in.

"How was your day?" he asked.

My anxiety from sneaking out made the words run from my mouth like a rushing spring. I told Shimmy all about the *We Rise* program, and how I had to miss the field trip to the hospital that morning with my cohort.

"Instead of learning from real doctors, I just sat in an empty classroom doing work I could have easily done with my eyes closed. It was a waste of hard-earned carfare," I complained.

Shimmy pulled the car to a stop and turned off the engine. I could hear loud music playing from in front of us and lifted my head up to the window to see where we were. A side street near a park.

Shimmy turned his body toward me so I could see his face. "You want to be a doctor?"

"An optometrist."

"Why?"

"My grandma went blind a few years ago, and I want to learn to fix her. Or people like her—probably too late for her to get her sight back, but I'm holding out hope."

"Never heard of a Colored doctor before."

"First off, I'm Negro, not Colored," I snapped, sitting up fully in my seat. "Mrs. Thomas says that Colored is a painful word used by segregationists trying to keep our race down."

"I'm sorry, I didn't mean—"

"And haven't you ever heard of Dr. Charles Drew?"

Shimmy looked so thunderstruck I couldn't help but suck my teeth. I was forced to learn his history, but he knew nothing of mine.

"He's a Negro surgeon and the founder of the blood bank." I stuck out my chin.

"You're smarter than the girls I know. Most of them are more interested in bagging a husband. Forgive me," he said tenderly, and his sentiment softened me.

"Come sit up front." He held up his forearm for me to clutch.

I hesitated, and then climbed over the seat, careful to keep my skirt down around my knees. When I slid into the passenger seat, I noticed that he smelled like a zesty aftershave. The front seat was wide enough for us to fit another person between us, and we sat a respectable distance from each other. Outside the window, I saw a thread of tall trees surrounding us on three sides of the lot.

"Are we near the Robin Hood Dell?"

"Yeah, on the far side of Fairmount Park."

"How did you find this spot?"

"When I was little, my grandpa used to bring my cousins and me up here to listen to music. He couldn't afford to buy tickets for all of us, so this spot was the next best thing. My grandmother would pack hot dogs and we'd get out of the car and dance under that streetlight"—he pointed—"pretending we were onstage."

Shimmy rolled the windows down halfway. The music came through loud and mostly clear.

"Free concert. I haven't been up here since he died."

"When was that?"

"About two years ago." He snorted, sounding like he was trying to cover up the sadness that had come into his voice. "Sure brings back good memories."

His story made me realize how much I had missed the closeness I had shared growing up with Nene, sleeping each night nestled in her bed. We sat in silence, listening to the call and cry of the instruments.

"This is a nice car," I offered.

"It's my old man's. Ma doesn't like him driving on Saturday nights, so she either lets me take the car or hides his keys."

"Why would she hide the keys?"

"'Cause he's always wasted." Shimmy chewed his lip. "How about your pa?"

I dug my fingers into my thigh. "He lives in Baltimore. Never bothered to marry my mother. She had me alone and I ruined her life."

"Don't say that."

"It's true." I hugged myself.

"I can't see you messing up anything." He turned his face toward me with eyes so warm, I felt a flicker of heat rise up my neck.

"You staying with your aunt?"

"For now. Till my mom calms down." I couldn't imagine telling Shimmy about the kiss and Leap, so I told him we got into a fight over money. It wasn't a total lie. Then we sat quietly, listening to the clip-clap music. Outside the car, there was a glimmer from the streetlights, and the shadows of the trees were large and luminous. I didn't see another car in sight. I knew what girls did with boys in off-road parking lots. For a fleeting moment my thoughts flashed to Inez, "fast ass."

Shimmy reached across me and opened the glove compartment.

"I brought you something." He passed me a small white box. I ran my finger under the Greenwald's seal. Inside were two chocolate drops.

"Noticed the other day you had a sweet tooth."

"Thank you." I held one out to him, and as he took it, our fingers grazed each other. A sensation that felt electric surged between us, and I trembled.

"You're cold."

"I'm all right."

He removed his heavy corduroy coat and draped it over my shoulders. The heat from his body was imprinted in the material and I instantly felt safe.

"Whatcha do today?" I lifted the sweet to my mouth, and when I took a bite, I left a ring of pink lipstick against the black chocolate.

"I went to temple this morning with my family. But my ma didn't like the rabbi's talk today, so she kept swearing in Yiddish on the way home."

My eyes got big. "Oooh, tell me a Yiddish curse word!"

"Like what?" He chewed his candy.

"Anything."

"I'm drawing a blank." Shimmy snickered.

"What does your mother say?"

He looked pensive for a moment. "*Du farkirtst mir yorn!*"

"What's that mean?"

"You'll be the death of me," he whispered. The air between us felt sticky and sweet. His eyes stayed on me for so long, I had to look away.

He'd certainly be the death of me if Aunt Marie found out. "How do you insult someone?"

"You call him a *dummkopf*, which means he's stupid." We both laughed and then finished off our candy.

"What else did you do today?" I balled the wrapper in my palm.

"Went home, ate and rested all afternoon."

"Rested? Lucky. As soon as I got home from my program, my aunt Marie put me to work doing Saturday chores."

"Yeah, we take a break from anything laborious on Saturdays, but Ma makes me do my chores on Sunday before I go to work at Greenwald's."

"Bet you aren't washing the walls," I joked, my hands still a little achy.

"No, but I definitely have to clean my room and mow the lawn."

He had his own room and a lawn that needed mowing. I slept on Aunt Marie's lumpy pullout couch while I waited for my mom to let me come back home, where she shacked up with her latest boyfriend.

"I'm glad you came, Ruby. I like talking to you. You're different."

"Never had a Negro friend before?" I blurted, before I could stop myself.

Shimmy's eyes drifted to the ceiling like he was searching for the right words. "It's more than that. You just have this confidence about you. I feel easy around you, like I can be myself."

Those words touched me in the center of my chest.

"Plus, you know music almost better than me."

I turned to face him. "When you played 'Rock and Roll' at the candy shop, I almost lost it. How did you even get that record into the jukebox?"

"It was just there, probably an accident. I wouldn't be surprised if Mr. Greenwald doesn't have it removed. He says that music is immoral and poison." He imitated the older man's voice and we both laughed.

"He doesn't want me playing it, but I do when he's not there."

"You do things you aren't supposed to a lot?" I watched his jawline tighten as he shook his head.

"I have a younger brother and sister, so Ma depends on me to be the man in the house when Pop's not around."

"I'm an only child."

"That must be lonely."

I shrugged. "I'm used to it. Plus, I grew up with an older cousin, Fatty. She was always dragging me into her stuff."

"So, you have a wild side."

"I wouldn't say that." We both giggled.

The music rose and fell, and we talked so much that we hadn't notice when it finally came to a stop.

Shimmy noticed it first. "Must be intermission."

We were silent for a minute, but it was a nice type of silence. Eventually, I asked Shimmy what he wanted to be when he grew up.

"An accountant, like my pop's brother. He's been grooming me, showing me things. I won't be as rich as you once you're a doctor," he teased me.

"Gotta get that scholarship first. It all starts from there."

"You will. Can't imagine anyone in your program being half as bright as you."

"You're sweet." We looked at each other at the same time. Our eyes clung again, and it felt so intimate, like a kiss. His fingers grazed mine on the seat between us, and then he left his hand there with our pinkies touching.

After what felt like ages, Shimmy glanced at the clock on the dashboard, breaking the trance.

"Damn it. I better head back. Ma will shout *feh!* if I get home after ten," he said, waving his fist.

"I bet that means she's pissed."

Shimmy nodded.

"I'm getting in the back seat, just to be safe."

"You worry too much."

"*Feh!*" I smiled. "You don't worry enough." I reached for the handle.

"Good one. The accent is perfect. Next time wave your fist," he said. "Stay right there." Shimmy got out of the car, walked around the front and opened the door for me. I stepped out into the night air. My whole body felt alive in a way that I hadn't experienced before.

"Thanks for coming." He took a step closer to me. A breeze passed between us, fresh and crisp. Shimmy reached for my hand and brought it gently to his lips and kissed it. I could feel electricity move through my belly, and then the sensation shot all the way up to the tips of my ears.

"I had a nice time." My voice came out raspy. We were still holding hands. I was holding hands with a boy. With Shimmy.

“Me too,” he whispered, and then he lifted the seat for me and helped me into the car.

We drove back to the neighborhood in silence. The memory of the wet imprint from his mouth still on my skin.

After Shimmy dropped me off back in the alley, I replayed every moment of our time together. When I pushed opened the door, I was shocked to see that Aunt Marie was not at Kiki’s working. She was sitting on the sofa dressed in her muumuu, going over her numbers pad.

“Where you been?” Her voice was hard around the edges.

She had a quarter glass of golden liquor next to her, and a pencil tucked behind her ear. The baseball game was broadcasting from her transistor radio. The Memphis Red Sox pitched against the Detroit Stars.

I stood there dumbstruck while she turned down the volume. “And why you coming in here all sneaky and smiling? Like a Cheshire cat.”

“I was—”

“With a boy, from the looks of it. Just ’cause you staying here with me, don’t mean you can come and go as you please. Who is it?”

“Why you not at Kiki’s?”

“Girl, I pay the rent. Don’t change the subject.”

I looked down at my toes and murmured. “I went to the store.”

“Don’t let your mouth mash the gasoline on an ass whooping. Come again?” She eyed me pointedly.

I swallowed hard. “I was with Shimmy.”

“Shimmy who? Wait—you mean to tell me you were with Shimmy, the landlord’s son?” Her voice thundered. “Girl, you done bumped your head?”

“We’re just friends.”

She took a sip of her drink with her eyes burning into me. “I’ma tell you like this. You done pulled a seat up to a game that your ass can’t win. Cut that shit off now.”

"Yes, Auntie."

"And don't you leave this house again without my permission, hear? These streets are dangerous for a flowering girl like you."

"Yes, ma'am."

"Chile, I ain't nobody's ma'am," she said as the telephone rang. "But I mean what I say."

I walked to the back and into the tiny bathroom. I didn't need to use it. I just needed some space to slip into the feeling of Shimmy's lips grazing my hand and recall that burn, wondering when I'd get to feel so good again.

Chapter Eight

THE INVITATION

Eleanor

True to his word, William had stood waiting outside Ware's department store at the end of Eleanor's first day on the job. He had a handful of pink and white lilies and an invitation to dinner. That evening, he kissed her for the first time on a park bench under the glow of the waxing moon, and from that day forward they fell into an easy rhythm. When Eleanor finished her shift at the university library, she'd study alongside him at the same table where she had watched his back for so many months. In between her classes and her double work schedule, William showed her *his* D.C., with frequent trips to the U Street corridor. They took in movies at the Republic Theatre, ate at all the best restaurants and danced like their bodies were made for each other. Two months had passed like this in an easy, wonderful blur.

Then came Christmas break, and Eleanor couldn't afford the seventeen-dollar round-trip bus ticket to Elyria, so Nadine invited her to spend the holiday with her family in Petworth, a D.C. neighborhood just northwest of Howard. When Eleanor returned to her dormitory, William was waiting for her once again, this time with a leatherbound book of Phillis Wheatley poems. It was the most thoughtful gift she had ever received.

They spent the rest of the day at his apartment, and between thank-you kisses, and his gentle hands sliding up and down her back, William invited her to brunch at his parents' house. He had whispered it so casually that Eleanor wasn't sure she heard him right.

"You want me to meet your parents?" she asked while leaning away, so she could see the expression on his face more clearly.

"What's wrong with that?" he returned with a sloppy grin.

"Well, suppose they don't like me?"

"Nonsense." He ran his finger along the edge of her collar. "They like who I like."

And now, one week later, they were in his car driving to the Pride residence for brunch, with Eleanor wondering for the umpteenth time if she had dressed well enough to make a good first impression. One of the nice things about her second job at the department store was that she'd managed a few frocks and a pair of calfskin pumps on her discount. With Nadine's keen eye for fashion, she'd purchased a secondhand wool wrap coat that fell just below her knees. Her lips were painted taffy pink, and her hair was styled in a small bouffant on top with loose curls around her neck. Eleanor had hoped that she looked sophisticated, like the city girls she watched on U Street.

William drove north on Georgia Avenue, and then west on Upshur Street heading into what he had referred to as the Gold Coast. Eleanor had never been this far north and noticed that the longer they traveled, the bigger the homes grew, the longer the driveways, and the more perfectly manicured the wide front lawns. He slowed the car when he reached Blagden Avenue, and then pulled into the circular driveway of what looked like a grand English castle.

"Welcome." He killed the engine, and Eleanor blinked several times, unable to believe her eyes. The place was enormous, and the oversized driveway was filled with several newer-looking cars.

"Is this where you grew up?" She swallowed hard, staring at the house in awe.

"Yeah. My family was one of the first to break the color barrier on the block. Now though, many of the homes are owned by Negro families."

The house was even more imposing up close. A turret soared from the top-right corner of the roof, and Eleanor could picture young William and his brother playing games of fortress. The front yard was expansive enough to get up a good game of tag.

The slate stairs fanned in both directions, and when they reached the foyer, an older man wearing a gray vest and stark white gloves greeted them with a hearty smile. "Master William. It's good to see you."

After a quick introduction, William asked after the man's son.

"Hitting the baseball like he's the next Satchel Paige."

"That's what I want to hear." William clapped the man on the shoulder and then handed him Eleanor's coat.

"You look lovely," he whispered, taking in her deep burgundy frock, with puffed shoulders and a high-waisted top. Eleanor squeezed his hand while hoping the butterflies in her stomach would subside. She had not felt this nervous in a long while. Even though she had known that William's family was much more well off than hers, she'd had no idea that he was white-folk rich.

Inside, the pinewood floors gleamed like glass under her feet and the ceiling soared above her head, with a crystal chandelier catching the afternoon light. They turned in to the parlor, where on the wall above the fireplace was a painting that Eleanor recognized as a piece from Jacob Lawrence's migration collection. She could only identify it because Mrs. Porter had shown her a recent article about Lawrence's work in a glossy magazine and had started a hunt to secure something of his for "her collection." Eleanor cocked her head, wondering if it was an original.

William interrupted her thoughts with two flutes. "You want orange juice or something stronger?"

"Orange juice, please." She took the flute while wondering if the something stronger wouldn't have settled her some.

While her father never needed an excuse to drink, her mother didn't consume libations on Sundays, for it was the Lord's day, and Eleanor hadn't really drunk much at all. She couldn't risk appearing off-kilter in front of these fancy people. While she sipped, her eyes took in the four white women giggling over champagne on tufted velvet chairs. William made the introductions, and the women were pleasant enough, but their presence caught Eleanor off guard. Maybe it was because she had spent so much time at Howard in the constant presence of Negroes, because it had never occurred to her that the brunch would be mixed companied.

William led Eleanor deeper into the house. Every room they entered had beautiful crown molding and detailed paneling. There were heavy mirrors on the wall and vases with sprays of exotic flowers in yellow and lilac and mint green at the very height of bloom. As Eleanor took in all of the elegant touches, from the glass end tables to the Persian rugs, she couldn't help feeling like she had stumbled into a place where she didn't belong.

William seemed to feel no such qualms. He came alive, his chest growing in size with each conversation. He introduced her to several more white people, and she continued searching for people who looked like her. How come his family didn't have *any* Negro friends? It was odd in a city so fraught with Jim Crow laws. Who were his parents anyway?

In the next room, string music from the phonograph chimed under the laughter and loud bantering between guests. Two older gentlemen—both of them white—clutching half-empty tumblers, were in the middle of a heated discussion.

"Country-ass Negroes, always have to drag us down with this slave history crap," one man said.

"I think it's important to remember where we came from."

"I think it's important to forget it and move on."

Eleanor's jaw dropped. White people talking about Negroes like that? In their own home? Before she could stop herself, she glanced up at William in shock.

"You'll have to excuse them." He gestured to the men, whose faces had started to turn red from their debate. "Those are two of my father's oldest friends. They were roommates at Howard. They argue about the same stuff at every brunch."

"Howard?" fell from her lips, her head swinging as if on a swivel back in their direction. The men were Negro? Eleanor opened her eyes wider but didn't see a trace of anything in their features that would mark them as such. Perhaps she had been wrong about the women in the parlor also. Before she could ask William, he reached out his arms.

"Dad." William embraced a man who was the same sandy-skinned tone as him and almost identical, except for the little relief of his belly and gray streaks in his hair and mustache.

"Eleanor, this is my father. Dr. William Pride Senior."

"Pleased to meet you."

"The honor is all mine." His father took her hand warmly in his. Eleanor immediately felt a bit more at ease.

"William, you never told me you were a second."

"I thought I did."

"I would have remembered." She tapped him playfully on the arm, as a sturdy, fair-skinned woman in a winter-white frock, embroidered with rhinestones, moved toward them. Her eyebrows arched up as she looked from Eleanor to William.

"Mother."

"William, I haven't seen you in—how long has it been? I couldn't even say."

"It's been a week, Mother." He leaned in to peck her cheek. She wiped imaginary dust from his lapel, but her eyes were on Eleanor.

"Feels much longer. You act like LeDroit Park is on the other side of the planet."

"I've been studying."

"Studying *what* is the question." She turned her full gaze on Eleanor.

"Nice to make your acquaintance, Mrs. Pride. You have a lovely home."

Eleanor offered a smile and her hand as she introduced herself, but his mother kept her red painted lips tight.

"Quarles?" She looked Eleanor over. "Are you one of the McLean Quarles?"

"I beg your pardon?" Eleanor looked to William.

"Mother, Eleanor's from Ohio."

"Oh." Rose Pride looked her up and down again, then turned her attention to a brown woman in uniform, who whispered discreetly into her ear. Rose nodded and put up two fingers.

"Which part of Ohio are you from?" she asked, cocking her head as if she wanted to hear better.

"A small town southwest of Cleveland."

Rose's expression looked as if she had tasted something bitter.

Just then, the woman in uniform stood tinkling a silver bell. "Brunch is served."

They followed his parents into the adjacent dining room. The table was elaborately dressed, with gold chargers and ivory linen. Lit candles and magnolia petals streamed down the center, on a silk table runner. A beautiful presentation of stenciled bone china was set before each guest. The table comfortably accommodated sixteen. William pulled out a high-back chair for her and then sat beside her. Eleanor watched as two of the women she had mistaken as white sat next to the red-faced men. Looking at them more closely, she could see the slight spread of the first woman's nose, and then the other lady's fuller lips.

It was then that Eleanor realized that she was in a room filled with white-faced Negroes. When she looked down at her hands, she gathered that she was the brownest person at the table. Only the two women serving in uniform and the man who opened the front door were darker. She listened to the guests as they chattered among themselves, and while their pronunciations weren't quite white, they weren't full-on the way her people talked either. As she watched, slowly the nuances of their Negro features came to life in the depth of their expressions, shape of their lips, breadth of their noses and richness of their laughs. Her initial impression had been wrong.

Mr. Pride called for grace.

Just as they bowed their heads, the sound of high heels clicked through the hallway. When Eleanor looked up, she saw none other than Greta Hepburn, with an older gentleman at her side, step into the room. Greta dashed straight to Rose Pride, kissing her on both cheeks.

"My mother sends her apologies. She woke up this morning with a splitting headache. She said she'll telephone you to make plans for lunch later this week."

Eleanor kept her face even, although her armpits began to sweat. Greta, wearing a lovely sapphire-blue frock with a wide bow at her waist, sashayed around the table bidding everyone hello. Her dress looked more expensive than Eleanor's entire wardrobe. When Greta finally took her seat, it was directly across from Eleanor and William. She tilted her head in a curt greeting, and then William's father blessed the food. As the first course of spring salad and tomato soup was being served, Greta looked at Eleanor with a curious expression.

"Eleanor, right? I didn't expect to see you here."

"Good to see you again, too," Eleanor replied, knowing full well that Greta knew her name.

Greta turned her attention. "William Pride, you owe me a tennis match. I haven't seen you at the Heritage Club in ages," she belted over scrapes of spoons and forks.

"It's been a while."

"Well, let's do it soon. Tomorrow?" she offered with a cheeky grin.

William dropped an arm around Eleanor's chair. "Things are a bit busy now, but a rain check?"

Greta looked from William to Eleanor and said, "I'll hold you to it."

The meal concluded with a fruit salad topped with mint ice cream, and then folks drifted away from the table. Despite the January weather, a few men slipped onto the back patio for a cigar around the firepit, while the women smoked cigarettes in the parlor. Eleanor didn't seem to fit anywhere, and found herself in the downstairs powder room, trying to make sense of it all. When she came out, Greta was waiting by the door.

"What's going on between you and William?" she asked through gritted teeth.

Eleanor remembered the spilled drink. "What's it to you?"

"Just curious—our families go way back." She eyed her, and then opened her compact and started powdering her nose.

"Yes, you said that."

Greta turned her gaze onto Eleanor. "Some advice, just between us girls. It would be wise for you to walk away from him. Save yourself the time."

Eleanor couldn't believe her audacity, but before she could open her mouth, Greta continued. "I remember your application to the ABCs detailing your busy position at the library. And then I saw you through the window folding sweaters at Ware's, too. My, I don't understand how you'd have time for a beau, what with all your *jobs*." She spat out the word "jobs" as if it was dirty.

"Just what are you saying?" Eleanor pushed her words out with fury.

Greta closed her compact and slipped it back into her clutch. "I'm just trying to save you the trouble. He's out of your league, dear one."

"You don't know me."

"Listen," she took a step forward, "you want to make the Alpha Beta Chi line next semester? Then you best follow my advice."

Eleanor took a step closer so they were eye to eye. "Sounds like a threat."

"There are plenty of men on campus for you to rendezvous with. William belongs to us," she said impatiently, and Eleanor thought she saw a speck of desperation in her honey eyes.

"Well, I guess that's for him to decide." Eleanor spun on her heels and went searching for William.

Eleanor was quiet on the drive back to campus as she relived her conversation with Greta over and over again. Just who did she think she was? And what did she mean by he "belongs to us"? Light-skinned folk? Or Negroes with more money than they could count?

"I'm going to do a little studying at the library. You want to come, baby?" William caressed her knee before grabbing hold of the clutch.

She declined, feigning a headache.

Nadine was painting her nails when Eleanor stormed through their door.

"How was it?"

And then she told Nadine everything. From the castle-like home, to the servants, to mistaking everyone for white only to discover they were all fair-skinned Negroes, to his mother's questions, and then finally, Greta's threat.

"That's old guard D.C. for you. William's family is the heart of the who's who, and Rose Pride is the pulse. She sits on every board and is the mistress of ceremony for all the important events."

Eleanor was silent. She'd known William's family was important, but she hadn't realized just how different they'd be.

"Don't let them get to you. If William likes you, Ohio, then that's all that matters." She held up the brush and started on her toes.

Eleanor pulled on a ratty sweatshirt and took the pins from her hair not feeling so sure. She flipped open her textbook and tried to study for her eight a.m. class, but the headache she faked with William felt all of a sudden very real.

Chapter Nine
CAUGHT UP

Ruby

The first half of tenth grade was nearing the end, and by the middle of January my mother still had not come for me. I did see her at Nene's house for our annual Christmas dinner, but she didn't talk to me much. She just sat sipping the special occasion corn liquor that Aunt Marie kept under the sink, while she and Leap played cards with Fatty and Fatty's latest boyfriend. Inez hadn't even bothered to bring me a present. Although I knew better than to expect much, I had used the allowance that Aunt Marie had given me and bought her three triangular plastic bracelets. In hindsight, I should have gifted the bracelets to myself because Inez hadn't even tried them on.

I thought by now her anger would have subsided. Usually, Inez would show up at Aunt Marie's a few days after dropping me off, with a peace offering of a new hairbrush, clip-on earrings or a sweater passed down from one of her employers. Then she and Aunt Marie would share a few cans of Schlitz and send me to Processed Willie's for fried fish sandwiches and tartar sauce. After a few hands of gin rummy, she'd say, "Go on, get your things." I'd hug Aunt Marie goodbye, and tuck my key away for the next time I was exiled.

But that didn't happen. Now the days had turned into months, and Aunt Marie and I were settled into a weekly routine. She had rearranged her schedule at Kiki's so she could stay with Nene on Friday nights and I could get to my Saturday enrichment classes on time. I hadn't been marked tardy since, and as Mrs. Thomas had suggested in our last meeting, I was working like my tail was on fire.

As a requirement for *We Rise*, we were tested at the end of each quarter to assure that we were educationally sound to continue on. Our second-quarter exams were coming up in less than a week. There was one in English comprehension and another in mathematical equations. I had an ear for language, but math was my Achilles' heel. Often when the numbers from my math assignments blurred into putty on the page, I found myself wishing I was less apt at art and English and better at science and math, especially if I was going to be an optometrist.

Regardless of my strengths, I needed to score a B+ or above on the exams to remain in the program, so all afternoon I sat at Aunt Marie's kitchen table working through sample trigonometry problems while listening to the steady patter of rain against the windowpane. The fumes from the furnace made me sneeze constantly and my nose was red from blowing it.

A light rap at the front door broke my attention, but I didn't move. Aunt Marie ran numbers out of Kiki's and had a few neighborhood customers who'd drop by the apartment with the bets they wanted her to play. If she wasn't home, they would wrap nickels or dimes in tissue paper and slip them under the door. I sat quietly waiting for them to leave, but nothing slid through. The knock drummed persistently.

"Who is it?" I made my voice deep.

"Ruby?"

The sound of my name got me up from my seat. I turned all three locks, removed the safety chain and opened the door. Shimmy stood in the hallway, his brown hair sopping wet against his forehead. I hesitated, and then let him in, grabbing a hand towel from the kitchen drawer and offering it to him.

"What are you doing here?"

"I've been looking for you for weeks. You haven't been anywhere. I thought you moved back to your ma's."

I walked to the bay window and closed it before the rain wet my canvas. Being nowhere had been intentional on my part. I had avoided anywhere where I might run into Shimmy. I stopped shopping on 31st Street on the days he worked, didn't linger on the front steps, and I purposely took the long way to and from my high school just in case he sought me out. Aunt Marie was right: no good would come from falling for a white boy—and a Jewish white boy at that. My attention needed to stay on my schoolwork so that I could go to college, and I knew Shimmy didn't fit into my future equation.

But now that he stood in front of me, fixing me with those eyes, and shivering wet, my will went weak.

"Take that wet coat off," I instructed, and then squeezed the towel through his hair. Our eyes locked, and even though I tried, it was hard for me to pull away. They were so green.

"Sorry for barging in on you. I just needed to know that you were all right."

"It's okay. Aunt Marie left for work."

He looked at my papers scattered across the Formica kitchen table. "What are you up to?"

"Studying for my *We Rise* exams, the program I told you about. The English I got, it's math that's driving me nuts."

He took a seat. "Let me see."

I picked up the worksheet packet and a pencil and carried it over to the sofa and handed it to him. Shimmy examined it carefully.

"I've been on the same problem for a half hour. I just want to give up. It's so hard." I flopped down next to him.

"It's not, actually. How are you with calculating sine, cosine and tangent?"

"Shaky at best."

"Okay, an easy way to remember is to first break it down to SOH, CAH and TOA. I thrive when I have a mnemonic device."

"What's that?"

"You know, when you put words to letters or create a song to help you remember the order of things."

"Oh, right. I never made it sound all fancy, but I know what you mean." I smirked, knocking my knee against his, and then I left it there as Shimmy continued.

"For trig I think of it as 'The Old Archaeologist Sat on His Coat and Hat.' Get it?"

I thought for a minute, "TOA, SOH and CAH."

"Yup, memorize that." He took my pencil out of my hand. "Can I write on this?"

"Sure."

Shimmy worked through the next three problems, explaining the relationship between angles slowly, and the cramp around my brain started to clear.

"I think I got it."

"It just takes practice. Math is muscle memory." He dropped the worksheet in my lap, and then I felt his hand brush against my knee. The warmth generated from his fingertips made the room go fuzzy.

"I see why you want to be an accountant. You're good at this," I said softly.

"Numbers just make sense." And then he was leaning his face toward mine and time stood still. My brain went to vapor as his nose grazed mine, and then his mouth sank against my lips. It was the sweetest second of my life, but then Leap flashed across my eyelids. Leap's hands pushed my face against his, Leap, Leap, Leap, and I yanked away from Shimmy.

"I'm so sorry." His eyes crinkled with confusion.

"No, I'm sorry. It's just—" My voice faded away.

"You are just so beautiful."

No boy had ever called me beautiful before.

"You are all I can think about," he murmured, and those words swept away the remains of my resistance to him. I blinked Leap away, forgetting that he was my first kiss, and breathed in Shimmy, pretending that this moment with him was the one that counted.

He took my right hand. "Don't disappear like that again. You've driven me plumb crazy."

"I won't."

Then he held my chin and I pressed in. His tongue tasted like Wrigley's Doublemint gum, and I left my eyes open, so that I could see that it was Shimmy and not Leap pressing his sweet lips against mine.

I was kissing a boy. A boy who liked me.

Outside, there was a crash, then a boom, and the lights flickered off. We pulled apart and Shimmy sprang to his feet.

"It's just the power going out. Happens often in a storm." I stood, rummaged around in Aunt Marie's kitchen drawer for a match and lit the candle she kept over the sink. Shimmy came up behind me and spun me against his chest. We stared at each other in the hazy, soft light. As he bent down to kiss me again, clunky footsteps crashed on the hall stairs.

"Damn it. That's probably Pop. He's been upstairs drinking with Mr. Leroy. Ma is going to kill me if we are late again." Shimmy moved away from me toward the door. "Can I come for you tomorrow night?"

"I don't know if I can get away."

"Well. I'll be in the alley at eight. I'll wait fifteen minutes." He kissed my cheek, and as I stood in the door, I heard him yell, "Pop, you all right?"

When I looked down the stairs, his father was slumped on the landing, feet stretched out wide. The whole hallway smelled of whiskey, or maybe gin. Blood flushed through Shimmy's face and neck and he shook his head. I watched as he reached down to grab his father under the arm and heave him up.

"Come on, Pop, Ma's waiting. Are you hurt?"

"Oh-kay," he slurred, patting Shimmy's face. "Good boy."

Shimmy held his dad around the waist and carefully guided him down the last flight of stairs. I closed the apartment door and then walked over to the window. The rain had slowed to a drizzle, and I wiped the condensation on the glass with my shirtsleeve.

On the street Shimmy opened the passenger door for his father, put a protective hand over his head and gently helped him into the car. The motion was as tender as putting a baby to bed. From the looks of things, I gathered that Shimmy did this often. He *was* a good boy. A good boy who liked me, even though we were so different. Shimmy stopped at the driver's-side door of his father's fine car and looked up. He waved and I pressed my hand against the window toward him.

In that moment, I knew that I wanted nothing more than to give what was budding between us a chance. Despite the odds, and despite Aunt Marie's warning.

Chapter Ten

BAD TASTE

Eleanor

Eleanor and a slim-waisted counter girl named Arlene were managing the women's section of Ware's department store when the bell above the glass door rang out. In floated Rose Pride, cloaked in a kelly-green cape with big bell sleeves. She was accompanied by an equally well-dressed woman of the same age, and the sight of Mrs. Pride standing just a few feet away made Eleanor's stomach quake. She hadn't seen her since their awkward introduction at brunch a few weeks before, but she'd thought about her plenty.

"Would you take them," she whispered to Arlene, who adjusted her name badge and then greeted them promptly.

"Welcome to Ware's, my name is Arlene," she sang.

While the women inspected the new arrivals at the entrance to the store, Eleanor ducked behind a coat display, out of view of the woman but positioned in a way that she could still see them. Rose's conversation with the other woman drifted her way.

"Honestly, as hard as we work for these children, you would think they'd do as we tell them." Rose picked up a satin sailor's hat.

"I often feel like a broken record," her friend chimed.

"Would you believe that last month, William brought this ragamuffin girl from the Midwest to brunch? When I asked her what her parents did, she said her father worked at a factory and her mother baked cakes."

A chill went down Eleanor's throat and she froze. They were talking about her. Eleanor watched from her hiding space as the friend cut her eyes at Rose and then shook her head in disgust. "William has as much in common with her as he does the gardener."

"No education whatsoever. Probably still eating hog maws and chitterlings, for God's sake," Rose cackled.

"Greta did mention something like that to me," sighed the friend. "I think that was the brunch I missed."

"Deenie, honestly, in our day, we did what our parents said. Especially when it came to choosing a mate."

"True. But you can't tell these young folks nothing. They think the world started when they were born. All traditions are old-fashioned to them."

"What's Greta have to say about William? Does she know anything about this Eleanor from *the Midwest*?"

"Well, she doesn't think it'll amount to much. William is merely passing the time."

Deenie—Greta Hepburn's mother, Eleanor surmised—moved from the skirt display to the blouses.

"For the life of me, I can't figure out why William and Greta aren't dating. We've done everything but build them a house."

Deenie shrugged. "I guess that's a question for William, dear. Greta is willing and ready. She's graduating from Howard in the spring, and suitors are calling. None as well suited as William, of course."

Eleanor bristled.

Rose handed a few blouses to Arlene, who carried them back to the dressing room.

"Well, sweet Greta shouldn't have to wait. I'll have to talk some sense into my thickheaded son."

Rose and Deenie followed Arlene back to the lounge to try on their clothes. Eleanor stayed hidden until the women were safely tucked away.

Once she heard the doors click behind them, Eleanor found her boss in the men's shoe section. The fragrance of shoe polish and leather filled her nostrils.

"Do you mind if I excuse myself for lunch?" she asked.

"It's a bit early," he said and tapped his watch.

"I'm feeling light-headed. I skipped breakfast," she pleaded.

Once he nodded, she took off for the break room, where she couldn't stomach more than a few carrot sticks. Rose Pride had called her a ragamuffin and insulted her parents. She had never felt so second class in her life, and for it to come from the lips of a Negro woman her mother's age made the cut feel even deeper. It wasn't right. The way they talked, William was a prince, trifling with a poor little handmaid.

Granted, her father did request chitterlings on New Year's Day, along with his black-eyed peas and collard greens, but that was beside the point. And why were they so worried about Greta? She was drop-dead gorgeous and could have any man at Howard with the snap of her fingers. The longer Eleanor sat there, the more enraged she became.

By the time her break was over, she had pulled herself together and pasted a smile on her face. Out the front window, she could see the two women strolling with several bags down 14th Street. It had just begun to snow lightly, and Eleanor wished she'd remembered to bring her galoshes. She had on her good shoes, and she couldn't afford to ruin them.

The rest of Eleanor's shift seemed to drag on forever. When it was finally time to punch the clock, she grabbed her handbag and hurried out into the winter chill. The crisp, brisk air did nothing to soothe the agitation that rested in the base of her spine.

"Eleanor," William called with his head thrown from the window of his car.

She had not expected him to come pick her up, nor did she wish to be a stain on his name. Since his mother didn't want them together, then she would make it easy for her. She continued traipsing down the sidewalk without responding to William's call.

But by the time she had made it to the corner, he'd pulled the car to the side of the road, gotten out and caught up to her. He grabbed her elbow. "Elly, what's wrong?"

The name of endearment and the concern in his eyes made her feel foolish, and her determination to walk away from him dissolved.

"Nothing." She lowered her chin.

"Something is definitely wrong. Let me take you home." He tucked her under his arm and led her to the car.

Without asking for permission, William took her back to his apartment. They had spent afternoons there in between Eleanor's work shifts and curfew every weekend since they had met. William had a roommate, but she had only met him once. He unlocked the apartment door and then reached for her coat.

"Why don't you have a seat, baby. I'll make you some tea."

William had a bevy of *Ebony* and *Life* magazines on the coffee table, and she flipped through one of the *Ebony* magazines without really looking at the pages. A few minutes later, William returned with a bamboo tray and a warm mug of peppermint tea with cream and sugar. He had so much class.

"So, you ready to tell me why you were ignoring me just now?" William reached down for her leg and gently dragged her foot into his lap. While she blew on her mug, he started to massage the ball of her foot through her nylons, hitting all the pressure points. She suppressed a moan.

"Babe?" He gazed at her. "What's up?" His brows were knitted in concern, his look so loving that Eleanor nearly quashed the whole thing. But she needed to know. She looked around the spacious apartment, taking in all the well-appointed furniture that could have been featured in the magazine she was holding.

"Did your mother decorate this place for you?"

"How'd you guess?"

"I see the resemblance in taste from the house you grew up in. So unlike mine." She said those last three words quietly.

"Well, if I give my mother an inch." He gestured at the artwork on the wall.

Eleanor looked down into her mug searching for courage. "Listen, I have enjoyed these past few months with you more than words can say. But folks like you don't want to see us together."

"Folks like me?"

She nodded. "With means. Living high off the hog, as my mother would say. I don't come from any of this." She gripped her mug tighter. "I grew up in a shotgun house. Do you even know what that is?"

He shook his head.

"It means that when you open the front door you can see clear through to the kitchen. All in one shot. My daddy worked my whole life at Ridge Tool Company. Biggest factory around. When he made it to operator three, he sat my mother down from her job as a school lunch lady. But she didn't sit long."

William's fingers stopped moving.

"She got in her mind that I was going to college, so she turned her love of baking into a business. Would be up all night mixing and stirring, and then out all day dropping off deliveries. And that's how I come to be here, at Howard. I don't have a fancy last name that can open doors for me. My mama's cakes and my daddy's factory work is what got me in the door. And a lot of studying and ingenuity on my part."

"I'm so glad you shared that real part of yourself with me. It means a lot."

"Well, I'm telling you all of this because I think Greta would be a better fit for you."

He snorted. "Greta? Where did that come from?"

"She cornered me at your parents' house last month, telling me to leave you alone. That you weren't my kind."

His brows crinkled. "Greta's parents and my parents have been shoving us together since second grade."

"And?"

"And nothing. There's no chemistry." He switched out her left foot for her right one. "I see her more like a cousin."

"Kissing cousins?"

"Where is all this coming from?"

Something cautioned Eleanor against telling William about overhearing the mothers' conversation at the store.

"It's just, if you were meant to be with someone else, you know, the girls you grew up with . . ." Her voice trailed off. She couldn't bring herself to finish with *the rich, fair-skinned, and connected ones*.

William paused. "Baby, I'm not caught up in all that class and colorism bullshit. It doesn't matter to me where you come from. I just want to spend time with you."

Eleanor bit her lip to contain the swell of solace she felt hearing that. But she still wasn't sure what to believe.

"Elly, look at me."

After a moment, she looked up from her mug and joined eyes with him.

"My family has their way of doing things, but I've never been one to get in line. I love you, and I want us to be together." His fingers moved from the heel of her foot and rolled her ankle. It was the first time he had ever said those words and she shivered with relief.

"Unless you feel different."

"I don't, I feel the same way about you. Just not trying to get my heart broken." Her voice was husky.

"Never." He kneaded her calf, made his way up to her kneecap, and then he was kissing her neck, her cheek, her chin. Finally, he found her mouth, with a hunger that she felt pulsate all the way down to the tips of her toes.

This was where she was supposed to push him away, but after enduring Rose Pride and Greta trying to tear them apart, she wanted nothing more than to connect with him. The rage that Eleanor had felt earlier in her chest morphed into a longing in the pit of her belly.

William's hands traveled, caressing the soft skin at the meeting of her thighs, and she gasped.

Breathlessly, he pulled away. "Forgive me. You're just so irresistible. I lost control."

This was as far as they had ever gone, but Eleanor was tired of holding back. Especially after today. She crashed against his lips, while putting his hand back between her thighs. The pressure from his thick fingers made her quiver, and after another bout of fitful kisses, she could not breathe. Her need to claim him was so big, so mountainous, she felt like molten lava in a volcano ready to erupt.

"Perhaps your bedroom would be better suited," she exhaled.

A flash of surprise passed through his inky eyes, but it was quickly replaced by desire. "You sure?"

She took his hand, blocked the good girl voice from her head and answered simply, "I am."

Scooping her up into his arms, William carried Eleanor down the hall, past the bathroom and into his bedroom where he placed her on his full-sized bed. Eleanor had never been in his room, and she could smell his bergamot scent everywhere.

"I need to see you, baby," he panted.

The streetlight outside his window lent the room a grainy glow. Eleanor sat up and slowly unbuttoned her cotton blouse. She slid it over her shoulders. William stood in front of the bed and watched as she reached for the clasp at the back of her skirt and then pulled it down over her knees, tossing it in a heap. She felt shy in her slip that hung with a trimming of lace at her knees.

"You are extraordinary." He unbuckled his pants and let them fall to the floor with a thud. Then he joined her on the bed and slipped her straps down her arms. Her breasts fell freely into the palms of his hands, and he buried his face in her talcum-scented cleavage. They clung and rolled. When Eleanor felt like every pore in her body was open and desperate to receive him, William reached into his nightstand and fumbled with a tin that had MIMOSA written across it. Inside was a condom.

Once he covered her body with his, he moved slowly. His tenderness made Eleanor feel like a precious tulip that he didn't want to crush.

"You ever done this before?"

Eleanor closed her eyes and grabbed his face and kissed him.

"I'll protect you always," William uttered, sinking further inside her. "You're my girl."

After a few pushes and pulls, their bodies became one. He stopped every few thrusts making sure she was okay. She was. In that moment, her yearning for him trumped everything, and when he shuddered against her she pulled him tighter.

While the sweat between them cooled, William ran his fingers through a tangle of her hair. She was wet everywhere.

"I've imagined that every night for the last few months."

"And?" Eleanor thought the intimacy would make her bashful, but it didn't. She propped her head in her hand and turned to face him.

"It was even better."

She kissed his lips, now dry and chapped. Suddenly she realized how much time had passed. She wanted to stay forever but told him she had to leave in time for curfew.

"It's the weekend, can't you make something up and stay the night?"

"And ruin my reputation? Laying with you was enough." She tapped his nose. Eleanor pushed the sheets back, but he grabbed her around the waist and cradled her to his bare chest.

"Make something up about staying with a girlfriend across town?"

"I'd be too scared," she said, but then thought about how Nadine did it all the time and got away with it.

Eleanor reached for William's robe hanging on the back of his door and then padded down the hall to the telephone.

Nadine squealed in her ear. "I'll take care of everything."

When she got back into the bed, William removed the robe and pushed his hips against hers in a way that already seemed familiar. She opened herself up again, feeling vindicated.

Chapter Eleven

SPRING FEVER

Ruby

I was making straight A's in high school and had successfully passed both my winter and spring exams for *We Rise*. I came in second behind Jonathan Draper, a know-it-all boy from South Philly who would have been cute if he got rid of his Coke bottle glasses and the pimples that dotted his forehead. A *We Rise* awards ceremony was scheduled in three weeks' time, for the first Saturday in May. It was to honor the ten left from my cohort of twelve who would be moving forward in the program. Now I only had to be better than eight other students to receive the scholarship, and I was so close I could feel the weight of the letter of acceptance in my hand.

The board members of the Armstrong Association, which sponsored *We Rise*, along with the chancellor of Cheyney University, would attend the ceremony, and I needed to present well. I had been begging Aunt Marie for weeks for my first pair of stockings to wear to the celebration. Up until now I had only worn bobby socks, and over our dinner of liver and onions with rice, peas and piping-hot biscuits, I pleaded once again.

"You're still too young." Gravy dripped from the corner of her mouth.

"Please, Aunt Marie. It's 1949 not '39. All the upper classmen wear stockings."

"Stockings are suggestive. Don't want you walking around here advertising yourself, making these men think you ripe for the picking."

I turned my fork over on my plate wondering why it was always my responsibility to worry over what grown men might be thinking. I had been hearing it all my life. Even back to when I lived with Nene, as a flat-chested eight-year-old, I was constantly reminded to be modest. Not to leave the bathroom without my robe on when an uncle or cousin or friend of the family was at the house, smoking cigarettes and drinking beer. Back when Nene could still see, she'd get eye-level with me and say, *If anybody ever put their hands on you in that way, tell me. I'll always believe you.*

Still, I hadn't told Nene about Leap touching me because I was ashamed that I had allowed it to get that far. Knowing Inez, she hadn't told either, seeing as how she took Leap's word over mine. If my mother had only cared enough about my future to make sure I had carfare each week, none of this would have happened. But with two kids gone from the program I was still in position, and I needed to wear stockings to show the people in charge that I was professional and that I would represent them well.

Aunt Marie's noes usually meant no. But I remained persistent, promising her everything under the moon if she would just say yes. I left pictures of nylons that I had cut out of *Jet* magazine on her nightstand before I went to bed.

The next day was Saturday, and Aunt Marie woke me up with a glass of tomato juice. "Go and put something nice on so I can take you downtown."

She had finally acquiesced, and I leaped up and kissed her on the cheek.

"Doing this for you, sweetness. Lord knows I hate interacting with those siddity folks downtown."

I dressed carefully, in my best box-pleated skirt with a seafoam-colored blouse that I tied at my waist. I wondered if Shimmy would notice when I wore my sleek new nylons. Our time together had become the highlight of my weeks, and when we weren't sneaking around in dark parking lots listening to music and eating chocolate, I was thinking about being near him, feeling the stubble on his chin. His warm breath against my earlobe, and his slick hands exploring under my blouse.

Our conversations flowed, and I never tired of hearing stories about his family. In comparison to me, even with his father's drinking, Shimmy was living a storybook life with both of his parents under one roof, and two younger siblings who seemed to adore him. In the front seat of their fine car, he would entertain me with tales about visiting his aunts and uncles in Brooklyn, cracking me up with his imitation of their accent by stretching his syllables with a high voice, and then dropping them down low at the end.

I marveled at his descriptions of skyscrapers, of going through the Holland Tunnel, driving through Chinatown, crossing the Williamsburg Bridge with its steel towers into Brooklyn, where the cultural patchwork of Irish, Italian and Jewish immigrants lived within blocks of each other. The farthest I had ever traveled was down to Atlantic City.

"Ready?" Aunt Marie sauntered into the living room, interrupting my thoughts.

When I looked at her, I gasped. "You look . . ."

"Like a woman? It's my costume among them highfalutin white people." She struck a pose, and I couldn't stop gawking at her flowy skirt and frilly, powder-pink blouse. She closed her tube of lipstick and dropped it into a tobacco-brown handbag.

"Don't get used to this, it's just an act. Let's go before my dogs start barking." She pointed to her heeled shoes.

I was so excited about our trip to the department store that I chattered nonstop, even though I could tell by the pinched expression on her face that Aunt Marie wasn't listening to a word I said.

"What's wrong?" I asked her as the bus rounded city hall, giving way to the row of fancy boutiques and department stores. There was Gimbels on the left and Wanamaker's on the right. Woolworth took up the entire corner.

"Nothing," she said, reaching up to pull the stop cord to halt the bus. On the street, crowds of people were moving to and fro. Most of the men were dressed in dark business suits and porkpie hats. The women had shiny blonde or brown hair and were dressed in jackets stuffed high with shoulder pads in shades of green, blue, brown and red. Pleated skirts ruffled around their knees as they clutched scalloped purses that matched their colorful gloves. I followed Aunt Marie two blocks, assuming we were going into Wanamaker's, but she kept on marching until we reached the five-and-dime.

"What happened to the department store?"

"Maybe for your birthday," she said.

My elbows slumped against my waist.

"Cheaper for the same thing. 'Sides those uppity salesladies don't know how to treat us. Ain't got time to be arrested for sucker punching a white woman today."

At that moment, I realized she was doing more for me than my own mother. This whole trip downtown took Aunt Marie out of her safe space. The costume she wore was just that, and she had done it all for me on a Saturday morning when she could have been resting up for her long night at Kiki's. As the light changed and we stepped down off the curb, I laced my arm through hers and squeezed.

"Five-and-dime is perfect," I said, putting on a smile. "Thank you."

She patted my hand. "After we get you those stockings, we can walk through Gimbels, so you can see all those pretty displays."

That perked me up. I would at least get to witness what the fuss was about. The five-and-dime was on the corner of the next block, and we went in and rode the escalator upstairs to the second floor. The women's brassieres, step-ins, girdles and all-in-one corselettes were tucked away in the back corner along with the nylon display case. A toffee-colored woman stood behind the counter and pointed out all my choices. My head spun. It was a much more confusing process than I had imagined. To fit into the right pair, I needed to figure my proportion and the denier, decide on the color and if I wanted seam or no seam, reinforced heel and toe or sandal foot, knit or mesh. Aunt Marie had wandered off, leaving me alone with my choices.

"What would you suggest, ma'am?"

She looked me up and down, then slipped a pair of gloves over her hands and opened the case containing the stockings. Each pair was separated by a thin piece of tissue paper. In the end, we decided on a crispy nylon taffeta garter belt and a pair of reinforced heel and toe knit stockings. Aunt Marie returned as the saleswoman placed them in a crisp white paper bag with gold lettering.

"Give her a second pair in case she gets a run in one of them."

Outside, I threw my arms around Aunt Marie in gratitude.

Not one for a lot of affection, especially not in public, Aunt Marie tapped my arm and then nudged me away. "You can pay me back by helping me clean Kiki's on a few Monday mornings while you out for the summer. Way for me to make a little extra money to help make ends meet."

"Anything," I said, grinning, gripping my bag. I could not contain my excitement. I didn't need Gimbels—this was like Christmas and my birthday rolled into one. I was chatting on about which of my skirts would look good with my new stockings when I stepped off the curb and bumped into someone's shoulder. I looked up and saw a thin white woman grimacing at me, a young girl in a gray wool coat by her side.

"Watch where you're going, *nigger*," she hissed as she grabbed her daughter tightly by the wrist.

I stumbled backwards, feeling as if she had punched me in the gut. No one had ever hurled that word directly at me in my life, and for a split second I felt completely dumbstruck.

"It was . . . an accident," I murmured finally.

The woman straightened her pillbox hat. "Now I must shower!"

"Not a bad idea. I can smell you from way over here," Aunt Marie said matter-of-factly. The woman looked at both of us and shouted, "Stay in your own neighborhood."

"I pay taxes just like you. Next time watch where you're going," Aunt

Marie called back before grabbing me by the hand and marching me off in the opposite direction. I followed her farther down the street toward city hall and into Gimbels, but my head had filled with lead.

The inside of the store smelled of sweet perfumes and creamy cosmetics. Everywhere I looked my eyes were met with sparkling hanging displays. The beautiful glass escalator that wound across three stories was like an invitation to heaven. But there was no magic in the moment for me. Instead of moving through the room wide-eyed, I felt the stares of every white person we passed. It was suffocating. The double-door exit was up ahead on the right, and I pushed out and onto the sidewalk.

An angry horn blasted at a passerby crossing the street, the traffic light turned from red to green, as the woman's voice echoed in my ears. *Nigger.*

Mr. Greenwald's mean face bore down on me. *You can't be friends with the likes of her.*

Mrs. Thomas's clenched teeth. *There are plenty of Negro kids who would kill for your place in this program.*

And then I was reminded all over again. What I'd known to be true from the moment Shimmy knocked on Aunt Marie's door. This thing between us would never survive. The world wouldn't permit us the light to grow. Shimmy and I would forever be sneaking around in dark parking lots, lurking in piss-infected alleys, with me always crouched down in the back seat. Our relationship was doomed from the start. Before I got hurt, I had to let him and the fantasy world we had created go.

The white bag with my coveted stockings slipped from my hand and onto a patch of dirt in the street. Aunt Marie stooped down and retrieved it, dusting away the grime. But I didn't reach for the bag.

"Can't let nobody steal your joy, sweetness, or you gon' live a miserable life. I done seen it. You show that ignorant woman by getting your education. Keep your eye on the prize. Forget about her."

I nodded like I understood, but the hurt had shattered into sharp pieces that scraped and bruised the inside of my throat. Knowing about racism and being abused by its wrath were two different things. Mechanically, I followed my aunt to the bus stop that would take us back to our cage in North Philadelphia. Where it had been decided for us that it was where we belonged. Crammed together like pigs in a stall so tight, it was impossible to dream or breathe. Every single day we had to fight for food, for carfare. And this trip downtown had shown me that we even had to fight for what should have been free: our dignity.

Chapter Twelve

LIGHT OUT

Eleanor

Making up excuses to stay overnight with William on the weekends became as natural to Eleanor as fitting women at the department store. When they couldn't meet in person, Eleanor monopolized one of the three telephones on the first floor of her dormitory, shooing girls away if they even tried to go near her middle stall. There was a forty-five-minute time limit per call, and William phoned every weeknight at nine o'clock sharp. Eleanor liked that he was a man of his word. Sturdy and dependable, just like her father.

Each night, he'd start with asking her about her day. And he never seemed to tire of the intricate details of her archival work with Mrs. Porter, or her complaints about Nadine leaving their small room like a typhoon had hit it each time she went out.

"Her mother needs to hire a maid or something to come by. I love her dearly, but the girl is a train wreck," Eleanor joked.

But as much as they talked, she avoided conversations about money; never disclosing when she'd been called to the bursar's office because her tuition was overdue, never complaining when she had been removed from the schedule at the department store because they had hired new girls who needed to be trained on her shift.

And the last thing she wanted William to think was that she liked him for his money. Her parents had raised her to be independent, and to make a way out of no way for herself.

Some nights William talked about his medical studies. He was in General Medicine and had to learn to master a little of everything. At the moment he was studying infectious diseases. How to spot them in a patient, the symptoms and how to treat them.

He'd tell her, too, about his younger brother, Theodore, who lived in New York City and attended Columbia Law.

"Teddy always said he didn't have the stomach for blood," William kidded. "Honestly, I don't much either."

"Then why do you want to be a doctor?" she asked incredulously, but William didn't hesitate.

"Pride family tradition. My dad is a doctor, his father was a surgeon, and my son will become one, too."

Tiny goose pimples pricked the flesh of her arms. William's family was truly unlike any she had known, and no matter how many months they had spent together, she still found herself periodically in awe.

Five minutes before they were due to hang up, William would say, "Okay, give me my bedtime story, baby."

This tradition between them started when he gifted her the Phillis Wheatley book for Christmas. Every night she'd read a poem or two from the collection before they bid their adieus.

"You should be an actress, like Fredi Washington," he would say sometimes after she finished.

"Nonsense," she'd say and blush.

"No, really. I can listen to your voice all night long."

"I think you are just smitten, William Pride." She'd hold the phone so tight that she could hear the background noise on the street outside his apartment.

"That too." His voice would vibrate through her ear, trickling down and settling in the space between her breasts, and she never wanted to part ways.

For spring break, Eleanor told her dorm mother she was going home to Ohio, but William took her to Highland Beach instead. A plot of land south of Annapolis along the Chesapeake Bay, Highland Beach had been established by Frederick Douglass's son as a beach town for the elite Negroes of Baltimore and Washington, D.C. She found the history of the place fascinating, and brought back seashells that she and William had collected from their long walks, barefooted on the beach. The time alone without curfew, dorm matrons and work schedules helped them to relax into each other. They talked for hours, and when they returned Eleanor couldn't remember her life without his affection.

Between her classes, spending time with William and working both jobs, Eleanor had lost track of her monthly cycle. Since she'd been rooming with Nadine, they had always been on the same schedule, but it had been days since she had walked in on Nadine shoving her Kotex belt back into her bottom drawer, with that expression on her face that said *thank goodness that's over and done with.*

Eleanor looked up at the calendar that hung on her side of the wall, the one her father had sent her with the four blue woodpeckers sitting on a log and Ridge Tool Company emblazoned on the bottom. She tried to remember the last time she had bled. Now that she was in an intimate relationship with William, it would have been prudent to keep track of how often they were together, but they had been careful over the last three months. Mostly careful. There was that one slipup on their last night at Highland Beach when they had run out of condoms, but William had pulled out and she had gone to the bathroom right after and washed her insides good.

As Eleanor was trying to calculate the day of her last cycle, Nadine walked in and closed the door with her foot.

"Ohio, you wouldn't believe the food fight I just endured in the cafeteria. It started off as a peaceful protest over meals being too expensive, but then turned into an outrageous mess." Her soft hair fell down into her face. "Did they get any in my hair?" She moved in close, shaking her hair in Eleanor's face.

"No," she replied flatly.

"You barely looked." Nadine turned her neck. "What is it?"

It was hard for Eleanor to push the words from her mouth. To confer with Nadine would make it real. She swallowed the lump that had swelled in her throat. "When did you last have your monthly visitor?"

Nadine's eyes expanded. She was so close that Eleanor could see the flecks of mascara that had flaked under her lashes. "Finished about a week ago. Why, are you late?"

Eleanor nodded, and the weight of the possibility caved in on her chest. "We're usually within a day or so apart."

Nadine sat down next to Eleanor and opened her gold cigarette case. After a long drag she offered, "Well, no need to panic. Could be a false alarm. You've been under a lot of stress lately, right?"

"Sure. Right." Eleanor's mind had already started racing and wrapping itself around a disastrous end. No period, kicked out of the dorm, dismissed from school, bus back to Ohio with no degree, parents too disappointed to look at her, illegitimate baby, damaged goods. And William. What would she say to William?

"Look, whatever you do, don't go to the school's nurse. Your business will be all over campus. I know a white doctor across town who sees Negro patients." Nadine placed her cigarette down in the ashtray and started fumbling through her purse for a pen.

"Here, I think this is his name. Look him up in the telephone book." She handed her the scrap of paper. "Go give them a call now before it gets too late."

Through sheer luck, Eleanor was given an appointment for the following day. She had to cut two classes to make it, and then ride the bus over to the northeast side of town. The tires seemed to hit every pothole, jostling her around in her seat until she felt sick. Motion sickness, she reasoned. But it also felt like something was taking hold of her body.

The appointment happened without much fanfare. Eleanor was instructed to give a urine sample and to write her name and date of birth on the plastic cup. The pale-faced nurse, who wore a baggy white uniform, instructed Eleanor to call the office on the sixteenth of May.

"That's two weeks. Why does it take so long?" Eleanor asked, panicked. For some reason, she had thought she would know the results immediately. There was no way she'd make it two weeks without worrying herself into an early grave.

The nurse touched her white cap. "Have you heard of the Hogben test?"

"No, ma'am."

"Seems they should explain these things in school." She scribbled something on her clipboard. "We have to ship your urine sample to a frog lab in Virginia. There they'll inject a female frog. If in the morning the frog has ovulated, that will mean you are pregnant."

It didn't sound like an accurate test.

"I assure you. It's never been wrong in all my years as a nurse. And I'm ancient," she said with a wink, and then handed Eleanor a yellow slip of paper.

In the two weeks that she waited, Eleanor tried not to fret about the results, instead throwing herself into preparing for her final exams. But on Nadine's advice, she didn't breathe a word of the test to William.

"Men only need to know what they need to know," she told Eleanor, and then, in typical Nadine fashion, she assured her that going to a cabaret would take her mind off things.

Since William was pulling an all-nighter for an upcoming medical exam, Eleanor had no excuse. She also didn't have much fight in her as she watched Nadine lay out a summer frock for her to wear.

Exactly two weeks after she'd gone to the doctor, Eleanor woke up early and slipped into the wooden telephone booth at the end of the hall, sliding the glass door closed behind her. She lost her fingering in the rotary dialer several times because her hands were shaking so much. When she finally got through, and after waiting on hold for what felt like ten minutes, the nurse came to the telephone and reported her results.

"Positive."

"What does that mean?" Eleanor asked, desperately hoping she had misunderstood.

"As in pregnant, dear."

Eleanor couldn't breathe after that. The walls of the booth seemed to close in on her, squeezing the blood from her brain. The nurse's voice became white noise. All she kept hearing was "positive." The results were positive. As in she was pregnant. How could this have happened? She was only nineteen, with two years left before she finished college.

"Thank you." There was nothing else to say, so she hung up.

It was early, and the girls who hadn't bustled out of the dorm for their eight a.m. class were still asleep. Eleanor sank down the side of the telephone booth, her knees huddled to her chest, and cried until her eyes were swollen and her legs had started to cramp. A shower would do her some good and help her to think things through, but she had no strength to move.

What Eleanor needed was her mother. She was the one person in her life who always knew what to do. But the news would crush her, because she had worked so hard to get Eleanor to Howard. Traveling up and down the highways, baking throughout the night, arguing with her father when he insisted that the money saved should be used to replace their battered car. The vehicle that they shared to make a living. With nothing left to do, she placed the telephone receiver to her ear and made the dreaded collect call.

Her mother accepted. "Sugar? What's wrong?"

"How do you know something's wrong?"

"'Cause its first thing in the morning. High-rate time. Now spill it before you run up my bill." She chuckled lightly, but Eleanor could hear the nervous undercurrent in her voice over the crackle of long-distance static that was often present during their calls.

Eleanor typically phoned home one evening a week after ten o'clock when the rates dropped. She could picture her mother in the kitchen standing at the stove wiping down the range. It was her nervous tic, and because of it, her stovetop always gleamed to shining.

"Mama."

"Yes?"

Eleanor felt a wave of fear, guilt and shame congeal into a ball in her gut that kept the words stuck in her windpipe.

"Spit it out, Sugar."

"I'm . . . pregnant." Her voice was so small, she felt like a child, humiliated for disappointing her mother.

The dead silence on the other end of the phone made Eleanor wonder if she had uttered the words too softly to stretch across the many miles between them. But then after two pops of static her mother asked, finally, "By that doctor?"

On their weekly calls, Eleanor had told her mother all about William. From their first date at the Lincoln Theatre, to him picking her up from work at the department store, and every detail of walking through his castle of a home and meeting his kind father and uppity mother. She had painted the picture of a fairy tale, and now it came tumbling down.

"He's not a doctor yet. But yes. It's William's."

"He'll be sure that it's his?"

"Ma! What's that supposed to mean?"

"Don't get testy with me. I know how these things go," her mother sighed loudly. "Ain't much to do but get married."

Eleanor twirled the white cord around her finger. "I don't want a marriage proposal like that."

"Well, you got it like that. What other choice do you have? Can't come back here with your head between your tail. God has given you a second chance, child. And this sounds like a good one. Best let that boy make an honest woman out of you and marry on up."

Eleanor was too young to get married. She had planned to finish college first, have a career in archiving and then say I do. This felt like the tail wagging the dog.

"I told you that his mother can't stand me," she responded sullenly. "She picked someone else for him to marry. She'll never approve."

She had made it a point not to return to his family's house for their many social affairs, because she couldn't bear to be around Rose Pride after overhearing her true thoughts about her. And each time William invited her, she had an excuse at the ready; she had to work, to study, she just wasn't feeling well. But now she had gotten herself into a fix. Two girls walked past the booth and Eleanor turned her head quickly so they wouldn't see her face. Once they were gone, the tears fell freely.

"Oh, Mama. I'm so sorry." Eleanor's voice broke and cracked.

"Too late for those crocodile tears now, girl. Should have thought about all this before you gave away your milk for free."

"Ma, why you got to say it like that?"

"You grown now. Can't sugarcoat the truth. Ain't nothing left to do but hope he man enough to buy the whole cow."

Eleanor's cry turned to hiccups.

"Wish I was there to hold you and fatten you up with a piece a pound cake." Her mother's voice softened, like warm butter. "But I'm not, Sugar, so you gonna have to trust that God's gonna see you through. You been praying?"

The line crackled. "No," she answered honestly.

"Well, that's the problem. Can't forget to invite the Lord in. He is bigger than all of this! He is your Creator and your Redeemer. Bow your head, child, let me pray for you."

Eleanor skipped class and crawled back into bed, with her secret burning a hole in her stomach. As she drifted off to sleep, she wondered if her thoughts would burn the secret out.

The next day William was sitting at his table in the library when she got to work. He now sat on the opposite side so he could face her during her shift. She rolled her cart of books over to his table.

"Missed you yesterday," he said and squeezed her hand. "What time are you off?"

"I work eight hours, but maybe we can take a walk during lunch?" She forced a smile that she knew didn't have the muscle to make it up to her eyes. What if he didn't want her, now that she was in the family way?

William touched her hand. "You okay?"

"Yeah, just a little tired is all."

"The walk will do you some good then. Come get me when you're ready."

Throughout her shift, Eleanor rehearsed in her mind how she would tell William the news. She had spent so much time in her head that she handed a student the wrong book and forgot to return to a patron who was waiting for her on the telephone. When Mrs. Porter chastised her for cataloguing two important finds incorrectly, she knew it was time to take a break. The anxiousness she felt at the idea of upending her life and William's whole world made her feel like she could throw up. Grabbing her purse from beneath the desk, she motioned for him to follow her. It was now or never.

Once outside, she could smell freshly cut grass and the azaleas planted along the path just beginning to bloom. They walked hand in hand to the farthest point on campus and sat on a wooden bench facing a willow tree.

"What are you so deep in thought about?" William slid next to her, wrapping his arm around her shoulders.

"Why do you ask?"

"You are never this quiet. Talk to me."

Eleanor fidgeted with the hem of her pleated skirt, still searching for the right words.

"Are you ill?" He made a show of feeling her neck for fever.

"I'm expecting," she blurted.

"Expecting what?"

Eleanor looked down at her fingers in her lap. "A baby."

William sat still for several seconds, as if in shock. Then he turned. "Are you serious?"

Eleanor nodded, sniffing back the tears that crowned her eyelids.

He stood abruptly. "Whoa. I wasn't expecting that. Fuck," he said between clenched teeth, and his word reverberated through her chest.

"I thought we were careful, mostly. I know this ruins everything. I'm sorry, William."

"You're not to blame," he mumbled, but as he paced in front of her, she could see the weight of her confession pressing down on his shoulders.

"Damn Highland Beach. When we ran out of condoms, I should have known better. I'm studying to be a doctor for Christ's sake."

The sight of William holding his head and walking back and forth made her feel awful. She should have kept her legs closed. The woman was in charge when it came to sex. This was all her fault.

Finally, William took several deep breaths and then sat beside her. Two squirrels chased each other on the grass in front of them. Eleanor watched as one carried something in its mouth and hopped up into the tree. She couldn't stand the thought of William thinking differently of her. Or more horribly, abandoning her. What if he claimed it wasn't his? Accused her of being with someone else?

"I guess we should get married then." He cut into her thoughts.

Stunned, she turned to him. "Because I'm pregnant?"

"That, and because I love you. And I'm pretty sure you love me, too."

Eleanor didn't know what to say.

"Hey." He tipped her chin so that their eyes met. "It's my job to protect you. The best way for me to do that is to make you my wife."

William had said exactly what she had wanted to hear, what would make this all work and allow her to keep her respectability. Offer them the life that she had often envisioned. But then she played the scenario forward and blurted. "But your mother . . . she'll never accept me."

"Don't worry about her. It's me and you, baby." He kissed her cheek and then rested his forehead against hers until their noses touched. Eleanor felt relief spread warmly through her whole body and then she was crying.

"I thought you'd be disappointed in me."

"Shh, it's all right," he whispered in her hair. When she had settled, William got down on one knee.

Eleanor covered her mouth, still in disbelief that this was happening to her. She glanced around to see if anyone was watching them, but there was nothing but a couple of pigeons searching the grass for seeds.

"I didn't hear your answer. Eleanor Quarles, would you do me the honor of being my bride?"

His deep, hearty words covered Eleanor like a quilt. He was offering her every girl's dream. This baby would have two educated parents. There was no question that she loved him.

"Yes. William, of course I'll marry you."

He leaned up and kissed her deeply. "Tomorrow we'll go pick out a ring. Oh, and I'll need to call your father and ask permission."

William wiped the dust from his slacks, and then pulled her up from the bench.

"Yes, he'd like that." Eleanor threaded her arm around his waist. "You sure about this? Marriage is forever."

"I'm sure we're going to be a family. And I'm sure that I'm the luckiest man in the world." He brought her hand to his heart and then kissed her fingertips.

On Sunday, William insisted that they attend his parents' brunch. Eleanor had not wanted to go. But now that they were going to be married, she knew she couldn't put it off any longer. Rolling her shoulders back, she took William's hand and walked into the palatial home with a fake confidence that she did not feel. If she were to be his wife, she would have to learn to mingle. The four women she had previously mistaken as white sat on the velvet tufted chairs, and Eleanor made it a point to ask how they were enjoying the good weather and to inquire about their plans for summer. William handed her a glass of tomato juice, and she could tell he was pleased, though he was quickly pulled into a conversation with one of his father's doctor friends.

The four women eventually decided to view the new flower beds on the patio, and Eleanor was left alone. To pass the time, she found a dark corner in the parlor to sit, where she occupied herself by looking through William's family photo albums that she found stacked on a bookshelf. There were pictures of William as an infant dressed in white, as a toddler on a tricycle, with his dad and brother on a fishing trip holding up his catch, underneath the Christmas tree in a velvet vest and knickers. Each picture he looked happy and healthy with his brother, mother and father. Rose Pride was young and always glamorous, and William Senior's chest was always puffed out with pride. That's what Eleanor wanted for their child, to be in a family full of love, happy and healthy.

When the meal was served, Eleanor took a seat next to William, pleased to find that Greta and her parents were absent. That made the food go down easier. She half listened to the bantering at the table of twelve, set against the soft instrumental music playing on the Victrola. After slices of coconut cake, coffee and cordials the guests started drifting off into various clusters around the house. The weather was nice enough for her to walk around the garden, and she found a bench against the backdrop of bushes on which to pass more time.

It seemed like an eternity before the final guests left, and when William came back outside to get her, she knew that it was time.

"You ready for this?" she whispered to him, and she thought she saw a flicker of something in his eyes. But he quickly smiled it away.

The four of them met on the back patio. One of the servant women in gray brought out a tray of tea, with shortbread cookies and cream.

"Why don't we have a seat," William gestured to the wrought iron patio table and the four matching chairs with thick pillows.

Eleanor's hand shook as she poured herself a cup.

"What are you majoring in, Eleanor?" Rose Pride held her teacup in a way that jutted her pinky in the air.

"History."

"Planning to be a teacher?"

"Actually, archiving in the library."

"Oh," she said, the conversation over. She turned to William. "Before I forget, there is a fundraiser next Friday for the Urban League. I need you to make an appearance."

"Fine," he said, and then cleared his throat. He looked at Eleanor and nodded. "Mom and Dad, I wanted to tell you that we have good news."

A stricken look crossed Rose Pride's face.

Without further preamble William announced, "We are getting married."

Rose Pride's red lips gaped open, and her eyes burned into Eleanor. "You must be pregnant," she spat.

"What she means is congratulations," William Senior offered.

"Are you?" Rose asked. "Pregnant?"

Eleanor couldn't seem to find her voice. This was not what she had anticipated. William took her hand above the table. "She *is* carrying my child, but even if she wasn't, we'd still get married."

"Bullshit." Rose threw her arms up.

"Darling!" William Senior exclaimed. "Eleanor and William, will you excuse us?" He yanked on Rose's hand and pulled her inside behind the sliding glass doors.

William linked his arm through Eleanor's. "She'll come around."

"She won't. Your mother acts as if I have bewitched you and ruined your life."

"Well, she's right about one thing—you have bewitched me," he said, then leaned in and kissed her cheek just as his parents returned.

"That's what got you in this mess in the first place." Rose looked at Eleanor pointedly. "When is the baby due?"

Eleanor reached into her purse and pulled out the note from the doctor.

"Well, then we'll have to move quickly. People in our circle talk, but I'll take care of everything." Rose Pride's face looked even more sour than on the first day they had met. Eleanor didn't know if she was making a peace offering or starting a war.

Chapter Thirteen

AFTERSHOCK

Ruby

It was rare for me to see Shimmy on Sunday evenings because Aunt Marie was usually home. But as soon as we returned from our trip downtown yesterday, Fatty came by to tell Aunt Marie that she had fallen behind on Nene's rent, again. She needed five dollars to settle the bill. I knew Aunt Marie had spent what little she had extra on the stockings I had begged for. But despite it all, Aunt Marie told Fatty that she'd take care of it.

Even though I could see the bags under Aunt Marie's eyes all afternoon as she iced the swelling in her bothersome left knee, at five o'clock sharp she dressed in a boxy burgundy suit and left for work on her night off to make Nene's rent.

Left alone in the apartment, I couldn't concentrate on my geography assignment. My mind was still reeling from my brush with the white woman from downtown, and I couldn't stop thinking about what I had to say to Shimmy. After chewing off the eraser from my pencil, I worked up the courage and called his house. It rattled my nerves to dial him up, even though we had devised a system where I would let the phone ring once and then hang up. I did so now, and within five minutes Shimmy phoned me back.

"Hello," I answered.

"Hey there," he whispered, "what are you up to?"

"Geography."

"You need me to help? I'm not only good at trig you know." He chuckled lightly. "I can make an excuse to get away."

"Yeah, come for me. What time?"

"Eight? Usual spot." His voice brightened.

At eight, I didn't make eye contact with anyone as I swiftly disappeared around the building and into the alley where Shimmy was parked with the headlights off. I kicked a can at my feet with my saddle shoe and stepped over a puddle that was either spilled beer or someone's pee.

"Hey." I climbed into the back seat, pushing aside a pink knit blanket and a Raggedy Ann doll. "Was your sister playing house in the car again?"

"She's always up to something," Shimmy said breathlessly, while reaching back to squeeze my hand. His touch was soft, and it made me second-guess what I had called him to do.

"We can drive to Smith Playground and find a place to park. I have the car till ten."

The purr of the engine vibrated beneath me as I sank into the buttery leather seat. I swallowed down the saliva that had suddenly filled my mouth. "I can't . . . do this anymore."

"Do what?" He crinkled his brows.

"This. Us." I snatched my hand back. "Keep putting myself in harm's way."

"Wait." He put his hands up in defense. "What's going on?"

I looked at my hands in my lap, and then told him about my encounter with the white woman downtown, and the uncomfortable stares in the department store. "Have you read the paper lately? Another Negro teenage boy was beaten to a bloody pulp in the Italian section of South Philly. Accused him of looking at a white woman. What would they do to us?"

"Ruby, I don't care about all that. All I care about is you." He leaned over the seat, bringing his face as close to mine as he could. Then when he couldn't get close enough, he turned off the engine, climbed over into the back seat and reached for me, but I held him off with my palms.

"You don't care because you don't have to, Shimmy. You live in a beautiful safe bubble, and the world says I don't belong there."

"So, we are taking our cues from the world now? What about how we feel about each other? It shouldn't matter what anyone thinks."

"She called me a nigger to my face," I said between my teeth. Shimmy grimaced like the word had stabbed him in the throat.

After a minute, Shimmy reached for me again. His comforting scent of Old Spice calmed me and I relented. His tight embrace gave me the permission I needed to release the tears I had been holding on to all day. When it was just the two of us in this car, I felt safe. The car was our world.

"I'm scared, you know. This country is crazy."

"I'll keep you safe."

"Until you can't." I pulled back against my seat. "Don't you know it's against the law for us to be together? What if your father finds out? Or Mr. Greenwald? They'll have my black behind, not yours."

His face looked tormented. "They aren't like that and things are changing, Ruby. You aren't the only one who reads the newspaper. Why, just a few months ago the Supreme Court of California found that the law banning interracial marriages violated the Fourteenth Amendment and struck it down."

"That's one state, all the way on the other side of the country."

"But it's only a matter of time, and we'll run away to California if we have to. Stop worrying, will you?"

My fingers trembled in my lap. Shimmy was the sweetest boy I had ever known. He had a big heart and a kind disposition, but it didn't matter what I said, how many facts I presented, he would never get it. He could not understand what I went through, attending a high school that only had used books with pages missing, and bathrooms that rarely had running water. He had no idea what it was like to go to bed hungry, to turn on the light to find that mice had gnawed through your dinner and left their droppings for you to clean, or to have to kiss your mother's boyfriend just for carfare to get to a program that *might* award you a scholarship to college—a scholarship that you needed so you wouldn't have to spend a life cleaning toilets like your mom. White people's toilets.

I knew if I didn't stop this now, I never would. "I gotta go. Take care, Shimmy." I opened the car door, walked out of the alley and took the front steps two at a time.

My heartbreak pricked against my skin like a consecutive pop from a rubber band. I wanted what Shimmy and I had to be easy. And since that wasn't possible, I needed my feelings for him to go.

Aunt Marie had brought me a leftover piece of cake from a birthday party at the club, and as I swung open the icebox to retrieve it, there was a bang on the door.

"Shimmy, go home." I slammed the fridge closed with my foot.

"Let me in."

Ignoring him, I dipped a fork into the plastic container and brought a corner of the white icing and yellow cake to my lips.

"Please. Don't leave me out here making a scene."

The cake tasted like a wet sponge, and I spit it out in the sink.

"Ruby." He called my name in a way that was like a magnet reaching through the door and pulling on me. My fingers undid the three locks and slid the chain back on the door, seemingly without my permission.

Shimmy's hat was in his hands. "I don't have all the answers. I don't know how to make this work. All I know is that I can't live without you. I'm willing to do what it takes."

He forced his way into the apartment and closed the door behind him. We stood toe to toe, eye to eye.

"I love you, Ruby."

And then we were kissing.

"I don't care who knows it." He held my face with his strong hands gripping my hair. Our mouths kindled when they touched, setting my skin on edge but the voices just got louder.

Nigger.

Stay in your own neighborhood.

Now I need to shower.

You can't be friends with the likes of her.

I pulled away and looked him in the eyes. "Do you know what my mother does for a living? She cleans up after rich white people. What does your mother do?"

He shifted from one foot to the other. "She's a housewife."

"Which means she doesn't work. Does she clean your house, or someone comes in to do it for her?"

A deep blush darkened Shimmy's cheeks.

"A woman with skin like me, I bet."

He looked away.

"What will your mother say when she realizes that you, her pride and joy, are in love with the help's daughter?"

"Ruby, we will cross that bridge when we get to it. Why are you trying to sabotage a good thing?"

"We are at the bridge, Shimmy, and it's best that we get off before someone gets pushed off. Mainly me."

Shimmy's eyes were so clear and so sincere and so full of hope. He wanted us to be together, desperately. But the world had shown me that what we wanted didn't matter.

"It's for the best, Shimmy. Just go."

He stood staring at me, but I no longer met his gaze. Then he reached into his pocket, put something on the kitchen table and opened the door without another word.

I listened to his footsteps, watched him through the window as he walked around to the alley and heard his car pull into traffic. The street was empty. I went to the table and picked up the brown paper bag he had left. Inside was an antique hair comb, adorned with garnet rubies.

"Rubies for my Ruby," I could hear him say. And it was beautiful. Placing the comb in my hair, I looked at myself in the bathroom mirror that hung over the stained porcelain sink. Staring back at me was the white woman's beet-red face, hissing at me. *Nigger.*

I removed the comb, ran into the kitchen and dropped it in the garbage. Then crashed the lid down, slamming it closed over and over again.

Chapter Fourteen

TO WHOM MUCH IS GIVEN

Eleanor

From the moment Eleanor told William that she was pregnant, their lives had accelerated. Rose Pride had climbed behind the wheel and driven all of their future decisions at maximum speed. It was Rose who had decided that Eleanor and William would wed on the last Saturday in June, at St. Luke's Episcopal, the Pride family home church, while Eleanor's waist was still small enough to conceal their secret beneath a silk tulle wedding dress. Rose had even offered to fly Eleanor's parents in on TWA for the ceremony.

But Eleanor's mother was already chewing firewood over the nuptials taking place in D.C. rather than Elyria, at the little church where Eleanor had been baptized and spent her whole life. So when Eleanor called to make the gesture on Rose's behalf, her mother coughed up flames.

"We can pay for our own tickets," she huffed in a voice that told Eleanor that they would rather travel by bus and stay in a rented room atop the

YMCA like poor little church mice than take a handout from her soon-to-be in-laws. She could hear in the way her mother had tsked against her teeth that she was thinking, *Those damn uppity Negroes!*

Although her sophomore year had ended, and she wasn't enrolled in summer classes, Eleanor had secured a month of summer housing in her dormitory leading up to the wedding. Very few girls stayed on campus over the summer, and Nadine had returned to her parents' home in Petworth, leaving Eleanor with the room to herself.

When Eleanor told Nadine that she was marrying William, Nadine had grabbed her hands and they jumped up and down until they were both breathless. Then she kissed her cheek and exclaimed, "You are going to be the talk of the town. Wait until I get my hands on you."

"You know you have to be my maid of honor."

"Ohio, with bells on girl, with bells on." Nadine had beamed. But as she carried her last suitcase to the door, she had admitted to Eleanor, "When girls get married, they no longer have time for their single friends."

"I'll always have time for you," Eleanor reassured her.

"I can't believe I'm going to have to endure a new roommate. I am sure I won't like her."

"And I'm certain she won't let you be as messy as me. So you better start picking up after yourself," Eleanor teased.

"Promise we'll lunch over the summer."

Eleanor had promised, and it was a promise that she had intended to keep.

The peace, quiet and cleanliness that she returned home to each evening gave her too much space to sort through the melancholy that hung around the outer edges of her mind. Alone, she weighed the possibility that maybe things were happening too fast between her and William. They hadn't even been dating a full year and already they were jumping the broom, and no matter how hard she tried, she couldn't escape the thought that twisted and churned deep inside her. She didn't have the gumption to ask but desperately needed to know: Would William Pride still marry her if she wasn't pregnant?

He'd assured her he would, but still, the question lingered, and she saw it floating in her bowl of oatmeal, scribbled on the tiles when she showered, in the books she read, flashing across her eyes when she closed them at night. Eleanor had lost the ability to be comfortable.

Rose Pride had insisted that she quit her job at Ware's because no one in her precious circle of friends could think that her son was marrying a simple shopgirl, college educated or not, but Eleanor refused to give up her job at the library. Mrs. Porter promoted her to be her full-time research assistant, which gave her more hours and much more responsibility for the weeks leading up to her wedding. They were in the midst of sorting through materials related to Frederick Douglass for the assemblage, and Eleanor had spent her whole shift running back and forth from the collection center on the second floor to Mrs. Porter's office on the third floor, carrying books, pamphlets and letters that had just been donated to them from a wealthy donor in Baltimore. When her shift ended, Eleanor crossed the yard feeling a slight ache in her abdomen and lower back. She had gotten used to the queasiness and was trying her best to deal with her inability to hold her breakfast down, the loss of appetite and just all-around crabbiness.

But this feeling, this was new. With each step the pain in her lower belly seemed to increase. Perhaps she had worked herself too hard. Tomorrow was Sunday and she would rest all day. Her pain would give her an excuse not to attend yet another brunch at the Prides', where she didn't feel like family. She hoped that their child would bridge the distance between them.

Eleanor had had no choice but to attend last week's brunch, because Rose wanted to make the engagement announcement quickly, so as not to stir up talk. Greta and her family had attended, and when William Pride Senior asked everyone to raise their glass to the happy couple, Greta gave Eleanor a look so cold that it sent an instant chill down her back.

Later, when Eleanor was coming out of the downstairs powder room, Greta was waiting for her, again.

"So, Eleanor. I must know. How did you manage to trap him?" she demanded, hands on her slim hips, jewelry gleaming, nostrils flaring.

Eleanor took a wobbly step back. "I'm not sure what you mean."

"Oh, you know what I mean." She sized Eleanor up and snickered. "You must be pregnant."

Eleanor refused to blink. "Jealousy doesn't suit you, Greta."

"And you will never be a member of Alpha Beta Chi. You will never fit in anywhere. I'll make sure of it." She moved in close enough for Eleanor to smell the champagne on her breath. "You aren't one of us. Go back to the rat hole you crawled out of," she sputtered. "With your cheap shoes."

Anger had pelted down on Eleanor so fast and hard that she couldn't do anything but laugh. "Get on with your life, Greta. There are plenty more fish in the sea, and you can keep the ABCs, I don't need any of you," she said and stormed off.

The memories of the fight with Greta, combined with the increasing abdominal pain, made Eleanor feel like she needed to lay down.

William's roommate had moved to Philadelphia to do his residency at Mercy-Douglass Hospital, and William had given Eleanor a key to his apartment. It was late afternoon, and William had gone to meet his father to shop for his wedding suit. There was an ease to being around William's things, even when he wasn't around. She walked the few blocks to his place in LeDroit Park, hoping the fresh air and sunshine would do her some good. Eleanor let herself in and went straight to the Frigidaire.

Twice a week, Rose Pride sent meals to William in color-coordinated Tupperware, and as expected, Eleanor found a container of chicken salad sprinkled with paprika. After spooning a few helpings into a bowl, she broke off a piece of French baguette from the breadbox. The pain continued to ripple in her abdomen and down her back. Had she really worked that hard today? After two bites, she had lost her appetite. Eleanor removed her skirt and blouse and laid across William's bed in her slip. Propping both pillows under her head, she curled in the fetal position and drifted to sleep.

Cramps stronger than the first day of her menstrual cycle—stronger than anything she'd felt before—jolted her awake. She reached for the water she had left on the bedside table and then stood up but quickly felt the need to hunch over.

Holding on to the wall, she made her way to the bathroom, where she sat on the cold seat and peed. The toilet paper that she brushed between her legs returned with a startling ringlet of blood. Eleanor closed her eyes as a familiar feeling came over her. She started humming the first hymn that came to her mind, "This Little Light of Mine," over and over. She wasn't sure how much time had passed when she heard William's key in the door.

"Elly?"

"I'm here." Her voice was somber.

William stood on the other side of the bathroom door. "I found my suit. I think you're going to love it." He rattled on about his time with his father, the shoes they selected and the people they ran into at the Whitelaw Hotel, where they had stopped for lunch. After a while he asked, "You all right in there? Why are you so quiet?"

A pain rumbled through her, making it difficult to answer. After several seconds passed, William cracked opened the door. "Baby?"

Eleanor was doubled over on the toilet and lifted her face to meet his.

Worry knitted his brows. "What's the matter? You don't look so good."

Her vision blurred. William was speaking, but his voice took so long to reach her, it felt so far away. He stooped down in front of her, bringing her eyes to his. "Tell me what you need. Is it the baby?"

William tried to help her to her feet, but she resisted.

"I'm bleeding."

He rolled up his sleeves and whispered that he'd be right back. Eleanor could hear him fumbling around in the kitchen and then something crashed to the floor. He returned with a wad of paper towels.

"Here." He folded them over and made a pad for her to place between her legs.

When he got her on the sofa, he covered her with a quilt. "I'll call my dad. He'll know what to do."

"No," Eleanor shrieked, not wanting to let his family in. "Call my doctor, his number is in my wallet."

William took his pointer finger and turned the rotary dialer on the telephone. It took him explaining what was happening at least three times, sweat beading on the bridge of his nose, before he handed her the receiver.

"This is Eleanor," she said formally, trying to mask the discomfort from her voice.

The nurse asked her to describe her symptoms, and she told her everything that had happened in the last few hours, ending with the blood seeping from between her legs.

Eleanor listened and then waited for the doctor, who asked another round of questions. She answered those too, thanked him for his time and hung up the telephone.

"What did he say?" William's knees rested against hers as they sat side by side.

With the back of her hand, she dabbed away the snot dripping from her nose that oozed with embarrassment. She wrapped her arms around herself and rocked. Eleanor had not even wanted the baby when she first found out she was pregnant. These feelings of hopelessness and loss that swooned around inside of her were all a surprise. What she should have felt was relief that her whole life wasn't going to be upended. Instead, she felt devastation that curdled into anger.

"What did the doctor say?"

"That you and your mom have gotten your wish."

"Huh?"

"There's no more baby," she choked.

"Don't say that."

"I've miscarried, so you can bow out gracefully. We don't have to go through with the wedding, and you can return to your perfect life as planned," she spat.

William put his hand over his mouth in shock. "How could this have happened?"

"Oh, it happens more often than you think," she responded coldly. "Did you even want the baby, William? This whole wedding thing?" She pushed his hand off her knee.

"What?" He looked at her incredulously.

"You heard me. Did you even want it!"

"Baby, calm down." He took her hand and held it firmly. "Naturally, I was surprised at first, but I've started looking forward to building a life with you. Why? You weren't?"

Of course she was. Marrying William would have been the best thing to ever happen to her. Securing a good marriage and future for herself with a doctor who loved her and could provide a stable life was beyond her wildest dreams. And not just any doctor, but William, whom she loved deeply and completely. Isn't that what every girl at Howard wanted? Why their parents sent them to the prestigious Negro college, to get a good education and find a mate that they could love and build a solid life with? Another cramp rolled through her body and she gasped.

William reached for her. "What do you need?" His eyes were tender and then he drew her into his arms, where she collapsed and allowed him to hold her until the sob that she felt in her chest burst free. She had lost the baby. The baby they had made together, and she trembled all over.

"I'm sorry. I feel like I've failed you." Her voice was small. "I don't even know where we go from here."

William dried the wetness under her eye with his thumb. "I'm not letting you get away from me that easily. Eleanor, I love you and I still want to marry you."

Her eyes glistened. What had she done to deserve such a kind, good man?

"We can try again. Everything will be fine, you just wait and see. That's a promise."

William's words were comforting, but for once, Eleanor wasn't so sure he was right. What she was sure of was that he didn't know her. Not well enough to make such a promise.

PART TWO

June 1950, one year later

Sometimes there are no words to help one's courage.
Sometimes you just have to jump.

—Dr. Clarissa Pinkola Estés

Chapter Fifteen

TAKING CARE OF BUSINESS

Ruby

My summer job going into my senior year of high school was to help Aunt Marie three mornings a week give Kiki's a deep clean. Although Aunt Marie hated doing domestic work with a passion, the money man she wrote numbers for had gotten busted a month ago in a police raid, and she needed to replace that income.

"Things are hot on the streets," Aunt Marie told me, "and I don't know who might run their mouth so it's best to lay low. Do something else for a while."

To hold us over, she accepted the owner of Kiki's offer to clean up the place, and she paid me fifty cents a shift to be her assistant. In a bleach-stained T-shirt and gym shorts, I wiped down the tables and chairs, while Aunt Marie scrubbed behind the bar. While we worked, she sang along to Fats Waller's "Ain't Misbehavin'" playing on the jukebox.

"When you mop the floors, get those corners good," she called to me from behind the bar. She had removed the many bottles of liquor and was sponging down the floor-to-ceiling mirror with dish soap, white vinegar and water. The mahogany shelves she polished with Murphy's Oil. I sloshed the mop in the soapy water, with a few caps full of ammonia. When I bent down to ring out the mop with my rubber gloves, a dizziness washed over me. I gagged and dry-heaved, then put my hand on the nearest wooden table to brace myself, belching up sour acid.

Aunt Marie's oil-stained rag swept over the bar top, but her eyes never left me. "Told you 'bout playing with fire, didn't I? Now your ass done got burnt."

Her frankness irritated me as much as the raw, red skin that rubbed against my cotton knit panties. I had caused the chafing by wiping too hard and too often, searching for my monthly visitor.

"Give me that damn mop." She came round the bar and snatched the stick from my hand so fast it caused a splinter. "Go sit your fast ass down somewhere."

Inez had called me a fast ass after that thing with Leap, when she kicked me out the house over a year ago. Coming from Aunt Marie's lips, the words stung like alcohol being poured into an open wound. Even though that time wasn't my fault, this time was, and I cowered in the corner under the picture of Nat King Cole, refusing to let all my shame and self-loathing out.

It had started with a handwritten note.

Philadelphia had been blessed with a warm day in March after a snowy February, so I decided to sit on the front steps with a small canvas and my color palette. Rowdy boys were playing stickball with a dismantled broom and a piece of a tennis ball. I was focused on painting the filling station across the street when out of the blue, Shimmy trudged up the street. My stomach did a pirouette at the sight of him, but I quickly turned my head, hoping he had not seen me. When I looked again, he had disappeared inside his uncle's paint store on the corner.

It had been so long since I laid eyes on him, heard his voice, felt his fingers caught in my hair. Smart Ruby should have retreated upstairs to the safety of the apartment, but the vision of him had weighed me down like iron to the cushion I used to pad my seat.

I tried not to think about him, to concentrate on my brush, dipped in green with a tint of yellow, as it stroked up and down the canvas, but my eyes kept darting toward the store every time I heard the swish and pull of the door, followed by the bell's ding. A few moments later, Shimmy emerged carrying a gallon of paint and a few drop cloths tucked under his arm. He didn't look my way when he strolled by me, but a piece of paper fell into my lap.

It had been ten months and four days since I broke up with him in Aunt Marie's living room, and that white paper burned feverishly in my palm. I didn't want to open it, but I didn't know how not to.

Mr. Greenwald is out of town. Meet me at the back door of the candy store at 7pm. Please come. I need to tell you something. Knock three times so that I know it's you.

Yours,
Shimmy

All the Jewish shops on 31st Street were closed on Saturdays, so the back alley behind the stores was deserted, except for an abandoned car with two flat tires, and a big blue trash dumpster that smelled of spoiled sardines. It was dark out. The sunny day had turned into a frigid March night, with the temperature dropping at least thirty degrees. My fingers were frozen as I timidly knocked three times.

The door spun open and Shimmy stood in the frame in a pair of dungarees, white collared shirt and a boyish grin on his face. He had grown nearly two inches in our time apart. His shoulders had filled out and his chest was defined. The string bean boy I had met had morphed into a stalk of a man. He reached for my hand and pulled me inside.

The lights were off, and the fragrance of the combined smell of chocolate, caramel, fudge and other sweets from the front of the store made me hungry. I followed him down a narrow hall and into a small storage room. In the middle of the floor was a makeshift table covered in a red checkered cloth. On top, there was a single candle lit, white Tupperware containers and plastic spoons. Two pillows were thrown on either side.

"Please, sit." He finally let my hand go, and when he did, I could still feel the warmth of his grip.

"What's all this?" I folded my arms over my breasts cautiously.

"Dinner. I brought you some matzo ball soup and challah."

I looked around the storage room at the shelves of boxes, bowls and stacks of supplies, while asking myself why I had defied my good sense of logic and reason by answering his call. No good could come from sneaking into the back of the candy store with a boy who should have long been out of my system.

"Please." He gestured to the pillow on the floor opposite him. "While the food is still warm."

My instinct was to say goodbye, but what tumbled out of my mouth was "I can't believe you went through so much trouble," and I felt myself being drawn to the pillow he had prepared.

"What have you been up to?" He took a bite, but I saw a slight tremble of his hands.

"Not much."

On the walk over, I had decided to keep my guard up. Only coming to hear what he had to say. Not to rekindle a friendship and definitely not a love affair. But with him so close, the hard shell that I had worked up around me had already begun to splinter, and then I asked the question that had been burning inside of me.

"Where have you been?"

My voice came out much more intense than I had wanted, and he put down his spoon.

"New York, taking classes at Brooklyn College. Why? Did you miss me?" His face flushed.

I giggled away his question, hoping my eyes didn't betray my truth. "Studying accounting?"

"Oh man, it's much harder than I thought. But I'm making it. What about you? Still chasing that scholarship?"

I straightened my back. "It's the only option for me."

"I didn't mean it like that." Shimmy covered my hand, and his eyes were a softer green than I had remembered. "It's in the bag for you. When do they make the official announcement?"

"I'm in the running is all I can say. There are still eight of us for only two scholarships." I fingered the braided bread. "What's college like?"

Going myself was all I could think about. Shimmy was the only person that I had known to attend a university and I was dying to hear everything.

"Hectic. Everyone has an opinion. There is always someone protesting something. Definitely more of a melting pot than here."

"What do you mean?"

"I go to school with people from all walks of life. And that's been good for me. Helped me shape my perspective. Opened my eyes a bit."

"Yeah? To what?"

"I think I understand you better."

I laughed. "You spend ten months away, and now you understand *me* better?"

He put a hunk of bread in his mouth and chewed. "That's what I'm saying. Living here, it was like I was trapped in my own little world. I only knew what my parents showed me. That was Jewish life, our little box. But up in Brooklyn, I had friends who were German, Italian, Negro and even Puerto Rican."

"What's that got to do with me?"

"I see you, Ruby." He ran his fingers up to my elbow. "You said I couldn't see our differences and that I was living in a safe bubble, and I understand that now."

Just the fact that he had even considered what I said touched me. The care in his voice pried me open, and as we slurped down our soup, I felt larger cracks split my protective shell. It did not take long before we had slipped into an easy rhythm, catching up on the parts of each other's life that we had missed.

"What happened with your mom?"

A lump formed in my throat at the thought of Inez. "I saw her over the holidays but that's all. I think it's fair to assume that Aunt Marie's is my home until I leave for college."

I had been practicing saying that out loud. *When I go away to college.* I had figured if I kept thinking it and saying it, it had to come true.

Shimmy unwrapped a chocolate-covered pretzel and handed it to me. "I know chocolate is your weakness."

I took a small bite and thanked him with my smile. "So good. Can't get these from the corner store."

"I brought a little radio," he said, as he reached up onto the shelf and fiddled with the stations until a song that I didn't know came on. Shimmy cleared away the makeshift table just as the song shifted to "Rock and Roll" by Wild Bill Moore. It was the song he had played on the jukebox for me on my first visit to Greenwald's.

"Wanna dance?"

"Right here?" I looked around the small storage space.

"Come on." He reached for my hand and lifted me to my feet.

Mama, oh Mama
I want to rock and roll.

Shimmy put his hands on my waist as we twisted our hips and bobbed our heads. The lyrics of the song spilled from both of our mouths. In that moment, I realized that I had been bottled up inside myself since he had been gone. All my time had been spent studying, throwing myself into *We Rise*, helping care for Nene, but I hadn't really been myself. This was the most fun I'd had in as far back as I could remember, and I felt free. We danced for so long my straightened bangs drew up on my forehead from the sweat, but for once I didn't care.

"What did you have to tell me?" Out of breath, I had remembered the reason I was there.

"Oh, that I'll be home every weekend now to help out Ma."

"What about school?"

"I've arranged my classes for the week to end on Thursday morning." His eyes lit up, and I could tell from the sloppy grin on his face that he had assumed that I'd be a part of his weekend package. As much fun as I was having, I still didn't think it was wise to go back. But before I could say as much, Shimmy's hands were on my hips, guiding me closer to him, and then he was leaning down and pushing my hair behind my ear, leaving a hot trail down the side of my neck.

I shuddered.

"Ruby." Shimmy had a way of saying my name that made me feel precious. "I missed you."

"Really? Even with all those sophisticated college girls?"

"None as smart or as beautiful as you."

"I bet the pretty little Jewish girls are pining for your attention like crazy."

"But I want you." He looked deeply into my eyes.

"Ain't nothing changed around here but the weather. While you were off broadening your horizons in Brooklyn, North Philly's still the same."

"Try with me." He brought me so close that all I smelled was him.

"When I saw you sitting on the steps today, it was like no time had passed. You are still right here." He pointed to his chest.

Even though I wasn't ready to admit it, I felt the same way. I had tried to entertain a boy or two at school in the time that Shimmy and I were apart, but I hadn't found any that were remotely as interesting as Shimmy.

Our eyes met, and I watched as his hunger for me settled between his brows. Ten long months apart, and I had not stopped loving Shimmy.

"You are under my skin," he whispered in my ear, and my knees buckled.

I had been so lonely before his note. And then we were kissing. It was the sweetest, most luscious kiss we had ever shared, but then ugly Leap flashed across my lids. I could feel his rough hands groping my breasts and him pushing his manhood against my thigh. I wrenched away.

"Sorry," Shimmy said. "I didn't mean . . ."

But I didn't let him finish, before crushing my lips against his. This time I put my hands in his soft, silky hair as proof. *Shimmy not Leap.*

Shimmy, Shimmy, Shimmy.

From that evening on, our time together went like this: on Friday afternoons, while Aunt Marie was at Nene's cooking her food for the weekend, I snuck Shimmy into our apartment. His father still drank with Mr. Leroy upstairs, so waiting on him was Shimmy's cover. Most weeks, Shimmy had to wrestle his father out of the apartment so that they were not late for Shabbat.

On Saturday evenings, while Aunt Marie was working at Kiki's, we took long drives in his father's car to a place where people couldn't see us. We talked for hours about everything.

Shimmy's dad was drinking more, and his mother had threatened to put him out on the street, but the kids begged her to let him stay. We touched each other for so long that every cell in my body was alive with longing, and we listened to music and had song battles to see who knew all the lyrics by heart. On the nights when Shimmy thought it was safe, we'd sneak into the candy store and hang out in the storage room.

I had not planned to lose my virginity to Shimmy on the floor in Greenwald's, on the red checkered tablecloth. But when he hiked up my skirt, I could no longer contain the tension that had been building inside of me ever since he walked into Aunt Marie's house to fix the sink. Without thinking about what could go wrong, what I might be giving up, I let myself go. I let him have all of me.

After our first time together, Shimmy had cradled my face. I liked the way we smelled afterward. Our secret was fragrant, filled with notes of our connection.

"I'm so in love with you, Ruby, it's hard to see straight."

I knew exactly what he meant, because as Aunt Marie would put it, I couldn't see for shit.

Aunt Marie finished cleaning the rest of the club herself, never even looking at me. Afterward, we didn't talk the whole bus ride home. When we got to the apartment, she put on a pot of water and made two cups of tea.

"Sit down," she said, finally cracking the icy silence between us.

I pulled a chair to the table and accepted the cup. Aunt Marie lowered herself into the chair across from me and wiped at her forehead with the kitchen rag she kept hanging from the stove.

"Edna from across the street told me Shimmy been sniffing round here. Is it his?"

Ashamed, I looked into my black tea.

"Goddamn it, Ruby."

My hope was that the stress from sneaking around with Shimmy, keeping up with *We Rise* and working for Aunt Marie had made my friend late. But the tenderness of my breasts, the way I couldn't hold anything down signaled otherwise. Aunt Marie had always been the type of person who knew things before folks opened their mouths, so her reaction was all I needed to confirm my deep-seated suspicion.

"White boys too good to use condoms?"

I kept my head bowed, because I couldn't stand the disappointment that I knew swam in her dark eyes. What difference would it make that the condom broke? I had been the family's piece of hope, the one smart enough to go to college, the girl to make three generations of tired, poor, Negro women proud.

When I still didn't answer, Aunt Marie sucked hard on her teeth. "Well,

I know someone who can make this go away. I'll find out if it's what you want?"

I knew enough about what happened to girls who got into trouble to know what she meant.

"Ain't that illegal?"

"Lots of things illegal. Don't make it wrong. You should know—sneaking around with a damn Jewish boy for Christ's sake."

I nodded, trying not to show that her words had landed hard against the side of my head.

"I need to hear your answer, girl. This ain't kiddie play."

"Yes."

"Yes, you want me to look into making it go away?"

"Please." I scrunched my toes up in my socks. If Inez had looked into making me go away, maybe her life would have turned out better. The heaviness of it all flooded me instantly, and before I could wipe the water from my face, Aunt Marie was on my side of the table, enveloping me in her girth.

"Auntie will take care of everything. It's going to be all right, sweetness."

The next evening, Aunt Marie came home early from work and announced, "Got you that appointment."

"When?"

She removed her chandelier earrings. "Tonight. Go in my room and rest for an hour, we'll head out round ten."

"I'm scared."

Aunt Marie's caramel-colored face looked ashen. Like she was weary down in her soul, and I regretted having to drag her into this. She squeezed my shoulder before I went back to her bedroom and stretched out, wondering what the procedure would be like. I knew it would hurt and I pictured a lot of blood. I didn't want to die trying to rid myself of a child that I did not want. Like Inez had not wanted me.

It was not lost on me that we were almost the same age when it happened. Inez had gotten pregnant with me at fifteen, and I had only made it one more year and some months before suffering the same fate. Aunt Marie always said the apple didn't fall far from the tree. Had Nene wanted Inez to go to college, too? Did she have a promising future that I messed up? I tried not to think about the thing growing inside of me as an actual person. I chose to look at it as a roadblock, one that was in the way of getting me to college. And I couldn't be detoured.

We caught the trolley, and then transferred to the 17 bus that carried us into South Philly. Once Aunt Marie pulled the cord signaling our stop, we walked three blocks to Tasker, and then ducked around the corner onto Gerritt Street, a tiny one-way with a broken streetlight at the corner. The house with the black-and-white awning and silver storm door was in the middle of the block. Aunt Marie knocked two times and then waited a beat, then tapped two more. A young girl with braids answered the door.

"Here to see Leatrice."

The child let us in. There was a man with gray whiskers passed out in a recliner, snoring in tune with the radio. An empty fifth of Inver House sat on the coffee table in front of him. Through the dining room, there was a door to the left that led to the basement. I followed Aunt Marie down the narrow stairs that shifted and groaned under our feet. At the foot of the steps, I saw a tucked-in twin bed on one side and a bar on the other. The room smelled of raw liver, dried blood and urine. A frail woman wearing a gauzy white dress with a scarf knotted on her head stood up, waving her palms at us.

"You can't be here." Her voice was high-pitched.

"Juney sent us. We have an appointment," Aunt Marie explained.

"Juney must ain't heard. White girl died last night on the table. Bled to death. People asking questions. Business gone cold."

My eyes grew big and a chilly sweat sprouted up and down my back. I didn't want to risk dying just to get rid of the thing. What was the point in that? I was ready to bolt, but Aunt Marie grabbed hold of my shoulder and pushed me forward.

"She ain't that far along. I'm sure this one be fine."

The woman called Leatrice shook her head. "Can't risk going to jail for nobody."

"Secret safe wit' me and I have cash. Please," Aunt Marie's voice pleaded. "I can pay extra," she said, which worried me, because I knew that she was having a tough time with the numbers business shut down. Where would the extra money come from?

Leatrice looked up at the ceiling like she was considering it, then looked me up and down. "Can't take the chance right now. I'm gonna have to ask y'all to leave." She took a step forward.

Aunt Marie raised her chest, like she wanted to make a fuss, but then she saw that Leatrice had moved closer to the table. Underneath a newspaper, I saw the barrel of a gun peeping at us. Being a gun-toting woman herself, Aunt Marie dropped her shoulders as she submitted to the implications.

"Come on here, chile," she said, ushering me back up the steps and back through the house. "We'll think of something," she told me once we got back to the bus stop.

As I stepped onto the bus, half of me was relieved that I didn't have to go through with it, but the other part worried sick over what would come next.

Chapter Sixteen

PAPER AND CLOCKS

Eleanor

Eleanor's face had grown round and curvy, and two juicy pimples rested on her chin. She snapped open her press compact and dabbed them with Max Factor's pancake. Then she brushed the face powder over her cheeks and forehead until her skin looked even and smooth. One by one, she removed the pink rollers from her hair, careful to keep the curls twirled with her fingertips. Her floral, royal-blue, ankle-length skirt hung from the back of her closet. She hoped it still fit. In the last week her belly had begun to protrude forward, and she could not resist dropping her palm, letting her baby know that she was still there.

Today was Eleanor and William's one-year wedding anniversary, and it had been a year filled with firsts. With the help of his parents, they purchased their first home, a three-bedroom in the glitzy Gold Coast section of Northwest D.C. It sat across the street from Rock Creek Park, and was a mere fifteen-minute walk from the house that William grew up in, despite Eleanor's protest that LeDroit Park, a fifteen-minute drive south of the Prides', would be a better fit and closer to the university. But the Prides had insisted that they live close by, and William agreed, so she had no choice but to smile and acquiesce.

The newlyweds had survived their first big blowup, spent their first Thanksgiving in Elyria with her parents and enjoyed a whole 365 nights of spooning in the same full-sized bed, in spite of Rose's suggestion that they buy separate twin ones. The couple had relished fifty-two Sunday mornings with the *Washington Afro-American* newspaper between them, until their coffee went tepid. Followed by a romp between their sheets filled with carnal pleasures so somatic that they needed a nap afterward.

It had been the best year of Eleanor's life. She delighted in waking up first to watch the way William's eyelids skipped up and down while he slept, savored the way his breath smelled of her after sex and hungered for the taste of his fingers in her mouth. Eleanor loved the feel of his socked feet covering hers under the breakfast table while they ate, and the warmth of his arms circling her back when they kissed, the smile of gratitude on his face each time she handed him his homemade lunch and the sound of his footsteps hurrying to reach her when he returned home each night. Married life delighted her. But tonight wasn't a celebration of their elation.

What their first year of marital bliss had earned them was another night at a premium table in a big fancy hall at yet another one of Rose Pride's must-attend affairs. As Eleanor painted her upper lash lines and fanned out her lashes, she couldn't remember if the event was for the ABCs, the Boules or the Links. With such plentiful invitations, they had all started running together in her mind. She did remember that Rose was being honored tonight for something or other, that was why despite it being their anniversary, William had insisted that they go.

"For Mother's sake." He had caressed her collarbone that morning, and then reminded her to send over a bouquet from Lee's Flower Shop.

It wasn't easy for Eleanor to keep track of the social calendar that Rose insisted on while still finishing her degree at Howard. She had taken extra credits over the summer and only needed a few more to graduate, but balancing the pregnancy, the new house and her studies was a struggle. As a result, she had only seen Nadine a handful of times, and she felt guilty about breaking her promise to keep in touch after she was married.

Eleanor was trying to latch the clasp of the gold tennis bracelet William had given her for her birthday when she heard his car pull into the driveway. He whistled to himself as he came through the side door and walked up to the bedroom.

"Elly! You are stunning," he said as he moved across the room to kiss her. "Happy anniversary, baby." He retrieved a small navy bag from behind his back.

"Oh, William," she said. "I don't need anything else."

"Open it."

Eleanor reached inside the bag, moved the tissue paper and found a box. She flipped it open and lifted a gold Bulova watch. On the back was an inscription.

Our time is for eternity,
Love WP

Eleanor beamed and then reached for his chin.

"We can stay here," she said and caressed his jawline. "Celebrate the old-fashioned way."

"Mmm. Don't start none, won't be none. I'll save my sweets for later." He squeezed her shoulder and headed for the shower.

William had started his first year of residency at the hospital and had been busy during her thirteen-week doctor's appointment that morning, and the leaflet that her obstetrician had given her to share with him was on the table. Eleanor picked it up and read it for the umpteenth time, even though she had committed most of it to memory.

The fetus was now peeing inside her, and if it was a girl, which she believed it to be, her ovaries were already filled with tiny eggs. Eleanor could not quite imagine a body already being groomed to give birth before it was even born. Her little one weighed about two ounces, had unique fingerprints and was covered in a fine hair called lanugo. Eleanor had looked up *lanugo* in her Oxford dictionary, before moving on to the most important sentence on the page. It was the very last line on the leaflet.

At thirteen weeks the mother has entered her second trimester, and the chances of a miscarriage are decreased.

She'd underlined those words with a blue ink pen. Seeing them now made her smile. She was out of the danger zone. Come January 1951, she and William would welcome their sweet-faced child, and she hugged herself at the thought of being a mother. A mother to William's flesh and blood, the baby that would bond them together for life, and damp away the doubt from Rose Pride's mind that her beloved son had married wrong.

When William walked into the kitchen, he looked like he had just stepped from one of the fashion pages of *Ebony* magazine. His hair was brushed, and his two-tone shoes were shining. Even after all their time together, it was still sometimes hard to believe that he was all hers. The man whose back she had admired for all those months was now her husband, and as Eleanor watched him move toward her, she felt like she had won the grand prize.

"What are you smiling about?"

"You."

In the car, William reached over and squeezed Eleanor's thigh. "Thanks for doing this tonight. I know it's our anniversary, but it means a lot to Mother, us being there. You understand, right?"

Eleanor nodded and then fiddled with the radio, until she found something more soothing than the bottom of the third inning with the Baltimore Elite Giants pitching against the Indianapolis Clowns.

William always prefaced these invitations with "for Mother's sake," but Eleanor knew that William enjoyed these posh events almost as much as Rose did. He was in his element at these soirees in a way that Eleanor was not. She hoped their child would bridge this one gap between them, once and for all. Two years ago, Eleanor hadn't even known that the Negro elite existed, and now she was a member of one of the most affluent families in D.C. She often had to remind herself to pretend that wearing a frock that cost more than her father's weekly wages was normal. As she moved through the banquet hall, she trained her face not to gawk at all the extravagances.

White-gloved waiters strolled the room, clutching silver trays containing champagne, crisp wine and succulent seafood hors d'oeuvres on toothpicks. Rose and William Pride Senior stood in the middle of two couples. Rose, as usual, was dressed in a silky one-of-a-kind frock, dripping with heavy diamonds and strings of pearls.

"William, darling, you remember Judge Mosley and his lovely wife? Their daughter, Beatrice, was a debutante at the alumni ball you went to in eleventh grade." Rose gestured for William to join their circle.

"Good to see you again," William said. "This is my wife, Eleanor."

William Senior added, "And today is their one-year anniversary. Congratulations." He raised his glass to them, and the Mosleys did the same.

"They are expecting their first child," Rose offered, and Eleanor noticed that her glass rested at half-mast.

"You must be so excited," Mrs. Mosley cooed, her gray hair bouncing against her shoulders. "Are you hoping for a boy or a girl?"

"Just a healthy baby" was Eleanor's standard answer.

"Well, may God bless you." The woman patted Eleanor's elbow.

"Oh, William dear, come with me. I want you to meet someone," Rose insisted before ushering William away and leaving Eleanor to fend for herself.

Alone, Eleanor made her way to her assigned table, where she sat and watched as the who's who of Washington, D.C., swarmed around each other. They buzzed with laughter, showing off brand-new suits, frocks, expensive jewelry and hats. She overheard chatter about new cars parked outside, and the summer homes on Martha's Vineyard and Sag Harbor that would take them far from the hot city's reach for the months of July and August. Eleanor longed for a familiar face, someone to pass the time with, but there was no one, and she recalled Greta's long-ago threat:

You aren't one of us. You will never fit in anywhere. I'll make sure of it.

In her first year of marriage to William, Eleanor had not made a single friend at these exclusive events. A few hellos and quick goodbyes, but nothing substantial. There were no invitations to tea, or baby showers, or lunch that she could grab onto. But with her baby growing inside of her, she could only hope that things would change. She moved her fingers in soothing circles under the table, reminding herself that she was never truly alone.

This one had to be the charm.

Eleanor and William had waited until after the wedding and honeymoon to tell his parents that she had lost their first child together at ten weeks. Rose gave her deepest condolences, but once she thought Eleanor to be out of earshot, she told William how she really felt.

"Perhaps we should get the marriage annulled and fix this whole mess," Rose Pride admonished him.

"Mother, there is nothing to fix."

"If she's not having your child, then what's the point?"

"The point is that I love her, and I need you to accept that."

"She doesn't fit."

"We fit just fine. I made a vow before God that I intend to keep. Now, drop it."

Eleanor didn't want to get caught eavesdropping while she stood just outside Rose Pride's den. When she turned to back away, one of the servants stood sweeping the floor behind her. She had heard the outburst, too, and offered Eleanor tight lips before fixing her eyes on the imaginary dust on her broom.

Rose was never outwardly rude to Eleanor. After all, control was her strong suit. When Eleanor became pregnant the second time, Rose hired a housekeeper to clean behind them once a week. She insisted that Eleanor give up her beloved job at the library, and even wanted her to pause her education, but Eleanor refused to give in to the latter. Her mother had worked too hard selling her baked goods to get her to Howard. Eleanor owed her a degree. To accommodate her new life, she had arranged all her classes on Monday, Wednesday and Friday to cut down on how often she needed to travel to campus, and then pushed on. She would finish the semester after the baby was born, but she would finish.

The sound of glass shattering pulled Eleanor's attention back into the room. A dark-skinned man with large eyes was apologizing profusely as he stooped to pick up a flute that had tipped from his tray to the floor. Eleanor looked for William and spotted him in the center of the room, standing in a circle with Greta Hepburn, her parents and his parents. Greta was chuckling, then put her ringless hand on William's arm as a pretense of steadying herself. Even from where Eleanor sat, she saw Rose's face brighten in Greta's presence. Greta was the daughter-in-law that Rose had wanted, and to Eleanor it felt like she was waiting in the wings for Eleanor to slip up.

She pinched her thigh in order to keep herself from imagining what Greta and William's life would have been like together, had William not met her, had she not gotten pregnant, had he not done the right thing by her, but she forced herself to let that nagging thought go. She flipped over her new watch and read the inscription again.

Our time is for eternity,
Love WP

When she glanced back up, William looked across the room and winked at her. The five-piece band had taken the stage, and the music played a steady upbeat rhythm as he moved toward her.

"Mrs. Pride, may I have this dance?"

Eleanor giggled despite herself and allowed her husband to spin her body across the dance floor. She nestled her face in his neck and whispered, "I love you."

They had barely made it through the door before William found the zipper at the back of her neck and tore her frock from her. The stairs to their bedroom would take too long, so they found their way to the living room. Pressed against the settee, William parted her thighs and sank into her flesh. They arched, clawed and moved against each other with the ache of that first-year fever that just never seemed to flicker out.

"Happy anniversary," William gasped, then collapsed against her breasts.

"Did I hurt the baby?" he asked, with his chest poked out.

Eleanor rolled her eyes playfully. "Always fishing for a compliment."

"You know I aim to please." He kissed her cheek.

"Well, accomplished." She retrieved her panties from the floor. "But our little girl is famished."

William stood naked in the dark living room. A sliver of moonlight caught the twinkle in his eyes. "Peanut butter and jelly sandwich coming right up."

It had become Eleanor's favorite midnight snack, and as William fumbled around in the kitchen, she licked her lips and thought, once again, how lucky she was.

Chapter Seventeen

HEAVEN HELP

Ruby

Aunt Marie had consulted with her "girls" at Kiki's and came home with several ideas to help me. Janice, who spun the 78 records on the jukebox, sent me a thermos of potent herbs that I was instructed to drink in one sitting. The concoction was meant to force a miscarriage, but instead I got the runs. Paulie from behind the bar recommended a scalding-hot bath that did nothing more than scorch my skin and kink up my hair. For three days straight, I had swallowed quinine, an anti-parasite pill courtesy of Sweetie Pie from the fry station, and I was in the middle of throwing my guts up when Shimmy knocked on the door. I dragged myself to open it.

He took one look at my blood-drained face and puffy eyes. "What's wrong?"

I couldn't look at him. My plan was to take care of this on my own, not burden him with it. Shimmy had enough going on keeping up with his college work and running back here on the weekends to help out his family.

"What can I do?" He touched my arms. "Do you need something from the pharmacy?"

A wave of nausea came over me and I reached for my knees. I wished that a few drops of Mercurochrome from M.D. Pharmacy on Columbia Avenue would make it all go away. If only it were that simple.

"I'm . . . pregnant," I whispered, fighting the sting in my eyes. It seemed that all I did these days was cry and feel bad.

"What?" Shimmy's voice cracked. "You're what?"

"You heard me." I glanced up, and his face had gone pasty white.

He started running his hands through his hair, something I had noticed he did when he was nervous, but I had no energy to comfort him. I walked hunched over to the couch.

"I've been trying to get rid of it, but nothing works."

"How could you've let this happen?" Anger rushed his words.

"Me?" I shouted. "Please stop acting like you weren't there."

Shimmy sank onto the sofa next to me and dropped his head in his hands. "My mother is going to kill me."

"Well, my chances of becoming anything but a maid are out the window. I'll have to kiss Cheyney goodbye." My voice quivered with frustration. I had ended up just like Inez after all.

Shimmy sat next to me as still as a statue, and I wanted to reach over and shake him. I didn't know what to expect now that he knew the truth about my situation. My heart wanted to believe that we were in this together, but Inez's story made me painfully aware of how easy it was for men to just walk away. My father jumped town, and he was the same color as me. I could expect even less from a white boy.

"But you don't have to concern yourself. This is my problem and I'll handle it," I said. "You should go."

Shimmy turned toward me. "Ruby, I'm not leaving you to handle this alone. What kind of person do you think I am?"

Comfort washed over me as he put his arm around my shoulders and embraced me. I blinked back the tears and offered hoarsely, "Aunt Marie's working on another lead in Delaware. She'll let me know tonight. I'm sorry, Shimmy."

"Like you said, I was there, too." He pressed his forehead against mine. "We'll get through it." Then he stood abruptly. "I hate to leave you like this but I gotta run."

"So soon?"

Now that everything was out in the open with him, I didn't want to be alone, and hated the desperate sound of my voice. I was afraid that if he left, he'd never come back.

"My pop is in the hospital. His legs swelled up really bad and the doctor said something's wrong with his liver."

"How long will you be around?"

"I don't know. Ma is falling apart, and the kids need me."

I needed him.

"I'll call you as soon as I can." He leaned down and pecked me on the cheek.

After a few minutes passed, I stood and locked the apartment door. I searched for something to soothe me, so I put on my apron and started to paint. I needed to disappear into Ruby Red's World, my personal sanctuary where I had control of everything, and stay there. Forever.

Aunt Marie, Fatty and I had worked out a schedule to care for my grandma Nene. Since I was on break from *We Rise* for the summer, my Saturdays were free to help out more.

"'Bout time you got here," Fatty said, meeting me at the door, repositioning her pageboy wig.

"What you talking about, you ain't even got to work today."

"Still got things to do. Running to the avenue to do some shopping and then I'm meeting a friend for a drink. Be back this evening." Fatty grabbed her purse, dropped in a tube of lipstick and was out the door.

The kitchen sink reeked from the overflowing dishes, and the trash smelled of musty collard greens. Even though it burned me up when Fatty left her mess for me to clean, there was a comfort in being back in the apartment where I'd spent the first eight years of my life. It was only a two-bedroom, and I had shared the back room with Fatty.

I crushed a cockroach with my shoe and made my way to Nene's room. She was in her rocking chair, padded with three pillows so it would be easy for her to get up. Her curtains were pushed open, and I could see the paint-chipped houses across the street and their rusted gutters.

"That you, sweetness?" Nene called to me.

"Mm-hmm. How you feeling today?"

"Oh, just dandy."

She had her family quilt pulled over her lap even though it was hot. Her nightgown was worn thin, but she insisted on one of us washing it by hand so that she could wear it daily. During the day, she perched sunglasses up over her nose, which I didn't understand since she couldn't see. A baseball game crackled from her rickety radio, and I reached over and fumbled with the dial.

"Gon' fix my hair?"

"I can. Let me get the comb and grease." I pulled out the right-side drawer where she kept her bobby pins, hair combs, oils and supplies. Nene had a slight smile fastened to her face as she listened to the game. I stood behind her and she rested her head against my belly as I raked the comb through her white brittle hair.

"Hot damn." Nene clapped her hands together. Ernie Banks of the Kansas City Monarchs hit a home run with the bases loaded.

The window was propped open with an old two-by-four, and a steady breeze caressed my skin. Dipping my finger in the hair grease, my mind wandered over to Shimmy.

An entire week had passed without a word from him. I knew he was dealing with his father, but I was dealing with the egg, and as each day passed it became harder for me to make believe that things would be okay. Aunt Marie still hadn't heard from the contact in Delaware, and thank goodness she hadn't brought home any more homemade remedies for me to try.

"How's that scholarship program working out?" Nene's raspy voice brought me back into the room.

"Pretty good. I should know something in a few months."

"That a girl. Be the first in our family to go to college. You make me so proud."

Guilt made my shoulders stiffen. "I ain't get it yet."

"But you on your way." She twirled a corner of the quilt with two fingers. "Last night I dreamt that I could see again and all the pain from my body, gone. Hallelujah! I was standing at the stove frying us up a fat piece of shad. Just a crackling and popping in the skillet."

"Nene, you the only one like that bony fish."

"Maybe," she said, and I could tell by the way her head got heavy in my hands that she liked the way I moved my fingers through her hair. We were quiet for a while. Nene and I could always be together in silence.

She sat herself up straight. "You know what they say when you dreamin' 'bout fish, don't you?"

It took my full concentration so that my fingers didn't stutter step.

Nene left her comment hanging in the air. I looked out the window at the pigeons pecking at the trash on the street.

"You can always tell me anything," she said softly.

My insides fluttered in response, but I couldn't bring myself to tell Nene the very thing that would crush her. She had already been down this road with Inez. I couldn't break her heart, too.

"Naw, Nene, nothing I know good. Except your hair is growing like weeds." And then I got working on the plaits at the nape of her neck.

When I pushed the door open to Aunt Marie's apartment, three dimes wrapped in numbered paper were on the floor, which meant her money man was out and she was back in business. Maybe now she wouldn't have to work so many shifts at Kiki's. I bent down and placed them in the jar next to the telephone, just as it began to ring.

It was Shimmy. "Meet me in the alley in ten minutes."

"Where you been?"

"Long story but I have a solution. Be there soon." He hung up the telephone.

I couldn't imagine what he'd come up with, but I was excited to see him. I changed into a clean blouse, and then stood in the bathroom mirror pinning my hair with the ruby comb he had given me on the day we broke up. Aunt Marie had fished it out of the trash those many months ago, and I now wore it all the time.

True to his word, Shimmy was in the alley waiting for me. He drove us to the back entrance of the candy store. After he kissed my hand, he led me inside. A single candle burned on our makeshift table in the storage room.

"What's all this?" I asked.

Shimmy reached into his pocket, and before my very eyes got down on one knee.

"What are you doing?" I gasped, as he held up a bow band gold ring.

"Marry me, Ruby."

I laughed, then covered my face with my hands. "Stop being foolish."

"This isn't a joke. I've thought about it long and hard and I'm serious." He held the ring up to me and I pulled him up off the floor.

"Have you lost your cotton-picking mind? I'm still in high school and your family will disown you."

"Let them." His face was dead serious.

"Shimmy."

"You love me. I love you. We are having a baby. It's what people do."

He was right, but not people like us. From opposite sides of the universe. My legs felt all of a sudden heavy and I sank down onto the floor.

Shimmy slumped next to me, resting his head in my lap with his ear against my stomach.

Oh, how I desperately wanted to believe him, but I had not been raised on fairy princesses being rescued by the handsome prince. No one I knew was living their happily ever after.

"You're my girl," Shimmy said, smiling up at me.

For the ease of the moment and to relieve all the stress I had felt in the past two weeks, I pulled Shimmy's face close to mine. Other than the back of his father's car, the storage room was the one place we could be Ruby and Shimmy. In that moment I needed to feel good, and Shimmy was the one person who could make me feel that way. Pulling him on top of me, I kissed him fanatically and reached for his belt buckle.

After the rhythm of our breathing had returned to normal, Shimmy threw a tablecloth around us.

"I'm scared to dream so big with you," I confessed.

"Don't be, I've figured it all out."

The back of my head was pressed into his chest with his arms threaded around my waist. As we cuddled, I listened to his plan of how he had worked out our future. Shimmy was so passionate and convincing that I began allowing myself the luxury of visualizing it.

"He'll need a good Jewish name like Samuel. I don't want a Simon Shapiro the second."

"Simon? Is that your real name?"

"I never told you that?"

"No. How could you keep that from me?" I squeezed his wrist. "And what if it's a girl?" I giggled.

"Then Ruth or Sarah."

"Heck no, Ruth sounds so old. Maybe Sarah though, it has a sweet ring."

I sank deeper into his embrace. My imagination had taken over, and I was picturing Shimmy and me in that park across from Inez's house pushing our egg on the swing, with our lunch in a woven basket on a beautiful blanket. I could almost taste the potato salad with just a squirt of mustard when I heard the front door close, and footsteps pound heavily from inside the candy store.

"Shit," Shimmy said, clamoring for his pants.

We exchanged looks, and just like that, I knew that Shimmy and me inside that park would never come to be.

Chapter Eighteen

THE RITUAL

Eleanor

Every morning before her feet grazed the white furry rug on the side of her bed, Eleanor kissed her fingers and then tapped her hand to her belly.

"Good morning little Pride," she whispered, while reaching for her day planner on her nightstand. With big, long strokes, she crossed off the previous day with a purple felt tip marker, celebrating another twenty-four hours with her baby still nestled inside her. Eleanor would then ease out of bed before William opened his eyes, brush her teeth, and pad down to the kitchen barefooted, to put on the percolator for their morning brew.

While William showered, she packed his lunch. Today, it was oven-roasted turkey on a baguette with mayo, and a few slices of dill pickle, topped off with two oatmeal raisin cookies. Some mornings they would sit at the kitchen table and sip their coffee together, before William headed off to the hospital for his residency. Wednesday was his early day, so Eleanor also packed his coffee in a thermos.

"Thanks, babe." He looked around the kitchen and Eleanor knew he was searching for his keys. She pointed to the hook next to the Frigidaire where she always hung them, and he smiled.

"How did I ever get along without you?"

"I have no idea."

He fastened his leather briefcase. "Classes today, right?"

"Yeah, should be done around five."

"I'll pick you up in front of the library. Take care of our baby." He kissed her belly and then headed out the back door.

As Eleanor pulled the screen door closed behind him, she could hear an airplane flying overhead in the distance. She stood in the doorway for a few more minutes watching the cars ride by, making sure William didn't double back for some forgotten item. Satisfied that he was gone, she closed the door and then climbed the stairs. Shuffling down the hall, she turned into the guest bedroom and closed the door behind her. A deep sigh of relief passed from her lips.

The spare room was naturally well lit and would suit her parents well when they came to visit after the baby was born. Her shoulders slipped down her back as she walked the few steps and opened the door to her prayer closet, then tugged on the string that switched the light on.

The closet was empty except for her hope chest and her high school choir robe adorned with satin yoke and cuffs. Eleanor pulled the choir robe over her arms and buttoned it. Her prayer closet was barely large enough for her to genuflect in, but each day she managed to shove her whole body inside, kneel with her hands cupped over her belly and pray.

She didn't pray the way they did at St. Luke's Episcopal Church, the way a proper wife of a soon-to-be doctor would pray. At St. Luke's, prayers were whispered by people sitting stiffly, their hands in their lap. In the closet, Eleanor worshiped with fervor, the way her mother and the members of Second Baptist Church in Elyria did. She had gotten away from daily prayer once she arrived in D.C, but now that she was with child, she had returned to it with daily precision.

Eleanor called out loudly, gutturally, with lots of "have mercies" and "I'm not worthy Lords," until she had exhausted herself with her begging. When she finished her praise, she reached into the hope chest her mother had given her after the wedding. It had been constructed with cedar by her father's hands, and then filled by her mother with two hand-stitched quilts, baby blankets and booties, silverware and table linens. On the side of the chest was a small vial of holy water that Eleanor used to trace the sign of the cross on her stomach, and that concluded her ritual.

William insisted that she call for a taxicab to transport her to campus, but Eleanor caught the streetcar instead. Even though she had married well, Eleanor had not gotten into the habit of spending money just because she could. With a little time to kill before her class, she decided to stop at the library. As soon as the double pane doors closed behind her, she heard her name being called.

"Eleanor, my goodness. I just spoke you up." Mrs. Porter waved to her while coming down the main stairs. Her hair was parted down the middle and curled tightly, and her black-and-white polka-dot dress hung loosely from her frame.

"Hello, Mrs. Porter." Eleanor held her bag with both hands, trying not to bounce on her toes from the giddiness she felt from running into her former boss.

"Marriage looks good on you, darling. Your cheeks are filling in nicely." She patted Eleanor's hand.

"Thank you," she replied, but she wasn't sure if fat cheeks were a compliment. Mrs. Porter didn't know that Eleanor was expecting, but it didn't seem like the right time to inform her.

"I was just telling my new intern, who isn't worth a darn, that I need your help with a few things. We just received a fascinating collection of musical compositions by Justin Elie of Haiti and Amadeo Roldán of Cuba." Her eyes shone like two copper coins as she threw her hands in the air.

"That's wonderful." Eleanor hadn't heard of either of the musicians, but Mrs. Porter's enthusiasm was infectious.

"Pages and pages of their work, personal essays and Amadeo's wife's diary. And there's more, you have to see this." Without waiting for Eleanor's response, Mrs. Porter took off at such a speed Eleanor had to be careful as she climbed the stairs following her. They walked up to the third floor, and then passed the restrooms into an office next to Mrs. Porter's. As soon as they walked into the room, the film of dust on the piles and stacks of boxes made Eleanor sneeze three times in succession.

"Helen Channing Pollock, daughter of the great playwright Channing Pollock, has given us her father's entire library. It is filled with his manuscripts of plays, magazine articles, lecture notes, theater memorabilia. The works."

"Pollock? Where's he from?"

"His mother was English and his father a Jew, so this collection will be housed in the Browsing Room. Not to be circulated, but it will be used for reference and research."

"This sounds far from the African diaspora."

"It is, but when wealthy white people feel strongly about contributing to the education of the Negro, as a partial atonement for the torment of the Atlantic slave trade, who am I to turn them down?" She winked. "The donation was also accompanied by a hefty financial contribution that we will use to continue the work for our collection."

The Moorland-Spingarn Collection always needed money. Mrs. Porter was known for calling up publishers and asking for donations. She had amassed friends all over the globe who were constantly on the lookout to acquire material on her behalf and send it to be archived.

"When you started working here in your sophomore year, you said you wanted to learn to be an archivist. I'm offering you a chance."

"But I'm married now," Eleanor blurted. She could hear Rose in her ear.

"Married but not dumb, darling. Look, I have evolved this library from a one-room study to a large-scale foundation, and I need your young eyes and brilliant brain to continue the work."

Eleanor looked over at the collection and felt her heartbeat quicken. She had missed the smell of vintage books, the feel of rare papers in her hands and long-forgotten music at her ear. Being back at the library would give her a bit more purpose while William was in residency.

"I'll pay you as a contractor. You could do twenty hours a week."

"Mrs. Porter, I'm expecting."

"A baby? Really?" She squeezed Eleanor's hands.

"Yes. Not many people know."

"Congratulations, that's wonderful. Well, then we'll consider part-part time, perhaps fifteen hours a week? I'll make sure you have a comfortable chair."

Eleanor wanted it, but Rose had insisted that she stay home and wait for the baby. It had been such a struggle just to convince her that Eleanor should finish her schooling. On the other hand, Eleanor's own mother had always told her that it was important for women to have a separate stash set aside in case of a rainy day. Wasn't that how she got to Howard in the first place? With the money her mother had tucked aside.

Mrs. Porter leaned in. "Let me give you a piece of advice. The way to a healthy marriage is to hold on to those pieces that make you you. I know how you feel about the library. Put that passion of yours to good use."

"I'd love to" slipped from Eleanor's mouth before she could talk herself out of it.

"Perfect. Let's stop by my office and work out a schedule for you. Welcome back." Mrs. Porter clapped her on the back. "I've added a few new classifications to our system that I can't wait to catch you up on. Dewey decimal system be damned."

In bed later that night, Eleanor told William about the position at the library. At first he resisted, saying he would provide enough so she wouldn't need to work, but after much coaxing and kissing, he began to listen. Eleanor made it clear: she needed this. Then she felt the baby move inside her and William pressed his hand to feel, too. He was so smitten that the conversation was over. Eleanor had gotten her way.

Chapter Nineteen

DEAD MEAT

Ruby

I had managed to pull my knit top over my head but had not fastened my brassiere when a paper-thin woman, dressed in a navy shift and white beret, entered the storage room. She looked around our make-do love nest with disbelief. Shimmy moved in front of me, as if he could block me from her sight line.

"Simon Shapiro"—the woman's whole body trembled—"have you lost your natural-born mind?"

"Ma."

"Don't 'Ma' me!" Spit flew from her red lips. "How could you betray our trust like this by gallivanting around with this, this *whore*?" She peered at me with so much rage that her words seemed to hit me like a blow to the chest. I tried to shrink from her vision by covering myself with my arms, but then she reached for the light switch, flooding the room with a spotlight on our secret. The smell of us that I had always loved suddenly made me sick to my stomach.

"Esther Hoffman called to say you'd been sneaking a Colored girl through the back door. I didn't believe it for a second. She must have mistaken my Shimmy for someone else. Well! I see how wrong I was!"

"Ma, I can explain," Shimmy pleaded, but his shoulders were hunched with shame.

I wanted nothing more than for the floor to open and sweep me away.

"Put some clothes on," she shouted. Then she turned her back and walked to the front of the store.

Shimmy and I dressed quickly and silently. I scrambled to my feet, smoothed my skirt and touched my hair knowing that not much would change even as I fingered it. Shimmy led and I followed him out.

Mrs. Shapiro was a petite woman with thin lips and dark shoulder-length hair. Her eyes were so black with fury that she looked like she would murder me on the spot if she were sure she could get away with it.

"Ma, this is not what you think it is," said Shimmy, taking a step toward her.

"How could you possibly know what I am thinking?"

"I love her," he said forcefully.

Shimmy's declaration in front of his mother surprised me. He hadn't taken the easy way out. He'd meant what he said about wanting to be with me. But I could see that his words didn't mean doodly-squat to his mother. She was looking at me like I was the filthy muck stuck to the bottom of her designer shoe.

"Foolish boy. You don't know what love is yet."

"I know how she makes me feel."

"I bet I know how she makes you feel," she said, summing up my voluptuous breasts and curvy hips with her hands. Like I was nothing more than an object—a *Negro* vixen—that tempted good boys like Shimmy into trouble.

"Get your things and let's go," she said as she grabbed Shimmy's ear.

"Ma." He stepped back and looked at me and then to his mother. "She's having my baby."

My heart dropped. Shimmy's confessing to his mother made it real. It pushed me one step further from my dreams of attending Cheyney. But then Mrs. Shapiro's face rearranged itself into horror. I had never seen another person so wounded before, and in that moment, I regretted for her sake ever taking up with her son. She dropped her head into her gloved hands.

"Ma, don't be upset." Shimmy reached to hold her up. "I will make this right. I'll marry her."

She recoiled from his hand like it was the head of a snake, hissing between clenched teeth, "Marry her? She's Colored, you blind fool."

"It's Negro, Ma, and that doesn't matter to us." He reached for my arm, but I had the good sense to pull away. I didn't want to add to his mother's dismay.

"What difference does it make? You are the heir of our family. How could you bring such dishonor to our name? As if your father wasn't already doing enough damage." She started murmuring words in Yiddish that I didn't understand.

"Stop it, Ma."

She gathered herself, fixing her gaze on me. "Little girl, go home. Tell no one about your situation. You will hear from me shortly." She took a step toward me, and I braced myself to be slapped, but she reached into my hair and snatched out the antique ruby comb Shimmy had given me.

"A thief too? I believe this belongs to me."

I hadn't thought it was possible to be more humiliated, but I was. I hurried through the back door as fast as I could. The garbage from the dumpster out back stunk something awful and I gagged, then threw up.

In a daze, I trampled through the neighborhood. I wished I could erase it all. I was disgusting, a slut. What the hell had I been thinking? This was damned from the start. Aunt Marie warned me, but I hadn't listened, and now I had gotten burnt, just as she'd predicted.

Despite the fact that it was a sticky July night, my body broke out in a cold sweat. I wandered the streets, which were crowded with people everywhere—sitting on the steps smoking cigarettes, leaning against cars with bottles hidden in brown bags, singing, cussing and trying to be heard over blasts of music.

There was a beer garden up ahead on the corner, and the blues floated through the opened windows. Three men stood outside passing a reefer joint between them while rolling dice on a piece of cardboard against the brick building. They snapped their fingers sharply after each throw.

"Hey, good-looking. Come over here so I can buy you a drink," one called out to me. He wore his hat low over his eyes and had a gold ring on his left pinky.

"With a body like that, I'll buy you two," said his friend wearing shades, and they all cackled and hooted.

I picked up my pace.

"You too good to stop?" the first man, with his hat slung low, called.

The man in shades snorted. "She too good for you."

That must have wounded the other man's pride, because next thing I knew Hat Slung Low started to follow me. "Hey. Hey girl. Don't you hear me talking to you?"

"Leave me the hell alone," I mustered with all the rancor I felt from my night.

The man stopped, stunned, and I took off running. I pumped my legs hard, turning corner after corner to make sure he wasn't following me. When I finally slowed down to catch my wind, I was a half block from Inez's apartment. How in the world had I ended up here, a place that had never really been my home?

As my feet carried me forward, I realized that it had been nearly five months since I saw my mother at Nene's for Fatty's birthday party. The celebration had been nothing more than boiled crabs with butter, brown liquor and bottles of beer, ashtrays overflowing with wet butts, slices of red velvet cake, and heated arguments over hands of Tonk. I had sat in a folding chair next to the phonograph, watching my mother grin up at Leap as she announced that she was having his baby.

"He wants a girl, but I'm hoping for a boy. Girls are too much trouble," she muttered to Fatty, and they slapped five in agreement.

Her words had made me shudder as I tried to make myself smaller against the wall in the corner.

Since she had not confiscated my key when she put me out, I trampled up onto the uneven porch and let myself in.

I walked in to find Inez standing over a pot that smelled like chili. It was a bit hot out for the dish, but it sure smelled good. Inez wasn't much of a cook, but chili was her specialty, and my mouth watered for the comfort of it. I shifted on my feet, waiting for something. A smile, a hug, her voice cooing that it was good to see me.

"What you doing here?" She held the wooden spoon in the air.

"I . . . I just wanted to see you," I admitted, realizing as I said it how true it was.

"Well, you see me."

Her belly had grown, and the thought that fluttered through my mind was that her baby and mine could grow up like siblings. *The apple don't fall far from the tree*, Nene always said. The idea sickened me, and I squeezed my fingernails into the back of the kitchen chair.

The smell of Leap's cigarette wafted from the next room, and I tried to put the memory of him forcing his tongue in my mouth out of my mind.

"Who is it?" he called out. Knowing it was me.

Inez said, "Nobody, honey. Dinner be ready soon."

She closed the lid over the pot, keeping her back to me. "Go on back to where you came from, girl. Roaming around in the middle of the night like you asking for problems. Ain't no room for you here."

"Mommy, I—"

She turned toward me. I wanted her to say something that would relieve the feeling that burrowed deep in my chest, but then her eyes cut through me.

"Get, now. And leave the key."

It fell from my hand onto the table, and I walked out of her apartment. No, that never had been my home. And I'd never want the egg inside of me to feel so alone, so motherless.

Chapter Twenty

STILL THE WATER

Eleanor

Eleanor made herself a cup of chamomile tea and then carried it back into the den. Over the past few weeks, she had found such pleasure in her work with Mrs. Porter that she had William lug a few bags and boxes home so that she could organize important pieces on the days she was not on campus.

Working on the library's collection connected Eleanor to the ways of her mother. She understood why she loved to bake. Kneading dough and pressing out pie crust weren't just a means of income; they brought peace and order to her life, and that's how archiving felt for Eleanor. When she read the essays of the ancestors, studied their photographs, drawings and linguistic codes, she felt charged to preserve history.

She loved reading about independent women in particular. Mrs. Porter had sent her home with the biographical pieces of Dorothy Creole's life to appendix and classify. Eleanor pulled the documents from the protective sleeve, then tucked her feet under her thighs on the sofa while she read.

Dorothy Creole was one of the first Black women in the Dutch colony of New Amsterdam on the island of Manhattan. She arrived around 1627, brought with the other enslaved women because the males needed wives, and the Dutch women needed housekeepers. Dorothy married Paulo d'Angola. D'Angola was the most common surname among the enslaved, and it meant that he came from Angola, Africa. One day in 1643, Dorothy went to the Dutch Reform Church to serve as godmother for a Black boy named Antonio. When the boy's parents died a short time later, Dorothy and her husband adopted him and raised him as their own. This is one of the first times when the public records show Black people stepping in to take care of each other.

Eleanor touched her belly. She couldn't imagine anyone else taking care of her baby besides her. She shuddered just thinking about it.

In 1644, Paulo petitioned for their freedom and won. As Black farmers they owned a two-mile stretch of land from what is now Canal Street to 34th Street in Manhattan. It was known as the Land of the Blacks. Although the free slaves were not treated as white, they were landowners. Blacks who were still enslaved looked at Dorothy and Paulo with hope. There was a way out of slavery.

Under the Dewey decimal system, Dorothy's story would have been classified simply under 326: Slavery and Emancipation. But like many of the subjects Eleanor filed, the story of Dorothy Creole contained multitudes. Eleanor wrote down: Slave, Former Slave, Adoption, Landowner, Estate Executor, Dutch/New Amsterdam History.

All she had left to do was write up a brief appendix and then she would return to bed. But somehow, she had managed to doze off, because the next thing she knew William was tugging on her arm.

"Babe, come to bed." He wiped his eyes.

Eleanor removed the documents from her belly, carefully placed the pages back into the protective sleeve and then followed him upstairs.

A few hours later, the doorbell woke her. Bedraggled in her bathrobe, Eleanor swung the door open and found Nadine standing on the front steps in a dress suit with a ruffled collar.

Her manicured hands rested on her hips. "Ohio, I hope you aren't wearing that to breakfast."

"Nadine." Eleanor ushered her out of the morning sun and into the vestibule. "It's so good to see you."

They embraced. With Eleanor married and living off campus, they hadn't seen much of each other over the past six months. Two weeks ago, they had run into each other in the library, and over giggles and hugs Nadine had pinned Eleanor down to breakfast.

"Why do you look like you just got out of bed? Did you forget about our date?"

"I overslept," Eleanor said apologetically. "Blame it on the pregnancy."

"Well, it's hot as the dickens out there. Let's skip going out to eat and I'll make you something here instead." She kicked off her pumps and pushed them in the corner.

"There's plenty of food. I just went grocery shopping," Eleanor said as she followed Nadine through to the kitchen.

"Perfect. Breakfast is the one meal I know how to cook."

"Aprons are hanging in the broom closet," Eleanor offered. "Do you know how to work the percolator?"

"I'll figure it out."

"Don't burn yourself, girl. I'll be back down soon."

"Love what you've done to the place, so much progress since you first moved in," Nadine called from the kitchen.

At the top of the stairs, Eleanor peeked over at the spare bedroom, but knew with Nadine visiting she had no time for her morning ritual. Instead, she said her prayers on her way into the shower, hoping that it would do.

The scent of bacon and fried eggs lured Eleanor to the table just as Nadine dropped slices of white bread into the toaster.

"Ohio, you look like a million bucks," Nadine exclaimed.

Eleanor wore her wrap dress with pearl buttons down the bodice and had pinned her hair in a neat updo twist.

"I have a doctor's appointment. Can't have my husband's colleagues whispering about his wife being shabby," she said to Nadine, but thought to herself, *especially with Rose Pride making it clear that she was not of their tribe.*

"My father loaned me his car so I can drop you off on my way."

"Perfect." Eleanor poured herself a cup of coffee while Nadine turned off the burners on the stovetop.

"Hope you don't mind me dirtying up your beautiful kitchen."

"Honey, please. It's nice to have someone cook for me for a change. Now, what's on your agenda for the day?"

"Right after I drop you off, I have to get back to my father's office. He's been riding my ass all summer. Remind me to never take a job working for my old man again." She slid a heaping plate toward Eleanor.

"I thought you two got along."

"As father and daughter yes, as employer to employee, not at all." She sat down with her plate and sipped her coffee.

Over their meal, Nadine caught her up on the happenings around town. Who was getting married and who had been dumped.

"I heard Greta took a job working at Dunbar High School. Maybe she'll manage to hook a biology teacher as a husband."

Eleanor dabbed bacon grease from the corner of her mouth. "I would definitely appreciate getting her out of my hair, but I doubt Greta's family would let her marry a common teacher."

"Well, she ain't getting any younger. Rose Pride still worshiping the ground she walks on?"

Eleanor told Nadine about the conversation she had overheard. Nadine was as furious as Eleanor knew she'd be.

"I'm hoping this baby will get her off my back." Eleanor took a bite of her toast. Nadine had slathered it in butter just the way she liked it. "Speaking of the baby, I was wondering if you would do me the honors and be the godmother."

"Really?" Nadine shrieked.

Eleanor nodded.

"William is okay with that?"

"Of course."

"It'll be my pleasure," she said, grinning. "I'm going to spoil that little one rotten."

"Not too rotten." Eleanor chided her.

Nadine looked down at her watch. "Shoot. We'd better get this show on the road. I don't want you to be late, and I can't bear sitting through another lecture from my father."

Nadine pulled up into the roundabout at Howard University Hospital. It was the same one where William worked but Eleanor never saw him when she came for her appointments. He was too busy with his residency rounds.

"Toodle-loo and don't be a stranger," Nadine called from the car window.

Eleanor waved and then made her way into the hospital. Immediately, she was overwhelmed by the odor of alcohol and disinfectant. She held her breath until she got into the elevator and rode it alone to the second floor.

The small reception area was freezing, and Eleanor regretted not throwing a scarf into her tote. Once she signed in with the receptionist, she sat and flipped through the latest issue of *Life* magazine, with little girls holding hands at the beach on the cover.

There were two other expecting mothers in the lobby. The one sitting diagonal to her wore a pants playsuit and her belly was so big that she threatened to burst out of it. Despite the chill, the lady fanned herself with her hand, while her little boy scrambled blocks at her swollen feet. The second woman wore a wrap dress similar to Eleanor's, and looked to be just a few weeks ahead of her on the pregnancy calendar. She caught Eleanor's eye and smiled politely. The big-belly woman was called back first.

Once she was gone, the woman with the nice smile leaned in and asked, "Your first time?"

"Yes." Eleanor cleared her throat. "You?"

"It is. When are you due?"

"Early January."

"I'm expecting this one to arrive around Thanksgiving."

"In time for the holidays."

"Such a blessing. We should exchange numbers. Once these babies get here, all of our childless friends will desert us. It'll be nice to have someone to talk to."

Eleanor was taken aback by her bluntness, but also soothed by it. She reached into her bag and jotted down her number.

"I'm Lois," the woman said and took the paper.

"Eleanor."

The woman was called back before she could give Eleanor her number.

"I'll call you," she said over her shoulder. "Nice meeting you."

A few moments later, a nurse called Eleanor's name and led her into a room, where she told her the doctor would be just a few minutes.

Eleanor looked at the generic posters of flowers hanging on the wall, wondering what her baby would look like. Would it have William's cute nose and her high cheekbones? And what shade would the baby be? She knew Rose was hoping for nearly white, but Eleanor thought a little color would do the family some good.

There was a swift knock, and then a man with wire-rimmed glasses and graying hair walked in.

"Mrs. Pride. Good to see you again."

"Dr. Avery." Eleanor sat up a little.

He washed his hands at the tiny sink while he spoke. "Today, I'm going to examine your stomach as a part of your eighteen-week assessment. If at any point you feel pain just let me know and I'll adjust my pressure. We'll also take a few measurements, and then I'll detect the fetus's heartbeat."

With his left hand, he gently palpated her abdomen. He then pressed hard around her pelvis. Eleanor's eyes were locked on the fluorescent light overhead, but she could feel the pad of the doctor's hand moving from side to side, top to bottom.

"Pinard horn." Dr. Avery held out his hand, and the nurse passed him a metal, hollow-looking horn.

"I'm going to push the Pinard horn into your stomach so that I can hear the fetus's movement and heartbeat."

Dr. Avery pushed the horn with a bit more pressure, and it forced Eleanor to look into his face. She watched as his brows knitted together. His skin was so fair, she could see heat gathering in his cheeks.

"Nurse, let me try the fetoscope."

She handed him what looked like a stethoscope, but it had a rounded bell at the bottom. With the plugs in his ears, he resumed pressing down on her abdomen with the device.

"When was the last time you felt the baby move?"

Eleanor drew a blank. She would have remembered if it happened during breakfast with Nadine, because she would have pointed it out to her.

"It's usually more active at nighttime. I don't remember too much movement today. Is everything okay?"

"We will need you to undress from the waist down." He removed the fetoscope. "I need to examine you internally. Nothing to worry about. Sometimes they are stubborn at this phase."

The nurse handed her a hospital gown.

"We'll be back in two shakes of a lamb's tail," Dr. Avery said good-humoredly, but Eleanor felt a pinch of panic rise in her throat.

Eleanor's hands shook as she removed her skirt and cotton panties, but she decided it was probably more modest for her to leave her nylons on. She tried chasing off her worrying thoughts but they had quickly mounted.

The doctor and nurse returned stone-faced. Her internal plea for her baby's safety echoed so loudly that she couldn't concentrate on anything they were saying. Their words washed over her as she felt her feet being guided into the stirrups, her thighs being separated, a cold instrument, deep fingers, poking, prodding, pulling.

"Ouch." She kicked her foot, but the plump-faced nurse kindly repositioned her, then kept her palm on Eleanor's ankle.

The lights overhead were giving her a headache. When the doctor pulled off his disposable glove, Eleanor saw blood on its plastic fingertip.

"What's happening?" Her eyes were wide.

Dr. Avery whispered something to the nurse.

"Is everything all right with the baby?"

"Give us a few minutes, Mrs. Pride. We'll be right back."

Eleanor noted his lack of eye contact. Something was wrong. The room felt even colder, and she ran her fingers back and forth against her shoulders.

When William was the first to enter the room, her throat closed up. He had never popped in on her appointments. His skin was ashen, and Eleanor tried reading his eyes.

"They called you? What's wrong with our baby?"

William's face cracked. "Dr. Avery said there is no heartbeat."

The bottom of her world fell out. "Make him check again." William reached for her hand but she pulled away. "No."

"Mrs. Pride, there is no fetal movement. I'm afraid that you've had a late miscarriage. I'm sorry." Eleanor hadn't even known that Dr. Avery was there too, until she heard his voice.

The air in the room stopped circulating, and Eleanor choked on her own saliva. Shaking her head furiously. "No. I'm out of the danger zone."

"We are so sorry," he replied. "It's rare but it happens."

"You're wrong. Please, check again," Eleanor said, grabbing her belly.

William tried to gather her in his arms, but she pulled away. "This isn't happening."

"We know this is difficult, Mrs. Pride, and we are so sorry for your loss."

He spoke softly to the nurse. "Please prepare the paperwork to have her admitted to L&D."

"Labor and delivery?" Eleanor shot.

"With late miscarriages, we have to deliver the fetus, expel it from your womb. We will induce your labor and need to move quickly."

Eleanor couldn't believe it was happening all over again.

"We'll get through this," William whispered. But Eleanor didn't want to get through it, she wanted her baby. Alive, in her arms, in her life, filling their home.

"I'm so sorry, love." His voice faltered, and Eleanor felt the volume of his disappointment. She had married well. He had married a malfunction.

The elevator doors opened on the sixth floor, and as Eleanor's nurse wheeled her through the hall, she was flooded with the groans of women in various stages of labor. Then as she was pushed into her room, she heard the faint call of a newborn hungry for its mother's milk. Tears sprang to her eyes and she hunched over.

It wasn't fair.

William had stopped to sign the paperwork. Somehow, the nurse managed to get her in the bed. Then Dr. Avery was there, explaining what would happen next.

"I'm going to start with administering Pitocin. Thirty drops every minute to get labor started. We should be able to remove the fetus in a few hours. I'll be back to check on you."

A new nurse hooked her up with the IV and then she was left alone. The blinds were open, and she could see the tree outside her window scattering pink petals in the wind. Tears stumbled down the sides of her cheeks. The door to her room slid open and William staggered in. The sight of him made her cry harder.

"There, there. It's okay." She allowed him to hold her.

"It's not." She pushed her face toward his. "It's all my fault."

"Don't say that."

Eleanor wiped her cheeks with the back of her hands. "I had a ritual, a routine. Every morning after you left for work. I went into my prayer closet and blessed the baby. This morning was the first time I skipped it. I woke up late and Nadine—"

"Elly, this is not on you."

"It is."

"It's an unexplainable act of nature. Don't blame yourself. You couldn't stop this from happening. Not even with prayer." He let her sob into his chest until she had nothing left.

Chapter Twenty-One

ULTIMATUM

Ruby

By the start of August, we still had not found a solution to my growing problem. Aunt Marie and I had taken a break from speaking on it, as if our silence could will it away. A few more times she brought home liquid tinctures that were supposed to cause the egg to dispel itself, but all they did was make me sick. If my calculations were right, I was coming up on fifteen weeks. My time for fixing this was running out.

We were in the middle of a three-day heat wave, and it didn't matter what I did to cool off, my skin was always damp. It felt like I was cooking from the inside. To escape the humid stickiness, the men on the block used a wrench to remove the stubborn cap on the hydrant. Running through the water plug was the closest that half the neighborhood got to swimming. Most of Philadelphia's city pools were "whites only," and even on the rare occasion that the lifeguard let us in, we had to be careful that they hadn't thrown nails at the bottom of the pool or acid or bleach in the water to dissuade us from coming back. We'd heard terrible stories.

I stood at the window trying to catch any piece of a breeze. Down below, children squealed in cut-off denims, their bare feet slapping the black tarred street. Sweat gathered between my heavy breasts and pooled at the base of my spine.

"Let me whip you in a game of gin rummy before I go off to work," Aunt Marie called from the sofa, shuffling a deck of cards. She wore a stretched-out bra with a pair of faded overalls thrown on top.

"You mean let me beat you."

"Girl, I taught you the game."

"And the student has surpassed the teacher."

"You a lie." She grinned, dishing the cards.

I had eased onto a pitifully flat pillow on the floor and was organizing my five cards by suit when we heard a knock at the door. The knocking had an urgency to it, like it was the law. Aunt Marie felt under the sofa to confirm that her .22 was where she left it, and then heaved up out of her seat. She squinted her eye against the peephole.

When I turned my head, I was surprised to see Shimmy's mother waltz through the door. Every hair on her head was smooth, and not a wrinkle could be found on her pencil skirt and knit blouse. Even though we were melting under the oppressive heat, she kept her lace gloves on and folded her hands in front of her.

"Mrs. Shapiro. Rent ain't due until the end of the week." Aunt Marie jutted her hip forward.

"My apologies for the intrusion," responded Mrs. Shapiro, and I watched her eyes sweep over the room. The faded sheets thumbtacked to the window as curtains, chipped paint pulling up from the walls, the cracks in the hardwood floor that trapped dirt seconds after we cleaned, our handwashed underpants and bras that looked more like dust rags hanging to dry on the backs of the mismatched kitchen chairs. I hadn't noticed the odor of last night's fried croaker and okra still lingering in the air, and the constant drip of the leaky faucet that Mr. Shapiro had yet to fix. I couldn't imagine how pitiful our living conditions looked through Mrs. Shapiro's sharp eyes.

"I'll keep this brief."

"Would you like to sit down?" Aunt Marie took our undergarments off the nearest chair and pulled it up.

Mrs. Shapiro's hand went to her throat, but she didn't move toward the chair. It felt like she was purposely avoiding eye contact, preferring to stare at a nail stuck in the wall above the stove. "I'm not sure if she has told you that I caught her and my son together." She addressed the nail. "We both know that they are too young to go through with any of this. It'll ruin their lives. With her being so smart. You are one of the *We Rise* scholars, right?"

"Yes, ma'am." I pulled myself up off the floor and stood next to the furnace so that I could see her better.

"Well, with the scholarship on the horizon, I don't think you want to lose out on such a prestigious opportunity."

"What are you suggesting, Mrs. Shapiro?" I could tell by the way Aunt Marie ran her thumb over her index finger that she was losing her patience with this white woman standing in our living space. Even if, technically, that white woman did own it. Aunt Marie paid the rent, so she called the shots.

"I want to help you make it all go away." Mrs. Shapiro lifted her chin and forced a smile finally directed toward Aunt Marie.

"Go 'head." Aunt Marie stared.

"Well, in the rare case that this sort of unfortunate thing happens in our community, we send the girls away."

"We ain't got no family down south if that's what you thinking."

"To a home for unwed women who have fallen into trouble." She looked at me for the first time. "I've inquired discreetly, and I found a place in Washington, D.C., that specializes in this sort of thing. It's expensive, but I am willing to take care of it."

"You want her to go there and do what?"

Mrs. Shapiro wrung her hands in front of her. "They will take the child and place it in a loving home with wonderful parents. It'll be the best thing for all parties."

"Best thing for you." Aunt Marie clucked her tongue.

"Honestly, I'm not even certain that it's my son's responsibility, but I'm willing to help."

I lowered my head and swallowed the scream that was rising in my throat: Shimmy was the only boy I had ever been with.

Aunt Marie piped up. "Bullshit. If you weren't certain your son was responsible, you wouldn't be here." She squashed a mosquito between her wide hands and blew it to the ground. "That boy's nose is wide open for this gal and you know it."

Mrs. Shapiro bristled. "Well, all I'm saying is this will free her up to get that scholarship and go off to college. Pretend like this awful thing never happened."

"How can you be so sure?" I croaked. "I mean, about the scholarship to Cheyney?"

"I'm on the board, dear. I'll make it so. As long as we can come to an agreement." She nodded at me.

"We'll talk it over." Aunt Marie stood with both feet planted in a way that suggested that the conversation was finished.

Mrs. Shapiro dabbed at her brows with the back of her gloved hand. "There are only four spaces allotted for Negro girls in the home. As of this morning, there is only one space left. We must move quickly . . . before things start to flower. Please don't take too long to decide." She reached into her purse and then held out a pamphlet to me. On the glossy cover was a photograph of a stately brick home.

"It really is for the best, dear. Do consider your future."

"I said we'll think about it," Aunt Marie asserted, and then walked toward Mrs. Shapiro until she turned into the hallway. "Good day."

Did Shimmy know that his mother had come to me with this proposition? I hadn't seen him since he proposed to me in the back of the candy store. He had called me on the phone a few times to check on me and to tell me that his mother had banished him to Brooklyn under the guise that his uncle needed his help, but we both knew she was keeping us apart. He had promised to get back as soon as he could and told me many times over that he wasn't abandoning me, that we were in this together. Yet I was here dealing with this alone.

Aunt Marie went to the leaky faucet and turned on the tap, let it run and then poured herself a cup of water. Beads of sweat quickly dotted her upper lip and started gathering on her forehead. She closed her eyes and swayed through her hot flash. Sometimes when she was having one, she told me she got little peeks into the future. I hoped that was the case now.

"What should I do?"

"You grown enough to open your legs to a Jewish boy, you woman enough to make a decision." She swallowed, and her curtness made me stiffen.

This whole situation made what Shimmy and I had shared feel vulgar and crass, instead of beautiful.

Aunt Marie dropped down and picked up her cards.

I carried the brochure back down to my pillow on the floor and opened it. The caption at the top read, "Mistakes Can Be Fixed and God Will Forgive." My eyes scanned the pictures of smiling white girls sitting under a tree with books in their laps.

I smoothed the trifold out on the table and tried a different approach. "How do I decide what to do, Auntie?"

"You ready to be strapped down with a baby you can't feed 'cause you ain't earning shit cleaning up after white people, or go on to college and become a doctor?" She dished a card, then signaled that it was my turn. "Hell, choice seems easy to me. Stay poor like the rest of us, or climb, scratch and claw like hell to get out."

Chapter Twenty-Two

WINDOW TO DARKNESS

Eleanor

Eleanor's entire body dripped in sweat and her bowels begged to be released. Although she was embarrassed, she could no longer hold it in. Soon, the smell permeated every corner of the room, and she was glad that husbands were not permitted during labor and delivery. The nurse wiped her quickly.

"Again," commanded Dr. Avery. "When you feel the cramping, push with the contraction."

She had refused the morphine that was meant to ease her pain. She deserved the punishment, wanted to feel every bit of suffering that came with pushing out a baby that she could not take home. Eleanor bore down and gritted her teeth until she felt a rush of water gush between her legs. Blinding pain rearranged her midsection.

"One more time," Dr. Avery called to her.

An animalistic cry roared from her lips, and then she felt something tiny slip out.

There was no cry. The room fell dead silent.

After fumbling between her legs, Dr. Avery handed the lifeless bundle to the nurse, who swathed it in a blanket quickly, but not before Eleanor was able to make out a tiny purple foot, perfectly formed, with all its toes and nails.

"Wait," she cried weakly, but the nurse turned her back and left the room.

"Try to get some rest now. You did well," Dr. Avery said and closed the door behind him.

How could one do *well* at delivering a dead child?

A second nurse swiped a damp cloth between her legs. "Ma'am, we have to deliver the placenta."

Eleanor used the last of her strength and bore down, pushing and grunting through the pain for over ten minutes before the placenta emerged. It felt bigger than the baby she had delivered.

The nurse placed fresh pads between her legs to catch the bleeding and then handed Eleanor two pills and a paper cup of water.

"This will make you feel better."

"Where's my husband? And where did they take my baby?"

"Just rest a bit, Mrs. Pride. I'll send him in shortly."

Eleanor couldn't endure much more. She swallowed the pills and was glad that they had the decency to kick in almost immediately.

When she came to, the room was dark. Eleanor looked around and then her hands went to her belly. She was thirsty, and she smacked her tongue around in her mouth and whispered:

"Where is my baby?"

She looked to the sliver of light that had pooled in from under the hospital door. Louder this time she called out, "Hello?"

Eleanor pushed herself to the edge of the bed and then tried to stand. The IV taped to her arm hindered her movement, so she yanked it out. "My baby."

Her legs were shaky, but she managed to make it to the door and open it. There were two women standing in the nurses' station sharing a tube of Ritz crackers.

"Mrs. Pride, what are you doing? You shouldn't be out of bed," one said, alarmed.

Eleanor felt a shock of liquid stream down her thigh. "Bring me my baby," and then her teeth began to clatter.

"She's in shock." The nurse rushed over and put her arm on Eleanor's shoulder. "It's all right."

"Where the fuck is my baby?" Spit flew from Eleanor's lips.

The nurse tried to guide her back to the room, but Eleanor pushed her arm off of her. "Bring me my baby. I want my baby, now." She sounded belligerent, even to herself, but her teeth wouldn't stop chattering, and the outrage wouldn't cease from tumbling from her lips.

Together, the nurses took hold of her, one on each arm, and dragged her back into the room.

Eleanor thrashed about on the bed. "I want my baby. It's my baby. My sweet baby."

They held her down. One of the nurses shot her with a needle. Eleanor opened her mouth, but her voice had deserted her. Her eyes stretched wide and then she collapsed.

Hours later, the morning sun pressed hard against the venetian blinds, creating a halo around the bouquet of flowers that sat on her windowsill. William was asleep in the chair beside her, still wearing his clothes from the day before. She turned her face on the pillow and watched him. What a disappointment this marriage must be for him. He probably should have run from her when he had the chance.

William stirred and, after a minute, opened his eyes. "Hey." He looked disheveled but beautiful at the same time. God, she loved him, and she hated that she was such a letdown. He had given her the world and she couldn't even bear him a child.

William ran his fingers over his hair, orientating himself to the new day. "You feeling okay?"

Eleanor's bottom lip quivered, and she shook her head. In an instant, William was on the edge of the hospital bed pulling her into his arms, squeezing her as tight as she could endure. A sob escaped his lips, but he quickly sucked it back inside. William was mostly even-keeled and not much rattled him. To see him emotional made her bawl even harder. She felt responsible for his grief.

"We'll get through this, babe." He leaned his forehead against hers and looked into her eyes. "You are young and so beautiful." He smiled demurringly. "And since I can't keep my hands off you, we'll conceive again in no time."

He kissed her lips, and as she sank against him, a swift knock clapped the door. William pulled himself to standing while straightening his shirt collar.

Dr. Avery entered the room. "Morning, Mrs. Pride. William. I'm sorry to disturb you." He pushed his glasses up the bridge of his nose.

Eleanor didn't even bother trying to pull her looks together for the doctor's visit.

"Doc, it's good to see you." William took a step forward and shook his hand.

"Well, I wish it was under different circumstances. As we expected, the fetus was stillborn. She had no chance of survival."

She. Eleanor had been right. She had been carrying her daughter. Dr. Avery's lips continued to move, but his condolences did nothing to soothe her.

"I know you did everything you could, Doc. We'll let Eleanor heal up a bit and then try again."

Dr. Avery's cheeks reddened. "Since this is your third miscarriage, Mrs. Pride, we recommend you don't try again. The next time could be life-threatening."

"You mean second," William corrected. "It's only her second."

The doctor looked down at his notes, and then over at Eleanor for clarification. She sat stunned. Guilt and panic webbed together inside her chest, constricting the words from moving over the lump in her throat. She should have known it would come to this, her deed in the dark held up to the light for William to see.

Closing the clipboard, Dr. Avery dropped his eyes. "Again, I'm sorry for your loss. Please let me know if there is anything I can do."

"I'm confused." William looked from Dr. Avery to Eleanor.

"I'll leave you two alone," he said, backing out of the room.

Once the door clicked closed, William turned to her. "Elly, what's going on? Why would he say third time?"

"Because."

"Because what?" He moved in closer. So close she could see two-day-old stubble peppering his chin.

"I . . ." She trembled and her mouth went dry. It was the secret her mother had told her to take to her grave. *No man wants to marry a soiled woman with damaged goods.*

"I got pregnant in high school after my first time and lost that baby, too."

William's face rearranged itself as if she had sucker punched him. "But I thought you were a virgin."

"I never said that." She couldn't look at him. It was true; she had not *said* it, but Eleanor was definitely guilty of implying it.

His nose flared and then he growled through gritted teeth. "How could you keep all of this from me?"

Eleanor had never seen him so upset and her hands flew to her face. "I just didn't want you to look at me differently. I'm so sorry."

William yanked up his jacket and tie from across the back of the chair. "I'm going to get some coffee."

"Please wait," she called out, but the door closed behind him with a thud.

Fresh tears streamed down her cheeks and Eleanor hugged her arms around herself. She didn't know which part she was crying for most. The loss of this baby. The loss of three babies. William finding out that she had given herself to another man before they met. That look of betrayal in his eye when he stormed out. Or that a baby would never exist between them, bonding them for life.

William was gone for so long that Eleanor's nurse had given her a sponge bath, checked her bleeding and changed her bed linen by the time he returned. Eleanor was wrapped in a clean robe and brushing her hair into a pin-up when he strolled through the door. He said nothing as he placed his empty coffee cup on the tray next to her and sat heavily in the chair beside the bed.

"Hey." Eleanor folded her hands in her lap. She knew that she had to walk through the fire and tell William everything, but she was terrified that they might not make it through the flames.

"Did you eat?"

"Not much."

"You need to keep your strength up."

"William?" She finally caught his eye. "I had only known that I was pregnant for a short time. Before I could figure out what to do, I miscarried. My mother said that it was God giving me a second chance. She said I needed a fresh start, and that's why I enrolled at Howard, instead of a university closer to home."

William was silent. His jaws clenched.

"I'm sorry. It's the only secret I've kept. Please forgive me."

William twirled his wedding band around on his finger with his thumb. "It's over and done with. All we can do now is focus on our future."

Eleanor breathed a sigh of relief. William wasn't going to leave her. They'd get through this together.

"No more secrets," he said, as the nurse rolled in dinner. Lumpy mashed potatoes with meatballs, green salad, orange juice, and hot water for tea.

Once the nurse left, William stood. "I have to get to work. I'll drop in to check on you when I can." He pecked her on the forehead, but his lips barely grazed her skin.

That night Eleanor slept fitfully, and when she awakened William was not in his chair. A pitcher of water and a plastic cup sat on the nightstand, and she was reaching for it when she heard a knock at the door. She expected to see a nurse doing rounds, but when Eleanor looked up, an older white woman stood in the doorway.

"Hello, Mrs. Pride, my name is Mother Margaret," the nun said, crossing the room with steady steps. She wore a black habit, and the skin under her chin hung just enough to make Eleanor think of a Thanksgiving Day turkey. A thick gold cross dangled across her chest.

"I understand you've been through an ordeal. I'm so sorry for your loss. May I?" She pointed to the chair.

"Yes, of course." Eleanor adjusted her blanket.

The woman pulled the chair up to the side of the bed and rested her hand on Eleanor's thigh. "You probably think this is the worst thing that could happen to you. But I am here to let you know that God works in mysterious ways."

"Excuse me?" Eleanor's head snapped. God had clearly forsaken her. He hadn't answered her prayers, and she had gone to Him on her knees for months.

Mother Margaret folded her hands in her lap and seemed to pause until she was sure she had Eleanor's full attention.

"Mrs. Pride. I run a home for unwed mothers not far from here. There is a limited number of quality babies being born to Negro girls who have gotten themselves into a fix. Most come from well-bred, educated families, a few are mixed-race."

Eleanor kneaded her blanket with her knuckles. "Why are you telling me this?"

"I know this is all happening very quickly." The nun reached into her black gown, producing a business card that she extended to Eleanor. "I am happy to meet with you and your husband once you leave the hospital. I think this alternative will suit you both well. It would be a shame for a thriving couple such as yourselves to lose out on the joys of parenthood."

Eleanor didn't want someone else's child—she wanted to have her own. She wanted a child with William's smile and her eyes.

The nun stood up and reached for Eleanor's hands. "May I pray for you?"

Eleanor wanted nothing more than to be left alone. She nodded yes, anything to make the woman leave.

Mother Margaret's hands were ice-cold and chapped, but her voice was strong.

"Hail, Mary, full of grace
the Lord is with thee.
Blessed art thou amongst women
and blessed is the fruit of thy womb, Jesus.
Holy Mary, Mother of God,
pray for us sinners
now and at the hour of our death.
Amen."

Mother Margaret made the sign of the cross and then touched her gold cross to her lips. "I hope that brought you comfort."

Eleanor nodded for the nun's sake, but she hadn't felt anything but sadness—and the overwhelming need to pee.

"Mrs. Pride, we are so thorough that no one besides your husband will need to know. Please do give it some thought. There is a baby that is right for you."

She closed the door behind her.

Eleanor flipped the business card over in her hand, then shoved it under her pillow.

Chapter Twenty-Three

WHAT'S RIGHT

Ruby

Over the next few days, I read the brochure on the home for "fallen girls" so many times I had whole sections of it memorized. Aunt Marie had given me her opinion, but I needed to talk it through with Shimmy. I had been trying to reach him since his mother's visit a week ago, but we kept missing each other's calls.

On Friday, I held out hope that this would be the weekend his parents would allow him a trip home from Brooklyn. Despite the heat, I pulled on a pink T-shirt and shorts, carried a novel outside and sat on the steps and waited. My head jutted up every time I heard the pull and swish of the door to the paint store, but there was no Shimmy. The water ice man came through the street wearing his cowboy hat. I paid a nickel for a cherry water ice that stained my fingertips and turned my tongue red.

By the time the sun moved to my side of the street, sweat had soaked through the back of my shirt. I packed it up and went inside, but the third-floor apartment wasn't much cooler. The heat, combined with my worry over what to do, made my temples throb. I decided to try Shimmy's home one more time. But his mother was the one to answer after the first ring.

"Have you considered my proposition, dear?" she asked by way of greeting. "Dear" did not sound like a term of endearment coming from her mouth.

"Ma'am, I was hoping to speak with Shimmy, please."

"Shimmy remains in Brooklyn indefinitely, but I assure you we are of one mind on this topic. He has admitted that he is not mature enough to go through with whatever you two were planning. This is the best option for both of you."

I paused. "Could you give me a telephone number that I can reach him at? The one I have keeps ringing."

"I'm afraid not." She was silent on the other end. "A piece of advice. When girls find themselves in trouble, it is best they make decisions for their benefit. Do consider your bright future. A child would only keep you from reaching your goal."

I swallowed the lump that had formed in my throat and uttered, "Are you sure you can guarantee the full scholarship for all four years?"

"Yes, I am certain." Her voice held promise. She wanted this as much as I did.

My knees shook. With Shimmy gone "indefinitely," as she put it, I didn't have a lot of options.

"Okay." My stomach rumbled as if in protest. But I forced the words that I had been thinking all day out. "Please make the arrangements," I conceded.

She sighed with elation. "Wonderful! You won't be sorry. I'll handle all the details and will be in touch shortly."

When I told Aunt Marie about my decision, she had the owner of Kiki's draw up a contract stating all the facts and promises we had agreed upon.

When she brought the papers home for me to sign, she explained her thinking.

"White folk got short memories. This way there ain't no room for funny business. Ain't trying to go to jail for kicking a white woman's ass." She tossed me a black ink pen.

As the week drifted by, I tried not to think about the egg growing inside of me. When I felt sick, I told myself that I was coming down with the flu. I tried not to think about Shimmy either. I had thought by now he would have at least called. It fired me up how easy it was for boys to slip away and leave the girl with all the responsibility of carrying the baggage. Shimmy would have no issues returning to college for his sophomore year, but I would miss the entire fall semester of my senior year of high school. Mrs. Shapiro said that I'd be able to take general classes while I was away, and that she would arrange with Mrs. Thomas to get all of my work sent for *We Rise* so that I wouldn't fall behind and would still be in position to receive the scholarship. It was also her idea to cover my absence with the notion that I was going to D.C. for a few months to partake in a prestigious internship. It's what I told Inez on the rare chance that she'd look for me while I was out of the city.

My time leading up to my departure was terribly lonely. I mostly stayed in the apartment with my paintbrushes and canvas, and even that didn't relieve me of the blues I was feeling. Or of the guilt and constant shame.

At the end of August, I was nineteen weeks pregnant when Mrs. Shapiro phoned to tell me that she would pick me up before daylight the following day and drive me to the home for unwed mothers. I suspected that the only reason she was taking me herself was so that she could confirm with her own eyes that I was there.

The next morning, Aunt Marie rose early and made me a sandwich with two slices of crisp scrapple to take along with me for the ride.

"Did you pack enough clean underwear?"

I gestured to my two muslin bags sitting by the door and nodded.

"Make sure you wash your panties out each night. Don't want you running around with dirty drawers and have them white folks talking 'bout you ain't got no home training," she fussed, and then just like that, my tear ducts burst and the waterworks fell.

"Chin up," Aunt Marie said. "You know you can call home anytime, little money McGillicuddy."

"But I'm scared," I murmured.

"Be strong. When you get back, you can focus all your energy on being the biggest money McGillicuddy this family has ever seen. Hear?"

I wiped my tears on her flowered muumuu.

"Go on now." She gave me a little push.

I picked up my two bags and clumped down the stairs. The blue Ford was parked in the alley. When I opened the back door of the car, I saw that Shimmy was in the passenger seat next to his mother. My heart split in two as he reached over the seat and wrapped his arms around me.

"This is not a social visit." Mrs. Shapiro clicked her teeth, while shoving Shimmy off me and back into the front seat. "Shimmy, must I remind you that you are only along for the ride because a proper woman should not travel on the highway alone. Please act accordingly."

She passed me sunglasses and a scarf for my hair. I realized they were my disguise.

As we drove down Broad Street, past city hall and the bronze statue of William Penn, Shimmy stuck his right hand through the seat and passed it back to me. I clung to his soft fingers like my life depended on it.

We drove in dead silence. Mrs. Shapiro would not turn the radio on because she said she had to concentrate on the road and the music would be a distraction. After what seemed like ages, Mrs. Shapiro instructed Shimmy to get the food from the picnic basket that they had brought, but she didn't offer me a morsel. Shimmy passed me back half of his pastrami sandwich on rye bread, and I could see her brows crinkle through the rearview mirror.

It was a clear day. I'd never been to Washington, D.C., before, and I recognized some of the monuments from pictures in my textbooks. And then, before I fully realized what was happening, Mrs. Shapiro was steering the car up a long driveway. At the end was a home that was huge and foreboding. It didn't look like a place I wanted to spend the night, let alone a few months. The reality of what I was about to do suddenly seemed very distant from the thing we'd planned on.

Mrs. Shapiro slipped from the driver's seat and dusted the front of her tan suit. Her jacket was belted at the waist and the sleeves were cuffed just below her elbows.

"Shimmy, come with me," she said as she added the final touch, a short black hat with a mesh net that stopped at her nose.

"I'll wait here with Ruby."

"You'll do no such thing."

"Ma, just give me this last moment. You've gotten what you want."

Mrs. Shapiro huffed, then marched up the driveway to the front door of the redbrick house. Shimmy turned around to me in the seat.

"Marry me, Ruby." His green eyes were clear, full of hope and innocence. I wished I could be as naïve as him.

"You don't have to go through with this. We can jump out of the car right now and run. You, me and the baby."

"Shimmy."

"I love you, Ruby."

"And I love you, but I'm learning that love ain't always enough."

"It is for me."

I squeezed his hand. Sure, it was enough for him, a boy whose parents owned the building that I rented in. What I had realized these past few weeks was that all people like the Shapiros had to do was make a phone call and anything they wanted fell at their feet. Whatever they didn't want went away. Like the egg. Love wasn't going to lift me out of my circumstances. I had to do that for myself.

Shimmy reached for me over the seat, and as I hugged him to me, I could see Mrs. Shapiro coming back down the driveway.

I whispered in his ear, "Your mother will crush our love. The world will stomp out our fire. I have no other choice, Shimmy. Please understand this, for me." I grabbed his face and kissed his lips, despite his mother watching. "Take care of yourself."

"Wait." Shimmy turned around in the seat, flipped open the glove compartment and pulled out a book of stamps. "Promise you'll write me."

I took the stamps and tucked them up my sleeve. Squeezing his clammy hand again, I stared into his eyes one last time and then pushed open the car door.

Mrs. Shapiro stood stiff like a guard.

"One last thing." She stepped closer so that only I could hear her. "My son is a fool, but I can see that you are a smart girl. Let him go completely, or the deal is off."

She held my gaze. I knew what needed to be done.

"Thanks for the ride, Mrs. Shapiro. Get home safely," I offered, and then turned my back on her and headed up the driveway with my shoulders as high as I could muster.

PART THREE

Mission of the House of Magdalene: *To assist the prostitutes, troubled, lost and fallen women and wayward girls.*

Chapter Twenty-Four

CRACKS AND CREVICES

Eleanor

Eleanor's eyes flashed open. Her cotton sheets were soaked through with sweat. She reached for the bottle of pills on the side of her bed. The little blue tablets offered her the only reprieve from the image that haunted her: a tiny purple foot being carried away. But when she turned the bottle upside down, it was empty.

In the three days that they had been home, William had only said what was necessary, and at night he kept to his side of the bed. When she woke up, he had already gone off to work, but today he had left a thermos of chicken noodle soup on the bedside table. She saw the food as a good sign and hoped that it meant they were on the mend. But then she remembered Dr. Avery's words: *We recommend you don't try again. The next time could be life-threatening.* How could they get past any of this without a child?

She dragged her slippers across the floor as she moved down to the kitchen, where there was evidence of William's hastily made breakfast. Eggshells littered the counter, a butter knife and crumbs from his toast. She tidied up, washed the pan and plate in the sink and then made herself a cup of Earl Grey tea with a dash of cream. When she settled in on the settee in the den with her hot mug, her eyes fell on the telephone. Since coming home from the hospital, she hadn't told a single person about her misfortune, not even Nadine. Eleanor knew that it was time to call her mother and break the news. But she couldn't bring herself to pick up the receiver. Saying the words out loud would make them true, and she wasn't ready for that. Eleanor had no energy for reading or archiving work, so she flipped on the television. The midday news aired, followed by the game show *What's My Line?* Episode after mind-numbing episode provided Eleanor a break from wallowing.

The sun had sunk and the *Texaco Star Theater* program was halfway through when she heard William coming through the back door. He dropped his briefcase in a chair with a thump and then found her curled up in the den.

"You're up." He walked over to her and put his hand on her head to feel for fever. After she'd returned home from the hospital, he had begun treating her more like a patient than his wife.

"How was your day?" She craved his conversation, but William didn't respond. He was too busy sizing her up.

Eleanor was still wearing the pajamas she had put on when she returned from the hospital. After three days, they were grimy, and her skin felt flaky and dry.

"Let me run you a bath. The hot water will make you feel better."

Eleanor didn't want to bathe and didn't think it was possible to feel better.

But William clearly thought otherwise. She could hear the tub filling. When he came back and reached for her hand, she didn't have the strength to resist his pull. Somewhere deep inside her it registered that she was lucky that William was still here after all she had put him through.

The bathroom was steamy with the smell of citrus. Hot soapy water sloshed against her skin as she slipped into the claw-foot tub. As she sank below the water, William tossed her a washcloth and then started for the door.

"Wait," Eleanor called. "Can you stay?"

William shifted on his feet. "I have some paperwork to finish up."

"Please," she croaked, lifting her eyes to meet his. William sighed, and then moved toward the tub and plopped down on the small foot stool.

They sat in uncomfortable silence. Eleanor pulled her knees to her chest while she gathered her nerve. "The guy from high school . . ."

"I don't need details."

"Well, what do you need? I can't stand this distance between us. Maybe if you knew what happened you could forgive me."

"It's just a lot to take in at once." He stretched his legs in front of him and she could see the sadness in his eyes. William was hurting as much as she was. It was his baby, too, and she had lied to him. There had to be a way to break down the shell he had constructed.

Eleanor held the wet cloth up to him. "Can you wash my back?"

He sat still for so long she wasn't sure he'd heard her, but then he rolled up the sleeves of his white shirt to his elbows. Timidly, he sponged her skin. The warmth drew grief from her pores. His touch and attention felt so good that she didn't even object when he wet the tips of her hair by accident.

"How do you know this song?" she asked, and William looked up, clearly unaware that he'd been humming along with the radio.

"My great-grandmother played piano. I listened to a lot of classical growing up."

"Did your mom force you to sing in the youth choir? Mine sure did."

He shook his head. "I was much too shy," he chuckled. "Teddy did though. He's the ham, always out front and center. He plays trumpet, too."

William dripped the sudsy water across her neck and shoulders and then down across her breasts. The heat made her nipples hard and she lifted her chest out of the water slightly. She knew he took her in by the way his breathing went shallow. Eleanor wanted her husband back.

"I always thought about playing an instrument."

"You still can." He reached into the tub and pulled up the plug. The water made a sucking sound as it slipped down the drain. "I'll set the table and meet you downstairs."

Eleanor rubbed down with sweet almond oil and then dressed in a fresh top and loose-fitting bottoms. She pulled her damp hair back into a ponytail and then trekked down to the kitchen, where a brown paper bag sat on the counter wafting the smell of tomatoes, oregano, garlic and basil. William pushed a paper cup into her hand.

"This is the best iced tea this side of the Mason-Dixon," he offered. "Taste it."

Eleanor sipped. The sugar and lemons went right to her head. "It's delicious."

"Told you."

She felt him coming back to her as she unwrapped the foil from her plate and was overwhelmed with the succulent sight of spaghetti with big, round meatballs. When she brought the fork to her mouth, the food tasted like love.

"Where did you get this from?"

"A new hole-in-the-wall that opened up a few weeks ago across the street from the hospital. The Italian family who owns it just moved from New York."

Eleanor ate half her plate before pushing it away.

"Saving room for dessert?" William reached into the bag and placed a slice of cheesecake between them. He dug his fork in, then nodded his head in appreciation.

Eleanor almost smiled. "Thank you. For all of this."

When they were finished with the cake, William put the leftovers in the Frigidaire and then dropped a business card in front of her. "I found this in your discharge bag."

Eleanor ran her fingers over the card, recognizing it as the one that Mother Margaret had given her in the hospital. In her fog of grief and guilt, she had forgotten all about the holy woman's visit.

"Oh, yeah. A Catholic nun came to pray with me. She said God works in mysterious ways, and that there was another way."

"For what?"

"To have a baby, I guess."

William looked at her expectantly. "Well, what did she say?"

"That she runs a home for pregnant, unwed women. Adoption I think is what she was suggesting."

"Is it something to consider?" He sipped his iced tea as he waited for her response.

Eleanor had never imagined adoption. She had desperately wanted to give William his own child. One that looked and acted like him, with their shared genes and facial expressions. A child that they'd bring up on the finer side of life like William. A child that would provide the glue that would bond her to him forever. Adoption was never part of the plan.

"I want to give you your own child," she whispered, feeling defeated.

"I wanted that, too, but after Dr. Avery's suggestion, I can't allow you to put yourself through that again. There's no risk worth losing you."

Her heart skipped; he still loved her. "What if he's wrong?"

"And if he's right? It's not a chance I'm willing to take."

Eleanor fidgeted in her seat. "I suppose we could consider other options. I just . . . this is not the way it was supposed to be."

"None of this is your fault. It's a freak act of nature. Don't blame yourself."

Eleanor looked down at the business card. The shame of not having a baby had crippled her, and William's words were a comfort. She didn't have to do this alone. Perhaps they should explore this other way. When they bought this house, it was with the expectation of filling it with children, toys, holiday memories and laughter.

"I just assumed that you wouldn't want a child that wasn't biologically yours." She moved the straw around in her cup.

"Listen to me." William caught her eyes. "I'll do whatever it takes to lift this sadness from you. Why don't we at least look into it?"

"Okay." Eleanor felt a slight ease in her chest. "I'll give her a call in the morning and make the appointment. No harm in gathering more information. Let's just see where it takes us."

William got up from his seat, and for the first time since Dr. Avery's news he pulled her into his arms and kissed her on the lips.

When Eleanor phoned Mother Margaret two days later to inquire, the nun insisted that if they were interested, they needed to meet with her quickly. William rearranged his work schedule and they set a meeting for the following evening. Eleanor knew it was wrong, but she still hadn't been able to bring herself to tell anyone about the miscarriage. She didn't lie, but when her telephone rang, she just didn't answer it. The shame haunted her, and although she knew she couldn't keep it to herself forever, she had decided to wait until after the meeting with Mother Margaret before she told anyone the truth.

William picked her up thirty minutes early for the seven p.m. meeting. She had dressed in a mint-green dress, with a nipped-in high-top waist, and leather peep-toe shoes. Neither said much on the way over. They parked on a side street just off MacArthur Boulevard in Northwest, and as they walked toward the office building, Eleanor clasped William's hand tightly to keep herself from shaking. The tree-lined street was quiet, and she could hear her heels echo against the concrete. The whitewashed building looked deserted, but when William pushed the door it clicked open. They rode the elevator to the fifth floor and knocked on the second door to the right, as instructed.

A voice rang out, telling them to come in.

When they stepped into the office, Eleanor saw the nun who'd prayed with her back in the hospital—Mother Margaret—and could smell years of wear on the dank carpet.

"I'm sorry it's a bit warm in here. The air-conditioning conked out a week ago, and I haven't gotten around to fixing it. Please have a seat." She gestured.

It was a small office, with a framed photo of the Washington Monument on the wall, next to a wooden cross. Eleanor moved a peppermint around in her mouth to calm her nerves, but she could still feel the pulsing at the back of her neck.

"I'm glad you called, Mrs. Pride. I wasn't sure that I'd hear from you."

"We haven't decided on anything. But I told my husband about your proposition, and we are curious to learn a bit more." Eleanor pushed a loose strand of hair behind her ear.

"Of course." Mother Margaret leaned forward and repeated what she had disclosed at the hospital and then added, "Our babies come from well-bred girls who have fallen into trouble. They are incapable of raising a baby on their own. They are happy to turn them over to good parents in exchange for a second chance at life. It really is that simple."

She flipped through the file on her desk. "What was your intended due date, Mrs. Pride?"

"January 3."

Mother Margaret pushed her glasses up her nose. "I have a Negro girl who is set to deliver around that time. She comes from a fine family. Highly educated and good-looking. It would be a match made in heaven."

Eleanor had been living in D.C. long enough to know that by good-looking she meant fair-skinned. A baby that would grow up to look like the Greta Hepburns of the world.

"I must assure you that we are so thorough in our procedures and so confidential in our record-keeping that no one will ever know that you didn't birth the child yourself. If that's what you want, of course."

Eleanor caught William's eye as her heart started beating wildly in her chest.

Mother Margaret said, "Don't take too long deciding. There are several well-meaning families like yours who would love to take home this baby."

"Can you give us a few days?" William asked.

"I can do anything you like, Mr. Pride. It would help, though, if you offered a small donation to our cause in the meantime. The operation is very expensive to run." She tapped the wooden box in front of her and smiled. Eleanor noticed that the smile didn't quite reach her eyes.

"Of course," William said as he removed his checkbook.

Mother Margaret stood and then showed them to the door. As Eleanor passed her by, she could have sworn she smelled a whiff of gin.

When they reached their home, William locked the back door behind them and then Eleanor fell into his arms. He smelled like a hard day's work, but she didn't mind.

Eleanor pulled away and leaned against the counter. "I'm scared. This feels like cheating."

"With all things considered, it might be our only way."

Eleanor turned her wedding band around on her finger. During the whole ride home, she had been thinking about Dorothy Creole, the formerly enslaved woman who adopted the boy and raised him as her own. When Eleanor had classified her story for the library, there was something about it that made her read it several times. Perhaps it was to prepare her for considering adoption herself.

"Listen, Elly. It doesn't matter where the baby comes from, just that we love it and raise it as our own."

"I don't want anyone to know," she blurted. Mother Margaret had offered them a confidential exchange, and for Eleanor that was the only way this would work. "About the adoption I mean. Let's pass this baby off as our own."

He scratched the side of his head. "You sure about that?"

Eleanor's voice cracked with emotion. "You have no idea what it's like, William. Marrying into a family like yours where everything and everyone is perfect."

"Whoa, slow down." His eyes widened.

"You're not a woman—it's different for us. I won't be able to live the rest of my life knowing that people are judging me and looking at our child differently. Like he or she doesn't belong. I just want to fit in. I'm tired of being on the outside," she hissed, much louder than she had intended.

It could have been the imbalance of hormones, but she had finally said it. She was tired of being on the outside.

William looked taken aback. "Baby, I didn't know you felt like that. I thought I was doing everything—"

"It's not you. It's your mother and her fancy friends," she sighed, and she noticed William bristle.

"I know my mother is trying, in her own way."

Eleanor kept her lips pursed. She didn't want the conversation to become about her relationship with Rose Pride. But she was sure that keeping the adoption a secret was the only way her dignity would remain intact.

"It's what I want. This must stay between us," she whispered, as the idea that had been forming in her head took shape. "I'm going to pretend to have this baby myself."

"That's going to be hard to pull off."

"I'll stay in the house for months if I have to. It's the only way for us to live as a family without everything we do being under a microscope."

William stepped closer and ran his hands up and down her arms. "Okay, however you want to do this is fine by me. I just want us to be happy."

Eleanor looked up into William's eyes and could see a glimmer of a new sparkle. "So, I'll phone Mother Margaret in the morning and tell her that we'll take the January baby?" Her hand flew to her mouth. "That sounds so weird, January baby." Eleanor giggled for the first time in a week.

"We will welcome baby January into our home and love it. Everything is going to be just fine." William pulled her face to his.

"Our baby." Eleanor squeezed him around the waist.

Now all they had to do was figure out how to pull it off without anyone finding out.

Chapter Twenty-Five

THE HOUSE OF MAGDALENE

Ruby

Before I'd even reached the side of the house, the silver storm door screeched open. A woman in a nun's habit stood in the doorway. Her face was stern and wrinkled.

"Welcome to the House of Magdalene. My name is Mother Margaret." She was an Amazon of a woman who towered at least four inches over me. Then she looked down her nose and ushered me inside. "Come along."

I trailed behind her down a short hallway that opened up into a wide kitchen. The room was muggy and smelled of simmering meat. Two blonde teenaged girls, both with heavy bellies that seemed far too big for their tiny frames, sat at the prep table peeling carrots and white potatoes. The one holding the carrots glanced over and then quickly darted her eyes away, but the stringy-haired girl with freckles knifing the potato gave me the tiniest smile.

As I followed Mother Margaret deeper into the house, I heard crying.

It was loud and insistent and made me increasingly uncomfortable. Mother Margaret's thick dress swished at her feet, and she seemed unbothered by the noise.

"This is the dining room, where you will take your meals three times a day."

Two long tables sat parallel to each other, and then off a bit to the left was a round table that held place settings for four. She then pointed out a classroom to the right, "for your weekly classes on etiquette, sewing, charm and Bible study."

We passed a small lounge with two sofas, where I would meet my social worker once a week. The floor creaked beneath her feet, and with each step the temperature dropped. I could feel a sudden coldness all the way down in my toes. We had reached the end of the hall, and Mother Margaret stopped and turned to me with a look on her face I couldn't read.

"This is the shaming room. It's where the bad girls go." She looked at me pointedly, freezing me in place with her gaze. "I trust you will not need to know what is behind that door."

"Yes, ma'am," I whispered.

"Yes, Your Excellency." Her eyes bored into me, waiting. After what felt like an interminable silence, I realized that I was meant to repeat the title. I did as expected.

Satisfied, Mother Margaret turned back and then climbed up two flights of stairs, stopping in front of an arched doorway with a dark wooden door. She turned toward me again, with her hands folded in front of her stomach, posture as erect as a statue.

"The girls go by first names only. No personal business is shared. The mission here is simple. To save your soul."

I had had to go to the bathroom ever since I arrived, but my fear had made me forget. Now, though, a drop of urine leaked out, and I pressed my thighs together to stop any more from flowing. Since carrying the egg, I'd never had an issue with holding my bladder—until now.

Without knocking, Mother Margaret shoved open the door. Once I stepped inside, I saw four twin-sized cots with two short chests of drawers against the blue-painted walls. Three of the beds were occupied by teens in various hues of brown and stages of pregnancy. When the girls saw Mother Margaret, they pushed themselves to a stand.

"Good afternoon, Your Excellency," two called out in unison. The other one stood but looked down at her feet.

"Ladies, this is Ruby. Loretta, please help her get settled."

Loretta stuck the piece of paper she had in her hand into the front pocket of her smock shirt and smiled. Her golden-streaked hair was pulled into a high ponytail, and just by the ease of her kind eyes, I knew that we'd get along just fine.

"Dinner is served daily at five thirty sharp. Please come down with your hands and face clean." Mother Margaret pointed to the small sink. "Cleanliness is next to godliness," she barked, before closing the heavy door behind her.

"Shit. She always coming up here unannounced," said the girl with the gap between her teeth. She wore her hair in two braids that bent out below her ears.

I carried my bags over to the empty bed and sagged into the cushion. The gap-toothed girl reached beneath her pillow and pulled out a pack of Lucky Strikes. She placed one between her lips and pretended to smoke.

"Calms my nerves." She gestured to the unlit cigarette. "They call me Bubbles. You met Loretta, but I call her Goldie 'cause how many girls like us you know with blonde streaks in their hair?" Bubbles giggled.

Loretta rolled her eyes. "Keep talking, and your baby will come out looking just like me. That's what my grandmother always said. The person who you're mad with is the one the baby looks like."

Loretta pulled from her pocket the paper she had stashed when I came in and unfolded it.

"That there is Georgia Mae." Bubbles pointed to the quiet girl, who had pulled her knees up to her chest and was picking at her toenails. "She don't talk."

The three girls ran the gamut on the color wheel, with Loretta being as light as butter cream, Georgia Mae's skin as rich as hickory, and Bubbles falling somewhere in the caramel middle.

"When you due?" Bubbles took another imaginary puff.

"End of January."

"I'm early January," said Loretta.

"Georgia Mae and I are November and December. That makes you the baby of the bunch. You'll have more chores to do." Bubbles puffed.

There was a lamp and Bible on top of the small chest next to the bed. Loretta pointed to the two drawers that were mine, and as I unpacked the few things I brought with me, the wailing started up again.

"What is that noise?" I looked up for an explanation.

"Just a girl who gave up her baby. Regret is a motherfucker." Bubbles blew out a fake puff.

"You'll get used to it," Loretta offered, tucking her letter back into her pocket. It was worn around the edges.

"That's why no matter what these crackers say, I'm keeping my baby." Bubbles returned her cigarette to the pack and tucked it under her pillow.

Loretta looked up at Bubbles with doleful eyes. "You know why we're here. It'll just be easier if you accept it."

"Humph. I'll accept it all right. By breaking my foot off in one of their asses," Bubbles boasted.

"It's best just not to think about it," Loretta said to me. "You have plenty of time before you go over. Just try to enjoy the moment like I do."

"Go over?" I asked.

"Over to the other side and have your baby," Loretta explained.

Bubbles snapped. "Reading the same old letter hardly seems like enjoying the moment."

"I miss Rucker. What can I say?" Loretta touched her breast pocket.

"You better off reading those boring books over there in the corner." Bubbles pointed to a bookshelf that I hadn't noticed. "Take your mind off things for sure."

Inside one of my bags, I had managed a few small canvases, brushes and a few tubes of paint, all of which I shoved under my cot. My body was suddenly so weary, it felt as if I had walked all the way here from North Philadelphia. I laid down. The girl's distressing cries continued, and I buried one ear in my pillow and covered the other ear with my hand.

A bell rang over the PA system that was wired into our attic bedroom. The girls stood, and we all took turns washing our hands and face at the tiny sink against the window and then filed out one by one. In the dining room, Bubbles headed over to the smaller round table that was set for four. There was a breadbasket, and a serving dish of the stew I had smelled when I arrived. Over at the long tables sat blondes, brunettes and one redhead, all of them white. I counted eight girls between the two long tables, plus the four of us girls from the attic room.

Mother Margaret stood in front of the unlit fireplace with her hands clutched in prayer. "Let us bow our heads please. Bless us, O Lord and these, Thy gifts, which we are about to receive from Thy bounty, Through Christ, Our Lord. Amen."

Spoons clanked against the bowls.

"White people's food." Bubbles reached for the salt and pepper shakers without tasting it.

We ate mostly in silence. Bubbles was right; the stew wasn't very flavorful, no matter how much salt I added, but I was too hungry to care. When we finished, I followed their lead and helped with the cleanup. Some girls went into the kitchen to wash and dry dishes, while others dusted off the chairs and swept the floor. In the kitchen, Bubbles scrubbed the pots clean while Loretta wiped down the stove. Georgia Mae and I collected all the trash, tied up the bags and carried them out to the cans at the back of the house.

When everything was tidy, Bubbles whispered to me, "Brace yourself. Next up is nightly devotion."

We all filed into the parlor. It had large windows with mahogany wooden beams on the ceiling. There were two stuffed sofas, which I headed for, but Loretta grabbed my arm.

"We sit over there," she said, pointing to the metal folding chairs set against the wide window.

"The sofa is for the porcelain girls." Bubbles tapped the inside of her palm.

I looked at her quizzically.

"It's what I call them ofays."

As the white girls crammed into the seats of the sofa, I caught her meaning. Mother Margaret walked in holding her Bible to her chest. Two medium-bellied girls distributed the stack of Bibles that were on the coffee table. Only two worn Bibles were handed to us, so I leaned over and shared mine with Georgia Mae.

Mother Margaret dropped the needle on the phonograph and a song played. Georgia Mae opened the hymn book that was under her seat and showed me where we were. I moved my lips over the words as the other girls piped out, "Be not afraid, I go before you always. Come follow me, and I will give you rest."

After two verses, Mother Margaret turned the music off and fixed her eyes on us.

"Will God forgive me for fornicating before marriage? How can I repent of my sins? Those are the questions you must ask yourself each morning, girls."

The room fell silent. I looked around to see what the other girls were doing, but their faces were like stone.

Mother Margaret opened her Bible. "Please turn to 1 Corinthians 6:18. Viola, would you read?"

Viola, a girl with blue eyes and dark hair, cleared her throat. "Flee fornication. Every sin that a man doeth is without the body, but he that committeth fornication sinneth against his own body."

"That means you, girls. You have committed the ultimate sin by giving into the temptation of fornication." She looked us over and I dropped my eyes. I had spent very little time in church, so I was ill prepared for the religious lecture from Mother Margaret that seemed to go on for ages. When she was satisfied that we had received her message, we were each given two sugar cookies and a glass of warm milk, then sent to bed.

When the lights went out, I pulled my knees up to my chest and wrapped my arms around myself. I was ashamed and scared. What had I gotten myself into? This home was not the girls' retreat I had read about in the brochure. Still, it was better than ruining my life. I just needed to keep my head down and get this over with.

Chapter Twenty-Six

TIGER MAMA

Eleanor

Eleanor stood at the sink drying the last of the breakfast dishes with her thoughts on her mother, Lorraine. It had been three weeks since she spoke to her last, and she knew she couldn't put it off much longer. Even though Eleanor was set on keeping the adoption a secret, lying to her mother about the baby wouldn't prove easy. But Eleanor reminded herself it was her mother who had taught her the importance of clandestineness for a fresh start. Plus, at least she and William were in this one together.

She had placed the last of the plates in the cupboard and was bracing herself to make the call when she heard a car door close. She looked out the window to see Rose Pride walking up the driveway. Before Eleanor could compose herself, Rose was tapping on the window of their back door.

"Good morning. I wasn't expecting you today," Eleanor offered as a greeting, but Rose ignored the formality and breezed past her and into the kitchen.

In one manicured hand, Rose gripped a shopping bag, and in the other a file folder. The peplum jacket and matching skirt suggested she had business to attend to today, and Eleanor felt shabby in her nondescript housedress, with no bra on underneath. Her hair was still fastened in rollers and tucked under a turban.

"William's already left for the hospital," she said, with the hope of discouraging a long visit. The kettle was already heated, and she had planned to sip lavender tea, while chatting with her mom. Then she had a few chapters to read on ancient civilization for her history course.

If Rose caught the hint of dismissal, she didn't show it. Instead, she placed her bag on the kitchen table and opened up the file folder, spreading out papers with diagrams and dates.

"Now, if *we* are going to pull this off, then we have to be smart about every step you make going forward."

"Excuse me?" Eleanor's hand flew to her throat. What was Rose talking about? Surely, she couldn't be referring to the . . .

"Since the baby arrives in January, let's work backwards."

"William told you?"

"Of course he did. You couldn't pull this off without me." She looked at Eleanor pointedly. "I had to jump on cleanup duty immediately. Thank goodness Dr. Avery was your attending doctor, and our families go back three generations." She reached into her bag and pulled out her reading glasses.

"Oh, and I'm sorry for your unfortunate loss. My William is positively devastated. That's why I'm here."

Eleanor was speechless.

"But as my mother used to say, when life gives you lemons you had better learn to juggle. And that's exactly what Prides do. So, come sit down so I can get you on board." She gestured for Eleanor to join her at the kitchen table.

William had told his mother when she had explicitly said that she didn't want anyone to know. What happened to it being the two of them against the world?

"Dr. Avery has assured me that no one from his staff will breathe a word of your unfortunate stay in the hospital. That gives us ample space to forge ahead with the plan."

"Plan?" She balled her toes in her slippers.

Rose pushed the papers across the table toward Eleanor. She took up the sheets and read. It was an outline of social appearances for Eleanor to make.

"If the baby is going to be born in January, I don't think you should show up for any engagements after October first."

Eleanor swallowed hard. It hadn't even been a full forty-eight hours since they made the adoption decision, and Rose was already taking command.

"It's a good thing I'm handy with a sewing machine." Rose reached into the bag and pulled out a nude pillow pad with thin straps. A padding to tie around Eleanor's waist.

"I also brought you the Lane Bryant catalogue. It's about the only one where you can get maternity clothes that will conceal your condition and keep you looking smart. I've flagged a few styles that will adjust easily for you." She held up the pamphlet with red tab marks. Rose didn't wait for her response and continued outlining her plan.

Eleanor would appear at a charity lunch in two weeks at the YMCA but would leave shortly after arriving with the excuse of feeling nauseous. Her final appearance would be at the dinner celebrating the six-month anniversary of Dr. Charles Drew's untimely death.

"It'll be a fundraiser to keep his research in blood transfusion alive," Rose explained.

There, Eleanor would appear long enough for people to see her flowering, but not long enough for meaningful conversation. These two events would give Rose enough ammunition to spread around that Eleanor was having a hard time with the pregnancy and needed to go on bed rest.

"William will make a few dinners without you, and keep the story going. I think it might be wise for you to go up to Ohio and spend a few months with your mother. Out of sight, out of mind. And then come back in time for the delivery."

"I'm not leaving my home," Eleanor said, with more bite than she intended. *Or my husband.*

Rose closed the catalogue. "Well, once folks get busy with the holidays they'll be minding their own affairs. You will have to miss going to New York for Theodore's engagement party over Thanksgiving. We can't risk it."

Theodore was marrying the daughter of a prominent New York attorney. Her mother was a well-known dancer who taught at Katherine Dunham's K.D. School of Arts and Research in New York City. Rose's face always flushed a pretty pink when she spoke of the union.

"I've got to run." She pushed herself to stand. "Lunch at the Whitelaw Hotel to discuss the ABCs fundraiser for underprivileged sharecropping girls in the rural South. In the meantime, start thinking of your color palette for the baby's room. I'm going to send a carpenter over next week to convert one of the guest rooms into a proper nursery. It'll be our treat," she said with a wink.

Rose removed a container of shrimp étouffée and left it on the counter. "It's William's favorite, I hope you like it, too."

"Thank you." Eleanor forced what she hoped resembled a smile.

When Rose's car pulled away from the curb, Eleanor felt steam rising in her throat. How could he? In the time they had been married she had never called William at the hospital, but she marched right over to the phone now.

"Elly, everything all right?" he said by way of greeting.

"You told your mother?"

"Told her what?"

"Really, William? Don't play simple with me. We agreed to keep this a secret."

"Oh, baby. She's going to help us through this."

"You should have asked me first."

"Please calm down. I didn't know it would bother you so much."

"Really, what part of 'secret' did you miss?"

He was quiet on the other end. "Can we discuss this when I get home?"

Eleanor slammed the phone down so hard that it fell to the floor. Rage coursed through her as she started yanking her rollers from her hair and then ran her fingernails over her scalp. She wasn't sure that Rose could be trusted. She had wanted them to annul their marriage, for goodness' sakes. Who else would Rose tell? Greta's mother? If William told her this, had he told her about the first miscarriage in Ohio, too?

Eleanor was too hot to call her mother or work on her Ancient Civilization coursework like she had planned. What she craved was fresh air and sunshine on her skin, but she was already worried about running into people. The baby fat was melting from her face and belly like lard in a hot pan. The risk wasn't worth it. Instead, she moved to the other side of the den and opened a box of records that Mrs. Porter had sent over the week before. Music had a way of soothing Eleanor's soul, and she sat cross-legged on the floor playing them one after the other, making notations of origin and instruments until her anger had receded a bit.

Once she slipped into the zone, the afternoon passed by swiftly. It wasn't until she gazed up at the clock that she realized it was almost dinnertime. A few minutes later, she heard the back door creak open. William was early and carried a box from her favorite bakery on T Street.

"Waving a white flag." He held the box in front of him, with a smile that Eleanor usually found irresistible, but not today.

"William, I thought I had made myself clear. That I didn't want anyone to know."

"Baby, I didn't know you meant my mother."

"Especially your mother. I told you how she and her friends make me feel. You should have asked me first." She put her hands on her hips.

"Listen, Elly, I want this as badly as you do. My mother feels the same way. I promise you she will not only keep our secret, but she will help us pull this off. We need her."

"This is about us, William. Not me, you and your mother."

Eleanor held out the schedule that Rose had drawn up for her, complete with diagrams of how big her belly should be for each public appearance.

William smirked. "She sure thinks of everything." He put the paper down and grabbed Eleanor around the waist. "My mother means well, and she will make sure everything goes off without a hitch. I can promise you that. I've known the woman all my life."

Eleanor sighed.

"We are going to bring a baby into our home and love it. That's all that matters." He kissed her on the lips and then tugged on her bottom one until she found herself submitting.

"What did you bring me?"

"Open it."

Eleanor unraveled herself from William's embrace and pulled the twine from the box. It was a heaping slice of carrot cake.

"If this is going to be convincing, I'm going to need you to put on a little weight." He tapped her on the backside. "Especially here."

Eleanor rolled her eyes as she pinched off a piece of cake with her finger. "Mmmm, if this is any indication of what you will be feeding me, I'll take one for the team."

Chapter Twenty-Seven

FORGIVE US, SINNERS

Ruby

A loud, buzzing alarm blared through the PA system, jolting me awake. It was still dark out. My cold feet slapped against the floor before I fully realized where I was. It only took a few blinks of my eyes for the previous day to flash before me.

"What now?"

Loretta stood at the sink brushing her teeth. "Pad your knees."

"For what?"

"To scrub the fucking floors." Bubbles wore dungarees with stained, ripped T-shirts tied around her kneecaps.

I rummaged through my drawer, looking for items of clothing that might do the trick.

"Hurry, the late crew gets stuck with the stair steps, and that's back-breaking," Loretta said, cracking open our door.

On the first floor, a few girls were lugging buckets of water. Georgia Mae went into the utility closet and handed out scrub brushes. Loretta's arms were filled with rags. Each girl took two. Mother Margaret's footsteps were heavy as she tramped from the kitchen into the parlor, where we all stood at attention. Most girls had their hair tied away from their face and, like Bubbles, had cushioned extra material around their knees.

Mother Margaret raised a megaphone to her lips and called for us to spread out. "Four of you in here, and then two girls to each of the other rooms."

I dashed behind Bubbles into the lounge as Loretta and Georgia Mae took the long stretch of hallway.

Mother Margaret's voice continued to loop. "Out there, they call you whores and sluts. Damaged goods. But in here, you can redeem yourself and pay for your sins. On the count of three, recite the Lord's Prayer like you mean it. One, two . . ."

Our voices merged in prayer. It felt like I had stumbled into a movie about orphans or badly behaved children.

"Louder. God can't hear you when you are mumbling."

The scrub brushes made sloshy, scratching sounds against the floors, while the prayer was called out in unison.

"Not too much water." Bubbles wrung out her rag in the murky bucket. "More elbow grease."

I followed her direction. We stayed on all fours, scrubbing and drying, buffing and polishing, while repeating the Lord's Prayer. It was the one prayer I knew. The one Nene had taught me to say on bended knee at night. I had not uttered it once since moving out of her apartment.

We kept at it for so long that my knees felt tender, my back ached, and I was hungrier than I had been in a long while. Hard labor had not been listed in the brochure.

"Ask God to forgive you for your lustful sins, girls. Your wicked ways. Pledge to him that you will do right by that innocent baby. Save the child from eternal damnation by relinquishing it to married parents who will raise it under the eyes of the Lord." She paused, then continued. "You are unworthy. Say it."

"We are unworthy."

"Forgive us our sins," she shouted.

"Forgive us our sins," we called back in voices that sounded off-key and miserable. This went on for what felt like hours, until my lips cracked with thirst.

Finally, Mother Margaret put the bullhorn to her lips and relieved us.

Exhausted, I reached for my bucket, and at the same time it tipped over in my direction. Dirty water splashed over onto the floor, and I blotted it as quickly as I could with my rags.

"Ooops," mocked a big-boned girl with red acne marks pocking her ivory face.

"Why would you do that?" I whined.

"Keep your mouth quiet or I'll do worse." She held a fist at me and then stomped in the puddle, making the mess worse on her way out the door.

"Bitch," Bubbles mumbled, but even she was too tired to do much more than dab at the soppy mess. "That's Gertrude. She's a lifer."

"What's a lifer?"

"She went over already, surrendered her baby, and now she is here paying off her debt by working in the laundry. We're all required to do payback work. Some stay longer than others."

"I didn't know that."

"There is a lot they don't tell you before confining you to the Gingerbread House."

I looked at her confused.

"It's what we call this place. Sounds sweeter than the House of Magdalene for Unwed Whores, don't it?"

On Sunday morning we met in the parlor for church, and after an hour sermon, we had time to ourselves. I spent mine painting Shimmy's hands reaching out for me. I missed him, and I missed Aunt Marie. I desperately wanted to be back home with her.

During daybreak devotion on Monday morning, a young nun arrived carrying a satchel. She wore a black jumper with a white collared shirt and a light veil that swung around her back. I heard a few greet her as Little Sister Bethany. She did not live in the Gingerbread House with us, but Bubbles told me that she was our teacher Monday through Friday. After a breakfast of clumpy oatmeal, we filed into the classroom, where she stood in front of the blackboard.

"Welcome, Ruby." She introduced herself, then held out her hand to shake mine. "We have a rotating schedule. Today is sewing. Do you have any experience?"

"Just a little," I offered. Nene used to take in sewing to make ends meet before she went blind, and she had taught me how to thread a needle and darn socks.

Small sewing kits were passed around with wicker baskets containing different textures of fabrics. Little Sister Bethany demonstrated a simple hem and then walked around the room inspecting our stitching as we tried mimicking her work. When class was dismissed, we were given watery chicken noodle soup for lunch. Each afternoon we were permitted two hours to work on our school assignments. Little Sister Bethany walked around the house checking to see if anyone needed help. The girls who weren't in school took that time to read or practice knitting or sewing. Once we finished, we did our house job; Mother Margaret assigned me the job of sorting and distributing the mail. When I looked around confused, a porcelain girl slid up to me.

"I'll show you how it's done. That used to be my job before I got transferred to tallying the spices and condiments in the kitchen."

"By spices you must mean cardboard and containers because that is the blandest food I've ever tasted in my life," I chuckled.

She introduced herself as Clara, and I recognized her as the freckled girl from the kitchen who smiled at me while peeling the potatoes when I'd arrived on Friday.

Clara had stringy brown hair and was rail thin. Her belly was grossly out of place on her tiny frame. It looked like she had shoved a beach ball under her blouse.

"We collect letters on Mondays. Then we put them in a box and mail them to an address in Raleigh, North Carolina. From there, the letters are transferred into new envelopes and postmarked."

"Why so many steps?"

She whispered, "Everything is done here in secrecy. They go to great lengths to protect our identity so that no one knows the sins we have committed." Her lips trembled before she pulled them into a smile. "You got it?"

"Yes."

She handed me a small brown box. "Here are the letters that just came in for distribution. Once you give them out, you can put the new letters you collect from the girls back in the same box."

There were ten letters. Each envelope was addressed in the same script, with a first name and the first initial of the last name of the recipient. As I stood in front of the living room reading off the names, each girl who retrieved a letter smiled and cheered like she had won a sweepstakes. After I called out the last name and closed the box, Loretta rushed up and grabbed my arm.

"There's nothing for me?"

I turned the box upside down to be sure, but it was empty. Tears gathered in her eyes and she ran off.

A few minutes later, done with my sorting duties, I went to see about Loretta. I found her laying on her bed reading the same crumpled paper she had been reading since I arrived.

"What's the matter?"

"My boyfriend. He promised to write, and it's been weeks."

"Maybe he got busy."

"Busy with Cissy Fontaine."

My cot creaked beneath me and I took off my shoes, folding my legs underneath me.

"She's been wanting Rucker since he and I started dating. Now that I'm in here, she can sink her claws into him." She tucked away a few strands of hair that had come loose from her bun. "Crazy thing is we only went all the way one time. One silly time and now I'm stuck dealing with this." She pointed to the pop of her belly. "He said we would get married."

"Why didn't you?"

"My mother said we didn't know his people and that they weren't our kind."

I nodded for Loretta to keep going. She sighed and then told me that her father was a dentist and her mother a social studies teacher. She grew up in a nice middle-class home, went to school and participated in social clubs with other nice girls who didn't do bad things.

"Or at least they didn't get caught." She exhaled. "Rucker doesn't live in our school district, but they accepted him because he plays basketball really well. Last year, he took our team to the state championship. All the girls liked him, but he picked me, captain of the cheerleading team."

I could totally picture Loretta at the top of the pyramid, in a short skirt, her cheeks rosy.

"My mother was already mad as a wet hen that I had the nerve to take up with the darkest-skinned boy in school. She was so furious that she had refused to let me go to the prom with him. Rucker had sent his high yellow friend Harold to pick me up, otherwise she wouldn't have let me out the house." Loretta's face pinched at the memory. "Months later when she found out that I had been with Rucker and that this was his"—she pointed to her belly—"she cried and locked herself in her room. The next day she told me to take her to him. My mother took one look at where Rucker lived, on the outskirts of town in a shotgun house, and turned the car around without even knocking on the door. Two days later, she told my daddy I had been awarded an internship in Washington, D.C. Then she brought me here. Said that I was to do as I was told, and when I returned home everything would go back to normal."

Funny we were both in D.C. under the guise of prestigious internships, and that we had both fooled around with a boy from the opposite side of the tracks. "Maybe his letter got lost in transition," I tried, but she just shook her head.

"On the drive up here, my mother told me to forget about Rucker. To get this done with so that I could focus on getting into Spelman College, just like her. They wouldn't even consider my application if they got wind of this whole mess." Loretta chewed on her fingernail. We were both quiet for a while and then she asked, "Is your guy still waiting for you?"

"Maybe, but it's definitely over."

"You love him?"

I nodded. "But it's complicated. My guy is more like you and I'm Rucker."

Loretta scratched the side of her ankle with the toe of the opposite foot. "What's that supposed to mean?"

I told Loretta about my time with Shimmy, how we met, fell hard for each other, and that it was his Jewish mother who brought me to the Gingerbread House and forbade me to see him again.

"A white Jewish boy?" Her bright eyes widened. "Girly! What did your mother say?"

My skin prickled. "We aren't close." I looked away, hoping she wouldn't pry.

"Shimmy's mom made me a deal. I come here, and she would ensure a full scholarship to Cheyney. I wouldn't be able to go otherwise. My folks can't afford it," I said in a way that suggested that I had two parents and a family like her.

"At least you get something out of it." Loretta hugged her pillow to her chest. I wasn't sure if she was feeling sad for me or herself. Then I remembered the stamps that Shimmy gave me. I had no intention of writing to him; Mrs. Shapiro had made clear what would happen if I did. I reached into my bag and passed the sheet of three-cent stamps to Loretta.

"Maybe you should try to write him one more time. I'm collecting the next batch of letters by dinner. If he doesn't answer this last letter, then move on."

Loretta took the stamps and pulled a pad from under her cot, dried her eyes. "Thank you, Ruby. I'll give him one last try."

"That's it and nothing more." I patted her thigh.

Chapter Twenty-Eight

EXPECTANT MOTHER

Eleanor

Eleanor gingerly ran her fingertips across the calendar that she kept in her top drawer. Today would have marked six months of pregnancy. Her feelings of loss still blistered, raw and tender. Although she had stopped crossing off days, she still kept track of the stages of pregnancy by reading the book *Expectant Mother* nightly.

She placed the calendar back in her drawer and then walked into her bathroom to prepare for another day. Bags had formed under her eyes, and as she stood in front of the mirror, she wished that her body had the decency to allow her to sleep. Eleanor woke up every morning around three to use the bathroom, despite no longer having a fetus resting on her bladder. Maybe her body was still adjusting, or she was experiencing phantom symptoms.

After splashing warm water on her face, she padded down the hall to her prayer closet for her morning ritual. Now when she put on her choir robe for daily devotion, it was for the baby that would be born of someone else's womb. On the floor of the closet, Eleanor went through her routine, but lately her heart hadn't been in it. When she raised up off her knees, she felt herself agonizing over if they'd be able to pull this off, and the thought of another woman carrying the child that she could not.

All that Mother Margaret disclosed about the young woman was that she was from a good family, that the girl was educated, pretty and unwed. As she moved down the steps to the kitchen, it wasn't lost on Eleanor that if she had carried that first baby to term in high school, she could have been on the other end of this, turning her child over to a married couple who couldn't give birth. She did feel grateful to be on the receiving end.

Eleanor set a pot of water to boil on the stove for her morning eggs. As she watched the water simmer and then bubble, she thought again about William's ability to love a child that wasn't genetically his. In the nearly two years she had known them, the Prides had always made such fanfare about their long lineage of educated, well-off, well-connected, light-skinned Negroes that she had a hard time believing that William and Rose could truly accept their bloodline ending because of her. Well, at least they had Theodore and his perfect fiancée. They'd probably have a baby without any problems.

The doorbell pulled her from her thoughts. Eleanor stopped in the hall mirror to double-check that the stomach padding that Rose Pride had made for her was in place. Satisfied, she opened the front door. The bright sun was momentarily blinding, and she blinked her eyes into focus.

"Mrs. Pride, good morning. Mrs. Porter asked me to deliver this to you." A teen boy wearing a wool cap held two stacked boxes in his arms.

Eleanor waved him in. "You can set them down in the den for me."

She rummaged through her dress pocket and handed him a dime. "Thank you."

When she had told Mrs. Porter that her doctor had restricted her travels until the baby was born, she had insisted that Eleanor keep working on small projects.

"You'll need something to keep your mind fresh," she told her over the telephone.

In order to keep working for the library and finish her degree at Howard, William had arranged for a messenger to deliver Eleanor's papers to school and pick up her weekly assignments from her professors. Eleanor didn't know what she would have done if she'd had to give up her archiving job completely, especially now that William was working twelve to fourteen hours a day at the hospital.

Even though it had only been a few weeks in hiding, the isolation was already getting to her, so when Nadine called an hour after the boxes had been delivered and asked if she could drop by with lunch, Eleanor was so desperate for company that she said yes before she could stop herself.

Fifteen minutes before she was set to arrive, Eleanor took her time relining her midsection with the pads, making sure they were positioned just right. Then she swapped out her simple housedress for one of the new wrap frocks that Rose had ordered from the Lane Bryant catalogue, finishing the look off with a ribbed cardigan. When Nadine arrived, Eleanor purposely answered with a handful of books so she could bypass a full body hug, leaning in for a cheeky kiss instead.

"Ohio, look at you." Nadine beamed.

"I'm so glad you dropped by."

Eleanor led her into the dining room just left of the foyer. It was a room they rarely used, but the wood table was big and bulky, and the perfect place to sit without worrying over being touched. A crystal vase of Gerber daisies sat between them. The table had been pre-set with green linen place mats and Eleanor's bone china dinner plates.

Nadine put down the food. "You didn't have to go to so much trouble for me. So formal."

"No trouble. What's the point of having nice plates if you never use them," Eleanor kidded.

"Well, how's it going?" Nadine unpacked a lunch of seafood salad, wilted spinach, cocktail shrimp, a hunk of good-smelling cheese and Ritz crackers.

"It's okay. I have these killer hemorrhoids that keep coming and going. Makes it hard to sit for long periods of time," Eleanor said, reciting what she had read of symptoms for six months of pregnancy.

"Well, at least you are keeping your pretty face. The women in my family's noses spread something awful during pregnancy. You look the same, except for your round middle," Nadine smiled.

Eleanor forced a smile back, resting her hand lightly on her padded belly. "The heartburn is a killer," she dropped another fact, "but it'll all be worth it."

"Yes, it will." Nadine popped cheese and a cracker into her mouth. She looked gorgeous as usual. "Have you thought of names?"

"William wants a William the third if it's a boy. How can I say no to that?" She'd made her voice a bit deeper and chuckled.

"And a girl?"

Eleanor winced. She thought of her stillborn daughter and shook away the image of her tiny little foot. "The verdict is still out."

"What about Emma or Emily? A daughter should be named after you. I'm Nadine and my mother is Nancy."

"Both very cute. I'll add them to the list." Eleanor forked the seafood salad.

"Don't forget to rub cocoa butter on your belly morning and night so you don't have to live the rest of your life with those awful stretch marks."

"Oh, I've been diligent."

"My mother has them, and she never lets me catch her in her panties and bra because of them. She says I've scarred her for life."

"Oh, but look what she got in return," Eleanor purred, making Nadine smile.

They settled into their meal, as Nadine filled her in on the campus life she was missing. Eleanor clung to every detail of every party that Nadine described, with a longing she hadn't anticipated.

"I ran into Greta Hepburn at Club Bali last Friday night." She waved her fork in the air.

"Has she found a man yet?"

"Not that I know of, but she was going on and on about Theodore Pride's engagement party in the Big Apple. Bragging about how she was spending Thanksgiving with her favorite family friends, and how much shopping she was going to do."

Eleanor felt her temples pulse. Greta was going to New York, while Eleanor had to stay home under the pretense of being too sick to travel.

"If she gets on your nerves in New York, just stick out your foot and trip her. Maybe that'll shut her up."

Eleanor faked a laugh. "I'll remember that."

They made small talk about the girls in their dormitory, who had made which sorority line and who Nadine thought would win homecoming king and queen. Eleanor felt a pang; she was missing out on the festivities of her senior year, but it would be worth it. Their baby would make it so. After they had stuffed their bellies to the gills, Nadine rose from her seat. "I better head out. I'm taking an evening statistics class twice a week to make up for the one I failed last semester."

"That's because you were partying too much."

"Well, I have to pass it this time or I won't graduate on time and my parents would never let me hear the end of it."

Eleanor didn't want to get up and risk a hug. "That food weighed me to my chair. Do you mind seeing yourself out? I'm going to sit here and read awhile."

"Of course not." Nadine pecked her on the forehead and said, "Take good care of my godchild." And then she was off.

As the door clicked behind Nadine, Eleanor thought about that darn Greta.

After everything, she was still a thorn in Eleanor's thigh that would not come out.

Chapter Twenty-Nine

SLUT

Ruby

I waited outside the lounge for my turn with the social worker, Ms. Jeanne. We met every Tuesday, and I had seen her three times since I arrived at the Gingerbread House. The windows were open because Mother Margaret said the mid-September air was cleansing. My sweater no longer buttoned over my belly, but I pulled it tighter across my chest. Clara had been called in ahead of me. She had gone over last week, and when she returned from the clinic two days ago, she looked like she had aged three years. The door to the office was left slightly ajar, and from where I sat, I could hear every word.

"You are unfit to raise a child, Clara. You have no job, no husband and cannot support this baby."

Clara sighed. "I will not give up my child. It's my baby—"

"It's why your mother sent you here. So that you could give this child a real future. Something you are incapable of offering it. You are only sixteen."

"My boyfriend said—"

"If your boyfriend was planning to marry you, you wouldn't be here. He's moved on."

"But we love each other."

"Love doesn't dry the baby in the middle of the night or give it a place to live. Your child deserves more than being a bastard. It deserves two parents who will provide a good home."

Clara whimpered.

"Clara, please, don't make this harder on yourself. Sign the papers."

"I can't, it's not right." Her voice cracked.

"You lost your rights the moment you decided to be a slut and open your legs to that boy in the back of his car."

The word "slut" seemed to bounce off the walls, echoing in my ears. A minute later, Clara stumbled out of the room, her eyes puffy.

I walked in and sat across from Ms. Jeanne. She wore thick black glasses and a gray blazer over a white blouse. A string of pearls rested at her throat.

"Ruby, how are you doing?"

"I'm fine." The tiny room smelled like mothballs, reminding me of my grandmother Nene's trunk where she kept her wedding gown and important papers. I longed for her deep in my bones.

Ms. Jeanne read my information off my file sheet like we were meeting again for the first time.

"You are sixteen years old? Turning seventeen in November?"

I nodded.

"From Philadelphia, carrying a child who is of mixed race, due end of January. When we met last week, you said that you understood why you were here."

The baby started kicking. I had felt it move every day now, but this time it was different, like a message from within.

"Yes. I understand why I am here."

The baby stretched along the bottom of my stomach and I couldn't help rubbing it, letting it know that I was there.

Ms. Jeanne continued talking. It was the same speech each week. Eat well, rest up, pray, don't forget why I was there, the baby deserved better than me. I gave her a faint smile to acknowledge that I understood.

"Good, glad we are on the same page. I'll see you next week." She offered me a butterscotch from a crystal dish on her desk, and then sent me on my way.

On Tuesdays, we had silent reflection the hour before dinner. We were supposed to find a corner and pray, but I spent my time looking out the window at the trees, watching the squirrels scurry about. I was on my way to the downstairs toilet when I bumped into Bubbles coming through the door that led to the basement.

"What were you doing down there?"

She looked surprised, like I had caught her stealing food after the kitchen was closed. "Just checking the laundry for fresh tablecloths before dinner."

Her answer didn't make much sense, but before I could dig deeper, we heard a loud scream.

"Noooooo. Noooooooo."

Two of the lifers were dragging Clara down the hall. Mother Margaret held a gold cross in her hand, following behind them.

"We had a deal."

"I changed my mind."

"Shame!" she bellowed. "It doesn't work like that."

"I have rights," Clara screamed at the top of her lungs.

"The only right you have is twenty-four hours in the shaming room." Mother Margaret held her cross up to Clara's face. "O Divine Eternal Father, in union with your Divine Son and the Holy Spirit, and through the Immaculate Heart of Mary, I beg You to destroy the Power of your greatest enemy—the evil spirits of Satan. Banish his hold on this child's mind."

Clara's dress had flown up to her waist, and I could see that her panties were streaked with blood.

Mother Margaret turned and roared at the lot of us who stood watching. "Go find a place to pray, now!"

But I felt rooted in place as the other girls scrambled off. Clara gave a bloodcurdling cry, and then was hurled into the shaming room. When the door slammed and locked in place, Clara banged and shouted like her life depended on it.

"When we meet again, you better be ready to sign those papers," Mother Margaret snarled and then caught sight of me. "Care to join her, Ruby?"

I backed down the hall and turned into the classroom on shaky legs. When I asked Loretta, she said that no one knew for sure what was on the other side of that door. But from the bone-chilling sounds of Clara's cries, I knew I never wanted to find out for myself.

Bleating sirens woke me up before the sun rose, and commotion could be heard downstairs. Loretta walked over to the window and opened the curtains to reveal flashing lights.

I told the other girls I'd try to figure out what was going on—I had experience creeping around from when I lived with Inez, as she didn't like me moving around after ten o'clock. Said it was bad for her nerves. I tiptoed down to the second floor, where the porcelain girls slept. Two were peeking out the door. When I made it to the first-floor landing, I saw two men dressed in white jackets on opposite ends of an orange stretcher.

"She's breathing but out cold," said the burly man to the other.

My heart stopped. Clara. I could see her freckled face and stringy brown hair. I covered my mouth to push back the vomit that had choked up in my throat, then hurried back up, not as quietly as I came.

"What happened?" the girls on the second floor whispered.

"It's Clara," I murmured back, then ran the rest of the way to the attic. Bubbles closed the door behind me. When I sank into my cot, I felt like Georgia Mae; the words wouldn't come out.

"Snap out of it." Bubbles shook my shoulders. "Tell us."

"She was being wheeled out on a stretcher. They said she was breathing, but she looked dead to me."

Georgia Mae moved on one side of me, and then Loretta sat on the other until we were a tight circle.

I didn't know how much time had passed before the morning bell rang and we filed downstairs. We all picked at our breakfast in silence, knowing that this was yet another secret we'd be forced to keep. The last twenty-four hours had made two things abundantly clear: we young ladies had come to the Gingerbread House to turn over our babies whether we wanted to or not, and Mother Margaret and her heartless crew would stop at nothing to ensure that we surrendered them. The ghosts of Clara's cries echoed against my ear. I wanted Shimmy to swoop down and bust me out of here. How come he got to go on living his life footloose and I was stuck in here dealing with our consequences? Resentment pooled in the pit of my stomach, and I put down my fork, unable to eat another bite.

Chapter Thirty

SOMETHING AMISS

Eleanor

Eleanor had turned off the television and was heading up for bed when her telephone rang. She looked at the clock, sighed and picked up the receiver.

"Hello."

"Do you have a mother?"

"Mama."

"Don't 'Mama' me. When was the last time you called home? It's been a month of Sundays at best." She tsked her teeth.

Eleanor sank into the settee, blameworthy as charged. "I'm sorry. Things have been happening so quickly I can barely keep up." *I lost the baby, I'm in the middle of an adoption while trying to figure out how to fake a pregnancy.*

"Ain't no excuse. You at least need to check in. Even if it's only for two minutes so that I know you alive in that big city. Anything could happen to you."

"Oh, Ma. I'm fine and well."

"How's my grandbaby? She must be just a-dancing in your belly by now," her mother sang, and Eleanor could picture her round cheeks and those deep creases that marked her forehead when she smiled.

"I just can't wait to hold my first grandbaby in my arms." The line crackled with the static that was common during their long-distance calls. "I bet she comes out . . ."—staticky static—". . . ooking just like you."

"Why do you say that?"

"Oh, all the babies in our family look like us. We got strong genes and my people are known to have hair thick as rope. Your daddy's genes are what softened your hair out a bit," she chortled over a break of static. "You know he's hoping for a boy. But I know it's a girl. I done seen her in my dreams, with a little button nose."

Eleanor pulled the knitted throw over her lap, swallowing hard. Was the baby she lost the same baby her mother had dreamed about? She shuddered.

Thank goodness, her mother hadn't required much more than an "uh-ha" and a "you don't say" to keep her going. The line continued to crackle with bits of static, but Lorraine blabbered on. About the items she had purchased for the baby at the five-and-dime, and how she had all the people in church praying each Sunday and Wednesday for Eleanor to have a safe delivery.

"Now, I know you had two false starts, Sugar, but don't let that spook you. The third time is most definitely the charm. You hear me?"

Lorraine's voice was filled with such hope, it further confirmed that Eleanor was right in keeping the secret. She was doing her mother a favor.

"From your lips to God's ears, Mama. I know you got a pipeline to the man upstairs, and it's strong as steel."

"You better believe it."

They said their goodbyes, and Eleanor folded the throw across the back of the chair and carried herself upstairs. It was late, after ten o'clock. She couldn't remember the last time she'd gone to bed with William.

He'd been working odd hours and sometimes napped at the hospital so that he could complete his residency on a fast track. His goal was to finish up as close to the baby being born as possible. Or at least that's what he told her.

Stop it, she chided herself as she fluffed her pillows and climbed into bed. Eleanor hated the voice of doubt that had started creeping from the corners of her mind, haunting her ever since William had taken on more work. How could she doubt him? He had married her despite her defects, forgiven her when he found out that she had been dishonest, and worked long hours to become a doctor so that he could make a comfortable life for them. As much as she enjoyed archiving, it wouldn't provide a quarter of what William would for their family. But still, she wondered, how much work was there to be done to keep him away for so long? She knew her isolation was partly to blame for her paranoia. She missed her life on Howard's campus. She was lonely, but deep down she knew that she deserved this bit of penance. Infertility came with a price.

Rose had arranged to drop by in the morning with a carpenter for the work in the nursery. "This is Bernie," Rose said as a way of greeting her.

He was a tall man wearing blue overalls and a white long-sleeved T-shirt cuffed at his elbows. His skin was dark, like Swiss chocolate.

"How do you do." Eleanor rested her hand on her padded belly. She had gotten into the habit of wearing the pads each morning when she got dressed, as a way to bond with the idea of the coming baby.

"Morning, ma'am," he said, but didn't make eye contact. Bernie carried a silver toolbox in one hand, and had a heavy belt hanging from his waist.

"Let's head on up," Rose said and prompted Eleanor to show them the way to the bedroom.

As Rose walked about pointing out all the upgrades, Eleanor bristled at the financial details that she tossed back and forth with Bernie. It was hard to wrap her head around the amount of money Rose was willing to spend on aesthetics alone. Her own mother had told her that when she was born, they didn't have money for a crib, so they had used a dresser drawer.

Rose handed Bernie a deposit check. "Well, I'm off."

Eleanor thanked her and pressed her lips together in what she hoped resembled a smile.

"Nothing's too good for my grandchild," she said and then made her way out the door, leaving her signature scent of Chanel No. 5 in her wake.

Eleanor stood staring at the kitchen cabinets, listening to the commotion coming from the nursery. She was not used to having someone else in the house with her. Besides that one visit from Nadine and Rose's occasional drop-bys, Eleanor spent her days alone. Should she go up and offer Bernie something to drink? His footsteps echoed overhead as he moved back and forth, and then she heard drilling. After several moments, she decided to leave him be. Mrs. Porter had sent over a book of poems by Phillis Wheatley, and a handwritten foreword signed by John Hancock that Eleanor had been looking forward to sinking into. The book was even earlier than the collection of Wheatley's that William had gifted her when they were courting. It had been so long since he had requested a bedtime story from her, and she missed that easy time between them. She made herself comfortable in the den and was halfway through the book when she heard Bernie's footsteps on the stairs. She stood, touched her pads and met him in the kitchen.

"All done for today. Be back in the morning."

"Sounds good. Thank you."

Eleanor watched him walk out the back door with his toolbox. His shoulders were erect, and he held his head high. She recognized it as the Negro man's pride. Her own father carried himself the same way. She had assumed that he had a car outside, but as she watched from the window, she saw he was marching down her street. She wondered where he might live, and what type of life was awaiting his return.

After his first day, Bernie reported to work every morning at eight a.m. sharp, and that forced Eleanor out of bed and through her morning ritual without giving her the time to feel sorry for herself. Bernie preparing the nursery for their upcoming baby reminded Eleanor to focus on the blessing of it all.

On the third day Bernie worked upstairs, Eleanor was taking a home test in the den when she heard him singing. She put down her pencil and listened. The tune was so unlike anything she'd heard, but somehow it seemed familiar. Then it dawned on her: it was music that she had come across in her archiving. Before she thought it through, her feet carried her upstairs.

"Sorry to interrupt." She stood in the doorway. Bernie was up on a ladder, removing the light fixture from the ceiling. "Are you singing Big Drum music?"

Bernie looked down at her, surprised. A waxy sheen of sweat covered his face. "How'd you know a thing like that?"

"I'm an archivist at the library at Howard University. I've been helping my boss secure music, books and artifacts from across the African diaspora." She beamed proudly. *She wasn't just some privileged housewife.*

Bernie climbed down the ladder slowly.

"How do you know it?" She rested her back against the doorframe. Dust was everywhere and the room smelled of wood shavings.

"I am from Grenada."

"I should have guessed," she said, though she only knew a few West Indian students at Howard. "How long have you been in the States?"

"Nearly eight years. Come here at seventeen."

"How do you like it?"

"Depends on the day." He climbed back up the ladder, dangling a sheer light fixture that was shaped like a white cloud.

"Well, I'll be downstairs in the den. Let me know if you need anything." She backed out of the room.

As the days passed, Eleanor was surprised by how easy conversations flowed between her and Bernie. They had discussed his culture and music at every passing, and by his second week at the house, she felt comfortable bringing a Big Drum record up to the nursery.

"Would you like to hear something I've found?" she asked, clutching the record to her chest."

"If it's not too much trouble."

Eleanor stepped into the room. Bernie stopped hammering the shelves in place on the wall. In just the few days he'd been working she could see the baby's room starting to take shape.

Eleanor put the record on the player and then remembered that it was more proper for her to take the only seat in the room.

"What do you think?"

"Sound like Carriacouan, funeral music. Something we play when honoring the dead," he said, his accent growing thicker. Bernie went on to explain the instruments that she heard and what part each played. They were so deep in analyzing the music that when she heard William call her name from downstairs she jumped.

"Excuse me." She stood abruptly. "My husband is home." She picked up the record, tucked it in her bedroom and then met William in the hall at the top of the stairs.

"Hello, my darling wife," William said, pulling her into his arms.

"It's so good to see you." Eleanor snuggled against him. Their time had been so limited lately. William was only home for a few hours at a time, often coming in the middle of the night to shower, change, catnap, and when she woke in the morning he was already gone. Eleanor hadn't realized how badly she had ached for him until she put her nose into his neck and smelled his skin.

"How come you didn't let me know you were coming home early? I would have made supper."

"Baby, tonight's the Dr. Drew memorial fundraiser."

It was one of the events Rose had put on her appearance calendar. "Goodness, I guess I've mixed up the days," Eleanor said, over the hammering that started pounding from the nursery.

"Ah, the nursery. I haven't had a chance to peek my head in there. Best if I go in and introduce myself."

Eleanor followed William down the hall and into the bedroom. William extended his soft hand and shook Bernie's calloused one.

"Nice to meet you," William said, smiling. "Looks like you've got your work cut out for you in here."

"You've got a house with good bones, sir. No trouble at all." Eleanor had always thought of William as tall, but she couldn't help but notice how much taller Bernie was.

Eleanor threaded her arm through William's as they walked through the theater to the ballroom. She was giddy to be out of the house, even if it was for one of Rose Pride's events. At least she was breathing the fresh air and, most importantly, holding on to her husband's arm. Everything in her life seemed brighter when he was by her side. She had missed him.

"You look lovely," he breathed into her ear. "I can't wait to get you back home."

She giggled. "Don't start none."

"Consider this my reservation for later," he said, and let his hand fall down her waist, and Eleanor melted against him as they sailed across the parquet floors.

They had been instructed by Rose to arrive five minutes after the program was set to start, so that they could get to their seats without anyone stopping them. Already seated at the many round tables were the who's who of Washington, D.C., and Eleanor watched as William waved to several of his colleagues. She saw a few women who had attended Howard with her, but just smiled as she held on to William and they made their way to the table. The stuffing around her middle felt secure, and the loose dress she wore created a tent that concealed her shape, but it was her face that worried her. She knew she lacked the pudge that came with pregnancy, so she had added extra blush to her cheeks to give herself that pregnancy glow. William led her to their table, across from his parents and two other couples that Eleanor recognized as friends of theirs. The master of ceremonies had gotten choked up talking about Dr. Drew and took a few seconds to clear his throat, then dabbed at his eyes with a white handkerchief before continuing.

"'So much of our energy is spent in overcoming the constricting environment in which we live that little energy is left for creating new ideas or things. Whenever, however, one breaks out of this rather high-walled prison of the "Negro problem" by virtue of some worthwhile contribution, not only is he himself allowed more freedom, but part of the wall crumbles. And so it should be the aim of every student in science to knock down at least one or two bricks of that wall by virtue of his own accomplishment.' These are the wise words of our brother, Dr. Charles Drew, just three years before his untimely death."

The man finished by listing all of Dr. Drew's accomplishments, and then the room opened up in applause while William's father and his two friends whispered back and forth to each other.

"Rumors are still flying around about Drew's death. I think it was confirmed that the car accident happened in a sundown town."

One of the men sucked his teeth. "Driving in the rural South is detrimental to any Negro man's health."

"You know the way segregated hospitals are. I heard they put him in a ward and left him unattended."

William's father leaned in. "My colleague said it was Duke. When they got Drew to the hospital, they were told that they couldn't admit Negroes and that he'd have to go across town to the for Coloreds only hospital."

"He was denied the blood plasma that he helped develop? Now, that don't make no sense."

"They must think that all Negroes are second-class folks."

"His life was snuffed out because he was Negro . . . The hospital had plasma, but it was labeled 'white only,'" William added as Don Shirley concluded his song and took a bow.

Waiters carrying baskets to collect donations floated around the room.

Duke Ellington walked onstage, followed by his twelve-piece band. They played while dinner was being served. Dinner was Eleanor and William's cue to leave. Rose looked across the table and gave Eleanor a nod.

"I think I better excuse myself. The baby is just not agreeing with me right now."

"Oh, Eleanor, we understand. We've all been there," said Rose's friend, whose name eluded her.

"We better go," William said, putting down his napkin.

"Oh son, I'd hate for you to miss saying hello to Minnie Drew and catching up with the family. Lewis is outside with our car. He can drive Eleanor home. I'm sure Eleanor won't mind," Rose said with a lightness to her voice.

This was not a part of their plan. The whole table was looking at Eleanor. She wanted William to come home with her; they had not spent quality time together in so long. But how could she go against Rose publicly? She was cornered.

"Darling, your mother is right. I'm just going to lay down. You stay and enjoy yourself and mix with your old friends. I'll see you later tonight."

"Are you sure?" he asked, and she thought she saw a quick flash of relief wash over his face.

"Of course." Eleanor took his arm and allowed him to help her from the table. As they passed through the doors, Eleanor looked up to see none other than Greta Hepburn gliding in wearing a dress that clung to her like a second skin.

When William came home much later, Eleanor could smell the after-dinner brandy that he had probably shared with the men around the bar. He reached for her, but she moved her shoulder and settled deeper into her pillow, pretending to be asleep. Eleanor couldn't remember the last time they had been intimate, but she was too angry to feel aroused. William didn't push it. He rolled over to his side of the bed. Once Eleanor heard him snore, she opened her eyes and stared up at the ceiling, wondering why he had not tried harder for her affection. She looked over at her husband, watching as his chest rose and fell.

Chapter Thirty-One

SILENCE THE LAMB

Ruby

For my seventeenth birthday, I spent the morning on my bruised knees scrubbing the floors and repenting for my sins. After dinner, we watched a movie called *Come to the Stable*, a comedy drama about two French religious sisters who went to a small New England town and got the people to help build a children's hospital. It was better than nothing. Gertrude, the acne-faced lifer who was charged with making popcorn, conveniently ran out when it got to us girls from the attic.

Before we were sent to bed, a chocolate cake with candles appeared on the round dining table, and I was floored when Kitchen Sister Kathleen suggested that everyone sing "Happy Birthday" to me. It was the sweetest thing that had happened since I arrived at the Gingerbread House, and the tastiest treat I had received. When we reached our attic room, I changed into my nightgown feeling content.

As I lay on my bed clutching the birthday card from Aunt Marie, the baby kicked, and I wondered if Shimmy was thinking of me. Did he even remember that my birthday was November 17? He had sent three letters since I arrived, but they remained unopened in the bottom of my drawer. The only way I could get through this was to block him out completely, and I had done it well until today. All afternoon, I had craved a chocolate-covered pretzel from his fingertips, the sugary smell of our spot in the storage room behind the candy store, the sound of his voice at my ear and the brush of his hands through my hair.

My daydream was interrupted by the sound of Bubbles jerking up from her cot. She turned a light on just as a stream of water gushed from between her legs, dripping onto the floor.

"Are you peeing yourself?" Loretta scooted back on her cot, looking horrified.

"I think my water just broke!" She doubled over her stomach.

"What does that mean?" I asked dumbfoundedly.

In the three months that I had lived at the Gingerbread House, no one had said a word about what happened when a girl went over. The girls would return to the house from the clinic tight-lipped, reluctant to share any details.

"Means the baby is coming." Bubbles bit her lips.

"I'll run for help." I moved toward the door.

"No," she hissed. "I'ma have this baby right here on my own. Then we jumping out the window together and going home."

Loretta clucked her tongue in a way that suggested that Bubbles was crazy.

"I told you I'm not giving these crazy nuns my baby, and I mean it." Her face was sober and eyes clear. "My grandmama was the midwife in her parish. I already stole some clean cloths, pads and scissors. Look under my mattress."

Georgia Mae lifted the left side, revealing Bubbles's stash of items.

"Bubbles, this is stone madness. You can't deliver the baby yourself." I crossed my arms in front of my belly.

"In the motherland women go into the bush, labor alone and then come back holding up a baby. I can do this. I will do this," she said, even as her face contorted in pain.

What she didn't say was that in those faraway villages, women died in childbirth all the time. I had read about poor countries in my world history book and knew the risks. Not to mention the consequences if Mother Margaret found out that we'd helped. She could call Mrs. Shapiro, I could lose my scholarship.

Loretta and I looked at each other, both without the faintest idea of what to do. But then Georgia Mae went to Bubbles and started rubbing her back. Her pain came about every ten minutes, and each time, Georgia Mae took a deep breath in and let it slowly out, gesturing to Bubbles to do the same, until they fell into a rhythm. I finally got my head out of the clouds, folded up some blankets and stuffed them under our door so that the noise wouldn't penetrate. It would also act as a barrier if Mother Margaret made one of her impromptu visits to our floor.

"Turn out the lights," Bubbles requested. "Better for them to think we sleep."

In the dark, the three of us rallied around Bubbles.

"Are you sure about this?" Loretta murmured.

"Goldie, I never wanted to come here in the first place. I'm only here because my daddy is the pastor of our church." Bubbles bit her lip like she had said too much.

Mother Margaret had given strict orders for us to not disclose personal details with each other. For the most part, we'd abided by the house's code of secrecy, but then Bubbles rolled her eyes and said, "Fuck it. Y'all the closest I have to family round here. I want you to know who I am." She looked at each one of us and then sank into her pillow.

In between the birth pains that rippled through her, Bubbles talked. Her voice took my mind off what was happening, and I was certain it did the same for her. Made her less afraid. She told us that her mother was the perfect first lady, prim and proper, and how every Sunday she played the part in her fancy hats and fine apparel. Bubbles had been sent to the home so that her slip in judgment wouldn't embarrass her parents in front of their precious congregation.

"When I missed two periods, Ray went to my parents and asked for my hand in marriage, but they told him no."

She readjusted the pillows at her back and told us that Ray was older, twenty-five to her seventeen. Ray had been married before and his wife had overdosed on pills. Everyone assumed that Ray had been the cause of her unhappiness, but he told Bubbles that it didn't matter what he did, she was just sad. She left behind a two-year-old daughter that Ray's mother helped Ray raise.

Bubbles squeezed my hand hard, and even in the dark I could tell she was experiencing a bad pain. After a deep breath, she told us that Ray worked as a janitor at her high school.

"It started off friendly. Hi and bye, that sort of thing. But then one day I ran into him at the county fair. I was walking with some friends, and he was trying to win his daughter a stuffed panda. When I saw him, I separated from my girlfriends and walked the fair with the two of them. I loved how sweet he was to me," she said, chuckling. "At first, he didn't want no part of me. Said I was too young, but then he quickly got over it."

The three of us stayed up taking turns comforting Bubbles throughout the night. Georgia Mae took a wet towel and put it on the back of Bubbles's neck to cool the sweat that wouldn't stop dripping. Bubbles moaned with her mouth closed, but I could tell things were getting worse, and after a while it was harder for her to contain the volume of her moans. Loretta told me to sneak down into the kitchen to get her something to eat.

With each passing hour, Bubbles's grunts got deeper, and her body writhed in pain. I plugged her pillow between her teeth to muffle her sounds, but then she pushed me away and threw up all over the floor.

"I can't do this," Bubbles said faintly.

Loretta kept up a steady rub on her back and shoulders. "You almost there."

"She is?" I looked at Loretta, who shrugged her shoulders in a way that told me she was just trying to comfort Bubbles. I was starting to seriously worry: What if Bubbles and the baby died right before our eyes? We didn't know what we were doing. Just when I decided that it was best to go for help, Bubbles said, "I feel it slipping down. Give me that damn pillow and help me get it out."

We sprang into action. I shoved the pillow back into her mouth and let her squeeze my hand as she cried out. Loretta stood holding an armful of towels and Georgia Mae squatted between her legs. The two of them did what looked like a dance of push and pull and push and pull, and then Bubbles roared like she was being split open. The bed shook and Loretta moved to keep it from knocking against the floor. When I looked down, Georgia Mae was holding on to a brown little thing covered in blood. Birdlike cries filled the attic room immediately.

Tears bursts in my eyes. Somehow, we'd done it. The four of us, with no training, had managed to bring Bubbles's baby into the world.

Bubbles looked on the verge of passing out, but then Georgia Mae placed the baby on her chest. As Bubbles brought her little girl to her face, I released more tears. I was in awe. I had witnessed a person coming into the world. Would I feel this way when I gave birth, too? I'd tried to think of the thing inside me as an egg, nothing more, but seeing Bubbles's baby made it harder. Suddenly I cringed at the reality of what I was at the Gingerbread House to do.

The baby hollered as Bubbles tried to get her swollen breast into her mouth. After a few tries and with Georgia Mae's help, the baby caught on and settled down.

"Joy comes in the morning." Bubbles's voice was raspy with fatigue. "I'm going to name her Joy."

The sky was still dark as mother and child drifted off to sleep. Blood was everywhere. How were we supposed to get this cleaned up without anyone catching us? But while I was frozen in fear, Georgia Mae was already fast at work balling up bloody linen. I got some water from the sink and wiped down the floor. We hid the bloody blankets behind one of the chests of drawers, and then Georgia Mae sponged off Bubbles and fixed her with two thick Kotex from the stolen supplies.

By the time the breakfast bell rang out over the PA system, I was exhausted. Loretta, Georgia Mae and I headed downstairs together. I had gone over several excuses in my head of why Bubbles wasn't with us, but when we got downstairs Mother Margaret was heading toward the door with a girl hunched over in labor. She called over her shoulder to Little Sister Bethany to hold down the house.

"I have some errands to run after I get her settled at the clinic. I'll be back sometime after dinner."

A day without Mother Margaret meant that luck was on our side. I breathed a sigh of relief as I sat down and ate my clumpy oatmeal, hoping the nourishment would make up for my lack of sleep. Since it was Sunday, we had church services with the old priest we had dubbed Father Time. The three of us sat in our little corner and dozed through his sermon, but he was likely too senile to notice.

Georgia Mae's muteness worked in our favor. She was essentially invisible, and slipped upstairs throughout the day with fresh pads and food for Bubbles to eat without anyone noticing. It wasn't until after dinner that Kitchen Sister Kathleen asked about Bubbles.

"Doesn't she usually clean the pots?" She tightened her thin lips.

"Her back is hurting so I offered to switch with her, just for tonight," Loretta spoke up then moved over to the utility sink.

Kitchen Sister Kathleen nodded, and then continued packing up the leftover turkey legs and gravy in clear storage containers. Once we had restored the kitchen and dining area, Little Sister Bethany made us sit for nightly devotion. We sang the same old hymns, but instead of the usual Bible verses, Little Sister Bethany read the story of the Tower of Babel from the book of Genesis. It was a welcomed reprieve. When we were finally permitted to return to our room, Bubbles was sitting up with the baby against her breasts.

"How is she doing?" I asked, leaning in to see her face.

"She's perfect in every way. Want to hold her?"

I nodded and she turned the baby over into my arms. She smelled so sweet. I felt a little tug on my breasts that startled me.

"Let me," said Loretta, and I passed the baby off to her. That's how the four of us spent our evening, passing the baby back and forth and fussing over her.

When she cried, we did our best to quiet her. Bubbles had just settled her down from a spell when we heard the doorknob turn in its hinges. It was way past the time when anyone would venture up to check on us. Had we been too loud? Did someone know about the baby? The blankets stuffed under the door restricted movement, but the person on the other end kept pushing and pushing until it slid across the floor.

Everything that I'd have to give up for helping Bubbles flashed before my eyes as the door opened. But it wasn't Mother Margaret. It was Gertrude, the acne-face lifer who had tipped over my bucket and denied us popcorn on movie night. The secret was out. She would report us to Mother Margaret, and Bubbles's baby would be taken away. All our hard work had been for nothing.

Gertrude looked around the room, and then her eyes fell on Bubbles rocking the baby. "You ready?"

Bubbles nodded and made to get up from her cot.

"Better hurry then, the coast is clear."

"What's happening?" I looked at Bubbles as she bundled up the baby.

"Gertrude's helping me bust out of here. Ray's going to meet us outside at midnight."

"What?" I said incredulously. "How do you know you can trust her? And what if he's not there?" I moved to stop her.

"Gertrude's cool, don't worry. It was all an act to cover our tracks. We've been planning this breakout for weeks. Ray's going to drop her off on our way. She's getting out of here, too."

Bubbles hugged Georgia Mae and then Loretta, who had started crying. "Thanks for helping me through this. I couldn't have done it without you three."

She grabbed me hard, and I whispered for her to be careful.

"Me and Ray gonna raise his girls together. It's the right choice, I can feel it in my gut."

I kissed the baby on her forehead, taking in her sweet scent for the last time. Gertrude opened the door, and then they were gone.

Chapter Thirty-Two

TELLING STORIES

Eleanor

Eleanor was not eight months pregnant, but if she were, her baby would be the size of a cantaloupe, weighing between four and five pounds. At this stage, she might occasionally see the baby's hands and feet protrude through her belly. The extra tooting of gas would turn her face red with embarrassment, especially in front of William. With D.C. being so cold and icy in November, she'd have to be more careful when out for walks, because her center of gravity would have shifted. But on *Expectant Mother*'s long list of pregnancy symptoms, there were two that Eleanor did not need to fake: insomnia and restlessness.

Sometimes when she was especially lonely, she wondered whether she'd really needed to go to such lengths to bring a baby into their lives, or whether she'd needed to hide the adoption. Perhaps she would have been looked at as a celebrated hero in the Prides' social circle for rescuing a child from an unwed mother. A modern-day trendsetter, not an infertile woman raising an illegitimate child.

The truth was that Eleanor didn't know anyone who had adopted. The whole idea had been foreign to her before meeting Mother Margaret. When she was growing up, children would come up from the South to stay with an aunt or grandmother and never leave. A childless, married woman would disappear for a season, and then show up at church rocking a baby. No one asked questions but people still whispered behind closed doors. Eleanor couldn't bear the thought of being on the receiving end of more whispers. She figured she was being talked about enough, as the poor girl from the industrial streets of Elyria whom the dashing William Pride had rescued. Or something close to that.

The home that Mother Margaret ran was largely for white women. The few Negro girls allowed must have the means to pay. Eleanor had spent a lot of time curious about these unwed girls. Where had they come from? Did they have any say in giving away their babies? Did it break their hearts, or had they willingly handed their infants over? When she was being honest, she knew she wanted to visit the place and have a peek at the house where her child was being incubated. But she was scared that she'd find out that life for the girls wasn't the easy picture Mother Margaret had painted for her, which would be more than she could handle. But being cooped up had given Eleanor plenty of time to daydream.

In her head she had started referring to the home as the House of Eve. Eve as in Adam and Eve, the first mother of all living things. She tried to picture what *her* Eve looked like. Was she tall or short, have long hair or bobbed? Was she carrying the baby high or low? And the question that plagued her the most: Was Eve happy to turn her baby over to the loving care of William and Eleanor for her second chance, as Mother Margaret had put it, or was that all hogwash?

It was the Monday before Thanksgiving, and William was set to leave for Theodore's engagement dinner on Tuesday afternoon. He had promised her all weekend that he'd be home so that they could spend time together before he left, but he had phoned each day with a delay. Today, he had been given a rotation in the emergency room and two children had come in with severe dog bites, and he didn't know when he'd be home.

Eleanor was used to being alone from her years in Ohio as an only child. With her parents working all the time, she'd had to learn to be independent. But this was different. Eleanor felt more isolated than self-sufficient. Howard was closed for the holiday break, so she didn't have any papers to write or library work to keep her mind occupied.

To pass the time, she cleaned every inch of every room in the house. When she was done, not a speck of dust could be found on any of the furniture or floors. Both her kitchen and two bathrooms smelled of bleach, and all the laundry had been folded and put away. Still, she had too much time left in the day.

A nugget of relief washed over her when she heard the telephone ring, and she dashed off to the den to pull it from the cradle.

"Hello, Sugar." Crackle, crackle, static.

"Mama!" she exclaimed, so happy to hear her mother's voice.

"How's it going?"

"Fair to middling." Eleanor snuggled against the settee with her feet folded underneath her.

"Is the baby moving around a lot? You eating your fruits and vegetables?"

"Yes, kicking up a fuss," she said, and then recited a few symptoms and stats she had read about for this stage of pregnancy. A bad wave of static crackled between them and Eleanor had to repeat most of it. As she fabricated her condition, pangs of guilt rumbled through her belly. She hated lying to her mother and reasoned it was for Lorraine's own good.

"Well, I hate to be the bearer of bad news, but Sister Pryor died a few days ago from a heart attack. Our little church is falling apart over it. You know she was everyone's mother."

Eleanor clutched her chest. It felt like she'd had the wind knocked out of her. "Oh, Ma. So sorry to hear that."

Sister Pryor had been Eleanor's babysitter when she was too little to go to school. She had fond memories of eating peach cobbler and listening to soap operas on the radio with her.

"I wish you could come home for the funeral. It would be good to see you, and I'd love to rub that baby in your belly."

"Me too, Mama, but the doctor says I can't travel in my condition. I don't even leave the house anymore. Just here waiting," she said over a pop of static.

"That's probably for the best. Can't ever be too careful, 'specially with your history."

Eleanor cringed. "You're right."

"Well, maybe I can come down and see you."

Eleanor could hear the longing in her mother's voice. She would have loved nothing more than to have her mother comb her hair, bake her a pound cake and pull her head into her lap.

"Mama, we agreed that it was best you come after the baby is born in January. That's when I'll really need you here. And you can stay longer. We are living in a construction zone right now, with the baby's room being set up."

"You doing all that for a baby who ain't gonna remember much of anything."

"Well, Rose insisted, and I'm just trying to keep the peace."

Her mother tsked her teeth. "Is she still all up in your business?"

Eleanor didn't want there to be tension between the sets of parents, so she lied, again. "No, she's simmered down quite a bit."

"Well, I called you this late 'cause the rates drop, but that don't make it free. I better go on and check on those apple pies in the oven."

Eleanor badly wanted to be able to tell her mother the truth about everything. Instead, they bid each other so long, but Eleanor clutched the phone well after the howler tone howled.

When Eleanor woke up the next morning, William was beside her in bed. She cuddled up to him and put her head on his chest. She loved listening to the sound of his heartbeat. He stroked her head, and then pulled her face to his and kissed her.

"Good morning."

"I miss this. Waking up to you."

"I do too." He traced his fingers down the side of her neck.

"Don't leave me." She climbed on top of him and ran her tongue along the edge of his ear.

"Baby," he exhaled, and then his hands were everywhere. He gripped Eleanor's hips and guided them toward his. They clung, sweating against each other as she locked her legs around his. After several breathless rolls and thrusts, William groaned and then collapsed against his pillow.

"I can't wait until my residency is over, so I can have more of you," he said, looking deep into her eyes. Her hair was damp against her forehead and her body tingled everywhere.

"Don't go to the engagement party." She ran her fingers across his stomach.

"I have to. You know that."

"Then I'm going with you." Eleanor threw the covers back off her feet and traipsed naked over to her closet.

"Elly, you can't," William stammered. "It's too risky."

"I'll be careful. Stay back at the hotel with my feet up while you go to the celebration. You can say that I'm resting."

William crossed the room and reached for her. "Baby, I'd love for you to come. Nothing would make me happier, but we are so close to pulling this off. It's just a few weeks more."

Eleanor knew that William was right. But she couldn't endure being alone for days at a time again. Not over a holiday. Not with Greta Hepburn prancing around waiting to sink her claws into William. She wanted him to stay with her, she wanted William to choose her, but she said none of this as they showered together and as she watched him dress.

William swept her up in his arms, kissed her lips and then rested his forehead against hers.

"Hey, don't look so down. I'll be back on Saturday and we'll have our Thanksgiving dinner then. Keep my side of the bed warm for me." He squeezed her hand, and then she watched the back she loved so much move away from her and into his world, the one where she still didn't belong.

Chapter Thirty-Three

SECRETS GIRLS KEEP

Ruby

Clara hadn't been returned to the Gingerbread House after she was taken to the hospital. Rumors swirled around, but the consensus was that she had tried to kill herself in the shaming room. Loretta said she had it on good authority that she had tied her shirt around her neck and tried to hang herself but only succeeded in passing out. Mother Margaret never said a word about Clara, but she did yell and lecture on Bubbles and Gertrude, who had somehow successfully escaped through the basement window. And Mother Margaret was madder than a pissed-on chicken.

The walls around our little prison were erected even higher. We were counted like preschoolers, our movements restricted. A guard was hired to walk the outside premises, and we were no longer allowed to return to our rooms throughout the day. We even needed permission to go to the toilet. All of the Gingerbread House girls were questioned several times, but Loretta and I stuck to our story.

"She must have slipped out in the middle of the night while we were sleeping. No, I don't think she had the baby."

No one expected anything from Georgia Mae, who got rid of the bloody sheets and afterbirth on garbage day. She had restored our attic room with no evidence that anything had happened.

Under our new confined system, the days drifted even more slowly than they had before. Things were even more miserable without Bubbles to make us laugh. I thought of her often. She was so brave to keep her baby and deal with the consequences; I'd never be that brave. Was I doing the right thing by giving my baby up? Should I have leaped from Mrs. Shapiro's car with Shimmy and run away with him? I'd been so focused on going to college and making something of myself that I never entertained that I could be like Bubbles and fight to have it all. But as quickly as these thoughts came, I shoved them to the back of my mind and locked them away. It was the only way I could get through this.

On the Tuesday before Thanksgiving, two girls went into labor within hours of each other, and Georgia Mae was one of them. The white girl was ushered out the back door into a van. When Georgia Mae made to follow, Mother Margaret stopped her.

"The clinic is for whites only. You come with me." Then Mother Margaret caught my eyes. "Ruby, why don't you come and help her get settled."

We followed Mother Margaret down three short steps and into her office. It was a cozy room with two large bookshelves, an oak desk and matching swivel chair. A framed painting of Jesus hung crookedly from the wall and the room smelled faintly of gin. Mother Margaret's habit swished around her feet as she opened the narrow door between the two bookshelves. The room inside was dark and windowless. It was barely a room at all—more like an oversized storage closet, containing only a twin bed pressed against the wall and a folding chair.

Mother Margaret thrust a Bible into my hand. "Read from 1 Corinthians, Ephesians and the book of Mark. The nurse will be called when it's time." She spun on her heels, closing the door behind her. I squeezed Georgia Mae's hand and placed the Bible under my chair.

Since Georgia Mae didn't talk, I rambled on, reciting stories from the books that I read. I rubbed her back the way she had done for Bubbles and mopped the sweat from her brow. Two hours later, Georgia Mae's pains had escalated to the point that she was hollering like something was ripping her apart from the inside. I hadn't known she could make such sounds. Eventually, a nurse came and sent me away. I was relieved; I wasn't eager to witness another birth so soon.

Georgia Mae's baby boy was born so fair-skinned that it was almost hard to believe that a girl with such rich, inky skin had birthed him. I was glad when Mother Margaret made it my job to check on her and help with the baby. While Georgia Mae recovered in that little back room, I brought her warm rags and clean pads, hot black tea and vegetable stew, then held the baby so that she could check her bleeding and relieve herself in the bathroom. She was given no medication, and I could see her pain in the depths of her eyes.

On the fifth day after Georgia Mae gave birth, I was on my way to Mother Margaret's office when I overheard her and our social worker, Ms. Jeanne, conversing.

"Georgia Mae Rowe has no parents. Her employer brought her in. A white lady from Roanoke. According to her paperwork, a distant aunt who lives in Richmond would like to adopt the baby," Ms. Jeanne said.

"Hmph, that child is too fair-skinned to live among poor Negroes. We have clients much better suited to raise that boy—clients who I'm sure would give a substantial donation."

I heard some papers shuffle.

"It's a few weeks too early for my D.C. doctor couple, and their baby will be Loretta's. There is a couple in New York that has been waiting patiently. The husband is a lawyer and I'm sure a prized boy would bring in extra—"

Just then, I dropped a spoon from the edge of the tray I'd been carrying.

"Who's there?" Mother Margaret barked.

I stepped into the room.

"Child. Do make yourself known as you walk about. Drop off the food and then get to class." Mother Margaret frowned.

I hustled through the door with the tray of tomato soup. Ms. Jeanne pushed back from her seat, watching me. With her keeping such close company, there was no way I could relay what I had heard without being caught. I wanted to warn Georgia Mae that her son wouldn't be placed with her aunt where she could see him from time to time, but instead would be sent to a family elsewhere, but there was no way. Besides, when I entered the room, Georgia Mae and the baby boy were fast asleep. I left the food for her on the folding chair, and Ms. Jeanne closed the door softly behind me. As I crossed back through Mother Margaret's office, she called my name.

"Yes, Your Excellency?"

"Mrs. Shapiro called this morning. She asked me to remind you not to forget why you were here and what's at stake. I know that Bubbles was your friend."

"I am aware, Your Excellency."

She looked me up and down with a scowl on her pinched face. "We will take care of Georgia Mae from here. You are dismissed from this post. Hurry along to charm class."

That night, when Loretta and I were alone in our room, I disclosed what I had overheard.

"We all know why we are here," she mustered lethargically. Loretta's nose had spread and it sounded like it was hard for her to breathe. "I just want to get this over with and go home. I can't take it anymore."

Between worrying over Georgia Mae and listening to Loretta's snores, I barely slept, but I cried for all of us in my pillow until it was soaked. How much more of this house of crazy could I take? My legs were restless, and I kept tossing them in and out of my covers all night. When it was time for breakfast, I told Loretta to say that I was in bed sick. Little Sister Bethany came up a few minutes later and took my temperature.

"What's wrong?"

"I'm just so tired," I said.

She looked deep in my eyes. "Rest, child. Please make sure that's all you do. We can't afford anymore incidents around here."

I nodded, turned toward the wall and fell into a deep sleep. I was dreaming about swimming in the ocean at Chicken Bone Beach in Atlantic City with Aunt Marie and her gang from Kiki's when the door to our room burst open.

It was Georgia Mae. Her shoulders drooped forward, and her thin top was damp with milk rings.

"What's wrong?" My voice was husky with sleep.

She collapsed into a heap on her cot. The cry that emerged from her mouth sounded like a wound that would never heal.

"Nooo" came from her lips, and I was startled that Georgia Mae had a voice. This whole time I thought she had been born special.

"Georgia Mae? What happened?"

"They. Took. Him. Away. They took my baby. My David."

I moved next to her on her cot and rocked her in my arms. Soon, the top of my gown was soaked in her tears. Finally her moans died to a muffle, and we sat in silence for a bit. After a few minutes, Georgia Mae turned her face up to the ceiling. Her eyes were dead, but her lips started moving.

"This my second child by that man." She dragged out the word "man" with venom. "I work in their nice house, filled with their fancy things. Cleanin' and chasin' behind their nasty kids." Her voice was hoarse but deep. She fell quiet for a while. So quiet that I thought she had retreated into herself again. Georgia Mae touched her hands to her stomach. It had caved in like a baked cake that had fallen just before it rose.

"First child I had by him at thirteen. Only had my monthly visitor two times before he catch me in the shed. That wife, she pretend not to know. Even when my belly grow. After the baby came, someone from the state show up at the house and took my girl away." Her voice quivered. "I named that one Charlotte."

Georgia Mae stared at the wall, never looking my way. Her pain weaved itself around me, choking me like it was my own.

"When he caught me again and my belly poked, that wife always pickin' on me. Say I'm a whore, called me prostitute. Always shoutin' mean things. Then she told me to get in the car and brought me here."

"You had an aunt that you hoped would take David?" I asked, recalling the conversation I had overheard.

She shook her head yes. "I scratched out a letter to my aunt when I got here, and she agreed. They all said yes, but they lie. All of them." She started crying again.

"What happened downstairs?" I asked.

She wiped her face with the edge of her shirt. "David was feedin'. It was late, middle of the night when I heard footsteps. Then three of them burst through the door. Two of those lifer girls held me down while the nurse snatched David right from my tit. He wailed as his milk leaked down my waist. When I tried to get up to follow him, they closed the door and locked me in. I banged and banged but they left with my baby." Fresh tears flowed down her cheeks and I pulled her tight.

"Ain't right to birth two babies and not have none."

After she told me everything, Georgia Mae lost her voice again. The next morning, she was moved from our room, down to the laundry with the rest of the lifers. Loretta and I didn't see her much, but when we did, she barely made eye contact. And I never heard her voice again.

Chapter Thirty-Four

STRANGE FRUIT

Eleanor

When the Thanksgiving Day Parade ended, Eleanor let the television run as background noise, while she worked on a 275-piece Whitman jigsaw puzzle that her father had sent her called *Off to the Chase*. It had a picture of a red-coated Englishman on a horse surrounded by hound dogs out on a hunt. Working a puzzle was a holiday tradition that she had shared with her father until she left for Howard, and as Eleanor's fingers moved over the pieces, pressing them into place, she felt at peace.

The sun was long gone when Eleanor drew herself a hot lavender bath, and it wasn't until she sank into the soapy water that her brain started clicking. It was as if the steam from the bath loosened the barrier she had constructed around her mind that blocked Theodore's engagement party out.

Knowing Rose, Eleanor was sure the engagement party was taking place at the fanciest venue where Negroes were permitted. The table would be set with elaborate sprays of flowers, illuminated with white pillar candles. All the guests would be draped in their finest clothing, trendy hats, gold watches and sparkly jewels.

Theodore Pride, whom Eleanor had only met a handful of times because he lived in New York, would sit at the helm with his lovely bride-to-be smiling up at him, much to Rose Pride's delight.

Her darling William would be wearing his navy morning suit that had been tailored just right. Greta would be seated across from him. Eleanor could picture it: Greta's straight hair twirling off her shoulders and a sweetheart neckline boosting her cleavage. Whenever William made one of his jokes she would lean forward and giggle, giving him a peek of what she had to offer. All while her eyes conveyed: *I am a much better lay than your wife. Let me show you.*

All the families present at the party were rooted in similar histories. They had attended the same universities—Spelman, Morehouse, Hampton and Howard—and run in the same social circles and intermarried for generations.

As Eleanor scooped water over her face, she tried to keep from imagining the worst. William loved her and that was all that mattered. She had a beautiful roof over her head, and they were having a baby. It didn't matter where it came from, the child would be theirs and they would love it. Nothing at that engagement dinner could change that, not even Greta.

On Friday, Eleanor ignored the turkey still in the fridge and made herself some Aunt Jemima pancakes. As she poured a dribble of warm syrup over her plate, she was startled by a knock at the back door. It was Bernie, peering through the glass. Eleanor hadn't put on her stomach paddings, so she turned her back and hurried from the kitchen, hoping he wouldn't get a glimpse of her flat belly through the sheer curtains. When she returned to let him in, she reminded herself to waddle.

"Bernie! I wasn't expecting you today," she said with too much glee in her voice, and she saw him blush under her attention.

"Sorry to disturb you. The boards for the shelving unit just came in and I wanted to make sure they fit while I had my friend's truck."

"Come on in, it's freezing," she said, closing the door behind him. "I was just having breakfast. Would you like some pancakes?"

He looked at her incredulously. They had become quite friendly over the past few weeks, chatting about music, his childhood in Grenada, her work at the library, but to eat together was too familiar. Eleanor bit her bottom lip, knowing that her loneliness had loosened her tongue.

"No, ma'am, I just ate. If it's all right with you, I'm just going to get the boards from the truck and carry them up."

Eleanor got out of the way and returned to her food at the kitchen table. Bernie hummed as he moved up the stairs, and the sound comforted her. After she wolfed down her pancakes and washed the dishes, she couldn't help herself from going upstairs.

"Mind if I sit?" She pointed to the rocking chair that had been delivered a few days earlier.

Bernie had rolled up his sleeves, exposing his muscular mocha arms, and she wondered for the umpteenth time about his family. Where did he live? Was he married with children? Or alone.

"As long as your husband don't mind," he said, then called over his shoulder, "the fumes and all from the paint."

"It's dry by now."

"It is but the smell lingers."

"I'll be fine. My husband went to New York for his brother's engagement party. I couldn't travel in my condition."

"You spent Thanksgiving alone?" Bernie moved toward the window and opened it, letting in a sliver of fresh air.

"All my family lives in Ohio. But it wasn't so bad," she added. "How was yours?"

"Not a holiday that we celebrate. I just got together with some friends and played cricket."

"Did you eat turkey and collard greens?" she chuckled.

"Naw. We had chicken, rice and peas. Few slices of avocado."

"Avocado?"

"You never had one before?"

"No."

"We'll have to fix that," he said with his singsong laugh.

As the minutes drifted into hours, they fell into an easy rhythm. Bernie sang his songs, and Eleanor handed him the screws, nails and hammer when he called for them. By late afternoon, all the shelving had been installed and the crib was nearly assembled.

Eleanor went downstairs as Bernie packed up, making trips out to the truck with his supplies. She was wondering how she'd spend the rest of the evening when Bernie returned through the back door with something in his hand.

"This is an avocado, ma'am." He held the dark green oval-shaped object out to her. "All you have to do is slice it in half, scoop out the inside and mash it with a little salt."

"Is it a vegetable or fruit?"

"Fruit. My mother always said, an avocado a day keeps the doctor away."

"Mine would say an apple." Eleanor brought the strange fruit to her nose.

"Well, since you brought it, I insist you share it with me before you go." She went to the drawer and pulled out a knife, a spoon and a cutting board.

"Do you serve it with crackers?"

"You can. Or vegetables, like carrots or peppers." He was a tall man, and his presence filled the space.

Eleanor reached into the icebox and pulled out a bunch of freshly chopped carrots. "My mother just told me that I needed to eat more vegetables."

Bernie picked up the spoon and dished a little avocado onto each of their plates. They stood at the counter, dipping carrot sticks in the avocado. It was creamy and much more delicious than she had imagined.

"That is good."

"Told you." Bernie chewed.

"So, do you have family here?" she asked innocently.

"Something like that" was all he offered, and Eleanor wondered, a sister, a brother, a wife?

Just then, the back door creaked open and William walked in, carrying his traveling bag. Bernie stepped back from the counter as William looked from one of them to the other.

"Honey, you're home early," Eleanor said. "I thought you said Saturday."

"Evening, Mr. Pride." Bernie nodded toward William, and then he carried his plate to the sink. "I had better go."

"Thanks for the avocado," Eleanor called after him as a gush of wind blasted through the open door.

William dropped his bag and locked the back door. Then he turned his attention to Eleanor. "What was that?"

"What was what?" Eleanor took another bite of avocado and carrot.

"You eating with . . ."

"Bernie. His name is Bernie, and he was just sharing an avocado with me."

"That all you do?"

"Are you serious?" She looked up at him, and when she realized that he was for real, her anger spiked quick as a hot flash. "You come in here accusing *me* when you've been off in New York doing God knows what?"

"I was at my brother's engagement party."

"With Greta," she spat before she could stop herself.

"What does she have to do with anything?"

"Oh, give it a rest. I know she still has a thing for you. Your mother won't let me forget it. I bet she was in your face all weekend, happy that you left your little pregnant wife at home."

"Unlike you I have nothing to hide," he said steely-eyed, and his meaning was not lost on Eleanor.

She hissed between clenched teeth, "And I was just being polite."

"Standing around the kitchen sharing food like old pals is more than just polite, especially when I'm out of town. He shouldn't have been here."

"Jealousy doesn't suit you."

"Dishonesty doesn't suit *you*," he said, grabbing up his bag and heading for the stairs. "You should know better."

It was crystal clear to Eleanor that this argument was about more than the avocado. She pushed her plate to the side and cut him off in the upstairs hallway.

"Have you ever spent a major holiday alone, William?"

"You knew what we were getting into when we started this."

"We? More like me, William. I'm the one cooped up in this house day and night, hour after hour, while you are out having the time of your life."

He unfastened the shirt buttons around his wrist, color rising in his face. "I spend my days and nights at the hospital so that I can become a doctor and support you. Plus, let's not forget that this was your idea to hide out in the first place."

"So as not to embarrass you!"

William stopped just beyond the doorway. Eleanor hadn't made their bed that morning and William looked at her and shook his head. "I'm tired, it's been a long day. Why don't you go back and finish your avocado?"

Eleanor wanted to reach up and choke him, but instead she shouted, "Why don't you take a long walk off a short pier!" then stormed out of the bedroom.

Chapter Thirty-Five

HOLIDAY BLUES

Ruby

Christmas fell on a Monday. The day before the holiday, Little Sister Bethany dragged in a skinny, four-foot Christmas tree that we took turns trimming with paper ornaments and strings of Cheerios and popcorn. Although Shimmy didn't celebrate Christmas, that didn't stop me from imagining spending the holiday with him, the egg between us as we lit our own tree and kissed under the mistletoe. But as soon as the thought entered my mind, I shook it from my head. Where would we have celebrated? The smelly alley?

I wondered what Nene was doing and wished that I could have a sip of the eggnog she made each year from scratch, and a slice of the ham with pineapples that was Aunt Marie's specialty. I even missed Inez, the sound of her laughter and how soft her voice could be when she was in a good mood. Keeping my spirits up was hard, because the whole house was draped in depression. Loretta moved robotically, her heavy sadness clinging to the air in our room.

At nightly devotion, Mother Margaret told us the story of Jesus's birth, and then after a bit of off-key caroling, we were allotted two drop cookies before bed. Loretta gave me hers. When we woke up the next morning, Mother Margaret handed us each a small wrapped box to open. Inside was a fake gold necklace with a dangling cross. Loretta dropped hers on the floor and then dragged herself to a chair in the corner.

Kitchen Sister Kathleen prepared a dried-out turkey with all the fixings, and we topped off the night with scoops of ice cream. The ice cream made me think of Shimmy and listening to "Rock and Roll" on the jukebox. If it weren't for that day, I probably wouldn't be stuck here. I'd be home with my real family. Now, with Bubbles and Georgia Mae gone, only Loretta and I were left in the attic room, but with her deep misery it felt like I was all alone.

The following Saturday we were in the kitchen snapping green beans when Loretta's birth pains started. They escalated quickly, and by the time Mother Margaret had summoned the tall nurse, it seemed like the baby was nearly out. A few hours later, I was permitted to visit Loretta and bring her dinner. She was in the same back room where Georgia Mae delivered, and as I waddled in, I couldn't stop picturing them holding Georgia Mae down and snatching away her baby.

"He looks like Rucker," Loretta said, holding him up so that I could see him.

"He's beautiful," I said, and he was. Fast asleep and bundled in a light blue receiving blanket, he looked like a baby cherub.

"I wish my mom was here." She teared up. "I hate that we have to go through this alone. It's just not fair."

"Everything will be fine," I leaned in and whispered.

"It's not. I see why Bubbles ran away. I wish I could do the same thing." She pulled the baby to her chest and her body shook with tears. "Rucker hasn't even had the decency to respond to my letters."

All I could do was pat her thigh and tell her over and over again that it was going to be all right, but I'm not sure she heard me. Then I remembered what I had overheard.

"When I was here helping Georgia Mae, I heard Mother Margaret say that your baby was going to a doctor's family. He'll be well cared for, Loretta. He'll have a good life."

She brightened just a little, but then she looked down at her tiny son and howled.

Chapter Thirty-Six

WHAT YOU ASK FOR

Eleanor

Their first big blowup as a married couple lingered far longer than it should have. Eleanor had inherited a stubborn streak from her father, and William didn't seem to have the time to make things right even if he wanted to. His residency became even more demanding, and he spent several twenty-four-hour shifts at the hospital each week, while Eleanor continued to duck invitations for visits from Nadine and a few other well-meaning girls from her dormitory at Howard.

Mrs. Porter took a two-week holiday to be with family in Montclair, New Jersey, so without her archiving work, Eleanor was left with very little to do to pass the time. She read books, reworked jigsaw puzzles and cleaned her already spotless house.

William walked through the door early on Christmas morning. Eleanor had gotten up earlier to make biscuits, crab cakes and sunny-side-up eggs to greet him. It was her peace offering, and one he gladly accepted. They wore pajamas, ate on breakfast trays in the den while listening to "White Christmas" by Bing Crosby and drinking mimosas. Eleanor rarely drank, so the bubbles went straight to her head, quieting the gruff voice temporarily. Rose had called, insisting that William join the family for Christmas dinner, but he declined and spent the whole day at home with her. Eleanor recognized this as an olive branch and accepted it.

Five days into the New Year, Eleanor awakened to find William in their bed. He must have come home in the middle of the night. It was still dark outside, and she couldn't figure out what had jolted her awake at such an early hour. Then she heard the shrill of the telephone ringing through the air. Eleanor pushed the covers off her and headed downstairs as fast as she could.

"Hello." Her voice wavered. She hoped to God it wasn't bad news regarding her parents.

"Mrs. Pride? This is Mother Margaret. Sorry to disturb your sleep, but I'm calling with news. You have a baby boy," she announced cheerfully.

"Oh, my goodness." Eleanor covered her mouth with her hand in shock. She had known this moment was coming, but to be standing in it, hearing it, was different.

"Congratulations. We are running all of the newborn tests now, and I'll give you a call back when we are ready for you to pick him up. He's a darling creature," she added.

"I can't thank you enough. You have changed our lives forever with this news."

"It's what we do here. Match well-deserving families with precious bundles of joy. Now, please keep this under your hat until I call again. I'll tell you when to announce that you are in labor."

"Yes, I will. Thank you."

Eleanor dropped the phone in the cradle and then ran up the stairs two at a time.

"Babe." She shook William.

He groaned.

"The baby is here." She trembled.

William was suddenly awake. Eyes wide.

"It's a boy. We have a son." Eleanor could hear the emotion that had welled up in her voice. "William Pride the third is here." She threw her arms around him and they rocked.

"Unbelievable."

"Mother Margaret said they were running tests and would call back soon."

William squeezed her so tight she could hardly breathe. "We have a son," he whispered in her ear. "Thank you."

The pride of pulling this all off welled up in her chest. It was finally over.

"I love you, baby. You're going to be a wonderful mom." He touched her cheek and then pulled her face to his and kissed her fiercely.

When Eleanor pulled away, she rested her head against his chest, listening to his heart thump. God, she loved this man, and now they would finally be complete. Inseparable, bound for life by the coming of their child, and the secret of how he came to be. One that would be carried to the grave. This baby would make them solid, and Eleanor would protect her family with everything she had. That was a promise.

Chapter Thirty-Seven

DARKNESS

Ruby

Loretta's son had been diagnosed with ptosis; a drooping left eye that made his face look slightly disfigured. When I brought in her lunch, she was rocking him to her chest, weeping.

I put the tray of soup in front of her and offered to hold the baby, but she shook her head.

"I heard Mother Margaret on the telephone this morning," Loretta choked out.

"What did she say?"

"She called an orphanage for him. Saying that with his lazy eye he was no longer adoptable. She's placing him in a home to rot away."

My egg started kicking and I put my hand against its foot. My belly had gotten so heavy that I couldn't stand for long, so I pulled over the chair.

"I came here to give him a better life; sending him to an orphanage is like sentencing him to jail. Do you know how many Negro babies spend their whole lives in those places?" Her bottom lip quivered.

"Do you think your mom will reconsider, and let you take him home?"

"Never, she would take her own life before she allowed this to blemish our reputation."

I pulled her into my arms and rocked her until she seemed calm.

After I left, I tried to think of something nice I could do for her. I decided to paint her a picture of the prettiest sunrise I could imagine. I'd use streaks of gold to match her hair. With my canvas and tubes of paint in hand, I ventured out onto the screened-in porch. It didn't take long before my fingers were stiff from the cold, but that didn't stop my brushes from flying with yellow and orange across the blank canvas. It had been ages since I had gotten lost in Ruby Red's World, and my mind was so deep inside my imagination that I didn't feel the cold or hear the door open. It was Mother Margaret, telling me we needed to go to the clinic.

I followed her inside.

"Why do we need to go? I was just with the nurse yesterday for my thirty-eight-week checkup and she said I was fine."

"Well, there's a new development. Please wash up and meet me by the back door in ten minutes."

Something felt off, and my thoughts swirled along with the paint that dripped from my fingers and circled the sink as I washed my hands. It had been so long since I'd left the Gingerbread House, so once we were in the white van, I turned my attention to the window and watched the city passing by.

I had always pictured the white girl's clinic as a big, grandiose building with multiple floors that stretched a full block. In reality, it was a basic one-story brick office barely the size of three Philadelphia row houses pressed together. We pulled into the alley, and I followed Mother Margaret past the reeking garbage dumpster. A piece of broken glass cracked beneath my saddle shoe. Mother Margaret looked both ways, then banged on the back door with her fist. A few seconds passed, and then a woman in a nurse's cap pulled the door open and we stepped inside.

The hallway was stark white, with fluorescent overhead lights that made everything appear sterile. As we walked, my stomach churned from the overwhelming smell of bleach. The nurse led us into a room at the end of the hall and told me to put on a medical gown. Up close, I could see that the nurse wore too much rouge on her cheeks and it made her look like a clown.

"Ruby?"

"Yes."

"Lay back, dear. Everything is okay. You don't have to be afraid."

But I was.

"I'll take good care of you. Don't worry." Her voice was so soothing that I didn't notice the needle in her hand until she pushed it in my arm.

Then came blackness.

PART FOUR

There are no good girls gone wrong—just bad girls found out.

—Mae West

Chapter Thirty-Eight

WAITING GAME

Eleanor

The telephone had not rung in three days. Eleanor knew because she had been hovering by it anxiously, spending almost all her time in or near the den since Mother Margaret called. William had gone to the hospital each morning with strict instructions for her to page him the moment she heard the news. Eleanor had even phoned Nadine and asked her to call her back to make sure the telephone was working properly.

"Seems to be working just fine to me," Nadine teased after Eleanor picked up. "Who are you waiting to call anyway?"

"It just hasn't rung all that much, that's all," Eleanor fibbed.

Eleanor hung up after finally relenting and telling Nadine she could swing by with breakfast someday soon. Bernie had returned to put the finishing touches on the baby's room the day before, but the ease with which they had previously spoken was gone. He had been quick and formal when she walked upstairs to check on him. Nonetheless, he had done an amazing job. The baby's room was cleaned and fully furnished.

There was nothing left for her to do. All the Evenflo bottles had been sterilized in hot water; the cloth diapers had been prewashed in Ivory Snow and were stacked and folded. Diaper pins overflowed from a mason jar, and she was set with two economy-sized squeeze bottles of Mennen Baby Magic to prevent diaper rash. All she could do now was wait on the call.

The day dragged on, and just as she decided to occupy herself with preparing dinner, William came through the back door carrying a paper bag filled with the fresh fruit she had requested. When he hugged her, she could feel the chill coming from his skin.

"Cold out there?"

"Freezing," he said. "Any news?"

Eleanor shook her head as she unpacked the bananas, grapes and red apples. "I hope nothing went wrong."

"I'm sure everything is fine. If I learned one thing from my rotation in pediatrics, it was that things can be pretty hectic."

"What if Mother Margaret took our money and this is all a hoax?"

"Everything will be fine. Just try to relax, honey. You go put some music on while I pull dinner together."

Eleanor did as she was told while enjoying the sounds of William futzing around in the kitchen. She was tempted to go in and help, but it wasn't often that he cooked, so she gave him space.

When the food was ready, they ate at the kitchen table. William had poured himself a glass of wine but she had refused. She wanted to have all her faculties when the call came in and it was time to race to their baby.

As William caught her up on his stint in the ER, she tried to give him her full attention, but part of her mind was still focused on all the things that might have gone wrong in the days since she'd spoken to Mother Margaret.

But then, just as she was securing the leftovers in Tupperware, the blissful sound of the telephone rang out.

They exchanged looks and then Eleanor dashed from the kitchen to the den. It was only a few steps, but she still sounded out of breath as she answered.

"Hello."

"Mrs. Pride?"

"Yes, Mother Margaret," she said loud enough for William to hear from the kitchen.

"Sorry to phone during the dinner hour, but I wanted to let you know that we have a slight delay."

"Is the baby all right?"

"Everything is fine. We are just backed up on our paperwork. I know you are both eager to start your new lives, and you should be able to pick up your baby soon. I'll phone again shortly."

After Eleanor hung up, she relayed the message to William.

"Well, that gives us just a little more time alone."

"I guess." Eleanor chewed the side of her nail. "What kind of delay? Mother Margaret was so vague. How long does it take to sign a few papers? Is something wrong with our baby?"

"Shh." William reached up and started massaging the back of her neck. "Trust me, the baby is fine."

Eleanor relaxed under his touch.

"You know," he whispered into her ear, "this might be our last night together without any interruptions. Might as well take advantage."

William's pressure was soft as he turned Eleanor toward him. He cupped her behind with both hands while pressing against her. "I want you." Eleanor could feel just how much he wanted her.

She felt herself going to putty in his embrace. Pushing her worries aside, she allowed William to lead her upstairs. He had made her a lovely dinner. They were finally in a good place and she wanted to return the favor.

The baby would be here soon enough, she reasoned. Everything was okay, they were in the home stretch. With each step she took, she tried to quiet her thoughts.

Against their cool sheets, with William's fingers in her hair, Eleanor looked into his eyes. She wanted to feel the hunger that usually came over her when he parted her thighs, but all she could think about was their baby.

Chapter Thirty-Nine

FORGET

Ruby

I drifted in and out of consciousness for what felt like hours. My head was foggy and my lower body throbbed. Each time I came to, an IV was plugged into my arm, connected to a long cord. There were three white people in the room and no one said anything to me about what was happening.

"Forceps," a male voice called.

There was a constant digging between my legs that made me squirm against the stiff sheets, but there was no escape. My feet were in stirrups, with a nurse holding each leg in position.

"Wait, stop," I managed, but my pleas fell on deaf ears. Clearly, I didn't matter.

"Push," the male voice said again.

I couldn't see him past the cloth that had been draped over my knees, and I didn't understand what was being asked of me.

"Scissors," he said flatly.

My stomach contracted in the worst cramps I had ever felt in my life. But that feeling was quickly canceled out by the searing pain, as my skin ripped from my bottom to the base of my vagina. I had entered hell, and I screamed as cold metal was thrust inside of me, pulling and yanking.

I balled my fists and hollered.

"Hush that noise," the nurse to my right hissed.

There was no one here to protect me. Her words stung, nearly as much as the incomprehensible pain that I felt pulsing inside of me. I was all alone. I hated Shimmy. I hated Mrs. Shapiro. I hated every white person who had their hands on me.

"Got it," he yelled, and then the most excruciating pain I'd felt in my life rippled through me. The room went blurry and I could feel myself slipping away. But then the sound of a baby's cry whirled me back. My head shook, and I opened my eyes as the nurse held the red baby with both hands before swaddling it in a green blanket. The cry was insistent, and I knew my baby was calling for me.

I had gone over. I was a mother.

"A boy or girl?" I whispered, but there was no response.

The man was still between my legs, and I could feel a needle pushing through my skin. Nothing was done to numb the jabbing. In and out, over and under, just like Little Sister Bethany had taught us in sewing class.

Then the doctor stood up. He looked at me for the first time, but there was no warmth in his eyes. "Try to rest," he said, before turning and walking out the door. The nurses followed close behind with the baby.

My tears were hot and immediate. To my surprise, I longed for my mother's embrace. I longed for Aunt Marie, too, but it was Inez I wanted more. But no one was with me. I was all alone. The resentment felt bitter between my teeth. I put my head back on my pillow and cried myself to sleep.

When I woke up, it felt like I had been to war. My lower body was on fire and the seat beneath me was soaking wet. The door opened to reveal the same nurse with the rouge on her cheeks. She was holding a small bundle.

"We need you to give her some colostrum."

I was frozen at the sight of my baby in her arms. Seeing the baby—my baby!—would make what I was about to do real. But the nurse was impatient, reaching down and yanking my flimsy gown open before I could say anything. She put the baby on my chest, and I felt a warmth spread between us. I was holding my child.

"A girl?" I looked up at the nurse, but her gaze was cold.

"Yes, a girl."

She grabbed my left breast with both of her rough hands and started shoving it in the baby's mouth.

"Don't get attached. You have five days with her. I'll return shortly to take her back to the nursery."

When I looked down into my little girl's face, all I could think was that she was mine. She was so light in my arms, and when she fell away from my breast, I unwrapped her from the blanket. I examined her frog-like legs, bony knees, tiny feet and pointy fingers. She had Shimmy's thin nose, but I could see me and a bit of Inez in her, too. But mostly, I saw Shimmy.

I brought her sleeping body to my mouth and kissed her everywhere. Part of me wished I hadn't seen her, because I knew in my heart that giving her away would be near impossible. But now that she was here, I couldn't look away.

"My little Grace," I whispered into her tiny ear. The name had just come to me, but as soon as I said it I knew it was hers.

When the nurse came back to retrieve Grace, I didn't want to let her go.

"Can't she stay here with me a little longer?"

"I said not to get attached. I'll bring her back for her next feeding. This is just a job. You are supplying her with the nutrients she needs in these next five days so that she will be strong and healthy. That's it."

She took the baby from me and left me alone.

I had lost a lot of blood during her delivery, so I was kept at the clinic for the entire five days I had with Grace. Every few hours they brought her to me and let me feed her. I unwrapped her each time and tried to memorize every detail about her. Sometimes as she sucked, she would lock eyes with me, and I'd wonder what was going on in that tiny little head. Did she know that we only had a short time together?

While Grace slept in the nursery, I passed the time wondering if I was doing the right thing. I knew what I had promised, but that was before I held Grace in my arms. She was no longer an egg, a problem to solve. She was my flesh and blood, and I loved seeing her face, smelling her breath and feeling her soft skin against mine.

But there was Mrs. Shapiro and the scholarship. I kept hearing Aunt Marie's voice. *You want to be poor like the rest of us. Stuck with a baby you can't feed.*

Then I thought of Inez, and how much she hated me. Blamed me for ruining her life and tempting her men. I couldn't imagine ever feeling like that toward Grace, but maybe Inez had told herself the same thing when I was born. I wanted my baby. I wanted to take care of her, and love her, and raise her up right. But where would I put her? Aunt Marie had been kind in taking me in, but I couldn't burden her with a child, too. We barely made ends meet each month.

At the Gingerbread House, I had seen what happened to girls who changed their mind and ended up in the shaming room. No matter how many times I turned a future with Grace over in my head, there was only one option, and I knew it.

When they brought Grace to me for the last time, I cried through the entire feeding. I wondered if she sensed my sadness from the shaking of my chest, as she cried, too, more than I'd ever seen. She would only settle down to suck for a moment before throwing her head back in a tantrum. We kept this up until I swallowed back my tears and sang to her.

"You are my sunshine, my only sunshine." It was the song that Inez had sung to me when I cried for Nene in those first few months of living in a new apartment with Inez and her boyfriend. I remembered the way she had made figure eights on my back while she sang to me. Inez could be nice when she wanted to.

The song calmed Grace, and eventually she gave in to the lull of sleep.

I was kissing the top of her curly head when the nurse walked in.

She reached for Grace.

I held her tight.

"I told you not to get attached," she said when she saw the tears streaking my cheeks. "She's going to a better place."

The Our Father prayer that I said down on my knees scrubbing the floors throughout my pregnancy tumbled from my lips. I squeezed Grace so close to my chest that she stirred. The nurse reached for her, but I couldn't let her go. Then the nurse pinched me hard and snatched her from my arms.

Chapter Forty

SO SLOW

Eleanor

After five days filled with anxiety and restlessness, Mother Margaret finally called again.

"Mrs. Pride, this is Mother Margaret."

"Good evening." Eleanor's fingers clenched around the receiver.

"I'm calling with good news. Your baby will be cleared for pickup tonight."

"Tonight?" she shrieked.

"Yes. I'll meet you at the same address at nine o'clock sharp. Please remember to bring your final donation so that we can continue our work."

"Yes, of course. We will be there."

William stood in the doorway and Eleanor ran into his arms. "Tonight, at nine."

"Told you to be patient." He touched her cheek.

"You did. This is unbelievable. I'm in awe."

"Let me shower the hospital off so that I can be fresh to greet our child." He squeezed her hands. "You did good, baby. Real good."

Eleanor was glad that they would travel to Mother Margaret's office under the cover of night. She didn't want to risk any of her neighbors getting a good look at her as she left the house, because she wasn't going to strap on her cumbersome pregnancy padding. When she held her son for the first time, she didn't want anything between them.

It was only eight o'clock by the time William had showered and dressed, and they both itched to leave. Eleanor suggested they take the long route to kill time. It had been a long time since she had actually left the house, and the night air felt good against her face as she slipped into the front seat. The car smelled like new leather, like William had just had it cleaned.

Eleanor watched as the scenery passed, nodding her head as the blues streamed from the radio. She had missed being out, and a peace came over her. They circled the city, passing the Capitol Building, the Washington Monument and the Lincoln Memorial before easing the car into a parking space on the same side street in Northwest just off MacArthur Blvd where they had parked during their first appointment. Eleanor walked slowly, her hand tucked inside William's, as they crossed the street to the whitewashed building.

"You ready for this?" He held the door open for her.

Eleanor simply nodded her head. She felt like she was going to meet President Truman for the first time and couldn't think of one intelligent thing to say to him. They rode the elevator up to the fifth floor, and William gave a light knock before pushing open the door.

Inside, the carpet still smelled dank and the wooden cross that hung on the wall was askew. Sitting on the desk was a Moses basket, and Eleanor's heart leaped at the sight of it. There in front of them was their son, waiting for Eleanor and William to take him home.

"Mr. and Mrs. Pride, welcome." Mother Margaret beamed at them, her hands clasped around the basket.

William removed his hat.

"Please, meet your new baby girl."

"Girl?" Eleanor stopped in her tracks. "Over the telephone you said it was a boy."

Mother Margaret stammered. "Did I? I must be getting feeble in my old age. Deary me, my apologies. I should have called you back to clarify. You have a girl." She pasted on a thin smile, touching the cross that hung around her neck.

Eleanor rubbed her hand over her face, not sure what to think. "That's a big mistake," she said pointedly.

"A girl is perfect," William interrupted, taking a step toward the basket. "Daddy's little girl."

They both peeked down into the basket, and Eleanor gasped. All her disappointment vanished at the sight of the tiny person balled up in the basket. She was beautiful. When she reached for her, the baby stretched her body long and then nestled herself in Eleanor's arms. She smelled so good, and already Eleanor could feel a tug and pull that made her woozy. William took her by the elbow and guided her into the office chair.

"She is lovely." William pulled his chair closer to her and moved the blanket down to the baby's chest. Perfect patches of curls sat atop her crown, and her lips puckered in her sleep.

The baby settled against Eleanor like it was the most natural thing in the world.

"Where is the lavatory?" William asked, trying to hide the emotion from his voice.

"Right down the hall." Mother Margaret gestured.

When they were alone, Eleanor whispered, "I didn't expect her to be so tiny."

"At birth she was six pounds even, and nineteen inches long."

Her sweet face was so pale that Eleanor turned her miniature ears over between her fingers to check for more pigmentation. They were a half shade darker, but not by much. Her mother would wonder why she was so fair, and Eleanor hoped that in the days to come she would flush with more color. But no matter what, she was their miracle. Eleanor closed her eyes and mumbled a thank you to Eve, for she wouldn't have this darling child without her.

Mother Margaret pushed a stack of forms across the desk toward Eleanor. "I'm so glad that Rose Pride contacted me about you two."

Eleanor opened her eyes, not sure she heard her correctly. "Excuse me?"

"When I met Rose and William for the first time, I knew that you'd be the perfect family to match with a child. And I was right. You are a lovely couple and will make the most wonderful parents. God bless you."

Eleanor tried to hide the shock from showing in her eyes. Rose and William had met with Mother Margaret? Without her?

"Oh, I need her name. Have you decided?"

Just then, William returned, drying his hands on a paper towel. "How about Wilhelmina?" He smiled down at Eleanor, and she was so taken aback that all she could do was nod.

"Fitting, strong name." Mother Margaret scribbled on the page.

William scanned the birth certificate and other documents while Eleanor rocked Wilhelmina in her arms, trying to make sense of it all. They went through the process of signing all the papers, but Eleanor couldn't do more than scribble her name while holding the sleeping baby.

"As I mentioned before, we close the birth records, which precludes the possibility of birth relatives seeking out the child. No information will be shared; she is yours free and clear." Mother Margaret stood and extended her hand. "May God keep you and your daughter. Go in peace."

Eleanor had walked into the building with only her and William to think of and now she was a mother. She had a daughter, someone who would depend on her for the rest of her life. The moment should have been picture-perfect, but the question that kept nagging at the back of her mind was: Why had William and Rose met with Mother Margaret? And why would they have kept this secret from her? Something didn't add up, but she decided not to ruin the moment with her questions. She would get to the bottom of it soon enough. Right now, she needed to concentrate on getting Wilhelmina home safely.

The distance from the building to the car seemed to have grown and Eleanor held Wilhelmina protectively in her arms, walking slowly so as not to stumble and drop her. When they reached the car, William opened the passenger door for her, but she decided to climb into the back seat with the baby. The two of them belonged together.

Chapter Forty-One

REDEEM THYSELF

Ruby

As I trudged up the long driveway of the Gingerbread House alongside Mother Margaret, my breath was ragged. I felt like my most vital organ had been removed from my body without my permission. Grace had been with me every second that I had spent in this place; to enter the house of hell without her felt like betrayal.

Mother Margaret's habit rustled as she stomped her foot impatiently. When I still didn't move, she placed her hand on the small of my back and shoved me through the door. The kitchen reeked of the same stew that had simmered on my first day at the home. My hand rushed to my mouth as I choked, and then dry-heaved.

As I passed through the downstairs rooms, the eyes of the porcelain girls followed me, silently begging to know what happened. But I did not want to give them anything, just as the girls who went over before me gave nothing.

What I wanted was to click my heels three times and let the black hole of sadness engulf me.

I knew the blackness well. I had seen Inez swallowed by it. Whenever her man of the month stopped coming home, she'd retreat into her bedroom with the door locked for days at a time, wearing the same powder-pink nightgown, chain-smoking cigarettes, Billie Holiday's record on repeat. During those times, she didn't care if I ate or went to school, just as long as I didn't bother her.

The stairs to the attic took the last of my energy, and when I barreled through our bedroom door, I ran right into Loretta.

"Ruby. You all right?"

My eyes must have said what my mouth could not, because she pulled me into her arms and held me tight.

"I know how you feel," she said softly.

When I let her go, I noticed the suitcase opened on her cot. "You leaving?"

Loretta dropped her eyes. She looked lovely, her hair combed loose around her shoulders, her face's earlier puffiness gone. The navy sweater looked good against her golden skin.

"My mom's coming." Loretta looked around our room to make sure she had everything.

Georgia Mae's and Bubbles's beds had been turned over with clean linen, their drawers emptied.

"We are going to stop on U Street for dinner and then stay the night in the Whitelaw Hotel. I can't believe I've been in this city for four long months and haven't seen one bit of the place." She chattered on, and I could tell that she was trying to pretend like we were here for another reason.

"Sounds like fun." I played along.

Once her suitcase was closed, she fastened it shut with a large gold buckle.

"What did you have?"

"A girl. Named her Grace."

"That's beautiful. Was it awful?"

"Worse."

Then Loretta's lovely eyes watered over. "We must carry this to the grave, Ruby."

Before I could answer, a knock interrupted, followed by Mother Margaret's voice. "Loretta, your mother has arrived to fetch you."

"Coming, Your Excellency."

Once we heard her footsteps traveling away from our door, Loretta walked over to me and placed a sheet of stamps and a slip of paper in my hand.

"Look, I know we aren't supposed to do this. But we should keep in touch. Promise you'll write me?"

I took back the stamps I had given Loretta. The ones Shimmy had given me. As much as I liked Loretta, I knew that it would be too painful for us to keep in touch. The only way to survive this heartache was to pretend it never happened. Bury it away, like I had done with Leap.

"Okay. Take care of yourself." I squeezed her hand, and then watched as my partner till the end walked out the door. Back to her life with two parents who loved her, and a future that promised that her sacrifice of giving up her son meant that it would be all right.

I was the last one standing.

The next morning, Mother Margaret entered the attic room with a new girl.

"This is Mary," she said.

Mary was cinnamon-colored with a well-defined nose. She wore a simple housedress that suggested that she was from the country. Her belly strained against the buttons.

"Do get her situated," Mother Margaret continued. "Tomorrow you'll have to report to the laundry, to give back to the house for your time here. It's a small price to pay for all that we have done for you."

"Yes, Your Excellency."

Mary looked around the room like a scared kitten dropped in a den of wolves.

"It'll be okay," I offered. "Just do what they tell you, and everything will be fine."

A part of me wanted to tell Mary the truth. About the humiliation, the pain, the heartbreak. But she'd know soon enough. She deserved to enjoy a bit of blindness before the storm.

Mrs. Shapiro must have paid a hefty fee for me to be in the Gingerbread House, because my sentence to the laundry was only one week long. Patty, the head lifer, had been in the laundry for nearly a year, so I knew I was lucky.

We were made to wear itchy beige, tentlike dresses that stopped below the knee. Patty woke us up at the crack of dawn each morning and marched us outside in the cold to exercise. When Patty blew her whistle, we had to run in place for fifteen minutes, and then do jumping jacks until I felt like my middle would fall out. This was to lose the baby weight, but the workout felt cruel so soon after I'd returned from labor. Once our morning exercise was over, we boiled and hand-scrubbed bedsheets, towels, maternity gowns and even undergarments, all before our first meal of the day. The food tasted like scraps from the table. As lifers, we were also the janitors, so we were called on to plunge the toilets, unstop clogged sinks, plug leaks and clear the gutters. I was black and blue from the inside out, and I hated myself for giving up Grace. Shame had gripped me so tight that it was hard to even eat.

On Saturday, we were loaded into the white van and driven a short distance to the Catholic church. There we waxed the floors, polished the pews and cleaned the bathrooms, readying the space for Sunday Mass. When we were finished, we had to get back down on our sore knees and pray for our sins. I prayed for Grace.

Because I was the only Negro girl in the basement, I slept apart from the other lifers, on a cot in the damp hallway where the pipes hissed all night. I imagined it was where Georgia Mae had slept during her sentence. I hoped the man she worked for wouldn't touch her again, but I also knew that hope had never gotten any of us very far.

Chapter Forty-Two

GREEN

Eleanor

The moment they stepped foot in the kitchen, Wilhelmina's cries went from a fuss to an all-out wail.

"She must be hungry." Eleanor handed the baby over to William. "I'll make up the formula."

Wilhelmina stretched out in William's arms. He glanced at Eleanor with a look that said he had no idea what to do with her.

"Just walk and rock her," she called over her shoulder.

The movement settled Wilhelmina for a few minutes but then she would howl again. Already, the sound of her hunger had stirred an instinct in Eleanor to soothe her, and she moved swiftly throughout the kitchen. She got to work mixing thirteen ounces of evaporated milk with nineteen ounces of water. She then spooned in one tablespoon of corn syrup. After it was all mixed together, she divided the formula into several bottles that she stored in the refrigerator. She placed the remaining bottle in the Evenflo baby warmer that she had purchased for one dollar and eighty-nine cents through the mail-order catalogue. All the reviews had called the warmer a lifesaver.

Eleanor tested the milk on the back of her hand and then reached for the baby, who was red in the face from hollering. She put the nipple in her mouth, and in a matter of seconds, Wilhelmina had settled down. Eleanor's shoulders relaxed as she moved into the den and nestled into the pillows on the settee.

"I better get some sleep since I have to report to the hospital in a few hours. You two going to be all right?"

Eleanor didn't glance up at him, but she mumbled that they would be fine.

William seemed to work even longer hours once Wilhelmina arrived. He said because he was only a resident, his request for time off had been denied. Eleanor filed his deception in the back of her mind; keeping up with the care of her new daughter took all her mental fortitude.

Willa, as Eleanor had dubbed her, cried constantly, no matter what Eleanor did to soothe her. Forty-eight hours in, Eleanor already felt like she was failing at motherhood. When Willa bawled, it took everything in Eleanor not to sit down on the floor and cry, too. Eleanor worried that Willa knew that she was not her mother, and was shouting out for "Eve," the woman whom she belonged to.

Gifts had started to arrive as the news spread of Willa's birth. Mrs. Porter had sent over a hand-knitted quilt with matching baby booties. Nadine sent a fussy dress for Willa and a bottle of perfume for Eleanor, with a note that said, "Don't sit around smelling like throw up, Ohio. Remember your man!"

Eleanor's mother was over the moon about the birth of the baby, but she and Eleanor's father would have to put off their trip to D.C. for a few weeks. On Sunday she had phoned to tell Eleanor that there was a shortage of employees at her father's factory, and he couldn't take off until February at best.

Caring for the house and a baby was more exhausting than Eleanor had imagined, and by their third afternoon together, coffee no longer had an effect on her. Eleanor was hanging on by a thread. The phone rang and she rocked the baby to her chest while she answered it.

"How's my favorite girls?" William asked.

"She's just quieting down after another crying spell. You think she's colicky?"

"I'll take a look at her when I get home."

"When will that be?" Eleanor asked, knowing she needed a shower.

"Soon. My parents just returned from their medical conference in Baltimore. They're dropping by with dinner for us."

Eleanor's jaw tightened. "The house is in shambles."

"They don't care about the mess. No one expects everything to be spotless with a newborn at home."

Rose did.

"They're just anxious to spend time with Wilhelmina. We've been keeping her all to ourselves."

"It's only been three days."

"Elly, they want to bond with her, too."

"All of a sudden you can make it home in time for dinner?" she retorted.

William paused. "Babe, don't be like that. I'm leaving the hospital by five. I'll help you soon as I get home."

Eleanor wanted to protest, but she simply didn't have it in her. She had not even combed her hair since Wilhelmina arrived. The last thing she wanted to do was host William's parents, but she had little choice in the matter. They were set to arrive at five thirty, and when Willa finally settled down for an afternoon nap, it was four fifteen.

Deciding that a shower was more important than tidying up, Eleanor hauled the baby's basket into the bathroom with her and turned on the hot water. When she was clean, she stepped out of the bathroom with a towel tucked around her body and the basket with Willa in her arms. She dressed in a simple pair of black slacks with a beige button-down blouse.

When Rose and William Senior knocked at five thirty on the dot, William had still not arrived home from the hospital. Wilhelmina had just stirred awake from her catnap.

"There she is." Rose had brought along a stuffed bunny, and she made its paws clap over the basket.

William Senior trailed Rose, carrying two paper bags that smelled of savory beef.

"Now, now." Rose reached for the baby.

"Look at this little face. What's the matter?" Rose cooed.

"She just woke up. I better warm the formula."

"Pity we can't give her breast milk. Wet nurses should have never gone out of favor," Rose said, and her words hit Eleanor right in the chest.

William Senior placed the food on the counter and then said he'd go make himself at home in the den. Eleanor could hear him flip open the newspaper.

Once the bottle was warmed, she tested it and then reached for the baby.

"Let me." Rose took the bottle from her. She was seated at the kitchen table and slipped the nipple into Wilhelmina's mouth. As Eleanor watched a satisfying look cross Rose's face, she felt an annoying trickle on her spine. Rose Pride always got what she wanted, no matter the cost. Mother Margaret's voice echoed in Eleanor's head.

I'm so glad Rose and William contacted me.

In that moment, Eleanor was sure that Rose had orchestrated the entire adoption, William acting as her faithful assistant. As she watched Rose light up with Willa in her arms, she felt the pebble of anger in her stomach start to stretch into a heavy rock.

Just then, William came through the back door, bringing in a burst of frost with him.

"Sorry I'm late." He kissed his mother on the cheek first, peeked at the baby and then came over to Eleanor. She gave him a tight smile.

"How was she today?" he asked as he removed his wool overcoat. Despite his long shift, he looked impeccable, wearing a cashmere sweater and slacks perfectly creased down the front.

"Fussy. She barely slept."

"Karo syrup is the key," Rose chimed.

"I added one tablespoon."

"Two tablespoons would coat her stomach and help her sleep," Rose added.

"But I read—"

"I'm married to a doctor and raised two healthy boys. I think I should know these things."

Eleanor bit her tongue and looked up at the kitchen clock. *How much longer until they would leave?* she thought as she moved to the cupboard and took down the dinner plates. William poured an aperitif for him and his parents and then ushered them into the dining room. As Eleanor set the table with linen place mats and her good silverware, she listened to them chat about the conference they had attended. The three of them ping-ponged back and forth with medical jargon and names of people Eleanor had never met. Sleepy and agitated, Eleanor reached for Willa, who had fallen asleep in Rose's arms faster than she ever did in Eleanor's.

"I'll put her down so that we can eat."

The quicker they ate, the faster Eleanor could get rid of them and finally confront William about his deceit. She couldn't hold back any longer. She placed Wilhelmina in her basket that she situated in one of the dining room chairs and draped her in a receiving blanket.

Over beef brisket smothered with onions and gravy, William's father asked him about his rounds at the hospital.

"I've just started a rotation in neurology. So far it isn't my favorite."

"Be careful of bringing the germs home."

"I wash my hands so much they're starting to crack." He held them up for his father to see.

"It won't be much longer before you've paid your dues, son. You'll be the third generation of a physician in our family." His father beamed.

"My pride and joy." Rose reached out and squeezed his hand. Eleanor rolled her eyes down to her plate. What a deceptive team the two of them made. Before she could eat three good bites of food, Willa started fretting. Eleanor stood to get her.

"Hand her to me," Rose insisted. "You need to eat so that you can keep up your strength."

Eleanor gritted her teeth but did as she was told.

"There, there, little one," Rose cooed. "Aww, she's opened her eyes for me." She nestled her nose closer to Wilhelmina. "Looks like she's going to have beautiful green eyes."

"The jury is still out." Eleanor picked at her food, but she had noticed her light eyes, too.

"You know, green eyes come from my side of the family," said Rose to no one in particular.

What in the devil was she talking about?

"My great-grandfather had green eyes. They usually skip a few generations," she chuckled.

The rock in Eleanor's belly felt like a boulder. Mother Margaret's voice vibrated in her ear. Why had they gone behind her back to instigate the adoption? Why not just introduce the idea to her and ask Eleanor if it was something she wanted? Unless there was something to hide. There was a motive in everything that Rose Pride did. Willa was no different.

Then it hit Eleanor like a ton of bricks. All those late nights at the hospital, William unreachable. Eleanor wasn't sure if it was the lack of sleep, or if the heat was turned up too high, but the room started to spin. As she put her hands on the table to steady herself, Eleanor looked around and it was like seeing them all for the first time. They were all liars. These people who were supposed to be her family had played her like a fiddle.

Green eyes come from my side of the family.

William had been unfaithful to her, and Wilhelmina was the product of this affair. Rose, the mother who had her hands in everything, fixed William's trouble with the adoption. She was a magician who could wave her wand and make everyone's problems go away. Wilhelmina was William's baby, not Eleanor's.

"How could you?" Eleanor's voice was a slow growl. Everyone turned to look at her.

"Honey, you okay?" William reached for her arm and she recoiled like he was on fire.

"You lied to me, William."

Eleanor couldn't believe that he had the audacity to look startled. How long did he think he could keep up this farce? She might not be a doctor, but she wasn't stupid.

"You and your mother."

Rose narrowed her eyes. "What are you talking about now, child?"

"Mother Margaret. She told me that you met with her. That you sent her to the hospital to plant the seed of adoption in my head. It wasn't a coincidence. You tricked me."

A look of panic crossed William's face as he and his mother exchanged glances.

Rose spoke in her placating voice. The one Eleanor had heard many times when she was forcing her way. "Because we knew you couldn't carry, sweetie. We were just trying to make it easier on you."

"So why not just tell me that's what you wanted me to do?"

"Because we didn't think you could handle it." She shrugged her shoulders.

"Elly," William said, but Eleanor cut him off.

"We. Everything is we. You against me."

"It's not like that, baby. I was just . . ."

"Doing what your mother told you to do. What are you hiding?"

He looked stunned. "Nothing."

"Then how could the eyes come from your side of the family, Rose? William, is this your baby with someone else?" She gave voice to her deepest fear.

"What? No. How could you say such a thing, honey?"

"Don't you 'honey' me." Eleanor stood trembling with rage. "They call first and say it's a boy, then we're told that there was some type of mix-up and then we were given a girl. A girl with green eyes, just like your mother's relatives. Do you know the odds of green eyes in a Negro child? Even if she is mixed-race."

Rose huffed. "You are officially delusional."

"And you are overbearing," Eleanor spat at Rose. It was the first time she had ever been disrespectful to her, but she did not take it back. She turned to William. "How can I trust anything you say?"

"Elly."

"Just stop it. This family is far too concerned with keeping up appearances. I can't take it anymore." She glanced down at the baby in Rose's arms and couldn't help seeing a resemblance. Eleanor stormed from the table. In the kitchen, she yanked the car keys off the hook. William appeared behind her.

"Eleanor."

"Please, just leave me alone." She pushed through the door. Just as she was about to slam it closed, she heard Rose calling out.

"The neighbors, dear." And then she added, in a lower voice, "You see, this is what happens when you marry a girl from the wrong side of the tracks."

Eleanor got behind the wheel of their car for the first time in months just as she saw William run through the back door.

"Baby, please wait," he called out.

Once the engine roared to life, Eleanor swerved into traffic without looking back.

Chapter Forty-Three

THE AFTERMATH

Ruby

By the time my one-week debt in the laundry had been paid, my hands were stiff, the skin flaky from the constant contact with hot water and bleach. I couldn't wait to see Aunt Marie. On the day of my release, Mrs. Shapiro did not drive to Washington, D.C., to pick me up. She had gotten what she wanted, and now that the papers were signed, I had been left to fend for myself. Thank God Aunt Marie wired me bus fare. One of the lifers hadn't heard from her family in months, and although her sentence was over, she stayed on and worked because she had no place else to go.

An hour before my bus was due to depart, Kitchen Sister Kathleen thrust a packed lunch into my arms for my travels, and I thanked her before walking out the side door for the last time. Little Sister Bethany had told me the day before that she would drive me to the bus depot, but when I reached the back door, it was Mother Margaret who held the keys to the van.

We drove in silence. When we arrived at the Greyhound Line bus station on New York Avenue, I thanked her for the ride and then stepped down, clutching the same two muslin bags that I had arrived with in August. The contents of the bags were exactly the same. I was the one who had changed.

I could hear the window of the van being let down, and then Mother Margaret called out. "The Lord gave, and the Lord hath taketh away. Blessed be the name of the Lord. Safe travels, Ruby."

My head didn't even turn back to acknowledge her, but my lips mouthed, "Fuck off, Your Excellency."

The tires screeched as she pulled away from the curb. I had been set free, but freedom didn't feel like I'd hoped it would.

When I arrived in North Philadelphia, at the corner of 29th and Diamond Street, it felt strange to be back home. My fingers were stiff and cold from gripping my bags against the early evening wind that whipped at newspapers and snatched cans and wrappers up and down the street. As I climbed the steps to the second floor, a stench drifted down from Mr. Leroy's apartment, and I wondered if Shimmy's father was up there drinking under the guise of collecting rent. This thought led me to Shimmy, but I shoved him to the back of my mind as I pressed open the door.

Aunt Marie's old floors moaned beneath my feet, and I was greeted by slips of paper folded around dimes. I scooped the numbers up off the floor and placed them on the coffee table for her to sort, before I fell back into the couch. It felt good to be home among Aunt Marie's mismatched furniture, with the sound of water dripping from her leaky faucet. I wasn't even bothered by the gassy smell of the old furnace that was only slightly masked by the boiled cinnamon potpourri. Instead, these familiarities comforted me.

Eventually, I peeled myself off the couch and made my way to the tiny bathroom. I turned on the faucet to the shower and it spit, then sputtered, while the pipes rattled. The water warmed, and I stripped off my bra and panties and stepped into the narrow tub. The steam unraveled the wall I had constructed, and as I scrubbed my skin, the pain I had suffered coagulated around my feet, refusing to go down the drain.

I cried. I wept for my baby, Grace, who would never know my name or recall my touch. Who wouldn't grow up with my voice at her ear, knowing that I had loved her. My chest heaved for my body that would forever be changed, for all the girls who had been forced to surrender their babies.

I cried for all the girls—for the ones who had been in love with the boys who had knocked them up, for the ones who were forced into the back seats of cars by boys they didn't know how to push away. One girl had even whispered about being raped by her older brother. I cried for her, too.

I cried for Clara, for Loretta, for Georgia Mae. I cried for Bubbles, who I hoped was doing okay, and I cried because I knew that hope was not enough.

When I had exhausted myself, I wrapped a towel around my puffy body, dragged my feet to the living room and went to bed. I slept fitfully, my arms cradled in front of me. Hugging the memory of Grace.

Aunt Marie was there when I woke in the morning. I opened my swollen eyes to the sight of her dressed in overalls and a baggy T-shirt.

"Welcome back, sweetness." She had a cup of coffee in front of her at the kitchen table, and her yellow numbers pad open.

"Morning."

"How'd you sleep?"

"Okay." It was cold. The furnace must have gone out again.

"Your mother asked about you. Nene too. I told them you were in D.C. at an internship. So you better come up with something good. Nene might be blind, but ain't nothing wrong with that old mind of hers." Aunt Marie chuckled, but it lacked the heartiness I was used to. Like she was trying to take my mind off all that had happened.

Aunt Marie had always been good at reading my feelings, and she crossed the room in seconds and wrapped me up in her girth. It felt good to be held and I crumpled against her.

"It's going to be all right, sweetness. You did the right thing."

We sat like that for a while, with Aunt Marie rubbing my back and letting me cry it out.

"I'm okay," I said.

"You sure?" She held me at arm's length.

Then she rose and poured herself another cup of coffee from the percolator on the stovetop. With her back to me, she pushed aside the makeshift curtain and reached under the sink. I could see her hands rattle as she tipped her flask of liquor into her coffee and then brought the cup to her lips.

Aunt Marie had picked up a second gig working at a new club on South Street, and between her work there and her job at Kiki's, she was gone every night of the week. I drifted through the halls of my high school feeling alienated, numb and disconnected. Senior pictures, class rings, basketball rivalries and plans for prom didn't excite me, and I mostly kept to myself. On Saturday I returned to *We Rise*, to a smaller cohort. We had been winnowed down to the six brightest of the bunch, and when I walked into the classroom for the first time in months, all the students turned and gawked at me. I stood frozen, clutching my books in my arm, blocking the small pudge that still hung around my stomach.

Mrs. Thomas's face opened. "Welcome back, Miss Pearsall. I trust your prestigious internship in Washington, D.C., went well?"

I swallowed. "Yes, it was an amazing experience. I learned a lot about . . . government."

"Wonderful, I will give you a chance in the next couple of weeks to fill us in on your experience. For now, we are working on narrative essay writing. Please sit down and get yourself acclimated."

I moved to an empty seat next to the window, wondering if Mrs. Thomas had been privy to my charade. If she was, she gave no indication. After class, I hung back and handed her an accordion folder containing every assignment that I had missed.

That evening, I sat at the kitchen table with a slice of peanut butter toast, alternating between a physics assignment and reading *Their Eyes Were Watching God* by Zora Neale Hurston. Filling my mind with literature and tough mathematical equations was a good distraction, at least for a few hours.

I was hunkered over the kitchen table, reading about Janie complaining to Nanny about wanting to want her new husband, Logan, when there was a knock at the door. Guessing that it was one of Aunt Marie's numbers clients, I kept on reading, but the knocking continued. I got up and opened it.

It was Shimmy.

My breathing shallowed at the sight of him standing in the hallway, his hair swept off his face.

"Ruby." He made my name sound like a prayer that had been answered. "Are you all right?"

Before I could get my bearings, he grabbed my face and kissed me hard and with deep affection. I was so famished for his attention that even though I knew it was best to shoo him away, I sank deeper into his strong arms. He smelled of the candy store and felt like heaven.

"God, I missed you," he said, pressing his lips on my cheeks, my eyelids, and then resting them again against my mouth. His tongue tasted like peppermint, and I allowed him to devour me and my sadness.

As I felt my longing threaten to take me to a place of no return, I shook myself free. That was foolish. I looked around the hall. Someone could have been watching me, and my deal with Mrs. Shapiro would have been over. I stepped back away from him, and an awkward silence passed between us. It was drafty, and I would be in a world of trouble if Aunt Marie caught me letting her heat out. But I didn't close the door on him.

"Are you doing all right?"

"I'm fine." I wrapped my arms around my waist to keep from reaching out for him again.

"I came to see if you wanted to go for a ride, so that we could catch up properly."

"I can't, Shimmy." I looked down at my bare feet.

It was part of the deal. I had to leave him alone completely or the scholarship was off. I had come this far, made the ultimate sacrifice, and I couldn't let up now. I had to see this through to the end.

"I think you better leave."

"Tell me what happened."

"Your mother said—"

"Forget about her for one moment. Please. I need to know."

All of a sudden, the wailing from the girls who had surrendered their babies echoed in my ears. I could see Grace being ripped from my arms.

"Go home, Shimmy."

"What did you have?" he pleaded. "At least tell me that much."

"A girl," I whispered.

"Can I at least come in? We should talk about this."

"Shimmy, I'm sorry. It's over." The last thing I saw before I shut the door was the hurt in his brilliant green eyes.

I stood with my back to the door, shaking uncontrollably. But I knew I had done the right thing. I had to move on. Even if it meant I would do so with only half my heart intact. I had lost the two people I loved most, Grace and Shimmy. I didn't need to be happy, but I could not be poor. All I could do was believe that the future I was moving toward would be worth it.

Chapter Forty-Four

OPEN ROAD

Eleanor

The moment Eleanor got behind the wheel of the Chevrolet Bel Air and pulled the car into two-way traffic, she knew where she needed to go. She navigated the car onto Interstate 70 and drove through the state of Maryland until she crossed into Pennsylvania. She was tired—so tired—but pangs of anger kept her alert. One second she was full of rage, the next she was weeping so hard she could barely see the black asphalt in front of her.

Somehow, Eleanor gobbled up one mile after another, with only one stop for coffee and to use the bathroom, halfway through Pennsylvania. It was close to two in the morning when she turned off the highway and drove into Elyria, following alongside the Black River until she navigated the car down her childhood street. Her family's shotgun house sat over a patch of well-tended grass. It still had the white awning with the red front door, and Eleanor breathed relief at the sight of it. It had been such a long time since she had returned home. The last time she saw her parents was during their first Thanksgiving trip as a married couple.

She flicked off the engine and contemplated sitting in the driver's seat until the sun rose so as not to frighten her mother, who was undoubtedly home alone. Eleanor's father worked nights, and she didn't want her mother to think she was a burglar.

A man stumbled across the street in front of her and she slunk down low in the driver's seat. Once he was out of sight, she decided to press her luck and knock. She banged her fist three times on the red door. In a matter of seconds, the front light flicked on and she could see her mother's eye at the peephole.

"It's me, Mama."

"Eleanor? Lord have mercy. What you doing out this time of night?"

The front door scraped the floor, making that swoopy sound that had always welcomed her home. Her mother stood in her faded housecoat with her hair up in pink curlers. She pulled Eleanor into her fleshy arms, and the familiar scent of Ivory soap and Dixie peach made the long trip worth it. Everything inside of Eleanor burst free.

"Oh Lord, get on in here, girl, before you catch cold all up your tail. You just had a baby. Where is my grand? And William?" Her mother glanced past Eleanor into the deserted street, and when she didn't see anyone, she tsked her teeth and pulled her into the warm living room that smelled of butter.

"Mama, there is something I need to tell you."

Lorraine looked her up and down. "Jesus Christ, what you done did now?" she said, and then turned toward the back of the house.

They bypassed the sofa in the living room, because that was for company. Even with the lights off in the dining room, Eleanor knew where to step without bumping into furniture. Back in the kitchen, her mother lit the two-burner stove and put on the kettle. Eleanor took a seat at the octagon table piled with catalogues, church programs, old magazines and advertisements. The kitchen walls were still painted a bright yellow, and the old flowery curtains still hung from the window overlooking the swatch of a backyard. Lorraine placed a mug of peppermint tea in front of her, and then lifted the glass top off the cake dish. Without asking if Eleanor was hungry, she removed the damp paper towel that she kept with the pound cake to keep it moist and cut her a healthy slice.

Homemade pound cake had always been the balm to Eleanor's soul, and as she took the first bite, the last few months pooled at the tip of her tongue. She sank inside herself and told her mother the story she had vowed to take to her grave. She left no detail out, and when she was finally finished, her mother reached across the table and smoothed her hair away from her face.

"Why don't you go lay down and get some sleep."

"You don't have nothing to say?"

"It's been a long drive, Sugar. We'll deal with it in the morning."

Eleanor was beyond exhausted as she stumbled down the narrow hall to the second bedroom. In the dark she could see the silhouette of her poster of Sarah Vaughan and her first date with William at the Lincoln Theatre flashed through her thoughts. How sweet and innocent their lives had been then, before they were weighed down with expectation, loss and life. Despite everything, she missed him. Eleanor crawled into her childhood bed, rounded her body into a ball and nestled her head into her pillow. She was knocked out before her feet warmed under the covers.

Eleanor slept until the middle of the afternoon. When she pulled herself from the bed, she found an old T-shirt from high school and slipped on a pair of gym shorts. Before she even reached the kitchen, she could smell ham hocks and beans simmering in the Dutch oven. Lorraine was hanging up the telephone when she shuffled heavy-footed across the linoleum floor. Her mother's hips had spread since Eleanor had seen her last, and her hair was more salt than pepper.

"Coffee?"

"Yes, ma'am."

Mahalia Jackson's "I'm Glad Salvation Is Free" floated from the record player in the dining room. Without even thinking about it, Eleanor started rocking her shoulders from side to side.

"How's everyone down at the church?"

"Fair to middlin'. Deacon getting old. Keep saying the same stuff every other week. We could use some new blood."

"Your cakes and pies still in high demand?"

"Of course, honey. Is the sky still blue?" Her mother grinned, stretching her right fingers open and closed. "Got a little arthritis in my hand, but it's only slowed me down a touch. Just gotta take breaks and take my time."

Lorraine placed a mug of coffee in front of her, light with carnation milk and sweet with sugar. Eleanor sipped as her mother leaned against the counter gripping her own cup with both hands.

"Where is the baby now?"

"Home."

"You left a newborn with a man?"

"I'm sure his mother is there."

"Still."

"It's not my baby, Mama. She said the green eyes come from her family. How could that be unless William was stepping out on me."

Lorraine lowered herself into the seat across from Eleanor and reached for her package of Camels. She placed the filter between her lips, lit the cigarette, then fanned the match until the fire went out. Puffing slowly, she said, "Sometimes when I would look at your father from the side, it was because my own eyes had gone crooked. Something you want to tell me?"

Eleanor's thoughts went immediately to Bernie. She had enjoyed his company and liked having him around, but it was nothing more than that.

"I told you everything, Mama."

They drank in silence.

Stubbing out her cigarette, Lorraine went back to the two-burner stove, and then returned with a heaping dish of ham hocks and beans. Eleanor demolished the bowl. The only thing missing was the cornbread.

Her mother emptied her ashtray in the garbage can. "William's a good man. A doctor. And he chose you."

"Money isn't everything, Mama."

"It ain't. But you done married well. Don't throw it away because William got a highfalutin, uppity mama who can't stop meddling."

"What if he was unfaithful?"

"Sugar, women have been through worse. Don't get so caught up in your feelings that you can't see the forest for the trees." She twisted her lips. "At the end of the day, you are his wife."

Eleanor carried her plate to the sink and started hand-washing it. "Where's Daddy?"

"He peeked in on you before he went back out this morning. They're still short on workers at the factory, so he's been working double shifts round the clock. Can't complain too much cause the money is good."

Eleanor sighed. It had been so long since she'd seen him. "What do you need me to do around here?"

"I got some cakes to deliver up in Lorain. Come on and take a ride with me, the fresh air will do you some good. You left a few things here at the back of your closet, go take a bath and get changed."

Eleanor stood.

"I sure am glad you here," she said, pulling Eleanor into her arms for a squeeze that made her pain ooze from her pores. "It's all gonna be fine. Just trust your mama on this."

Chapter Forty-Five

BITTER TASTE

Ruby

I had been home for a full week before I saw Inez. Secretly, I had been waiting for her to come looking for me, but she had not even called Aunt Marie's since I returned. When the dismissal bell at school rang on Friday afternoon, I decided to take a detour and walk down her block.

When I got to her building, I saw that she wasn't home. All the shades and curtains in her third-floor apartment were drawn. Inez didn't like to run up her light bill, so during daylight hours she relied on sunlight only. If I turned on the lights before five, I would get hit over the head with her hairbrush, even if it was to do my homework.

It was sunny but cold, and I stood waiting under an old oak tree across the street. My feet must have spread during pregnancy, and I could feel my baby toes cramped and pinched against the leather. When my fingers felt numb in my pockets, I finally saw her pushing a baby carriage up the street.

I watched as she lifted the baby up and carried it with one hand while dragging the carriage up the steps with the other onto the front porch. Inez pressed her foot against the tire break of the stroller and then unlocked the door. I don't know why I didn't call out to her, but instead I waited until I knew she was in the apartment and settled before I crossed the street and rang the doorbell.

"Who is it?" she called through the intercom.

"It's me, Inez. Can I come up?"

Pause. "What you want? I ain't got no money."

"I don't need nothing. Just wanted to see you."

The intercom fell quiet. I waited by the door for so long that I thought she wasn't going to let me in. Then, finally, I heard the buzz. I took the stairs two at a time like I always did and pushed open the door.

The place smelled different. A mix of soiled diapers, cigarettes and cheap air freshener.

"The baby's sleep, so don't come up in here making a whole lotta noise, you hear?"

"Yes, ma'am."

Inez stood in a pair of dungarees with a striped smock top, bent over the kitchen sink with her hands scrubbing chicken parts. Her hair was pulled up in a knot at the top of her head.

"You making dinner already?"

"I like to get it out the way while she's down for her nap. Leap likes to eat when he get home from the shipyard at five thirty."

"How's he doing?"

"Why you asking?" She narrowed her eyes at me.

"Just making conversation."

"We're doing fine. Going down to the justice of the peace to get married soon." She held up her hand and showed me a thin band. "It's just a promise ring for now. The real thing coming soon," she said, picking up the knife. I watched as she lifted the skin on the chicken and scraped against the yellow, slimy film that clung to the meat.

I took a seat at the kitchen table and reached for a butterscotch in the candy dish.

"When did you get back?"

"Last week."

"And you just now dropping by?" she said, which confused me because she always seemed like she didn't want me around.

I didn't know how to respond, so I stayed quiet.

"Marie said you was at an internship."

"Yeah, for the government," I said.

Inez turned and looked at me. A long silence passed between us. It felt like she knew it was all a fabrication but that she didn't want to use up her energy playing detective.

"Well, you better be getting on down the road. Leap will be home soon."

I didn't want to leave so quickly. "Can I see the baby first? Aunt Marie told me you had a girl."

"Named her Lena, after Leap's mama. She's in your old room. You can go back and peek on her. But quiet. If you wake her up all hell will break loose."

I tiptoed as softly as I could down to the back room. My old furniture was unchanged, and my unicorn poster that I won for a summer reading challenge still hung on the wall over my twin bed. A wicker bassinet was wedged between the wall and the dresser in the corner. The baby was nestled under a dull yellow blanket, and as I leaned in to get a better look at her, the smell of her flushed me with memories of Grace. All my senses were alive at once and my breasts throbbed. I wanted to pull her to my chest and cradle her, but instead I ran my hand along her belly.

I had spent the past few years thinking that my mother didn't love me. Maybe she didn't, at least not in the way I had wanted. But now that I had birthed a child and had given her up so she could be raised better than me, I saw things a bit differently. Inez had left me with Nene all those years because she couldn't take care of me. Just like I couldn't take care of Grace.

When I walked back into the kitchen, Inez was rubbing a chicken breast down with oil.

"She looks like you," I offered weakly, and that was a fortunate thing. No little girl should have to walk around looking like Leap.

Inez pressed her lips together at the compliment, then her eyes went dark. "Look, like I said, things are diff—"

I cut her off. "Can I ask you a question?"

She nodded, and I continued before I could second-guess myself.

"Were you in love with my father?"

The knife slipped from her hand and made a thump on the tiny counter.

"Love ain't a strong enough word to describe how I felt about Junior Banks." She paused. "I worshiped the ground he walked on. We went to high school together and I always knew he was out of my league, but I couldn't get him off my mind." She smacked her lips.

"His family was high yella and his daddy had money. Maybe those things made me want him more. I don't know, but I used to think if I made myself pretty enough, and did whatever he said, I could make him fall in love with me. I had a head for numbers, so I used to daydream about helping out at their funeral home keeping the books. We'd be one big happy family." Her eyes glazed over, and she paused like she wasn't sure that she wanted to continue. I waited patiently.

Then she mumbled, "You was conceived in the back of Junior's daddy's car. I thought by giving it up, I could make him love me. But then he disappeared. And his mama laughed in my face, dismissing me like I wasn't shit." She spit the words out, and I could tell the memory still haunted her. She furiously shook salt and then lemon pepper into the bowl of chicken.

"When Junior left me high and dry, I ain't have a pot to piss in or a window to throw it out." She took the chicken out of the mixing bowl and started lining the pieces up on the baking tray. "But now with Leap, things is different."

"I'm happy for you," I blurted. As I said it, I realized it was true.

"Marie always loved you like you were her own. You'll be fine with her. Safe."

That last word hung in the air. I wondered what it would be like if the tension between us simply vanished. I wished we could find some middle ground. Inez opened the oven and pushed the tray of chicken inside, then wiped her hands on a towel.

"Before you go, some mail came for you." She pulled a drawer open and then rummaged through a few papers. Then she thrust an envelope onto the table.

Cheyney State College was emblazoned in royal blue on the envelope. Could this be the letter that would change the direction of my life? The fruit of so many sacrifices. I picked it up and dropped it in my shoulder bag.

"Thank you."

"Go on now, before it gets too dark out. You know how these fools around here get to acting when the sun goes down."

I stood up, childishly longing for Inez to come over and hug me, but a shrill cry from the baby shattered the space between us.

"Got damn it," she mumbled under her breath, but then a smile crept onto her face. She dropped the towel and hurried down the hall to her child.

The last thing I heard was Inez cooing, "Who's a good girl, Mommy's baby . . . ," as the door closed behind me.

CHAPTER FORTY-SIX

REVELATIONS

Eleanor

The next morning, Eleanor found a note on the kitchen table from her mother telling her that she had gone over to check on Sister Clarise, an elderly woman at the church, and that she'd be back in a few hours. A breakfast of eggs, bacon and biscuits was left on the stove under a sheet of tinfoil. Eleanor gobbled it down. She had not called William since she had arrived, and she had an urge to talk to him. She picked up the phone but dropped it back on the hook without dialing the number. What would she say?

For as far back as she could remember, there had been a pile of *Ebony* magazines stacked in a corner of the living room, and Eleanor wandered into the room and picked up the January issue. A fighter plane was on the cover, and she flipped through the pages, and had stopped on an article called "The Abortion Menace," when she heard a soft knock on the front door. Eleanor had hoped that her mother had not spread word that she was in town, because she wasn't in the mood for a parade of company. She placed the magazine on the coffee table and looked through the glass hole. Her throat constricted at who she saw.

"I know you are in there, Eleanor. Please, open the door."

Sighing, she turned the knob.

Rose stood on the slender wooden porch in a floor-length black mink coat and a matching hat adorned with a leather flower. She looked like a movie star who had been mistakenly dropped off at the wrong house, in the wrong town, in the wrong universe.

"Are you going to invite me in?" Rose blew on her hands. Eleanor knew that her mother would have her hide for being rude. She stepped aside so that Rose could enter her childhood home. Rose's eyes appraised the shabbiness of the furniture in the front room. Taking in every nick and scratch from the years of use. Eleanor's parents didn't believe in replacing things until they were broken and beyond fixing. Whereas Rose replaced things with the seasons.

"So, this is where you come from?" Rose draped her coat and gloves over the arm of the recliner.

"How did you find me?"

"Sometimes a woman just needs to go home. Been there a time or two myself."

Eleanor gestured for Rose to take a seat in the recliner, while she sank across from her on the orange sofa.

"Would you like some coffee or tea?" she offered, remembering her manners.

"No, thank you."

There was a family portrait of Eleanor with her parents on the table, and Rose picked it up and studied it. Eleanor was sixteen in the photo. It was two years prior to her attending Howard University. Before she found out that Negroes like Rose Pride felt she'd been born on the wrong side of color, class and wealth.

"I know you think I'm a monster for orchestrating the adoption. I just wanted what was best for my son. And for you."

"You don't care about me, Rose. With just the two of us here, you can be frank."

Rose cleared her throat. "I won't lie. You were not my first choice for William. But, you have certainly grown on me. Let me tell you a little story. Do you have a few minutes?"

Eleanor nodded.

"My grandmother, Birdie, was born a slave. Her white father owned an infamous slave jail in Richmond and her mother, my great-grandmother, Pheby, was his mistress. Birdie was the only one of her three sisters who outright refused to pass for white. They went up north to attend college, but Birdie decided that she was going to stay back in Virginia and uplift her people. She married a doctor, my grandfather, who was so fair that he could have also passed for white, but he chose not to as well. My grandparents were able to build wealth and retain it because their near whiteness opened doors for them."

Eleanor wasn't sure why Rose was telling her all of this. What did it matter?

"We held ourselves apart from the common sharecroppers who were uneducated, black and dirt-poor. And why shouldn't we? We had nothing in common with them. We were trying to get ahead and stay ahead. I'm sure you see us as *uppity*, but this was the only way to assure that our children and our children's children could build a legacy."

"What does this have to do with me?" Eleanor asked sharply.

"All I want is what's best for William. I'm his mother. I just . . ." She swallowed, more nervous than Eleanor had ever seen her. "Eleanor, I just want to protect my boy."

"No matter who gets burned in the process?"

Rose swallowed. "Now that you are a mother, you will understand."

"I am not a mother."

"How can you say that? My son loves you. He has done all of this for you."

"He did it for you."

"Eleanor." She leaned forward in her chair. "I've had Greta Hepburn picked out for William since he was four years old."

Eleanor wrung her hands in her lap. So that was it. She was here to offer her money to divorce William once and for all.

"But your spunk, tenacity and stubbornness are the things I've grown to admire most about you. You don't back down, not even to me."

"Why are you here, Rose? Just spit it out, please."

"I did have a hand in getting Wilhelmina to you, but William is not her biological father. You must believe me. It's a well-kept secret that the Magdalene home has a small market of well-bred Negro children for those who can't naturally conceive. I was simply using my connections and resources to give you both what I knew you wanted most in the world. To start a family."

"Why didn't you just tell me? Why go behind my back?"

"Because I knew that if you knew it had been my idea you would have rejected it."

Eleanor had to admit that Rose was right about that.

"It was me who was dishonest. Don't make William and certainly not that sweet baby girl pay for my transgression."

Rose reached into her clutch and pulled out a pearl bracelet with a gold clasp.

"This was my grandmother's. I wanted to pass it down to my daughter, but I only had boys. As my first daughter-in-law I want you to have it. It's my way of asking if we can start over. Turn over a new leaf."

Eleanor was taken aback. She took the bracelet in her hand and ran her fingers over it. It was stunning.

Rose got to her feet and slipped back into her coat.

"William misses you. Please don't stay away too long. And Wilhelmina needs you. She needs her mother."

She took one last look around the living room and then let herself out. Her perfume stayed in the air long after she had gone.

Eleanor stayed in the same spot on the couch thinking about her conversation with Rose. She replayed it over and over in her head. Eventually, she put on her coat and went for a walk through her neighborhood. She walked past her old high school, the track that she ran on after school most days, the bleachers where she let her first boyfriend feel her breasts. She walked past the butcher and the fruit stand. This is where she was from. She could taste her roots on her tongue. When she returned to her parents' street, she saw a shadow on the front porch.

Eleanor heard a soft cry as she reached the middle of her block and it touched her at the center of her core. She picked up her pace. The first thing she saw was William's back, but this time instead of being bent over books in the library, he was bent over their baby.

A swelling of surprise, love and joy pulsed through her chest. When Eleanor started up the steps to the porch, William stood. He opened his mouth, but no words came out. Eleanor moved into his arms. William cupped the baby in one arm, and Eleanor with the other. The three of them locked in a fold.

"I'm so sorry." He kissed her cheeks and then settled on her lips. "Somehow I felt justified in going behind your back with this because you never told me about the first miscarriage. It was stupid—I know two wrongs don't make a right. Please forgive me." He pressed his lips against hers. His mouth was warm and tasted like home. "I rushed here when my mother called and said you might be ready to see me."

Eleanor squeezed his waist and then reached for Wilhelmina. "Rose wanted you to come get me?" Eleanor smiled to herself. Maybe Rose was turning over a new leaf as a mother-in-law. *Maybe.*

Eleanor brought the baby to her heart, before unlocking the door and letting her family inside.

Chapter Forty-Seven

SIGNED AND SEALED

Ruby

I waited until I got back to Aunt Marie's house before I loosened the flap on the envelope. My hands were unsteady as I brought the letter to my face.

> *Dear Ruby Pearsall,*
>
> *Congratulations! We are pleased to announce that you have been awarded a full four-year tuition scholarship on behalf of the Armstrong Foundation* We Rise *program of Philadelphia. The financial award is contingent upon maintaining a grade point average of 3.0 or above. Please review your contract for more details. To accept this award, we must receive the completed acceptance form enclosed no later than the first day of March.*
>
> *We are excited to have you and look forward to welcoming you on campus in the fall of 1951.*
>
> *Sincerely yours,*
> *Geraldine Clair Davis*
> *Admissions Director*

A lump formed in my throat. Mrs. Shapiro had made good on her promise. In a few months, I would go off to college. In that moment, I yearned for the type of excitement that would make me jump and shout, but the news that everything I had sacrificed for had come to fruition didn't feel like I had imagined it would.

I flopped on the sofa and stared at the thick linen stationery until the words started running together, begging my body to feel something.

When Aunt Marie got home and I showed her the letter, she did all the praise dancing for me.

"Sweetness! You did it. You gonna be the first one in our family to go to college. I'm so proud of you." She took my arms and swung me around the room, eyes shining with pride.

"You know Nene gonna want to have a seafood dinner to celebrate you."

"I hope Fatty has figured out how to fry fish like Nene by now," I said, attempting lightness. I wanted Aunt Marie's glee to infect me.

"This will change your life. You won't have to struggle like the rest of us, out here trying to make a dollar out of fifteen cents. You are going to make us all proud."

Aunt Marie went to the record player and dropped the needle and while she swayed to the sounds of Dinah Washington, I knew that the only way I could do this was to take Mother Margaret's suggestion.

The only way forward was to forget.

EPILOGUE

Thirteen years later, July 1964

Eleanor

Eleanor sat in the den, sipping a cup of coffee that had grown tepid. She considered the new arrowroot-color wallpaper. It was a recent change to their decor. All the magazines were raving about the color, but Eleanor was not sure that she actually liked it. Rose said it made the right statement, so Eleanor had let it be.

William's undergraduate and medical degrees from Howard University hung above the mantel. Eleanor's eye fell on the spot next to it that held her own college degree and her most recent Archival Award of Excellence certificate, and the sight of both tickled her with pride. The television was on low as a breaking news banner crossed the bottom of the screen. Eleanor leaned in.

It was the fifth day of the race riots in Harlem. An off-duty white police officer had shot and killed James Powell, a fifteen-year-old unarmed Black teen. The city was in an uproar and the riots had spread to the surrounding boroughs. Eleanor made a note to phone her sister-in-law after dinner to check on Theodore and their three kids. Perhaps she should ask if they'd like to escape the city for a bit and come for a visit.

"I look ridiculous," Willa shouted as she marched in from the kitchen, bringing her signature scent of lavender with her.

She wore a yellow sundress that Eleanor had purchased from Woodies while out shopping with Nadine. It had looked loose and flowy on the mannequin, but the dress hugged Willa too tight.

"Goodness me, I must have picked up the wrong size." Eleanor crossed the room and lifted the label in the back of Willa's dress. It was the correct size, or at least the size Willa wore three weeks ago. Her body seemed to be developing right before her eyes. At thirteen, she had more curves than most grown women.

Willa turned toward her, red-faced. "Why am I like this?" Her lovely ringlets bounced against her shoulders.

"Like what?" Eleanor feigned innocence.

Willa pointed to her busty breasts and slapped her wide hips. "You have those itty-bitties, and I get stuck with these sandbags. How is that possible?"

Eleanor blinked. "Body shapes run back a few generations. Just like your green eyes, sweetpea."

"I'm such an oddball."

"You are beautiful."

"I want to look like you. Tall, slender, brown, not like this." She pouted as her eyes filled with tears.

"Willa, calm down." Eleanor reached for her, but Willa stormed out of the room and stomped up the stairs.

"I'm not going to lunch with you and Daddy," she called, and then slammed her door shut.

Eleanor should have run after her and insisted that she accompany her, but she didn't have the strength to wrestle her into a dress that fit and drag her out of the house. William would be disappointed, though.

Eleanor sighed and decided to at least try. When she got upstairs, she realized that Willa had gone into the spare bedroom and was hiding in her prayer closet, again.

"Sweetheart, come out of there."

"No!"

"Let's find another dress for you to wear. Daddy will be distraught if you don't come to lunch."

"Tell him I'm sick."

"Wilhelmina Rose Lorraine Pride, come out of that closet right now!"

The door opened slowly, but Willa remained seated.

"Darling, are you coming or not? Your father doesn't like it when we are late."

"I'm not going."

"What do you want me to tell him?"

"I said, I'm sick."

"Very well. Mind yourself, I'll be back soon."

Eleanor walked away from the bedroom and down the steps. She picked up her linen purse and glided out the door to the car.

When Eleanor arrived at Howard Hospital she took the elevator up to the top floor. As her kitten heels clicked across the white tiles, she said hello to a few of the nurses on duty before walking back to her husband's office. As assistant chief of staff, William had a well-appointed corner suite. Eleanor could hear voices from the office floating down the hall.

"Darling." William beamed when he saw her, and then stood from behind his desk. A woman in a white lab coat with a stethoscope hanging from her neck sat in the seat across from him.

"I'd like you to meet our newest doctor on staff, Dr. Pearsall. She's an optometrist and has just arrived from Philadelphia."

The woman stood and reached out her hand to Eleanor. Eleanor shook it. Her touch was soft and somehow familiar. For whatever reason, Eleanor had a hard time making herself pull away.

"How do you do, Dr. Pearsall?" Eleanor looked at the woman's face. Although her mouth smiled warmly, the feeling had chilled just below her dark eyes.

"I'm just fine. Happy to be here. Please, call me Ruby."

"Where's Wilhelmina?" William broke into Eleanor's thoughts.

"Pretending to be sick. I think she's suffering from summer fever." Eleanor chuckled. "She sends her regrets and asks that we bring her back some dessert."

William grinned. "Dr. Pearsall, would you care to join us for lunch? We are heading over to a new bistro that just opened up on U."

Dr. Pearsall appeared caught off guard and quickly shook her head. "Thank you for the invitation, but I need to go down and get settled."

Then something on the wall above William's head caught her eye. "That's a beautiful painting." She pointed.

"Oh, our daughter is quite the artist." William lit up.

"She has an eye," Dr. Pearsall said, still staring at it. "Well, I better get on my horse. It was nice to meet you, Mrs. Pride."

"Likewise," Eleanor said, smiling, and then watched the optometrist walk out the door.

Author's Note

My late grandmother became pregnant with my mother at age fourteen and gave birth to her at fifteen. It was 1955, and having a child out of wedlock was the ultimate sin. So they hid her pregnancy from everyone. Even to the child she gave birth to. My mother did not know her mother was her mother until she was in the third grade; she had been raised by her grandmother, and it had never been openly discussed. My grandmother told me that she was the black sheep of the family. Both she and my mother shared a feeling of deep-rooted disgrace, and as I was growing up, I could see it play out in their turbulent relationship.

My mother does not think there was love between her parents. She describes it as a onetime hookup. My grandfather did not make my grandmother an honest woman by marrying her. He couldn't. His family was very light-skinned and from the "right" side of the tracks. She was mahogany brown and from the lower-class section of North Philadelphia. Like oil and water, they were not intended to mix. My grandfather married someone else, with whom he went on to have children, and my grandmother and mother were stuck with the burden of this lifelong embarrassment.

The idea for *The House of Eve* started with a what-if. What if my grandmother had had money and opportunity, and when she found herself pregnant and in trouble she was sent away to a home for unwed mothers? To erase the humiliation of bearing a child out of wedlock, and to be able to return to her life in North Philadelphia and start over. Like it never happened. Searching for the answer to this question, I read *The Girls Who Went Away* by Ann Fessler, who so graciously answered all my emails about this moment in history. I found articles about women who had been forced to surrender their babies and I found these two particularly helpful: https://www.washingtonpost.com/history/2018/11/19/maternity-homes-where-mind-control-was-used-teen-moms-give-up-their-babies/ and https://washingtoncitypaper.com/article/273834/wayward-past/.

The astonishing fact is that between 1945 and 1973, 1.5 million women in the U.S. lost children to forced adoption in homes for unwed mothers. I say lost because they were forced to give their babies up. Until 1973, abortion was illegal and punishable by imprisonment for both the mother and the doctor. Unmarried women were also pressed to give up their babies because there were no IVF treatments, and the only way for married couples who suffered from infertility to have a child was through adoption.

But in trying to connect the dots between my grandmother's story and the research, I didn't find the story I wanted to tell, because of all the stories of women I uncovered, I couldn't find a single story about a Black woman. When I asked around, I was told that Black women went down south to hide out, and then left the baby with a relative. Or they had the baby and dealt with the consequences because there was no other option. My mind couldn't accept that this was it. Black women's lives have never been a single narrative. There had to have been a small group of elite Black people who could not conceive but still wanted a family. How did the stories of wealthy Black families dealing with infertility play out in the 1940s and '50s?

In order to find the story, I needed to understand the lives of these Black families. I read *Our Kind of People* by Lawrence Otis Graham. This book was instrumental in laying out the life of people like the Prides—families that could trace their roots back to three generations of education and financial privilege.

When Eleanor first appeared to me, she was full of rage and desperate to have a child. I had recently watched Toni Morrison's *The Pieces I Am* documentary, in which she says that she didn't know that Black folks separated themselves by color until she stepped foot on Howard University's campus in 1949 from Lorain, Ohio. I started wondering: What would a woman like Eleanor do when she found herself married to the son of one of the wealthiest families in town but could not give him a child? What would her desperation to fit in cause her to do?

Shimmy was born from my mother's memory. She told me that when she was a girl living in North Philadelphia, she grocery shopped on 31st Street, where most of the shops were owned by Jewish people. I read an article by Allen Meyers, who wrote *Strawberry Mansion: The Jewish Community of North Philadelphia*, which confirmed that Black and Jewish people lived in close proximity, and through goods and commerce engaged in everyday life.

When I first start writing a novel, I often feel like I have all these beautiful Christmas ornaments, but I need a tree to hang them on. After a drive to Washington, D.C., to see the site of the Florence Crittenton Home, a home for unwed girls and women, I got the goose bumps that tell me that I'm making a connection with voices that want their story told. Marginalized voices that have been silenced. I learned that these homes were started for prostitutes, fallen women and wayward girls, but when I looked more closely, I learned that the houses had been filled with girls who merely had sex and ended up pregnant. Sometimes they were in love, sometimes raped, but no matter what, they were shamed. I had found my tree.

I'm drawn to writing historical fiction because I feel charged to tell the truth about American history, whether grim or happy. A few people who appear in the story are based on real-life heroes. One of these is Dorothy Porter Wesley, a librarian, biographer and curator who over the span of forty years built the Moorland-Spingarn Research Center at Howard University into a world-class research collection. When she realized that the Dewey decimal system had only two numbers for Black history, one for slavery and one for colonization, she created space in the system for African-American productivity by classifying the work by genre and author. The *We Rise* program that Ruby attended was based on an initiative called *Tell Them We Rise*, which was designed by Ruth Wright Hayre, the first African-American woman to teach full-time at a high school in Philadelphia. This program allowed 116 students selected in sixth grade to attend college for free if they stayed in school. Louise D. Clements-Hoff, the artist who introduced Ruby to art, was a Philadelphia painter and educator. Georgia Mae, Ruby's mute suitemate at the Magdalene home, was also based on a real character. In 1959, Georgia Mae Rowe gave birth at the age of fourteen to her second child in the St. Gerard's Maternity Home in Richmond, Virginia. She had become pregnant by a twenty-seven-year-old white man who was married with children. Georgia Mae requested that her son be given to an aunt, but because her son was fair-skinned and her aunt dark-skinned, the request was denied.

I wrote this book for women like Georgia Mae, my grandmother Yvonne Clair, my great-grandmother Addie Murray and every woman who was forced to surrender her child either because of race, age, sexual abuse, shame or coercion. You are not alone. *The House of Eve* is for you.

Acknowledgments

I would like to thank God for bestowing His calling and purpose on my life loud and clear, and making me brave enough to walk by faith even when I am afraid. To my mother, Nancy Murray, for letting me root around in your history, exposing family scars and giving me my stories. I have needed all of it and all of you. To my father, Tyrone Murray, for your love and guidance and constant example of strength and family; your belief in me is my super power. To my second mom, Francine Cross Murray, for your advice, wisdom, and always keeping me on my toes; you complete our family and I love you. My ancestors for constantly watching over me: William and Geraldine Murray, Mary Meadows, Yvonne Clair and Gene DeShazor, Nadine and Resce DeShazor, Tommy and Lucy Getter—take care of our PJ, who I miss dearly. To my super sibs and first loves, Tauja, Nadiyah, and Talib Murray. Qualee and Quasann Abram, Armani, Aarick, Devin, Deuce and Darren Johnson: you make my heart sing. Pacita Perera for being my guiding light and first reader always. Glenn Sr., David and Marise Johnson, and Luqman Abram, for being the best in-laws a girl could want. The entire Murray clan, especially our patriarch, Uncle Edgar, and matriarchs Aunt Frances and Aunt Sally, and all of my beautiful cousins, especially Tina Bembery, for keeping us together. To cousin Mary Beverly and Aunt Constance Henderson, for being our pillars. I have the best friends on the planet; thank you all for your constant love and support and big hugs to the Midlo chapter of J&J. To Claudia Bates Physioc and all the beautiful Belles for teaching me how to save myself from drowning.

My dearest agent and friend, Cherise Fisher, for your fierce protection and our deep connection. With you by my side, all things are not only possible but inevitable. Wendy Sherman for having the vision and wisdom that keeps us all on track. All good things from here! To the best editor duo in the land, Carina Guiterman and Lashanda Anakwah, it means so much that I can trust you with my heart. Thank you both for shepherding this novel to its best. Hannah Bishop, I've never had it so good, girl, you slay, and Emily Varga, thanks for teaching me what I'm worth and making sure everyone else knows too. Stephen Bedford and Alyssa diPierro, thank you for the best marketing plan I have ever received. Jonathan Karp and Tim O'Connell, I'm so grateful to you both for rallying the troops and providing the perfect title change. Together, you've made me feel like I have found a home. The best is yet to come.

To all of the independent bookstores, librarians, teachers, book clubs, bloggers, influencers, reviewers, and readers who lovingly show up for me, read my novels, and are ambassadors at spreading the word: thank you. I could not do any of this without your support. It takes a village and I am grateful to Marita Golden for your sensitivity read and for teaching me the art of craft at the Hurston Wright Foundation. Benilde Little, my first teacher; Victoria Christopher Murray, Kristin Harmel, Kate Quinn, Robert Jones Jr., Janet Skeslien Charles, Patti Callahan Henry, Julie Cantrell, Nomi Eve, Drexel University, Story Summit, Kimbilio Fellows, James River Writers, and Tall Poppy Writers for being a part of mine. Pens up to my writing students, thank you for making me better.

For my beautiful children: Miles, you make my heart burst with pride; Zora, you are the perfect firecracker and the world is not ready—burn, baby, burn! Lena, you are the Light, the keeper of our stories, and more talented than you know. You three are my greatest creation. To Glenn, my beloved husband, who has never wavered. Started from the bottom now we here. *Rock solid, ten toes down—you can't move what's rooted in the ground.* The promises do come true. I couldn't love you more if I tried.

About the Author

Sadeqa Johnson is the award-winning author of four novels, including *Yellow Wife*, a 2022 Hurston/Wright Foundation Legacy nominee and BCLA Literary Honoree. Originally from Philadelphia, she currently lives near Richmond, Virginia, with her husband and three children.